LIBERATORS

LIBERATORS

A Novel of the Coming Global Collapse

James Wesley, Rawles

DUTTON
— est. 1852 —

DUTTON
— est. 1852 —
Published by the Penguin Group
Penguin Group (USA) LLC
375 Hudson Street
New York, New York 10014

USA | Canada | UK | Ireland | Australia | New Zealand | India | South Africa | China
penguin.com
A Penguin Random House Company

LIBRARY OF CONGRESS CATALOGING-IN-PUBLICATION DATA

Rawles, James Wesley.
Liberators : a novel of the coming global collapse / James Wesley, Rawles.
pages cm
ISBN 978-0-525-95391-3 (hardback)
1. Survival—Fiction.   2. Financial crises—Fiction.   3. Suspense fiction.
4. Dystopian fiction.   I. Title.
PS3568.A8437L53 2014
813'.54—dc23
2014020037

Printed in the United States of America
1   3   5   7   9   10   8   6   4   2

Set in Arno Pro

DISCLAIMERS

This is a work of fiction. All of the events described are imaginary, taking place *in the future*, and do not represent the world as we know it in the present day. It does not reflect the current geopolitical situation, governmental policies, or the strategic posture of any nation. It is not intended to be commentary on the policies, leadership, goals, strategies, or plans of any nation. This novel is not intended to be predictive of the territorial aspirations tactics of any nation or any planned use of terrorist tactics. Again, it takes place in the future, under *fictional* new leadership of many nations. Any resemblance to living people is purely coincidental. The making and/or possession of some of the devices and mixtures described in this novel are possibly illegal in some jurisdictions. Even the mere possession of the uncombined components might be construed as criminal intent. Consult your state and local laws! If you make any of these devices and/or formulations, you accept sole responsibility for their possession and use. You are also responsible for your own stupidity and/or carelessness. This information is intended for educational purposes only, to add realism to a work of fiction. The purpose of this novel is to entertain and to educate. The author and publisher shall have neither liability nor responsibility to any citizen, person, or entity with respect to any loss or damage caused, or alleged to be caused, directly or indirectly, by the information contained in this novel.

This novel is dedicated to my excellent wife, "Avalanche Lily,"
for her inspiration and encouragement.

There is no king saved by the multitude of an host: a mighty man is not delivered by much strength. An horse [is] a vain thing for safety: neither shall he deliver [any] by his great strength. Behold, the eye of the LORD [is] upon them that fear him, upon them that hope in his mercy; To deliver their soul from death, and to keep them alive in famine. Our soul waiteth for the LORD: he [is] our help and our shield. For our heart shall rejoice in him, because we have trusted in his holy name. Let thy mercy, O LORD, be upon us, according as we hope in thee.

—PSALM 33:16–22 (KJV)

DRAMATIS PERSONAE

Phil Adams—Defense Intelligence Agency counterintelligence case officer with the Defense Clandestine Service (DCS) Task Group Tall Oak, Washington at Joint Base Lewis-McChord, Washington.

Jacob "Jake" Altmiller—Hardware store manager in Tavares, Florida.

Janelle (McGregor) Altmiller—Real estate agent in Tavares, Florida. Wife of Jacob Altmiller. Sister of Rhiannon (McGregor) Jeffords and Ray McGregor. Daughter of Alan and Claire McGregor.

Lance Alan Altmiller—Son of Jacob and Janelle Altmiller. Eleven years old at the onset of the Crunch.

Terrence Billy—Garbage truck driver, Williams Lake, British Columbia. Member of the Secwepemc tribe.

PO3 Jordan Foster—Navy SEAL BUD/S student, United States Phil Bucklew Naval Special Warfare Center (NSWC), Naval Amphibious Base Coronado, California.

Larry Guyot—Owner/manager of Guyot Railway and Engine Maintenance, Ltd., Prince George, British Columbia.

Jerry Hatcher—Cessna 180G bush pilot, Bonners Ferry, Idaho.

Dustin Hodges—Deputy sheriff, Bradfordsville, Kentucky.

Peter Jeffords—American missionary from New Hampshire.

Rhiannon "Rhi" (McGregor) Jeffords—Missionary originally from Bella Coola, British Columbia. Wife of Peter Jeffords. Sister of Janelle (McGregor) Altmiller and Ray McGregor.

Sarah Jeffords—Daughter of Peter and Rhiannon Jeffords. Seven years old at the onset of the Crunch.

Hal Jensen—Section chief, DCS Task Group Tall Oak, Washington, Joint Base Lewis-McChord, Washington.

Joshua Kim—NSA security officer, Washington, D.C.

Jean LaCroix—Son of Megan LaCroix. Three years old at the onset of the Crunch.

Leo LaCroix—Son of Megan LaCroix. Five years old at the onset of the Crunch.

Malorie "Mal" LaCroix—Younger sister of Megan LaCroix. Former machinist in Kearneysville, West Virginia.

Megan LaCroix—Intelligence analyst NSA contractor at Fort Meade, Maryland. Divorced mother of Jean and Leo LaCroix.

Ken Layton—Former mechanic and member of the Northwest Militia.

Stan Leaman—Dairyman from Anahim Lake, British Columbia.

Sylvia Leaman—Cousin of Stan Leaman. Sixteen years old at the onset of the Crunch.

Kevin Lendel—Member of the Northwest Militia.

Alan McGregor—Retired cattle rancher, Bella Coola, British Columbia. Father of Ray McGregor, Janelle (McGregor) Altmiller, and Rhiannon (McGregor) Jeffords.

Claire McGregor—Wife of Alan McGregor. Mother of Ray McGregor, Janelle (McGregor) Altmiller, and Rhiannon (McGregor) Jeffords.

Ray McGregor—Afghanistan War veteran and military historian. Originally from near Bella Coola, British Columbia. Living near Newberry, Michigan. Son of Alan and Claire McGregor. Brother of both Rhiannon (McGregor) Jeffords and Janelle (McGregor) Altmiller.

Brian Norton—Defense Intelligence Agency counterintelligence case officer and electronics expert with DCS Task Group Tall Oak, Washington at Joint Base Lewis-McChord, Washington.

Scott Paulsen—Defense Intelligence Agency counterintelligence case officer and Russian linguist with DCS Task Group Tall Oak, Washington at Joint Base Lewis-McChord, Washington.

Lamar Simons—Mayor of West Hamlin, West Virginia.

Rob Smith—Cessna Amphibian float plane pilot, Tavares, Florida.

Chad Sommers—Grandson and adoptive ward of Ron and Tracy Sommers. Eight years old at the onset of the Crunch.

Ron Sommers—Rancher and former Marine Corps 3002 ground supply officer, living near Alta, Wyoming.

Tracy Sommers—Wife of Ron Sommers, living near Alta, Wyoming.

Clarence Tang—Defense Intelligence Agency counterintelligence case officer and Chinese linguist with DCS Task Group Tall Oak, Washington at Joint Base Lewis-McChord, Washington.

Aaron Wetherspoon—Retired U.S. Navy chaplain.

AUTHOR'S INTRODUCTORY NOTE

Unlike most novel sequels, the storyline of *Liberators* is contemporaneous with the events described in my four previously published novels, *Patriots*, *Survivors*, *Founders*, and *Expatriates*. Thus, you need not read them first (or subsequently), but you'll likely find them entertaining. For those who have read them, you will find that this novel ties together the four previous books. My regular blog posts are available at: http://www.SurvivalBlog.com.

LIBERATORS

1

EXIGENT CIRCUMSTANCES

The backbone of surprise is fusing speed with secrecy.

—Carl von Clausewitz

Seattle, Washington—October, the First Year

To Phil Adams, it seemed that his life had become jammed in "fast-forward." Even though his job as a contract counterintelligence agent with Defense Clandestine Service (DCS) Task Group Tall Oak, Washington at Joint Base Lewis-McChord was already fast-paced, recent global socioeconomic events were spinning out of control. The mass media was abuzz about the inflation jumping above 100 percent, annually. Federal debt obligations had reached absurd numbers, the stock markets had reached dizzying heights, and there were rumblings about foreign repudiations of U.S. Treasury paper.

As he drove toward a routine security paperwork inspection with a defense contractor, Phil Adams had his attention glued to the car radio. He punched the radio's scan button often, jumping from news report to news report. The stories that he heard this morning were the worst yet: rioting in Detroit and Cleveland and rumors of mass demonstrations being planned by "community activists" in many other major cities. Phil muttered to himself, "This is starting to damage my calm."

Then Phil got a call on his cell phone from his manager, Hal Jensen.

"I need you to either get back to the Section office or get to a STU phone, pronto!" Hal said.

"I'm on my way to Peregrine Systems for a quarterly," Phil answered. "I'm just a two-minute drive from there. They've got a secure phone. I'll call you in five mikes or less."

Just three minutes later, Phil called Hal on the secure line. "What's so urgent?"

"I just got a priority tasking via the high side. We've been ordered to fully update and upload all of our electronic holdings, clean our Section out of the SCIF, degauss and destroy all of the Tall Oak local classified holdings, and turn over the entire SCIF to the FEMA staff. I've also been directed to close out all employment contracts—both full-timers and the ad hocs."

Phil was stunned. After a long pause, he replied, "Okay, I'll make some excuses here and be back at the office ASAP."

Phil drove back to JBLM—still listening to the bad economic news on the radio. Phil was thirty-two years old, of average height, with a handsome face, brown hair, blue eyes, and short-cropped hair that was turning prematurely gray. The gray hair was an advantage on post, where everyone seeing him in civilian clothes assumed that he was either a field-grade officer or a senior NCO who was off duty. Even though he wasn't tall, soldiers had a tendency to step out of the way when he walked down the hall. His physical bearing triggered immediate respect.

As he walked into the Tall Oak Sensitive Compartmented Information Facility (SCIF), he could immediately feel the tension.

Hal spelled it out tersely: The economic collapse had forced a drastic cutback in federal programs. For the first time ever, intelligence agencies had their budgets axed, and the deepest of those cuts were made to agencies with contractors. They were to destroy all of their holdings and shut down the Section. Their communications equipment would all be handed over to the FEMA staff. However, three of their computers designed specifically for handling SCI traffic would be useless to the FEMA staffers without their removable hard drives. But that was of little concern to the departing Tall Oakers.

Tall Oak had one locked storage cage in the far end of the building that was used to hold their Field SCIF gear. This cage contained some dusty equipment in plain view: two pallets of coiled concertina barbed wire, three folding tables, a half dozen folding chairs, a bundled GP small tent, two sledgehammers, a shovel, a four-wheeled utility cart, a two-wheeled dolly, and a tall stack of galvanized forty-gallon steel trash barrels that could be used as burn barrels. None of this gear had been used in recent memory, and the only time that Phil ever saw it was when he was escorting visiting inspectors. In the context of their work, the Field SCIF gear was essentially a collection of relics and an administrative nuisance—just a few more items to count each time that they had to do a PBO inventory.

Fortunately, with digitization, the volume of hard-copy classified material that DCS Task Group Tall Oak stored had decreased in recent years. Most of their holdings were in the form of magnetic media that could be destroyed by degaussing them—passing them through an intense magnetic field. But the task of destroying all of the paper documents would still be enormous.

Since the SCIF had only three crosscut paper shredders, Jensen decided to set up a temporary Field SCIF in the motor pool area behind the building to burn most of the documents. Stringing the three strands of concertina wire went quickly. They didn't bother staking it down. Inside the concertina wire enclosure, eight burn barrels were set up in a semicircle. Green plastic Scepter cans of diesel fuel were hauled out and used to stoke the barrels since documents stacked more than five pages thick did not burn well, just by themselves. There were also fire extinguishers nearby, if needed.

Many cartloads of documents were wheeled out of the SCIF and down the hall to the burn barrels. The flames were a hazard (since the barrels had to be stirred regularly with a length of pipe), and the smoke was irritating. Intermittent rain showers made the work miserable as wet ashes began to cling to every surface.

As they worked, Phil's coworker Clarence Tang listened with earbuds to news reports on a compact FM jogging radio, which he had strapped around his upper arm. He relayed the news headlines tersely and sporadically, half shouting, "There are still riots in progress in New York, Chicago, Atlanta, Dallas, and Los Angeles. Now in California there are also riots and looting in Oakland, Stockton, and San Francisco. So far there is just sporadic looting in Portland and downtown Seattle. They say that Vancouver, BC, seems almost normal, except for a couple of protests by 'the usual activists.' They're describing the freeway traffic like it's rush hour, but at midday. Seattle traffic is definitely slowing down, and they may be closing Sea-Tac airport since there are riots in so many destination cities. Seems like most metro areas with populations over a half million are in trouble. Part of Miami is in flames, out of control."

Phil discovered that the reinforced concertina wire–handling gloves worked well at protecting his hands when he stirred the drums of burning documents. Meanwhile, inside the SCIF the bulk degaussers were kept humming, demagnetizing various media. The various "wiped" removable hard disks, disk drives, and tape cartridges were then carried out and smashed with sledgehammers, and then burned for good measure. Hal even had them burn the stacks of generic classified document cover sheets, even though they themselves were not classified. (Jensen always held a "belt and suspenders" attitude about some things.)

Next, they checked the serial numbers of all of their handguns and locked them in one of the GSA high-security drawers. Unlike the others, Phil kept his holster, because it was his personal property. He reminded Hal that he had a SIG P228 at home and asked if he could keep his two issued spare thirteen-round magazines.

Hal nodded. "Sure. Keep them—and here are three more for you. Magazines are classified as 'expendable' items and aren't even listed in our Property Book. Consider them an early retirement gift from Uncle Sam."

An inventory of all badges and credentials followed. Finally came the SCI debriefing for Phil, Brian, Clarence, and Scott. It seemed strangely surreal, as they sat and watched the same debriefing DVD that they had shown to countless others. They were all exhausted, sweaty, and grimy with ashes, and they smelled like diesel fuel. Once they had signed their DD Form 1848 debriefing memorandums (which reminded them that they were still bound by the strict terms of their DD Form 1847-1 SCI nondisclosure agreements for the rest of their lives), they were officially read off of SCI.

While they were signing their debrief/nondisclosure agreements, two members of the FEMA staff arrived. These men seemed confused and uncertain of what they should do in the Mother of All Emergencies. They soon gravitated to the television and watched CNN, transfixed, like millions of other Americans.

After signing out for the last time and a few handshakes out in the hall, the Tall Oakers simply drove off to an uncertain future.

Phil returned to his apartment exhausted. He grabbed some leftover sushi takeout boxes from his refrigerator and ate, sipping a bottle of lemon-flavored sparkling spring water. He then resumed organizing his gear—a process that had started a week before. Most of his field gear was sorted into a stack of forest-green Rubbermaid storage totes. Alongside it were his two Pelican long gun cases and nineteen military surplus ammunition cans, six cases of MREs, a tan military surplus water can, and two white cardboard case lots of Tannerite binary exploding target powder.

Phil had two vehicles: a 2012 Chevrolet Malibu, which he used to commute to work, and a 2015 GMC Canyon midsize crew cab four-wheel-drive pickup truck. Just a few months before the Crunch, he'd traded in his blue 2009 GMC Sierra for the Canyon. Outwardly, it looked similar to his old Sierra pickup, but it was scaled down for better gas mileage. Immediately after buying it, he purchased a T.A.G. Crown-S camper shell for his pickup, a common accessory to have in western Washington's wet climate.

When he first bought the Canyon pickup, it had seemed fairly roomy. But when he did a test load using his storage totes and gun cases, he could soon see that he would have to rethink his "Get Out of Dodge" packing plan. While his plastic totes could be stacked two-deep in his Sierra pickup, there was not quite enough room in the Canyon, so he had to buy a set of half-height totes to use for the second layer.

In his final preparations, Phil had to be selective about what was going with him and what he'd abandon in his apartment. He first pulled a few useful items out of his car, like road maps, a tire-pressure gauge, a digital recorder, a Maglite flashlight, and some road flares. Then he filled up the back end of the pickup almost completely, and crammed some clothing and his extra sleeping bag in the gaps around the bins and ammo cans. He also loaded up both of the seats on the right side of the pickup's cab. He left only the driver's seat and a driver's-side rear seat open, knowing that he'd need room to recline his seat to sleep on the long trip ahead.

He always made a habit of leaving his pickup topped off with gas. This served him well today, since every gas station within fifty miles of Seattle had enormous queues of waiting customers.

Although technically Phil still had DCIPS termination paperwork to complete, as far as he was concerned, that could wait until "normal" times. He said to himself, "They have their SIGs, they have their badges and credentials, and I've been read off. Everything else is just piddly paperwork. That can *wait*."

2

THE HISTORIAN

Fear not, but trust in Providence, Wherever thou may'st be.

—Thomas Haynes Bayly

DuPont, Washington—October, the First Year

Phil Adams had met Ray McGregor when they were both deployed in Afghanistan, stationed at Forward Operating Base (FOB) Robinson, in Helmand Province. They both had a fascination with military history. They struck up a conversation in a MWR tent when Phil noticed that Ray was reading the book *The Bear Went Over the Mountain*, a history of the Soviet army's invasion of Afghanistan. They were both Christians, and both were politically conservative and viewed politics with a jaundiced eye. They became fast friends.

After leaving active duty, Phil Adams became a counterintelligence contractor at Joint Base Lewis-McChord, in Washington, but he kept in contact with Ray via e-mail and Skype. Ray was the oddball of the McGregor family. After his service with the Canadian army, Ray studied military history at Western University, in London, Ontario. But he had dropped out in his senior year to work on a book about World War II veterans in Michigan. Often living in a fifth-wheel "Toy Hauler" camping trailer towed by his pickup truck, he'd first encamped in Ypsilanti, Michigan, and later in Newberry, in Michigan's Upper Peninsula.

With the exception of some things that he'd left in storage at his parents' ranch, everything that Ray owned fit in his pickup and Toy Hauler trailer. This trailer held his enduro motorcycle, a hydraulic wood splitter, two chain saws, fuel cans, and his various woodcutting tools. He also carried a small emergency food reserve in the trailer, which included two Rubbermaid tote bins filled with canned foods and three cases of Canadian military individual meal packs (IMPs). These were packed in heavy-duty plastic-foil retort pouches and were the equivalent of U.S. military MREs.

Ray had already toured the inside of a B-24 at an air show in Georgia. That plane was the world's only restored flying B-24J, owned by the Collings Foundation. But Ray also wanted to see where they were produced, so he made arrangements via e-mail and completed the short drive to the Willow Run plant. Originally built by the Ford Motor Company, it was an enormous five million square feet in a 1.25-mile-long building. The size of the building was awe-inspiring. At the height of production in 1944, the plant was producing a Liberator at a rate of one every sixty-three minutes, twenty-four hours a day, seven days a week. By the war's end, the plant had produced 8,685 B-24s. At one point, forty-two thousand people worked at the plant.

After a change in ownership and several repurposings, the plant was finally shut down in 2010. Ray walked through the empty shell of the building, accompanied by a security guard as his tour guide, in the summer of 2013. The guard, who drove Ray between sections of the building in an electric golf cart, was part of a skeleton crew at the plant. The guard was mostly quiet during Ray's hour-long tour, though he mentioned that most of the people whom he drove around the plant were retired Ford and GM employees. Some of them, he said, had made M16 rifles there, for GM's Hydramatic Division, during the Vietnam War. But a few were "the real old-timers," who dated back to the days of B-24 production. As the golf cart hummed them back to the guard office for Ray to sign out, his guide mentioned one last fact: "The lore here is that the turntable two-thirds of the way along the assembly line was put in for tax purposes. That gave each B-24 a ninety-degree turn before final assembly. That way, the company paid taxes on the entire plant to Washtenaw County, because the county taxed at a lower rate than Wayne County did. The airport, you see, is in Wayne County. And you know, General Motors still pays five million a year to Ypsilanti Township in property tax on this building and the 335 acres it sits on."

Ray was sad to hear that the plant was scheduled to be demolished, and GM was faced with $35 million in environmental cleanup costs.

Other than a few articles that were published in *Military History* magazine, Ray was a failure as a history writer. He had never found a literary agent, and his four uncompleted book manuscripts had never been published. He made most of his meager living cutting firewood.

When Ray moved near Newberry in Michigan's Upper Peninsula, he kept his trailer parked at a sprawling farm that belonged to the Harrison family. Four generations of the Harrisons had lived on the farm. Ray had met them when he began a series of taped interviews with Bob Harrison, who had been a B-24 bomber pilot in World War II.

Ray's own great-grandfather Samuel McGregor was a cattleman. He had been a remittance man from near Greenock, Scotland—a city west of Glasgow. He settled in British Columbia in 1913, and Ray's family had been there ever since. Ray had two sisters, Rhiannon and Janelle. While Janelle and her husband, Jacob, ran a hardware store in Tavares, Florida, Rhiannon had moved with her family to the Philippines to do missionary work.

The last e-mail that Ray sent to Rhiannon before Internet service was disrupted read:

Dear Rhi:

Things are getting bad here, even in the Upper Peninsula of Michigan. I parlayed the last of my cash into food and fuel. The inflation is so crazy that to wait just one day would mean that I'd only get half as many groceries for my money.

I talked with Mom and Dad, via Skype. (I'm not sure how it is in the P.I., but here in the U.S. the phone lines are getting flaky AND are jammed with calls.) Dad said that they are doing okay, but they sound befuddled by the economic situation. Dad asked me for advice on finding a stock that would be safe to invest in. Ha! I suggested putting all of their remaining cash in food, fuel, salt blocks, baling twine, and ammo.

My old friend Phil Adams told me that I need to "Get Out of Dodge," ASAP. The plan is for Phil to meet me at the ranch. I'm not sure if I can get enough fuel to get out West though. I think I can trade some ammo for fuel . . . I also have a few silver dimes and quarters, but those are effectively now my life savings. (They are now worth a fortune, at least in terms of the Funny Money U.S. Dollar.)

I'll be praying for both you and Janelle and your families.

May God Watch Over You,

Ray

3

DAILY GRIND

Of all the modern notions generated by mere wealth the worst is this: the notion that domesticity is dull and tame. Inside the home (they say) is dead decorum and routine; outside is adventure and variety. . . . The truth is, that to the moderately poor the home is the only place of liberty. . . . It is the only spot on the earth where a man can alter arrangements suddenly, make an experiment or indulge in a whim. . . . The home is not the one tame place in the world of adventure. It is the one wild place in the world of rules and set tasks.

—G. K. Chesterton, *What's Wrong With the World*

Charles Town, West Virginia—September, the First Year

After serving in the military, Megan LaCroix did her best to keep everything in perspective. It was amazing what conditions a human being could get used to. The right wheel well of the Ford 350 Econoline that she was riding in always prevented her from really getting comfortable on the long vanpool commute from Charles Town, West Virginia, to Fort Meade, Maryland. By the time she hit Frederick, Maryland, she could think only of how incompatible her long legs were with the van. But on days that she did not have to drive, the front passenger seat did offer a power port to plug in her old clunker Toshiba laptop. Megan would access her favorite blogs before leaving the house in the morning and then save them in a date-indexed folder for that day so that she could read up on the blogs and news feeds that she liked, such as the *Paratus Familia* blog, Patrice Lewis of Rural-Revolution.com, ChrisMartenson.com, and others. Most of her news links came from the DrudgeReport.com, and that particular morning took her a few extra precious minutes to get all the news feeds on Governor Martin O'Malley's new Comprehensive Safe Citizens Firearm Safety Act, which had caught her attention. Even though she was not a Maryland resident, she did work in that state and ultimately it was its restrictive gun laws that caused her and her former husband, Eric, to choose Kearneysville, West Virginia, as a place to put down roots and raise their family. It was the early 2000s when they were first stationed at Fort Meade/NSA-Washington (NSA-W) together, and they wanted to live away from the hustle and bustle of the Beltway where gas was only $1.43 a gallon and credit was easy.

Megan was a former Marine, and while in the USMC she had been a Marine Corps intelligence specialist. Her career started out rough with an unexpected emergency leave during boot camp, but she quickly excelled in her MOS during her first duty station at Company I in NSA-Hawaii. It was there that she had met Eric Turner, a Navy CTR3. After they'd gotten married and started their family in Hawaii, their respective career detailers assigned them both to Fort Meade, Maryland, otherwise known as NSA-Washington. This was the headquarters of the NSA. Megan was assigned to Company B and continued to progress professionally as an analyst.

Now life was much different for her; she was divorced, a single mom of two young boys, and she was underwater with her home's value. When her lease was up on her BMW 325i she simplified her life by buying a 1996 Honda Accord for two thousand dollars cash. The car seemed like it always needed something, but despite its multiple kinks would always start up, thanks largely to the maintenance and repair work of Malorie LaCroix, her younger sister.

Although it went against her nature, Megan eventually stopped paying her mortgage. She had tried to communicate with her bank, Bank of America, but they were impervious to working with her at all. So she got their attention the only way people could before the Crunch, by mailing them her house keys. Megan still kept up on the taxes and made sure that the power bill got paid, but she didn't feel bad about no longer paying the mortgage. By then Bank of America was essentially a "federal utility."

The federal government tipped over the critical domino that would lead to the inevitable Crunch with the passing of the Troubled Asset Relief Program (TARP) Act. This essentially threw open the doors of the U.S. Treasury and the banking cartel would "plus up" all the bottom lines of their franchise constituents. Banks were no longer concerned with meeting the bottom line; they had access to the tap where the money comes out and "too big to fail" meant all the new "wholly owned subsidiaries" were indeed getting theirs.

The Fed chairman was running the printing press in high gear while the Treasury secretary was trying to find a higher gear yet. Between the two of them they perpetuated their predecessors' invention. One Beltway pundit called it "Ben and Tim's self-licking ice cream cone." This was a monetization scheme euphemistically called Quantitative Easing, wherein one part of the government sold its debt to the other part of the government. It was an on-going travesty that far eclipsed the brief Fannie Mae and Freddie Mac disasters. The American people, for the most part, lay down for it, and although there was substantive pushback from conservative and libertarian pundits, few elected officials were willing to stop the music. It was, after all, creating a semblance of a "recovery," and the stock market was soaring.

As the commuter van cruised along, Megan read up on the new gun-grab legislation. "Here I am commuting two hours each way and barely making ends meet, and MOM wants to grab more guns from law-abiding citizens. Soon only the criminals will be able to carry guns," she mumbled to herself.

Chuck, the man whose turn it was to drive that morning, heard her speaking and said, "What was that?"

"Nothing," Megan replied, "I was just talking to myself." She knew better than to open that can of worms with Chuck. Chuck was a committed liberal who had searched on eBay to find a "Kerry-Edwards" sticker to round out the "Hope and Change" motif he had on the back of his Toyota Prius.

The morning commute from Charles Town, West Virginia, to NSA-W averaged two hours, and starting the day with the alarm clock's buzz at 3:30 A.M. was torturous. The lack of sleep was aging Megan well past her biological age of her late twenties, though not wearing any makeup allowed her to streamline her morning routine. If she hit the rowing machine for twenty minutes, took a shower, downloaded her news feeds, and grabbed a piece of toast with peanut butter on the way out the door it was a good day.

——————

Malorie LaCroix was usually awake by 6:00 A.M. She would get her young nephews, Leo and Jean, ready for the day, pointed in the right direction to do their chores, fed, and in their seats to start homeschooling by 8:00 A.M. sharp. She had motivated them by saying that they could eat only after the animals did—a lesson underscored when they had to memorize II Thessalonians 3:10 one morning on empty stomachs after refusing to feed and water the chickens and sheep.

Megan's modest three-bedroom house on six acres offered her the solace on weekends that she desired along with her two sons and Malorie, who lived with them. Kearneysville was a small, quiet town in Jefferson County along Route 9 between Charles Town and Shepherdstown.

Megan bought the house with Eric, who wanted to live out in the country to raise their family. Kearneysville had a downtown consisting of a bank, a post office, an insurance agency, a used car dealership, and a Presbyterian church. The gun laws were much less strict than in neighboring Maryland, and West Virginia offered an incentive for new residents to move in, enticing young professionals with lower taxes.

Megan was able to briefly tune out Chuck and Carol bantering about some superficial topic by listening to the AudioHopper.com downloads that she had remembered to check her RSS feed for last night. AudioHopper.com was a collection of short podcasts that were popular blogs read aloud and recorded for busy people on the go. As she stared out the window watching the fall colors streak by, she thought about how different life was for her now. She had never imagined she would be in this position: divorced with two young boys, struggling on one income in a job she hated, all while stepping up preparations for an uncertain future.

The commuter van was on I-70 now passing Mt. Airy and traffic was mercifully light. Megan scrolled through more news feeds about North Korea's saber rattling.

Chuck eased off of the highway to the Canine Road exit and got the van in the queue for the Vehicle Control Point (VCP). The morning pair of DJs on the radio played off each other's apathy while reading the morning news. Silver was up to forty-four dollars per ounce, France and Poland were petitioning the EU to ban all U.S. GMO crops, oil was trading at $142.88 a barrel, and the stock market was climbing above sixteen thousand points on the Dow Jones Industrial Average.

As Chuck lowered the radio, he said, "Sounds like the president's reinvestment in the economy really achieved the jobs objective—sixteen thousand thousand points on the Dow! I bet somewhere in Alaska, Sarah Palin is looking for a Russian visa." Carol giggled, which only encouraged Chuck. "Don't bother rolling your eyes, Megan. We're only joking about your Caribou Barbie."

The NSA cop at the gate dutifully scanned everyone's badge. One of the advantages of driving in the commuter pools was that the parking was much better. Any car that got on campus after 7:30 A.M., depending on where they worked, would have to park a long way off and negotiate their way to one of the entry points into the Puzzle Palace.

Megan always took the stairs, seven flights up to her office in OPS2A. Her coworkers were not especially cheerful; there had been a lot of lost time and wages with the newly implemented furloughs.

Megan surveyed the milieu in the office and thought, "Wow, they sure are getting a lot of mileage out of this sequestration—it's still a net increase in spending over last year!" She quietly got to her cubicle before Heidi, the head of the section, spotted her. Megan logged on to the four accounts she had to monitor: NIPRnet, SIPRnet, NSA-Net, and JWICS.

Anywhere within NSA, people noticed the rift between those who wear the blue badge (those trusted civilian servants of the government) and the green-badged personnel—the contractors. For most green-badge people their professional aspiration was to achieve a blue badge by any means. The illusion was that blue badgers were secure, couldn't possibly be fired, and would retire with full bennies from Uncle Sugar forever—guaranteed by the full faith and credit of the U.S. federal government. However, as the news of the economy only worsened, the furloughs only seemed to clue in the thousands of people who worked for the Agency. Everyone, blue or green badge, could not help but notice that the goose that kept on laying the golden eggs might not be able to keep pace forever.

As Megan brought up her NSA-Net ("high side") account, the lead story on the NSA-Daily home page was about the budgetary crisis stemming from the lack of an actual budget being passed. As usual, Republican senators were getting the yellow journalism treatment for their unwillingness to just spend the tax. All NSA-ers were urged to contact their elected officials to ask that they pass a budgetary measure to continue to fund national security efforts, especially in the wake of the brewing turmoil with North Korea. "Wow, nothing like appealing to fear," Megan said to herself as she began to triage her in-box.

4

CHOOSE CIVILITY

At its core, then, political correctness is nothing more nor less than the unjust intimidation of others into thinking and speaking a certain way. As such, it is pure totalitarian mind control.

—David Kupelian

Friedman Auditorium, NSA-W, Fort Meade, Maryland—Six Months Before the Crunch

April was usually warm and humid in central Maryland, but this was one of those countertrend cold snaps that lead to more than a few global warming jokes around the water cooler. It was the monthly Equal Opportunity, "Choose Civility," and counter-complacency strategy meeting for Megan's department. Megan was not one for touchy-feely subjective policies, but such was the way of the federal government in those days. "If you want their money, you have to put up with their rules," she said to herself as she found a seat in the Friedman Auditorium toward the back left. "You never know, I may even be able to make an early discreet exit, this way."

Megan had given up soft drinks more than two years before, but she was going to need something to keep herself awake for another "insomnia proofing" EO meeting. The speaker giving the talk this morning was late, and the improv MC, who looked like a model for a Calvin Klein ad, was making small talk and asking for everyone's patience as he gave some statistics about the new Howard County program called "Choose Civility."

Megan had routinely endured the "moonshine" jokes from her colleagues jeering at the recycled glass jars she used to transport green tea with her to work. Today she was grateful for having given up the chick purse for the "maternal urban assault pack," as Malorie called it. The large satchel allowed her to carry a lot of valuable things with her, including an Altoids tin filled with small survival items; a six-inch nonmetallic knife with the sheath sewn to the inside of the bag for easy presentation; a Gideon's pocket New Testament, paper maps of the Maryland, Pennsylvania, West Virginia, and Virginia areas vacuum-sealed in a pouch; a made-in-America Maglite LED XL50; and, of course, baby wipes. "No mom should be caught without them," she would tell herself. She also carried her green tea sweetened with local honey in the outside pocket of her satchel.

Joshua Kim was a rather laid-back NSA cop. He had made an easy transition from U.S. Air Force Security Forces NCO to work as a "blue badger" at NSA. He still believed in "to protect and to serve" and was driven by an innate sense to help people, which was counter to the training that most law enforcement officers received these days. Typically he arrived before the morning pass-down brief and get breakfast. Getting in early meant that he could traverse the campus easier before the traffic, get a cup of Starbucks coffee from the Sodexo kiosk, and catch up on the news headlines, albeit from the Communist News Network (CNN)—he was sure to keep his filter on.

Joshua happened to be on the Headquarters Building rotation that morning. After being called in to settle a parking dispute between two senior executives over who could get the last coveted parking spot near the Headquarters Building, he resumed his hall patrol. Preferring the stairs to the escalator for the free daily exercise, he would inconspicuously time himself by starting to hum the melody of a hymn on one hallway and seeing if he could finish it by the time he reached the end of the hall on the next floor. It was not uncommon that he was stopped by someone asking for directions; the NSA campus could seem like a maze for a newbie who didn't know how to carry a map in his head. He finished "How Great Thou Art" in the Elvis Presley style, ascended the third-floor stairs, and took a right at the top landing to enter the Friedman Auditorium.

Joshua saw Megan sitting toward the back of the auditorium and noticed the satchel by her feet and the unintended gleam from the glass jar peeking out from under her satchel's cover. Unconsciously he had switched from internally singing to audibly humming the melody of the next hymn at the top of the third-floor landing. When he approached Megan to inquire about the glass jar, she recognized the tune first and reflexively asked, "Excuse me, but is that the tune to 'Be Thou My Vision'?"

"It is. I didn't realize I was humming out loud. I was hoping to ask the questions here, though. Is that a beverage in your bag?"

"Yes, it is—Officer Kim, you caught me," Megan admitted, surreptitiously glancing at the name badge on his uniform.

"I'm going to have to ask you to remove it from the auditorium immediately; the signs posted at the entrance prohibit food or beverage."

"Since you asked so nicely, I suppose that I could throw it away. My office is a long walk from here."

"However you remove it is fine with me."

Megan's hand disappeared for a brief second under the flap to grip the jar, and she blushed a bit as she excused herself past Joshua at the end of the row. Joshua had not previously noticed, but she was wearing a long skirt, what he guessed to be a merino wool top, and Dr. Martens boots, which was not typical of the fashion that most women donned while at the NSA. Joshua had made it down the aisle to the front of the auditorium and was on his way back while the improv MC was starting in on "equal access to marriage rights" in his sugary, heavy lisp. Megan had just come back from her walk of shame to duck into her row when Joshua was returning up the aisle. He was impressed with her modest choice of attire and decided he might try small talk with the woman he had just admonished about the beverage.

"Are those Dr. Martens Aimees?"

"Actually, they are. Are you still asking the questions here, or am I allowed to ask one myself?"

Normally cops eschew sarcasm, but this girl clearly had a knack for it, and he was intrigued and—if he was honest with himself—also attracted to her. He was unfiltered now, and answered with an unconscious eyebrow raise.

"Why were you whistling such an old church hymn earlier?"

"Usually when I'm on foot patrol I pick a hymn and sing it in my head to give me an informal time hack on how much ground I'm covering. 'Be Thou My Vision' was the last song that we played at church on Sunday. Plus the tune was so hauntingly beautiful it stuck with me since then. Why the Dr. Martens?"

"You know, usually cops have one hand on their pistol while standing behind the B pillar when they talk to the common citizen. I wear Docs because I learned in the military that the only reliable transportation you will ever have is—"

"Your feet!" Joshua could not believe that he overrode his professional manner to interrupt her like that.

"Yes, Officer Kim. Your feet are the only means of transportation that one can depend on. So I always wear shoes that I can get around in if need be. You can say that I like to be prepared. What church do you attend?"

"I can tell that you're not into this guy's presentation here."

"He's not even the featured speaker. As a former Marine, I have a thing about punctuality. It's seventeen minutes after the scheduled start time. Moreover, I just do not get why we have to be lectured on why we should accept the 'alternative' lifestyle as legitimate, and if I somehow disagree I have committed the last sin left in society, the sin of intolerance. So are you dodging my question?"

"No, this just isn't the right venue, and I'd like to speak with you, the common citizen, as you say, in a more informal setting. I take lunch around eleven-forty-five. Would you care to meet me in the OPS1 cafeteria?"

"I usually bring my own lunch, but I'll consider it. After all, out of the two of us, you're the only one carrying a pistol here. I suppose that makes your argument somewhat persuasive."

"Don't let the pistol persuade you, an argument ad baculum is not persuasive at all—it simply does not follow. A man persuaded against his will remains unconvinced still."

"Ad baculum. Where did you learn Latin?"

"I went to Catholic school. Eleven-forty-five, I usually sit at a table by the round couch across from Einstein Bros. Bagels—look for the guy with the pistol, and I'll save you a seat. Good day, citizen."

Megan smiled and shrugged with noncommitment as he walked away. She wasn't used to someone who was not put off by her sarcastic defenses and could even dish it out himself. As the featured speaker, a black female who was assistant deputy to the NSA general counsel on EO, finally took the stage a full twenty-three minutes late, Megan mentally checked out of the indoctrination and realized that Officer Kim was both in shape *and cute*.

Perhaps she could bring her lunch to the OPS1 cafeteria today after all.

5

WORKFORCE

Parsimony, and not industry, is the immediate cause of the increase of capital. Industry, indeed, provides the subject which parsimony accumulates. But whatever industry might acquire, if parsimony did not save and store up, the capital would never be the greater.

—Adam Smith, *The Wealth of Nations*, Book II, Chapter III

OPS1 Cafeteria, NSA-W—Six Months Before the Crunch

Megan was sitting in the OPS1 cafeteria at eleven-forty about where Officer Kim had described he would be sitting. She didn't see him there, but she hated to be late so she unpacked her food and was peeling her hard-boiled eggs from her pasture-raised chickens when Joshua walked up carrying his tray and said, "I wasn't sure if I would see you or not."

"You know how I feel about being late, and besides, that briefing left me worn-out thinking of how I was being held there against my will. Any chance I had of a daring daylight escape vanished when I had a conversation with an Agency cop about my contraband beverage—I forgot to thank you for that, by the way, Officer Kim."

"Well, we're certainly off to a great start. Please, call me Joshua. Do you mind if I sit down?"

"I'm Megan LaCroix, pleased to make your acquaintance. Not at all, please have a seat."

Trying to lighten the mood yet not sure what to say, Joshua asked, "Do you always brown-bag it?"

"Pretty much. I come from a long line of Quebecois who refuse to pay what Sodexo charges for food."

"Yeah, I've heard people joking about how some of the cafeteria employees look like persons of interest in their areas of operation. You mentioned that you were an ex-Marine."

Megan was somewhat taken aback by the characterization of how people look when she triangulated in on another push button of hers. "That's *former* Marine. You're an ex-Marine only if they kick you out—the Big Chicken Dinner so to speak. Once a Marine, *always* a Marine."

"I sit corrected." Joshua was rather self-conscious now. He hoped that his subtle use of sarcasm resonated with her in some way, and he looked to change the subject. "By the way, Agape Community Church."

"That's where you attend church? Where is that?" Megan asked.

"Not far down 32 in Columbia, or the People's Republic of Howard County, I should say. It's the large brick building on the hill on the right that reads GATHERING PLACE on the outside."

"Oh my, that's a *Christian* church? I got the vibe that it was religious in some way, but I thought that it was a Unitarian place of worship or something since there is no cross on the building. I would have never thought that it was Catholic, though."

Joshua laughed. "Yeah, we get all kinds of questions about that. It's one of the gotchas of living in Merry-land, where the do-gooders use the pen more mightily than the sword. I'm *not* Catholic, but I was raised in a Catholic orphanage in Nashville, Tennessee. The lack of a cross actually goes back to the days when a man named Rouse founded the municipality of Columbia and passed an ordinance that no one faith group could have a single-purpose building for worship."

"Okay, you've officially piqued my interest. I want to hear more about the orphanage, but first, define 'single-purpose.' If I own a bowling alley in Columbia, isn't that single-purpose?"

"Wow, you *do* have the gift of wit," Joshua retorted.

"Malorie, my younger sister, tells me that it's my spiritual gift."

Not exactly sure how to proceed, Joshua continued, "Yeah, but bowling alleys do not make spiritual, nonphysical claims, so they are of little trouble to those looking to build the utopian state. Actually, public schools are more like temples of social thought than any modern church."

"Interesting choice of words. I must say that I agree with your sentiment on public schools. Seems like the liberals own the whole system, which is why we homeschool our kids."

"Whoooah, perhaps I shouldn't be having lunch with you alone." Joshua sensed that he was inadvertently crossing a line at that very moment. "Are you married?"

"No, I'm actually divorced, but thank you for asking. Had you reacted otherwise in some opportunistic way, I would have thought much less of you. My sister, Malorie, and I were both homeschooled, and she lives with me now and helps take care of my children—hence my reference to 'our' children."

"Homeschooling, that's cool. I've never really given it much thought. I mean, after all, we pay taxes to the system, so we should probably use it. Do they learn Latin, too?"

"Of course, how else will they be able to read the classics?" Megan said.

Joshua adjusted his body armor so that it would not choke him as he ate his soup and said, "Hmmm, the classics—too many memories of ruler-toting nuns, perhaps more on that later. Anyway, Agape Community Church was planted as a Great Commission Church and the building is shared jointly with a Messianic Jewish congregation. The building is also rented out for private parties, weddings, that sort of thing. I actually play bass in the worship band at Agape in a rotation and this is our week to play. Service starts at ten-thirty on Sunday mornings." Joshua realized he was leaning forward in a very interested way, but thought it was best to check his body language lest she think he was too pushy. He sat back for a moment before continuing. "Would you care to come? Since the building is not single-purpose we have to tear down all the sound equipment after service, so if you wanted to join us for lunch we usually shoot for around 1:00 P.M."

"It sounds lovely, but I don't make this commute on the weekends. It sucks the life out of me during the week, so to avoid it two days a week provides my sanity standard. Besides, it gives me a chance to catch up on the chores around the homestead and to play with the boys. Thank you just the same, for the invite."

"Homeschooling and homesteading? Maybe I shouldn't be having lunch with you after all, Ms. Megan, the glass-jar-smuggling homebrewer."

"Yeah, check the NSA-Daily tomorrow. Maybe Big Sis Janet Incompetano will have something about us right-winger homeschoolers up there. You can never be too sure about people who eschew debt and have their kids memorize the Declaration of Independence. Sounds like the exact type of citizen I would want to turn my Gestapo on."

Joshua was picking up on the fact that sarcasm was gold with Megan and that she could dish it out as well as take it. He decided that he definitely wanted to get to know more about her. Megan was different from a lot of the twenty- or thirty-somethings eligible bachelorettes at NSA. She was confident, dressed very modestly, and witty. "So where do you work?"

"OPSEC, Officer Kim. You are not read onto that compartment of Megan yet." Megan, a single mom, had perfected her poker face without having an alpha male around and raising two boys. She wanted to see if Joshua was only after one thing, and to find out if she pushed, whether he would push back or simply lose interest. Megan had had to sit and listen to a lot of other single moms at the Agency cry on her shoulder because they had fallen for men who valued the chase but not the catch.

Sensing that this was a test, he decided to lay a marker on the table and show that he was still interested. "Referring to ourselves in the third person, are we?" He tilted his head twice over his left shoulder to point in a specific direction, "You know, there are Occupational Health shrinks right over in the next building; I can see about getting you an appointment."

Megan burst out laughing while trying to cover her mouth and not spray any homemade sprouts. She wasn't used to someone absorbing her darts so well, but regained her composure and confided, "I'm a threat analyst for SADCOM."

"SADCOM?" Joshua furrowed his brow. "You mean "SOUTHCOM, as in Southern Command?"

"No, 'SADCOM' is what the people who work for CENTCOM call their parent organization. While they look romantically at their counterparts in SOCOM and refer to that as 'HAPPYCOM.'"

"I see, maybe. No, wait, I don't get it."

"Just about everyone who works for CENTCOM doesn't like it, myself included. I'm employed by contract for the Agency, but I work in an office that has a liaison officer (LNO) capacity to CENTCOM on behalf of the National Security Agency. I basically analyze the area of operations and assess our ability to gather intelligence in foreign areas that are nonconsensual to our exploits." Megan paused for effect, carefully trying to get a read on Joshua, and then continued, "I basically push paperwork from one side of the desk to the other."

Joshua saw that she was, in fact, a real person with real hurts, so he trod carefully, seeing if he wanted to dig deeper or not. Not knowing fully what to say, he keyed in on an earlier part of the conversation and said, "Sounds like that is rather unfulfilling for having to give up so much time during the week to work and not be home with the kids. Did you say that you had boys?"

"Yes, two sons. They are everything to me, and the reason why I get up in the morning to do this at all is for them." Megan kept it on a professional level and said, "I was a signals analyst in Company B of the Marine Cryptologic Support Battalion here at NSA-W. Before that I was stationed at the RSOC in Kunea with Company I, with my ex-husband, Eric—you don't have to ask, yes, he is an 'ex,' not a 'former' husband. You might say that he earned his Big Chicken Dinner with me." Megan caught herself in an uncharacteristically unguarded moment and couldn't conceal her flash of anger. She felt that she had said too much, and decided not to reveal anything else.

Joshua didn't want to say something stupid, nor did he just want to fill the space with empty pleasantries. So he smiled and said, "I generally walk through your section in the late mornings. Do you mind if I knock on the door and see if you would like to do lunch again next week?"

Megan was not one to live for others' approval, so she had stopped feeling sorry for herself years ago. If Joshua was willing to link up again for lunch, then that was worth exploring, based on her initial impression of him as a thoughtful and seemingly kind Christian. She thought it over for what felt like an awkwardly long pause and said, "Okay, Officer Kim, we can do that. But I have to ask you not to stop by the office. A lot of my office mates hate their lives and long to turn their lives into the soap operas they so diligently DVR every day. My SID is 'mclacro,' you can find me on SEARCHLIGHT. You never know, I might even reply."

Joshua was smitten. He nodded and said, "Have a good day, Miss LaCroix."

6

DIFFUSED RESPONSIBILITY

Now, I'd like to ask people in the room, please raise your hand if you have not broken a law, any law, in the past month. . . . That's the kind of society I want to build. I want to guarantee—with physics and mathematics, not with laws—that we can give ourselves real privacy of personal communications.

—John Gilmore

Odenton, Maryland—Six Months Before the Crunch

Subject: Lunch?
Unclassified: FOR OFFICIAL USE ONLY
Megan,

Hello. I hope that this finds you well. I have been thinking a lot about our lunch meeting and I would love to meet again to talk and get to know you better. How about lunch sometime next week? Do you like Korean food? Looking forward to it,

Joshua

Unclassified: FOR OFFICIAL USE ONLY

She replied:

Re: Lunch?

Unclassified: FOR OFFICIAL USE ONLY

Joshua,

   Okay, I'm game. I do like Korean food, as a matter of fact. I don't eat
out very much, but some of the girls here in the office rave about Mona's
Gourmet Carry Out on Annapolis Road in Odenton. They say that it is
best to call ahead and place your order or else Congress is more likely
to pass a budget before they get your food to you. I can take at most
one hour for lunch. Give me a call on my high side phone: 962-4589.

Megan

Unclassified: FOR OFFICIAL USE ONLY

Megan was a confident woman and she knew better than to call men. She
and her sister, Malorie, grew up as the apple of their papa's eye and they never
felt incomplete without a man's attention, especially if it was the fleeting kind
of attention. Most women who were single moms would find themselves compromising proper judgment when it came to dating candidates and subsequent physical intimacy just because they felt less appealing to men because
they had children. Megan was content to keep on working to provide for her
boys whether or not the phone rang. But she did hold her breath when the National Secure Telephone System (NSTS) phone did ring five minutes later.

   "Four-five-eight-nine, this is Contractor LaCroix."

   "Megan, hey. This is Joshua. Is this an okay time to talk?"

   "Well, I was just about to lower the ocean levels, win the war on terror, save
the San Francisco Salt Marsh Harvest Mouse, and secure world peace with
this PowerPoint presentation, now that the fonts are in cornflower blue instead of ocean blue."

   "Right, be sure to hit Save. You wouldn't want to trust the fate of the free
world to the default settings on that, would you? Hey, about lunch, I was going
to suggest Mona's Gourmet Carry Out, so I'm glad that you mentioned it. I'll
be at the range this Thursday and Friday for my weapons requalifications.
What day works for you next week?"

   Megan noticeably lowered her voice so that she would not be adding fuel to the gossip inferno in her office. "Do you get to Mona's by cutting across Fort Meade and going out the Mapes Road gate, to Telegraph Road?"

"Yes, that's usually the route I take."

"Well, how about Tuesday, then? I usually like to hit the thrift store over on post and it's only open Tuesday through Thursday. You can find some good stuff there sometimes."

"Done. What sounds good to you? I can phone in the order."

"Surprise me, I'm not picky."

"Okay. How about we meet by the PG-165 facing Canine Road out the gate for OPS2B Tuesday at noon?"

"Sounds good. See you then."

It had been so long since Megan had been on any sort of a date that she did an Internet search using DuckDuckGo.com for "conversation starters" when she got home and added that to her morning reading for the next few days' commute. If Joshua was worth adding to her life, she wanted to get past the superficial pleasantries that usually transpire before the magical third-date threshold was crossed. Since the women in Megan's office were notoriously generous with the gory details of their love lives, she knew it was generally acceptable for a woman to "give it up" after the third date. If Joshua wasn't several orders of magnitude off that standard, she would never have replied to the e-mail in the first place. But the dating sea had a lot of sharks swimming around in it, and she wanted to be sure that she could get to know him as a real person.

On Tuesday, Joshua was fifteen minutes early to meet Megan. He thumbed through his pocket testament to read through a psalm while the band Switchfoot quietly played in the background. Megan, notoriously punctual, was walking through the turnstiles at three minutes until noon.

"Hello, Megan, good morning. How have you been?"

"Good morning to you as well, at least for the next two minutes. I'm well, buckled up, and excited for some Korean food. Hey, that isn't an I6 I hear. What are you running in this rig?"

"I didn't know that you were into trucks. That's a small-block Chevy, naturally aspirated with a mild cam and a HEI distributor—not too flashy, but rock-solid reliable."

As they proceeded slowly down Mapes Road, passing the Defense Media Activity, Megan said, "My sister, Malorie, got the motorhead gene; mine is a bit more recessive. She is very handy with a wrench and would love to pick your brain about your Jeep. Is that a four-inch lift on here?"

"I went modest; I could have gone with a six-inch lift, but I wanted a reliable vehicle versus a finicky trailer queen. Hence the simplicity small-block, and I have a spare circuit board for the HEI distributor in a small tin in my toolbox, uhhhh . . ."

"You carry a what?" Megan feigned an incredulous tone; she wanted to cut to the quick and sort Joshua into either the "keeper" or "do-not-bother" category.

"Well, the Chevy 350 is the most popular engine in the world, parts are ubiquitous, and these engines are a cinch to work on. However, I started to read certain blogs and I realized that the whole world is deeply connected and the linchpin is electricity."

"Hmmmmm, sounds like you've been doing some threat analysis; one of the blue badgers in my office is getting ready to retire—maybe you could apply?"

"I should have taken into account that you were a threat analyst before I opened my mouth . . ."

"Joshua, please don't be shocked about my inquisitive tone; I *really do* want to hear more about your thought process." Megan gripped the roll bar instinctively as she had on so many trips out in the backwoods of Maine with her family as the Jeep slowed down and turned right into the seedy rear parking lot of Mona's Gourmet Carry Out.

"This Jeep is my sole means of transportation. I maintain it meticulously, but I got to thinking that the stretch of land between Baltimore and Quantico is such a huge target—what if some rogue terrorist group were to pull up in Baltimore Harbor and set off an EMP? Or if those same people were to fly a small aircraft on approach to Tipton Airport and set it off over the NSA campus? Most cars, say ninety-five percent, would be dead—but I could be back on the road in twenty minutes."

Joshua was sure that he had just put himself on the weirdo do-not-return-phone-calls list, but little did he know that Megan was very impressed with his "prepper indicators" and that his stock value had just gone way up with her.

As they entered Mona's Gourmet Carry Out, Megan immediately noticed that they accepted only cash, a sign of a good place to eat. "Wow, everything looks great," she said. "What did you order for me, by the way?"

"I ordered the Kimchi Bokkeumbap for you; it's reliably very good."

"What's your favorite thing on the menu here?"

"I'm Korean by ethnicity, but I never grew up in the culture. I much prefer fried banana peanut butter sandwiches on account of my origins, but I do love the Beef Bulgogi and the Spicy Korean Beef Soup combo here."

Megan was in full analyst mode. "I couldn't help but notice your facial features."

"You mean that I don't look very Korean? You're right. I did some study on this—all of us orphans are obsessive about our origins—and I concluded that my mother must have been Chinese, or perhaps my father and/or mother were ethnically Chinese, but somehow I ended up with a Korean surname."

Joshua carried the tray back to the table, and they sat down. Megan did not want to waste any time during their lunch hour so she started out by asking, "I really want to hear more about you. So tell me, are you from Memphis?"

"Since I was raised in an orphanage, where I'm 'from' is quite relative, but I claim Tennessee as home. I'm an average guy, I live off of Haviland Mill Road near the Brighton Dam in a rented room above a garage, I name Christ as my Lord and Savior, and I can't relate with anyone on the first ten pages of *Details* magazine." Joshua paused for effect, arranged the items on his tray, then continued, "I was left on the doorstep of a Memphis Catholic church when I was a newborn. My birth parents were never identified. They only left a note with my name, 'Joshua Kim,' and I was raised in an orphanage in Nashville."

Joshua pleasantly noticed that Megan was proficient with chopsticks as he continued, "I was raised to be Catholic and all in all I would say that my upbringing was pretty good. I had a lot of different exposure to other cultures, growing up. We had one nun from Ghana who taught us classical literature, a Jesuit priest from Bolivia who taught all of the math and physical sciences, as well as a nun from France. Eventually, I learned enough French to pass the CLEP for college credit when I was a junior enlisted airman."

"*Vraiment? Tu parles le Français? Je suis Quebecois.*"

"So you're telling me that I'm winning back some cool points for the tin foil hat comment about my spare HEI distributor?"

"You're all right with me, Officer Kim. We happen to believe in spare parts and putting things away for a rainy day at our house, too. Please continue with your story."

"Well, if you've never been to an orphanage, it is rather hard to explain. The one thing that got me through was my best friend, Dustin. He and I were inseparable; we basically are *brothers*. He lives in Kentucky now, and we still talk all the time."

He paused for a moment, and went on. "One summer we both earned a trip to a boys' summer camp that the local Diocese puts on every year in southern Illinois. We were both pretty nervous about the new setting, but since we had few worldly possessions and we were also used to daily routine we adjusted quite well. The first afternoon we got our bunk assignments and there was this one shy boy prone on his stomach flipping through an off-road truck magazine. He was tall and skinny with red hair and was pretty much minding his own business when a few kids who were sent from a rough Chicago parish decided to raise their collective testosterone level and bully this kid reading his magazine. The boys reached over him, grabbed the blanket on the other side of the bed, folded it over to envelop him, and in one motion jerked him down onto the floor. Two kids held him while the other two had bars of soap in a sock and started to hit him. Well, these kids did not factor in Dustin or his high sense of justice—probably what makes him such a good sheriff's deputy now. Anyway, Dustin swept the legs of the nearest kid and delivered a sound knee to the right side of his torso, taking the wind out of him. Without missing a beat he grabbed the back of the shirt collar of the other boy who was hitting the kid, who appeared to be the ringleader, and put him right down on the ground with his knee on his chest, and said, 'Get!' It was really something to see, at eleven years old."

Joshua took a quick bite, and then continued. "Dustin does not suffer bullies or fools at all. The other two, who were holding the blanket, saw the trend and decided that they did not want any part of Bunkhouse Justice 101, and promptly left. Dustin and I helped the kid up and asked him if he was okay. His name was Ken Layton, and ever since he's been one of my best long-distance friends. All three of us got to be great friends over those three weeks at camp. Ken told us all about drive trains and differential ratios, which started my long and expensive hobby of off roading. Turns out that Ken could also shoot pretty well, too. On the .22 range, he consistently took the top scores even with those old worn-out bolt action rifles. I'm getting long-winded here, but Ken went back to his house in Chicago and Dustin and I faithfully wrote back and forth with Ken for years, first by snail mail, and later by e-mail. Ken later met a guy named Todd Gray, who planted the seed with Dustin and me on preparedness."

"Preparedness?" Megan was nearly finished with her lunch and Joshua had not really touched his, but she was enjoying his story.

"It's the concept of redundant options. It's like insurance."

"I've heard of that." Megan figured it was time to lay a marker on the table here. "I first realized that the world was not capable of growing exponentially ad infinitum when I came across a link on the website peakprosperity.com called The Crash Course by Chris Martenson."

Joshua asked, "You like Chris Martenson, too?"

"Indeed," Megan said. "He made too much sense to ignore. I just wish that I had started listening to him years ago. Eric was into guns, but not prepping. They are not coterminous."

"I've got to say that the whole idea of one rifle and a backpack in the woods or a pallet of MREs and a box of ammo in Laurel, Maryland, are dangerous myths."

"Guns are useful tools, but I figure that they truly solve very few problems in and of themselves. That's why Malorie and I have been studying all we can with permaculture and how to produce nutrient-dense food reliably in quantity. You may want to add the 'survival seed pack' to that list of dangerous myths. You've seen how crazy it gets when Snowpocalypse hits the D.C. area every other winter."

"When I-95 or I-70 closes, there aren't enough supplies on the shelf, the trucks can't get through to deliver more, and people panic. All of this happens in the *good times* when there is law and order present."

Megan knew that Joshua was speaking honestly and even reluctantly about things that most people never got to hear about, so she was careful to sound empathetic. "You're correct: Batteries, flashlights, camping gear, toilet paper, disposable diapers, and bottled water are all the first to go."

"That's right. In law enforcement we see this all the time, even if most cops never put all of these philosophical thoughts together into a coherent concept. We still see incrementally the best and worst in society."

The conversation was moving at a brisk pace and Megan was fully engaged now. She asked, "That is what some would call the creep of 'positive law.' When the government becomes the guarantor of all things, then they *must enforce law positively*; that is to say, 'The Constitution is a living document, the law is whatever we say it is, subject to change at any time.' When that happens, there is no other end result but that the haves are systematically robbed by degree until wealth redistribution becomes 'economic justice' and legitimate civil rights are exchanged for 'social justice.'"

"I couldn't have said it better myself," Joshua replied. "Sounds like you and I have been reading the same books! Then, in times of relative peace, we hardly notice the thin veneer of cordial civil conduct, and all it takes is one natural disaster like an ice storm and fights break out over disposable diapers, flashlights, or bottled water."

Joshua continued. "Here's a better question: How many cops does society need when we reject God's law? I liked the term that you mentioned, 'positive law'; I think that it explains a lot. We are all trading away our legitimate rights for what the government claims that they can provide for us—security. This is false and it preys upon man's deepest fear of the unknown, and I consider myself a hawk. There is no way to have just law outside of God's revelation, but modern society is way too enlightened to be bothered with 'thou shalts and thou shalt nots,' so we degrade into what we want. The trouble is that there is no referee to decide whose wants are correct and it inevitably deteriorates to a power struggle. So in the Congo, six million people have died over the *inability to agree*, tens of thousands in the Darfur region, and yet our callous government could care less. All the while our government is more concerned with the Facebook posts of Americans than Iran's nuclear weapons development."

Megan nodded. "I agree; the legitimate offensive parts of our government seem to be shifting focus from international to domestic."

After letting that sink in, Megan continued. "Take your example of who is defined as good and bad according to the law: Heck, you and I are probably guilty of violating a dozen laws every day that we *don't even know about*. And what if someday my Christian homeschooling resource web search—all permanently archived on some server—is classified as a 'hate search' because it's Christian and outside of the liberal public fool system? They can reach back in time and start to use the force of law to prosecute me because the 'moving target,' as you put it, shifted to make the 'Christian Right' into Public Enemy Number One. You think that I'm kidding?"

"No, I don't," Joshua said. "I did read that article, and it's getting harder and harder to tell the good guys from the bad guys. So far this 'Global War on a Noun' has only proved how much money we can spend; I don't believe that it has solved anything other than to manage crises by in-box, spin up the abhorrent DHS, and put tens of thousands more people on the government payroll."

"Right! And the deterioration of society is marked with waypoints like Nanny Bloomberg wanting to ban salt, oversize sodas, and trans fats, all the while presiding over a city government that's bankrupt financially and morally."

Megan shifted in her chair and glanced around the room, just now realizing that her enthrallment with Joshua and the animated conversation had left her completely unaware of her surroundings—who was sitting where, who might be listening. In her line of work, her peripheral vision was like a sixth sense, and she realized at this moment just how much she liked Joshua, to have ignored the world around her with such abandonment.

"Joshua, I've thoroughly enjoyed our conversation, but it's almost time for me to get back to work."

"Sure," Joshua said. "I'm sorry that I didn't get to hear more from you. I kinda felt like I was doing all of the talking there. May I take your tray?"

As Megan stood up she said, "Yes, thank you. I really enjoyed this, can we do it again?"

"Of course! How about next Tuesday?" Joshua wanted to try out his new developing sense of sarcasm as he held the door open for Megan. "If you like chicken, how about we try eating at 'Cluck U'?"

Joshua and Megan had decided to continue meeting for lunch a few times a week. After a month of this Joshua phoned his "brother" Dustin Hodges in Kentucky to tell him about Megan. After going through their usual list of topics of sports scores and getting ready for bow season this year, Joshua broached the subject of Megan and described her circumstances, personality, and worldview.

"Sounds like she has her head on straight. You obviously have a deep interest in her. What are your thoughts?"

Joshua knew that he could fool a lot of people, but Dustin was not one of them. He paused before saying, "That's just it. She is not *like* most of the ladies at work. We've been having lunch together now for a while, and I can sense that there is some real hurt under the surface. I'm not sure if I am man enough to help her. I mean, the ex-husband, the two boys, her sister . . ."

"Little bit of advice, partner: Never think that you can help a woman deal with something like that. If she has not taken up smoking or some other addiction, she likely already has a line on how to fix it herself. Women tend to talk about the thing for the sake of the thing, where you and I as guys are talking about this to try and find a *solution*. Women are weird that way. Has she told you about her ex?"

"No."

"I'm guessing that you are gentleman enough to not bring up the subject." Joshua grunted an affirmation and Dustin let out a long exhalation. "Then I think that you're going about this the right way. Two points of observation: She is not going to expose the most vulnerable part of her life, that being her sons, unless she's really sure that you are worthy of that level of trust. Secondly, you had better not burn that bridge if she is a keeper. Is she a keeper?"

"I really believe that she is. I know that it seems too soon to tell, and that there is this rule somewhere that you have to date for longer than we've been seeing each other, but to be honest with you, Dustin—"

Dustin interrupted. "You'd better be honest with more than just me, Josh! Are you being honest with yourself?"

"Honestly, I love her. At least the version of her that I have in my head. When I'm brought into the rest of her story, then I might feel different or perhaps stronger—but I really think that she is the one."

Dustin knew Joshua very well, and he wanted to give him the assurance that he heard every word that he said, and to give him an out if he wanted to end the conversation. So Dustin ended with, "Brother, I'm really glad that we had this talk. *Seriously.*"

7

THE CROSSING

How complacent we become when we sit secure, hedged round by laws and protections a government may provide! How soon we forget that but for these governments and laws there would be naught but savagery, brutality and starvation!

For our age-old enemies await us always, just beyond our thin walls. Hunger, thirst, and cold lie waiting there, and forever among us are those who would loot, rape, and maim rather than behave as civilized men.

If we sit secure this hour, this day, it is because the thin walls of the law stand between us and evil. A jolt of the earth, a revolution, an invasion or even a violent upset in our own government can reduce all to chaos, leaving civilized man naked and exposed.

—Louis L'Amour, *Fair Blows the Wind*

East of Seattle, Washington—October, the First Year

Phil's drive across the Snoqualmie Pass was nerve-racking. Though the pass was clear of ice and snow, there was heavy traffic, of all descriptions, heading east. Overloaded vehicles were the norm. He noticed that many drivers were hunched up close to their steering wheels, looking tense.

Although it would have been far more direct to take Interstate 5 north to British Columbia, he knew from AM radio reports that the border crossings had at least a three-hour delay. And of course the guns that he was carrying would have put him in handcuffs immediately, given Canada's draconian gun laws.

He was heading for the town of Oroville, Washington. Normally a five-hour drive via the Snoqualmie Pass and Highway 97, it took him nearly seven hours with the heavy traffic in the first stretch. The traffic had lightened up considerably north of Wenatchee, and it was almost normal when he got north of Omak.

As he drove, he punched the radio's Seek button regularly and often switched from AM to FM, trying to catch as much news as possible. Reports were filled with frightening incidents of galloping inflation, large-scale street protests and riots in most major American cities, emergency executive orders, bank closures, and a full-scale panic on Wall Street.

He knew that Oroville was along a "porous" stretch of the border that had often been used by narcotics smugglers. Four years earlier, he had investigated an industrial espionage case where a set of mil-spec composite aircraft wing tooling had been smuggled across that stretch of border, destined for mainland China. The perpetrators were never caught, but Phil had filed the border crossing location away in his memory as a useful tidbit.

He arrived in Oroville late in the day, and low on fuel.

As he waited his turn in the long queue at the Cenex gas station, he removed his Garmin GPS receiver from its dashboard bracket. He programmed the leftmost loop of Meadowlark Road into the GPS. After twenty minutes in line, he reached the pump and was horrified to see gasoline priced at twenty-eight dollars per gallon and CASH ONLY. Despite the high cost, he filled his tank completely. The 26.5 gallons cost him $742. There were police officers responding to some sort of scuffle inside the station's convenience store, so he didn't dare go in.

The new routine at the station was interesting: Gasoline was no longer self-serve. Since the digits on the pump's display couldn't accommodate more than $9.99 per gallon, they had it marked "$2.80," with a handwritten sign above that read: MULTIPLIED BY 10. An attendant carrying an FRS walkie-talkie would approach each car near the head of the line to preapprove it to buy gas or diesel, which meant showing him at least five hundred dollars in cash. Then, once at the pump, payment was demanded in advance. Meanwhile, an armed security guard stood by, holding a Mossberg shotgun and watching the proceedings closely.

Phil timed his arrival at the border for precisely 5:00 P.M. He hoped this would coincide with a shift change for border patrol agents on both sides of the border, so there would be a lower chance of encountering a patrol vehicle. All that stood between him and Canada was one hundred yards of grassy meadow and a three-strand barbed-wire fence in the middle of it.

Across the border was a web of roads that had been punched in and graveled for a housing development that never happened because of the economic downturn that began in 2008.

Phil's hands were shaking as he walked to the fence, holding a pair of compound aircraft snips. These high-leverage cutters made quick work of the fence wire. Heavily tensioned, the wires whipped back as they were cut just to the right of a cedar pole H-brace. (He realized that someone would eventually have to repair the fence to prevent cattle from becoming illegal aliens. Cutting it there would make retensioning the fence wires much easier for whoever did the repair.) The T-posts were spaced twelve feet apart, so it wasn't difficult to fit his pickup through the gap in the fence. He eased the pickup forward and across the uneven pasture ground, whistling nervously. He wondered about cameras and sensors but trusted that the law of averages was on his side.

Only ten minutes later he was driving through Osoyoos, British Columbia. He didn't dawdle, but he was careful to observe the speed limit signs. He wanted to be outside of the fifty-mile-wide border enforcement zone as soon as possible.

His GPS trip planner estimated a 630-mile drive to reach his destination of Bella Coola, which would take about thirteen hours in normal driving conditions.

Reaching the point of exhaustion, he pulled onto a small road that went into Crown land. He followed the road for several hundred yards and then pulled off on a logging road, where his pickup could not be seen.

Shutting down the engine, he assessed his situation: He'd apparently made his border crossing undetected. The gas gauge read just over a half tank. He didn't have any Canadian currency, but he did have a handful of pre-1965 U.S. silver quarters and dimes, as well as one half-ounce Canadian Maple Leaf gold coin that he'd bought during a dip in precious metals prices in late 2013. He prayed that it would be enough to get him to the McGregors' ranch.

Phil spent a fitful night trying to sleep in the cramped cab of his pickup, with his sleeping bag draped around him. He was still feeling tense from his journey, and it was also chilly. Worried about wasting precious fuel, he didn't start the engine to run the pickup's heater. In the end, he got only about four hours of sleep. At first light, he stepped out of the cab and relieved his bladder.

As he continued west of Kamloops, it was obvious that he was in an Indian tribal region. The local Indians, called "Aboriginal," "Indigenous First People," or "First Nations Peoples" in British Columbia, were hardworking and fairly self-sufficient. But the same signs of neglect that characterized tribal housing in U.S. reservations were obvious here. Many houses had wrecked cars up on blocks in their front yards.

On an empty stretch of Highway 97, he spotted a GMC pickup abandoned by the side of the road. He backed up and stopped to look at it. The truck had obviously been stripped. An orange adhesive Royal Canadian Mountain Police (RCMP) MOTOR VEHICLE ACT DERELICT NOTICE sticker was on the windshield, with a July date, and two initialed updates in August and September. The pickup was missing its passenger-side door, tailgate, spare tire, and two wheels. The hood was raised. Phil walked over to it and leaned in to see that the radiator, fan, and water pump had also been stripped from the engine.

Walking around to the back of the truck, he saw that the license plate was still there, and that its inspection sticker was valid for another seven months. That sticker, he surmised, was what had kept the truck from being towed away, to date. He used his Leatherman tool and removed the screws from the license plates. Carrying the plates to his truck, he debated whether it would be safer for him to continue to travel with his Washington plates or to switch to the BC plates.

Just before reaching the town of Cache Creek, he pulled onto a quiet side road and switched the plates. He continued on, and then stopped at a Shell Canada gas station. His GPS travel planner told him that gas stations would be few and far between for the rest of his drive to the Bella Coola region. A large hand-painted sign declared: NO GAS—SORRY.

He pulled up to the pump and was greeted by an elderly First Nations man, who was wearing jeans and a stained Edmonton Oilers logo sweatshirt with frayed cuffs.

The man said, "We're closed."

"How about if I pay you in gold?"

"Nuggets? Some of them is fakes."

"No, this." He held up the half-ounce gold coin, tilting it intentionally to reflect the glint of the rising sun. He had it turned so that the Maple Leaf logo side of the coin faced the man.

The old man smiled and came over to examine the coin. He exclaimed in the Chinook jargon, "Skookum!" (This was one Chinook word that reached deep into the interior of Canada.)

Phil nodded and said, "I only need half a tank, but this is a half-ouncer, so that's enough gold for at least a couple of fifty-five-gallon drums."

"I'll trade you that half tank, plus thirty-five gallons in cans."

Phil shook his head, still smiling, and said, "A half a tank, plus thirty-five gallons in cans, plus ten silver quarters in change would make it square. Have you got any Caribous minted between 1952 and 1967—the eighty percent silver kind?"

The old man scratched his chin and said, "Yeah, but do you know what five-gallon cans—*empty* cans—are selling for these days? They're plenty scarce. Right now I'd rather trade you more silver Caribous than I would gas cans."

Phil grinned and said, "That's my offer—I'm sticking to it."

The old man laughed and said, "Okay. *Huy-huy.* You got yourself a trade."

The odd assortment of gas cans fit in the bed of the pickup only after some gear was moved to the rear driver's-side seat. There simply wasn't room for one bin, so Phil unpacked it and wedged all of its contents into nooks and crannies both in the cab and in the bed of the pickup. As Phil did so, the old man noticeably ogled the ammo cans and gun cases but didn't say anything about them.

Of the seven fuel cans, no two were alike. Some of the gas cans looked ancient, while others were fairly new plastic containers. One of them had the annoying CARB-compliant nozzle, which had been mandated in recent years, but the station owner assured him that none of them were "leakers." In a separate transaction, by trading back one of the silver Canadian quarters, Phil got an assortment of nozzles so that he'd have one for each type of can.

Now confident that he'd have more than enough gas to get him to the ranch, Phil set off again. The old man waved good-bye with his right hand, while his left hand was thrust into his front pocket, clasping the gold coin.

8

CUP OF JOE

A mighty fortress is our God,
A bulwark never failing;
Our helper He amid the flood
Of mortal ills prevailing.
For still our ancient foe
Doth seek to work us woe;
His craft and power are great;
And armed with cruel hate,
On earth is not his equal.

Did we in our own strength confide,
Our striving would be losing,—
Were not the right man on our side,
The man of God's own choosing.
Dost ask who that may be?
Christ Jesus, it is he,
Lord Sabaoth his name,
From age to age the same,
And He must win the battle.

—From the lyrics to "A Mighty Fortress is Our God" (a hymn written
by Martin Luther, paraphrasing Psalm 46)

LaCroix Homestead, Kearneysville, West Virginia—Two Months Before the Crunch

Megan had put the boys down for an afternoon nap, which meant that they would spend forty-five minutes giggling and likely not sleep, but it was worth the effort if they did. It was Saturday and Malorie was busy doing side work fixing vehicles to earn some money for herself. She usually took clients by word of mouth only and arranged parts and consumable supplies during the week, giving her the opportunity to work nonstop on a Saturday when Megan was home.

Megan was moving some electric fencing in quiet reflection when she caught herself saying out loud to the curious sheep nearby, "I need to decide about Joshua." She pounded in the grounding rod and set the charger on the fence before heading over to Malorie. She rarely disturbed her sister when she was working to earn money; Megan was well aware what Malorie had given up to come be with her. Megan grabbed two cold National Bohemian beers from the refrigerator on the back porch and headed out to the shop.

There exists a nexus of unspoken communication between sisters that is not understood outside of that relationship, a connection that meant not having to say anything before introducing a topic. Megan saw Malorie's legs sticking out from underneath the F-250. She turned down the volume on the radio, touched the cold bottle to Malorie's calf to get her attention, and said, "He's a good guy and deserves my decisiveness."

"I know that you don't get personal over high-side e-mail, and it's only been five months since you started having lunch together. Where does that leave you?"

"That's just it, I don't know. I'm very hesitant to have him come to Kearneysville to meet you and the boys—it's a huge risk. What if the boys don't like him, or what if they really do like him and then the relationship deteriorates between us? You know that I do all that I can to protect Leo and Jean, and if I bring Joshua across the boundary of my life to their lives it changes things."

"I haven't met him." Malorie grabbed the right-side mirror to help herself up from the creeper. She wiped the sweat from her forehead, took a long swig from the bottle to counteract the August heat, and asked, "What would Papa say about him?"

"Joshua is not a logger, and he was raised in a Catholic orphanage, not the backwoods of Maine. I doubt that he could set a choker line or sharpen a saw chain, but he is very grounded and a good Christian man—I think that Papa would approve once he got to know him."

"You weren't there when Papa died in that logging truck rollover, but those few weeks before the accident he seemed to know about his impending death—he became quite chatty."

"Papa? *Je ne comprends pas.*"

"Yes, Papa! He would still continue to drink a lot after Mom was killed by that drunk driver, but he somehow sensed that his time was short and would give me these long monologues on life and what was important. It kept me up until late doing my homework, but I would trade all my frustration then for another opportunity to hear him again now. Do you remember what his favorite saying was?"

"I think so—it was, 'I already told you no.'"

"Not that one." The two sisters enjoyed a long laugh together before Malorie said, *"Le génie est une longue patience."*

Megan cocked her head and offered, "It would seem that after five months I'm becoming impatient perhaps?"

"You don't give yourself enough credit. Things broke down with Eric before he asked for a divorce, *n'est-ce pas?*" Megan nodded and Malorie continued. "It's been three and a half years now since Eric left, Leo is five, and Jean is a precocious three. If nothing changes in your situation, then you are not going to progress past where you are now. Those boys need an opportunity, more than the pittance Eric pays you every month. I know that you're having a lot of trouble trying to reconcile how much you disagree with what the Agency is doing domestically and the fact that you have to work for them to make ends meet. Someday that will have to end, because you will not be able to live with yourself if you stay there. Moreover, Leo and Jean need a mother and a father—you don't expect me to teach them how to pee on a tree, do you?"

They laughed, and without saying any more Megan collected the bottles and put them in the recycling bin while Malorie slid back under the truck to finish replacing the universal joints. Megan reached into her pocket, pulled out her cell phone, and stood on the corner of the property where she could get the best signal and dialed Joshua. After two rings, he answered, "Hey, good lookin', how are the chores coming along? Did the boys go down for a nap?"

"Joshua, would you like to come over next Saturday? There's a great coffee shop that I'd like to take you to after you have a chance to meet Malorie and the boys. Can you come for lunch?"

"I will move heaven and earth to make it, if need be."

The following Saturday, Joshua was prompt. He had two Hot Wheels cars in his cargo pocket and he carried a plate of vegetable rolls for lunch. Megan came out of the house with the boys holding her hands while Malorie emerged from the shop with grease on her arms.

Seeing Malorie for the first time gave Joshua the opportunity to compare Megan alongside her sister, and their differences were apparent immediately. While Megan was a classic beauty, Malorie was taller, with sharper facial features. She could have worked as a model. Both sisters were brunettes with blue eyes, although Malorie's hair was a shade lighter than Megan's. Megan's hair was longer, reaching the middle of her back, when unbraided. Malorie had the fashion-model cheekbones, but Megan had the prettier smile. They both had pale complexions and a strong LaCroix family resemblance that was distinctively French—so much so that both would have fit in without comment if they were included in a "Beauties of Quebec" calendar.

"Did you find the place easily?" Megan asked.

"I did." Joshua took a knee to be on the same eye level as the boys, and he said, "Hello, you must be Leo and you must be Jean. My name is Joshua, it's a pleasure to finally meet you." The boys knew enough to offer their extended hand to shake Joshua's, but had not learned the art of eye contact or a firm grip yet. "I heard that you boys liked to eat your vegetables, so I brought these veggie rolls for us to have with lunch."

None of the interaction was lost on Megan, who was warm but not overly affectionate with Joshua in front of the boys. She was not experienced in how to navigate the situation and Joshua was very cautious to pick up on her signals and tread lightly. Malorie came over, and after she was introduced said, "Cool Jeep. Megan tells me that you did a small-block Chevy swap."

"I had it done, since I'm not set up at my apartment to do that kind of work. Everyone recommended Sam up at Mid Atlantic in Glen Burnie. I went to talk to him because originally I thought about swapping a 4BT Cummins into the Jeep. Sam knew his stuff and said that the twelve-valve 6BT was likely a better candidate and would work with the longer wheelbase on my Jeep. But in the end, those drive trains are heavy, require a lot of suspension work to accommodate the extra weight, and are expensive and hard to come by, so a small-block swap was less expensive, by a large margin. I love it. I'm guessing that Megan told you about my spare HEI circuit board?"

"No, she left that part out. But you can be sure that your stock value went up with her when she heard that, though! Going for EMP-proof?"

Joshua smiled and said, "I'm guessing that the analyst gene is dominant in the LaCroix DNA."

Megan asked, "Who's hungry?" and the boys responded loudly and raced each other round to the back porch. The five of them sat down at the table, where lunch was served. Megan looked at Joshua, squeezed his hand, and asked him if he would pray before their meal.

After lunch, Malorie offered to clean up and put the boys down for a nap. Joshua discreetly asked Megan if it would be okay if he left the Hot Wheels cars on the couch where the boys could find them after their nap. Megan kissed the boys and left with Joshua to go get coffee at the Black Dog Café.

As Joshua pulled down the driveway, a chicken strutted out at the Jeep and then ran off of the gravel driveway. Joshua looked over at Megan—realizing that he had never seen her in jeans before but certainly wasn't disappointed—as he said, "Leo and Jean are great boys! Very polite, and they listened to their mother very well; I know that you're proud of them, as you should be."

Megan smiled and her piercing blue eyes caught his. "Butter me up all you want, but you're still buying the coffee."

As they cruised along the back roads, Joshua slowed down to enjoy the scenery and found that comfortable RPM in fourth gear that allowed him to hold Megan's hand and not have to shift. The weather was perfect and the whole firmament seemed to resound with praise toward its Creator with lush green in every direction that they could see. Joshua eased the Jeep into the dirt parking lot close to both the farmers' market and the Black Dog Café. "Aw, too bad the farmers' market is only open on Wednesdays; I could really go for some fresh vegetables and local honey!"

Joshua continued to hold Megan's hand as they walked up to the door of the Black Dog Café. He held the door for Megan, and she waved to Marcy as they walked in. Megan looked over to Joshua and said, "I am going to the little girls' room, just get whatever Marcy recommends for me—she knows what I like." He nodded back and walked up to the counter to order.

Joshua brought her coffee, some freshly baked goods, and a tea for himself back to the table where Megan was sitting. He was hoping for a long afternoon of conversation with her, because there is really nothing like falling in love at a coffee shop. It would have been nice to take her to Montreal, but Charles Town, West Virginia, was as good a place as anywhere to talk for a few hours.

"It was nice to finally meet Malorie. She really seems to know her vehicles. And your boys are quite handsome and well-behaved—I can say that now that I've made good on buying you coffee, *ma chérie*. They certainly seem like a lot of fun. Are they a help around the homestead?"

Megan averted her gaze and traced her finger across the lace holes of her Dr. Martens unconsciously as she answered. "I think that they've had to grow up faster than I would hope. I was expecting the Thomas the Tank Engine stage to last a lot longer than it has, but the boys really have become good workers around the homestead. Auntie Malorie cracks the whip between snacks, hikes, games of tag, and extra stories." Megan smiled, locked eyes with Joshua, who was listening attentively, and said, "They don't understand *why* Eric isn't there, but they do very much realize that he's absent."

Joshua reached out and put his hand on her hand, gently squeezed it, and did not say anything as Megan continued. "Hawaii was paradise. Eric and I were very much in love as newlyweds. Eventually, we both came down on orders together—compassionate assignment, of course—to come to Fort Meade. It was hard to get promoted in the Marine Corps when you're having children—that is a fact. So I was passed up for two promotions and was seemingly locked in at being a corporal. As an NCO I had plenty of responsibility, but as an E-4 it's hard to live on such a small paycheck. Eric was in the navy and we were fortunate to be stationed together. The world was our oyster, or so we thought. We found this house in the country and we bought it. Eric wanted to raise the boys far out of the pressure cooker of the Beltway metropolis, but then not long after we got settled into our new routine and duties, Eric came down on orders to deploy again as a 'Sand Sailor.'"

Joshua asked for clarification. "Sand Sailor? I'm afraid that I haven't heard the term before."

"It's navy slang for a 'fish out of water' or a sailor who is deployed in the desert. It's almost always used as a pejorative term."

"I see." Joshua thought it best not to interrupt her.

"So he was on orders for a whole year; our oldest son was two and starting to toddle around. We thought that he would go over, get his ticket punched, and be in a good spot for his next promotion—such a simple plan. All the while I would be home saving the extra money and paying down our mortgage. Eric said that he liked the job okay, and the long days made the time go by so that he didn't have to think about missing Leo and me as much. But as the time went on, he was not staying grounded in true godly things. He stopped going to chapel services and there was a noticeable decline in substantive letters from him. I guess that the targeting mission really got to him. It's one thing to process signals impersonally as strictly empirical data; it's another to track someone's life and be responsible for steel on target when the boys in black show up to shoot people in the face.

"Somewhere between the ones and zeros of Johnny Jihad's life and the 'actionable intelligence' derived from the analysis—we lost Eric. To deal with that stress, the office would generally play television shows in the office on those huge flat-screen monitors that they used for shift-change briefings. They showed everything from *Seinfeld* to *Friends* to *Desperate Housewives*. You can't take in that level of pop culture and not be affected by it.

"Eric eventually started to notice a female Air Force senior airman attached to his section. She would bring him up on chat more often than necessary and comment on certain scenes in the television shows. Seems like histrionic crass girls with 'daddy issues' are beacons for extracurricular activities. Toward the end of the deployment he called and said that he wanted to discuss the 'dissolution of our marriage,' which could not have come at a more inopportune time because I was pregnant again, but had been reluctant to tell him because things were deteriorating so quickly."

"Wow, so you went from deployment widow to single mom and pregnant?"

"It was illogical. Yes, he wanted to chase his sweet young complicated thing and I was holding down the fort with all the responsibility. You can say that we had a 'mismatch in our commitment level' to the relationship. He initiated the paperwork on his end with the JAG office, and I signed it, and that was that. I was here, pregnant, alone, and a single mom. I called Malorie, and she dropped everything to move down to West Virginia. I could hardly afford the live-in nanny anyhow. I took the option to separate from the Marine Corps and I became another green-badge contractor. I ended up with the house and the leased car, while he took his porn collection, his truck (with the payments), and *all* of the guns. I changed my name back to my maiden name of LaCroix, and the rest is history. That was three years ago now."

Joshua squeezed her hand and said, "I'm sorry you had to go through such a terrible ordeal, Megan, but I want you to know that you haven't scared me away. Knowing what you've overcome, I'm even more amazed by you."

9

TOLERANCE

Farming looks mighty easy when your plow is a pencil and you're a thousand miles from the corn field.

—President Dwight D. Eisenhower

Millinocket, Maine—Four Years Before the Crunch

Malorie LaCroix went on to trade school after she finished high school early and worked as a first-year apprentice machinist at Millinocket Fabrication and Machine, Inc., in Millinocket, Maine. She was more conversant in French than her elder sister, Megan, and after translating some French machinery manuals for Millinocket, Malorie eventually developed a side business doing French-to-English technical translation. She was an avid 4WD enthusiast, preferring older Ford eight-lug pickup trucks to all other modes of transportation. She was nineteen years old and already had a local reputation for building trucks for several people around the state.

Malorie was single and, like her older sister, grew up in a stable family home where her parents loved each other. Their father, Cedric LaCroix, was a lumberman in the northern woods who might be away at camp for weeks at a time, but while he was home he doted on his girls. After an accident late one winter that would have broken most men, he was left injured, with a permanent limp, and no longer able to have children. Since then, he had always joked that he would have to raise his girls like boys, so both Megan and Malorie would learn to sharpen axes with a stone, rebuild chain saws, and drive a skid steer during the summers, and in the autumn they would rack, hunt, pack out, and process deer. No matter how hard he worked them, both Megan and Malorie knew that they were the object of their father's love.

With that level of confidence, the sisters never needed to be reaffirmed by other boys. So why should they care if they never were asked to go out by the football players for pizza after a game or to an unsupervised party out by the lake, which usually meant underage binge drinking and propositions for sex. Malorie had consoled way too many women who had given away what they could never get back.

Megan and Malorie were both homeschooled up through their eighth-grade year in the classical tradition of education. Their mother, Beatrice, had them memorize huge portions of the Bible as well as read nearly all of the classics, the writings from the Scottish Enlightenment, and the Founding Fathers. Beatrice would tell them, "You never know when these books will be outlawed, so read them now. The Founding Fathers were not clairvoyant; they just read their history and decided what kind of government they did not want." Cedric did not have an education beyond the eighth grade, so he was insistent that he would work as hard as he could so that Beatrice would be able to stay home to educate the children properly. He would drill them on their memory work every night after dinner that he was home to ensure that they were getting their money's worth from homeschooling.

After Malorie completed the eighth grade, she had attended the local high school as her sister had for ninth through twelfth grades and, like her elder sister, pursued intellectual interests after her other schoolwork was complete. Since Beatrice worked part-time at the local library in Sherman, Malorie would catch a ride there from Katahdin High School and hang out in a quiet corner consuming volumes of da Vinci, amazed at his mechanical acuity, his use of physics, and his contributions to mathematics.

Megan had joined the USMC a year after high school and was away at Parris "Paradise" Island for boot camp when their mother was killed in a head-on collision with a drunk driver on her way back from a prayer meeting at church. Malorie was only fourteen years old and although no one can ever be prepared for that, she had a lot of growing up to do in a big hurry. Her father, who was always as tough as nails and the quintessential north woods logger, wept bitterly over Beatrice's death. The other loggers said that when he got the news that she was killed, he set down his saw and was never the same again. Cedric and Beatrice had been junior high school sweethearts and he had never known any other woman. When she died, he transferred his love to the bottle and drank heavily. Megan came home on emergency leave to mourn her mother's death.

Five years later Malorie was at the Bridgeport mill checking her part drawing for the proper tolerance, carefully aligning the cutter for tapping a through hole on a structural flange mount, when she heard her name being called from the front office. "Malorie, phone is for you."

"Phone? Whoever calls me at work?" Malorie asked herself.

It was Megan on the other end. "Malorie, Eric divorced me. *J'ai besoin de toi! En ce moment.*"

"Okay, I will pack up tonight and be there late tomorrow evening."

10

VOLUNTARY DISPLACEMENT

Slap some bacon on a biscuit and let's go! We're burnin' daylight!

—John Wayne as Wil Andersen, in The Cowboys (1972)

NSA-W Headquarters—October, the First Year

Joshua watched the news while having breakfast in OPS1 cafeteria, but in the spirit of *fairness* the powers that be had decided to put Fox News on only one day per week and to give more time to MSNBC and CNN. This morning the CNN headlines were all bad.

"If it wasn't for the fact that they make you watch CNN in an airport, who would voluntarily watch the Communist News Network, anyway?" Joshua mumbled to himself. The ticker rolled by with the following text:

"U.S. Dollar Declared 'Trash' by Foreign Investors."

"National Gasoline Price Average Now Over $6.13 per Gallon, $10 a Gallon in Sight."

"Boston, Houston, and Fresno Pawn Brokers Are Asking for Police Protection."

**"CDC Reporting Preliminary Concerns of a Resistant
Strain of Influenza Virus Seen in Charlotte, NC."**

**"CBO Score for New Budget Proposal Is 'Untenable with
Current Revenue.'"**

**"President to Meet with Minority Opposition Leadership
on New Security Measures."**

Joshua took in the news and methodically processed it as he finished his oatmeal. His mind was already racing from his conversation with Dustin over the phone last night, and the onslaught of bad news was only briefly interrupted by the camera crew going on location to a Humane Society rally in Lansing, Michigan. After a few commercials, the cheery news anchor was back to cover the president's meeting this morning with a joint session of Congress.

"The president is in an emergency session of Congress and pleaded with them to pass the Omnibus Patriot Safety and Security Act this morning. [Audio cuts to president.] 'I have asked Congress to pull together and do the right thing for America. The debate has been robust, and we have heard from both sides of the aisle. I have listened to all the concerns and now is the time to act to secure America in this new age of multifaceted threats.' Watchdog groups on Capitol Hill are saying that this is an overreach, and while no comment has come from the president himself, his press secretary had this to say last Tuesday: 'This is only a temporary measure granting certain powers to the president—it has a thirty-day sunset clause—unless we are unable to resolve the present crisis.' The eighteen-hundred-page bill is likely to see a vote before the close of business today."

"Yeah, right, that 'unless' is a pretty big gamble to take with the Constitution! We've all seen their record on not reading two-thousand-page-long bills. Don't these clowns work for us?" Joshua asked himself.

On his way to the office, Joshua walked past the murals of law enforcement personnel doing their mission on the NSA campus adorned with the words, "Train, Defend, Protect, Deter, Authenticate and Respond." He was on his way to the Security Operations Control Center (SOCC) to check in to his shift, fifteen minutes early, as always. Joshua drew his weapon and attended the shift change brief. Afterward he logged on to a high-side terminal to quickly check e-mail, and he was glad to see among the usual all-users "no reply" e-mail that there was actually a message from Megan waiting for him:

Subject: Parler Affairs
Unclassified: FOR OFFICIAL USE ONLY
Joshua,
    Please stop by when you are able.
C'est avoir de très l'importance.

M.

Unclassified: FOR OFFICIAL USE ONLY

The day was far from business as usual, the buzz in the news feeds translated into heightened national security posture. As an implementation of additional security measures, NSA-W was conducting random vehicle checks even for blue- and green-badge personnel and 100 percent vehicle checks for all visitors. This effort required extra officers to be dispatched to the VCPs, and Joshua found himself assigned for the late-morning shift. Around 1300 he was able to come to Megan's office, but only for a brief moment.

Almost as soon as Joshua knocked on the door, Megan was ready for him and suggested they go down the hall to speak in private.

"Joshua, I'm really worried," Megan began.

"About?"

"Where have you been? You haven't heard?"

"Let's just say that I got your e-mail this morning, then responded to a 'hey you' tasking to go and acquaint myself with the greater central Maryland area's glove compartment contents."

"Fair enough. Well, you know how they recently blocked DrudgeReport .com from the NSA unclass web servers. Well, I checked a personal e-mail account late this morning. It was a message from Malorie about what we had discussed last night."

"Which was what? Megan, I can't stay very long here."

"The president dismissed four conservative Supreme Court justices this morning."

"What? How?" Joshua was truly perplexed.

"By executive order. Evidently, that new Omnibus Patriot Safety and Security Act gives the president the power to do pretty much whatever he wants—*and they haven't even passed it yet.* Those judges were all that stood in the way of a judicial challenge to these emergency presidential powers. Did you see that they're recalling all close-air-support aircraft from Saudi and 'redeploying' them to CONUS? Officially the secretary of the Air Force is just calling it a 'contingency.' I read that in a SADCOM report this morning."

"That is likely classified and we can't speak that way out here. Besides, this whole situation is nuts! Have you seen the financial reports? 'Whither do we go?'"

Megan, quick on the uptake, said, "Yes, I know. Nietzsche would have been very proud of our positive-law-strewn, failed Republic."

Joshua replied, "This morning I asked a colleague about having to take all that extra online training for security of classified information. He didn't seem the least bit put out by having to change all of the passwords to every account we have access to. It just didn't faze him that the same people that dole out our paychecks don't seem to be spying on the North Koreans, but are monitoring my SMS traffic instead!"

Joshua continued, "How far down the rabbit hole does this go anyway? Data can always be historically analyzed and made to say anything."

Megan smoothed the wrinkles on her skirt and said, "It would seem that there are a lot less libertarian patriots and a lot more sheeple collecting a paycheck from Uncle Sam in this big glass house. If they couldn't see the shackles forming around the feet of their fellow citizens now, when would they ever notice?"

Joshua let out a breath loudly, almost whistling, and then said: "I don't know. *Four* justices? Who knows what other powers were granted to the president in the new law? Outlaw homeschooling? Ban firearms? Make us a one-world-government subject to the UN?"

"So do you want to stick around and see what happens?"

"What are you talking about?" Joshua reached out to grasp her hand.

"All I need to do is to go back in that office, send one e-mail to tender my resignation, grab my satchel, and I'm out the door." Megan was completely serious.

"I e-mailed you this morning because I already discussed it with Malorie last night," Megan continued.

"What you're talking about here is pretty radical. I like you, Megan. I *really* like you. I find you fascinating. You let me meet your sister and your boys, which is something special, to be sure—but what you're saying has *huge* consequences for me."

Megan focused her piercingly blue eyes on him and said, "Look, I used to think of myself as trapped by Eric. When he called and broke the news to me about his escapade I knew that there was no way I could pay for the house without his salary, so for about thirty seconds I was willing to *overlook* his indiscretion while I lay on the kitchen floor crying with the phone in my hand. The very next moment, Leo crawled in, and I decided that I would not let him ever see me crying over their father. I told Eric to move on and that I would have his trash packed when he got back to the East Coast. I was not going to be trapped by a man. I was a woman given a charge by God to raise those boys and with His providence I was going to do exactly that. I started putting my money into tangibles, preparations, and the livestock that I knew we would need to raise for food. I called Malorie, and the rest you pretty much know."

"You know that I feel a strong connection to you and your boys—even your sister. But what are you proposing?"

"Five minutes, I'm in that door and back out again *pour toujours*. I can call Malorie on the ride home, and we can be ready to get out of Dodge by tomorrow morning."

"Go where?" Joshua's passion had given way to the onset of anger. "Your native Maine is a thousand miles at least from here and your Accord is not ideal transportation. What family do you still have there anyway? Winter is coming, and if the power went out you would not be in a position to cut enough firewood to survive. Once you were there, I'm sure that you could find some pocket of backwoods Maine where you speak the local dialect and blend in; heck, you may even get across the border to Canada. But it's the getting there that is your biggest hurdle. You'd have to get through Baltimore, Philadelphia, northern New Jersey, New York City, and then Boston—in case you haven't heard, law and order is not in vogue there anymore."

Megan smoothed her brown curly hair back and said, "You're right. I hadn't thought of the urban deathtraps en route. You've seen what it's like leaving this area on a holiday weekend with the traffic; the situation now is ten times more hopeless."

"Maybe not, because I'm actually one step ahead of you on this one."

"How so?"

"Will you marry me?"

"Sure, we could ask the Honorable Clarence Thomas to perform the ceremony, I hear that he has a lot more free time these days."

"Look, I knew that you were marriage material ever since we met for lunch after the morning I busted you in the Friedman Auditorium. Moreover, I'm a serious Christian looking for a godly woman. I'm also smitten with your boys. Maybe it's my upbringing in the orphanage, but I don't want them to be without a father—I've seen what that can do to a boy trying to figure out how to become a man."

"How long do I have to think about it?"

"Probably about as long as it takes for me to go turn in my weapon and come up with a convincing excuse why I need to leave early today. We could beat traffic if we left now."

"And for the ring?"

Joshua pulled out a zip cuff and handed it to her. "I wasn't sure what size you were, but this is adjustable."

Megan walked up to the turnstile and swiped her badge across the reader, and the green light lit up with the accompanying audible relay click allowing her to pass. The sun seemed to shine especially warm that early autumn afternoon and the air seemed to be that much more refreshing knowing that she had picked the day and time when she left—rather than stick around and hope for the best. She envisioned an ostrich with its head in the sand getting shot in the butt and giggled nervously as she realized the magnitude of what had just happened.

Joshua pulled up to PG-165 with the Jeep passenger door facing her; the small act of chivalry was not lost on her. She handed him her green badge without saying a word, and he knew it was destined for the box holding the rest of the visitors' badges. "Uncle Sam will want his ID back," she said to herself.

"Ready to go?"

"Not without my effects."

"What?"

"I need you to go over to the visitors' overflow parking lot, by the static guardrail display, which is where our commuter van is parked. Chuck did not want to wait in the long vehicle line this morning, so he parked over there and we simply walked across Canine Road through the visitors' center gate. I have some things in there that I don't want to do without."

Megan reached into her satchel and found a spare key to the van. She pulled out a scrap of paper and scribbled a note to the van pool saying that she had a family emergency and would be taking some unexpected time off. Next, Megan went around to the rear of the van and opened up the two doors. There in the back was a wooden crate with some stenciled Chinese characters that Joshua could not recognize next to the words "Snew Chain Made in China." Megan reached for the tire iron to break the metal bands securing the wooden crate closed. Inside the crate Joshua was pleasantly shocked to see Megan discreetly pull out a rough cotton cloth bag that she briefly opened to give him a peek at the collapsed AR-7 inside. Taking up the rest of the space in the wooden crate was one hundred rounds of carefully packed .22LR ammunition and a small cleaning kit. She put the contents in her satchel as she commented, "One of my friends from B Detachment was a Chi-ling"—Chinese linguist. "She works in one of the shops that deals with tracking new Chinese communications technology or something like that. Anyway, I had her print out the Mandarin characters for 'snow chains' and then I made the stencil misspelling to hopefully give the box enough credibility to not be opened should we have a random vehicle inspection like you were doing this morning. Since they usually cancel work when it snows, I thought it would be good cover with low probability of ever having someone who wants to open it. The rest of the van pool thought that I was just being overly cautious. This van is the only thing that keeps me going home nightly to my boys, so I prepare accordingly."

Also in the back of the truck was a .50-caliber ammo can with one of those tamper-evident serialized metal one-time-use bands that was used to seal the door on a cargo truck. Written in a black marker across the top was BREAK-DOWN BOX. Megan just smiled and said, "A girl has got to be prepared, you know."

"So, as an NSA cop ..."

"*Former* NSA cop—you just quit, didn't you?" Megan quipped.

"Not formally; if the SOCC knew what I was doing right now, I would likely need that zip cuff back for my own wrists. But as I was saying, you can't bring firearms onto the NSA campus. Should I even ask what is in the ammo can, Miss LaCroix?"

"You are not read on to that compartment. Just kidding. It's a fuel pump from a junkyard for the same year as this Ford Econoline van, along with a forty-five-foot roll of wire with alligator-clip terminals and thirty-five feet of three-eighth-inch tubing. Malorie fabricated it all for me, soldering the connections, and then mounted it to a piece of plywood cut the same size as the side wall of the can to give extra static electricity protection if I had to use it. The fuel pump is for extracting fuel out of a tank if ever needed and there was no grid power. I also keep a can of Slime fix-a-flat, a tire plug patch kit, a spare serpentine belt for this van, multitip screwdriver, pliers, a 'shifting spanner,' as our Brit friends say"—she held up an adjustable wrench—"a tube of RTV silicone, a small LED Maglite, a road flare, nonemergency contacts for every county sheriff's department between here and home, and a small box of blade fuses."

"Megan, I have certainly grown to love you, but after seeing you produce a gun that was hidden in plain sight this whole time, I love you all the more."

"I think it was God's providence that brought us together. Let's saddle up; we're burning daylight here, cowboy."

Unceremoniously, Joshua's Jeep pulled out of the overflow parking lot and turned right onto Canine Road, and then headed toward Columbia on 32.

"I don't take it lightly that you trust me; I want you to know that I'm committing myself to the success of you and your boys. I've done my growing up and lived life. Leo and Jean are likely going to grow up in some austere times ahead—you know it and I know it. To that end, I wanted to tell you what my plan is.

"You remember me telling you about my buddy Ken Layton, from the Catholic summer camp that I went to years ago? Well, he and his wife, Terry, have been hooked up with this guy named Todd from Idaho. He said that if things ever went really bad, that he and Terry were going to drive out West to 'bug out.' He's been trying to tell me for years about the survival retreat, but I just thought that was all Chicken Little–type stuff. I mean we made it through two World Wars and the wheels have not fallen off of the bus yet, so what was he talking about? As it turns out, he has been texting me these past few days in one last attempt to reach out to me. Ken, Dustin, and I have always loved each other like brothers, so I don't discount Ken's sincerity and his fervor to try and win me over to his point of view."

"Do you think that we can really make it all the way to Idaho?" Megan asked.

"No, I don't. At one time, Ken even got me on a three-way Skype call with this Todd guy. I was rather incredulous, his screen name was 'End of Beans,' and he didn't use the camera. Ken later told me that it was a play on the phrase 'The end of the world as we know it' except that Todd was an accountant so I guess he managed to merge all that weirdness into one tidy screen name.

"Todd wanted me to sign up for the mutual assistance group package and was even willing to have Terry send me a buying list of where to start based solely on Ken's recommendation and that he knew that I was a cop. I politely thanked him and said that I had a lot of years of service in and that I was going to stick it out here in Maryland at least until I retired. With all of the redundancy built into the government, we should fare better than everyone. That was my thinking then, but today is a different day."

"The suspense is killing me here. Where are we going?"

Joshua took a long drink from his stainless steel REI bottle, offered some to Megan, and said, "Dustin invited me to a picnic."

"You quit your job to attend a picnic?"

"Dustin, who is of the same mind as Ken, called me last night and wanted to catch up since the last time we talked a month or two ago. He asked me about you."

"*Moi?*"

"I told him that I was falling in love with you. He said that if the situation ever worsened—how does he put it?—'When the Schumer hits the fan,' that I should proceed directly to his house for the picnic, and that I should bring you with me as my wife. The implied task is to '*Get here, Wingnut!*'" Joshua smiled as he retold the story. "He sometimes adds 'Wingnut' to the end of the sentence to tease me about not joining another branch of the military.

"After Ken's text messages and Dustin's call last night, I packed that footlocker you see in the backseat, just in case. All I have at my apartment is my music stuff, a crossbow, a used couch, some thrift store kitchen stuff, and my laptop. I'm not a materialistic person, except for my Jeep. I just can't live without you, Megan; I want to spend the rest of my life with you."

"Well, whisking me away out of the belly of the beast was a good start."

"So, here's the turnoff to cross the Potomac—whoa, that's a lot of flashing strobe lights up there! I wonder what that's all about." Joshua reflexively reached for his holstered pistol, but he remembered that he had turned in his issued pistol and that his personal one was in the footlocker behind them.

Joshua was still wearing his NSA police uniform and he silently prayed that he would have favor with this checkpoint. Families with overloaded cars trying to get somewhere were unpacking all of their belongings on the side of the road for police dogs to sniff and rubber-gloved personnel from the Department of Homeland Security "Field Operations" to go through.

"Megan, go ahead and get your ID out. And keep that AR-7 wrapped up. The laws about even having a gun in your car in Maryland are not Second Amendment friendly."

After half an hour, Joshua inched up to the Maryland state trooper and the Frederick County policemen who were conducting the checkpoint.

The young trooper said to Joshua, "Identification, please. Where are you going?"

Joshua did all of the talking. "I am taking my fiancée here back home to West Virginia."

"You're not from West Virginia, Officer Kim?"

"No, sir, I live in Howard County, but I'd like to think I could live out this way one day."

Reciting as if he'd said it many times before, the trooper said, "Any of the following are declared contraband as of 2:00 P.M. EST by order of Governor O'Malley: magazines of any caliber that can hold eleven or more rounds; any physical gold, silver, or platinum not in worn jewelry form; any cash in excess of fifty-five hundred dollars, or durable goods of that same amount. Do you have any of those items?"

"No."

"Just that footlocker with you is all?"

"Roger that."

"Here are your IDs, have a good night."

The Maryland state trooper thought it odd that Joshua would be this far from NSA, but ultimately it was Megan's West Virginia driver's license that got them through the checkpoint. Joshua didn't ask what the situation was, and the trooper didn't tell him anything except that it was "Just a precaution, on orders from the governor's office."

"Well, it appears that you successfully just emigrated out of the People's Republic of Maryland, Officer Kim."

"Better a year early than a day late." Joshua sighed.

They arrived at Megan's house an hour later, just before dinner.

11

YOU CAN'T GET THERE FROM HERE

Do not by any means destroy yourself, for if you live you may yet have good fortune, but all the dead are dead alike.

—The Horse Hwin, in *The Horse and His Boy* by C. S. Lewis

LaCroix Homestead, Kearneysville, West Virginia—October, the First Year

None of the roads they traversed from the Maryland checkpoint to Megan's house were unfamiliar, but the collective sense of urgency and uncertainty was very high between them. They listened to the radio and said little, except for what the immediate actions would be when they arrived at the homestead. Joshua pulled in the driveway and Megan hopped out of the Jeep. After he triple-checked his mirrors to make sure that there were no kids behind him, Joshua instinctively backed up the Jeep toward the house. He opened all the doors and the hood (Malorie would likely want to inspect the Jeep from headlight to taillight), grabbed his footlocker, and headed into the house.

Malorie and Megan had already made most of the arrangements for a quick exodus in the weeks before. Since their original plan was to head to Maine, they intended to pack the Honda Accord's trunk very lightly. That afternoon, Megan had called Malorie before leaving her office to say, "Malorie, *il est temps. Je serai à la maison bientôt. Je t'aime.*"

After she had hung up the phone with Megan, Malorie acted immediately and called the nearest neighbor with a homestead up the road. She offered them all of the livestock to raise or slaughter as they wished, including the fifteen laying hens they had. Malorie also said that whatever was still in the house after twenty-four hours was theirs to take. Malorie had the boys' items packed and both of their bug-out bags ready by the door.

When Megan walked in she saw the boys prone on the floor zooming their cars back and forth in what looked to be the most intense race in the history of mankind's pursuit of speed. She got down on her hands and knees to kiss them, while they stayed fixated on their race. With all of the pending turmoil, it was nice to know that they still thought that everything was normal. Malorie was in the kitchen making dinner when she looked up and caught her sister's eyes. They didn't need to say anything, for they were in lockstep already. They exchanged a quick hug and continued working.

Joshua came through the front door, set down the footlocker, and joined the race with the boys for a few minutes before helping Malorie get dinner on the table. Dinner was solemn. Not a whole lot was said in front of the boys about what would be happening in the next few hours. Megan bathed the boys while Joshua did the dishes and helped clean up from dinner.

Malorie had gone into the basement to dig out one of Eric's old large-framed backpacks. "I assume that is for me?" Joshua asked as he moved from the kitchen to the dining room, where Malorie was laying out the contents of her bug-out bag.

"Yes, it is. I saw that you didn't have a bug-out bag with you, so I'm going to lay mine out here on the table. You can make yours match or customize it as you see fit, cafeteria style. We should have extras of all of these items in one of those tubs over there—help yourself. What do you have for weapons?"

"I have a Glock 19 in my footlocker with five magazines and a thousand rounds of ball ammunition. I also brought my Remington 870 with a hundred double-ought buck shells and my scoped .270 for long-range work with about three hundred rounds for it. I knew that we wouldn't be able to take it all, so I brought what I knew would be necessary."

"I think that we'll be fine if we split the load between us." Malorie looked solemn and then added, "I'm guessing that we won't be able to drive the entire way there for whatever reason, so dismounting becomes easier if you pack for that contingency."

Joshua answered, "I agree; wow, that is quite a spread there. It sure does look like you have fine-tuned that load quite a bit." Without knowing it, Joshua was in for an education in bug-out bags.

Malorie continued, "This is my ten-by-eight tarp in dark earth tones, and Megan also has one just like it. We can put zip ties around the edges in the grommet holes to make a large sleeping bag. Which brings me to this little Snugpak Jungle Bag—small, light, perfect for what we would need.

"Nature is a cruel and unforgiving teacher, and chance favors the prepared gal. You only have to be caught once in the woods in Maine, cold and wet after dark, to realize how insignificant you are in the forest. We have two little boys that depend on us for everything; we're not taking any chances. Go ahead and grab an extra few boxes of .22 long-rifle ammo if you believe that you can manage. We can always trade it or use it for my sister's AR-7."

Malorie heard the boys being wrangled into pajamas upstairs and she smiled as she continued, "We each have one of the McNett Outgo microfiber towels. They are big enough to dry an adult and a child each, and they also come with this mesh pouch that comes in handy to put our toiletries in. Over here I have a small bunch of zip ties held together with this bread bag tie, grab whatever size is clever. Here is a military lensatic compass, indispensable, in my opinion. I'm not sure if we have an extra one of these, though."

Joshua replied, "No problem, I actually have my old one from my Air Force days in my footlocker over there."

"Great, redundancy is key. Next I have about ten one-gallon Ziploc bags and fifteen or so quart-size bags. I find that they are helpful for organizing little things at the end. Megan swears by these Maglite LED XL-50 flashlights, so be sure to grab one for yourself. Each of us also has a small strip of kitchen sponge that we've bleached out and let dry in the sun. It's useful for collecting rain water or can even be lowered on a string to a water source that is out of reach, like a well casing, if need be. We each have a multitool, and I see that you have one there on your belt. Grab a boonie hat for yourself over in that bin; you don't want to be sunburnt out there.

"Grab one stainless steel spoon for yourself and a canteen cup if you want one. Do you have any junk silver—you know, the pre-'65 stuff?"

"Actually I do. I have a roll of quarters and a roll of dimes. Plus fifteen Maple Leafs concealed in a belt, and ten of the one-tenth-ounce gold American Eagle coins also concealed the same way."

"Cool, you're hired. Okay, here is where Megan and I divide the one-of items. I carry the collapsible fishing pole and the Go Berkey water filter. Since it's only a one-quart capacity, please grab the only other one we have over there to take with us in your pack. At a halt we'll be able to process twice the amount of water. Megan carries the extra ammo and extra food. We have to assume that the boys cannot carry much of anything except for perhaps a quart of water."

Joshua wanted to key in on a detail here and asked, "Splitting the load should be easier with the three of us. You mentioned ammo. What calibers do you have?"

"We've standardized our calibers between us, knowing that something like this could happen one day. So we both have Smith & Wesson .357s, which can shoot a variety of rounds, like .38 S&W and .38 Special, as you may know. I also managed to get an M1 Carbine for each of us. Megan has her AR-7 and I have a twelve-gauge Mossberg 500. We bought all of those guns without paperwork through private sales, so in some instances beggars can't be choosers. These should be adequate for what we would need them for, though."

A chorus of "Auntie Malorie" broke out from the top of the stairs, and Joshua smiled and said, "Sounds like you're needed for tucking-in detail."

Joshua stood there alone next to the dining room table. As he packed things in his developing bug-out bag, he thought of what it must be like to live in a house where you have parents who care for you so much and where you're tucked in every night as an individual. All of this was foreign to him, but he imagined that he could get used to it.

Malorie and Megan came down the stairs together, and Malorie asked, "We haven't discussed it, but I assume that we're taking the Jeep and not the Accord?"

"Joshua, what are your thoughts?" Megan said.

"Actually, I was going to suggest it. The Jeep has more ground clearance, and we don't know what we'll encounter between here and Kentucky."

"So we're headed to Kentucky? Is Maine out of the question, then?"

Megan filled Malorie in on their earlier discussion about the impossibility of making it through all of the chaos in the northeastern cities, each one a potential if not certain death trap. "You weren't there, Malorie, but Joshua and I barely made it out of Maryland today; we wouldn't have without his uniform and my West Virginia driver's license."

"The world has changed," Joshua added. "I got a text on the drive here from my buddy Ken Layton in Chicago, who said that he and his wife, Terry, are packing up their Mustang and Bronco tonight to leave for Idaho at first opportunity—but he sorely wished that he would have left yesterday! They're without power and they can hear gunfire throughout the city in just about any direction."

"Okay, Kentucky it is. Who do we know there?" Mal asked.

"We've been invited to a picnic, Mal. And not to bury the lead here, but Joshua and I are engaged."

"Wait, you're getting married now, too?" Malorie was quick on the uptake, but this was a lot for her to process all at once.

Joshua decided to put a marker of his own down on the table. "Nothing matters more to me than you and those boys. I am prepared to give my life so that they have a chance to survive. I never had a family, but they do, and it's worth throwing ourselves headlong in that direction to sustain their existence rather than stay here and gamble ours away."

Up until then, no one had heard from Joshua regarding his motives; it wasn't the kind of thing most people asked about, but everyone tried their best to detect. It was Megan who spoke next. "Sounds like we're all of one accord with our purpose."

Joshua wanted to lighten the moment with levity and said, "Accord? I thought we were taking the Jeep?" They all laughed out loud as the stress of the situation unwound in a split second. "Malorie, I left the hood up, thinking that you'd want to inspect our means of transportation."

"I'll get started right now. Can I bring it into the shop, where there's light to work?"

"By all means, sister-in-law, *mi* Jeep *es su* Jeep. The keys are in the ignition." Joshua smiled and Malorie, who had never forgiven Eric, smiled back. Malorie had been repacking her bug-out bag while they were talking, and dropped it off by the door as she left.

Megan looked at Joshua and said, *"Merci beaucoup."* Joshua didn't say anything. He just embraced her for a long hug followed by a long kiss. He had longed to kiss her for months now, and since they were going to be married eventually, he would have gotten the chance. But today was the day for realizing eventualities.

12

CONVEYANCE

In the day of prosperity we have many refuges to resort to; in the day of adversity only one.

—Horatius Bonar

LaCroix Homestead, Kearneysville, West Virginia—October, the First Year

After the kiss, Joshua looked deep into Megan's eyes and knew that he was where he was supposed to be, doing what he was supposed to be doing, and most important—she was the one he was supposed to be with. Rome was indeed burning, but God's provision had given him the out, wisdom gave them the unction, and courage gave them the impetus to stay ahead of the Golden Horde. If Joshua were to try to explain leaving his job to a coworker or government career counselor, it would not have made sense, but God's workings are different and seldom coincide with positive law, corrupt authority, or lifetime guarantees for Federal Reserve notes.

Malorie's head appeared out from under the Jeep on the creeper. "This thing is dry and rock solid. No leaks, all of the bushings are tight."

Since you decided to go with one of the world's most ubiquitous drive trains, I happen to have a few new parts over there in those bins. I know that I have at least one serpentine belt and some filters as well. We'll see what we have room for at the end and pack accordingly.

"Speaking of, if you're ready we can pack up now and then try to get some sleep before we leave in the morning."

Joshua said, "I'll grab the fuel cans from around back."

With the ladies having most of their items prioritized and packed ahead of time, the work went quickly. The fuel and water were separated by a small tub of tools that Malorie packed. After a short discussion they decided that Joshua would drive and switch off with Malorie, who would be in the passenger seat. Megan would be in the backseat with the boys; the drivers could change out as needed. In total the distance was 550 miles, and no one expected it to be an easy trip. Since this was all a very new experience and no SOP had been established, they decided that all weapons would be loaded and rounds in the chamber with the safety on.

Malorie took a shower and went to bed; Megan sorted through some last-minute kids' items, very grateful that her sister had diligently scanned all of the baby pictures and made double backups of them on password-protected USB sticks for posterity. Joshua cleaned and lubricated all of the weapons and set them by the door, before taking a shower and retiring to the couch. He and Megan would be married eventually, but he insisted on maintaining a prudent separation until it was right to sleep in the same bed together.

13

DEPARTURE

In recognition of cybersecurity as a national priority, the US Cyber Command was chartered to protect our national interests in cyberspace. Although support for this national initiative is gaining ground, it is imperative, going forward, that we broaden our understanding of the science that underpins cybersecurity. We must form collaborative public and private partnerships and devote more attention to understanding security science.

—Keith B. Alexander, General, U.S. Army (Commander, U.S. Cyber Command and Director, NSA/Chief, CSS), *The Next Wave*, Vol. 19, No. 4, 2012

LaCroix Homestead, Kearneysville, West Virginia—October, the First Year

The alarm sounded early on Malorie's phone. She pulled on her BDU pants, wigwam socks, and USMC Danner boots. Then she slipped on an Under Armour long-sleeve shirt and put on a merino wool shirt. The October mornings were chilly in West Virginia, especially with the high humidity and being so close to the river. "Best to dress in layers," she said to herself.

Joshua put the battery back in his cell phone and walked out to the corner of the property where Malorie had told him that he could get the best signal. Joshua called in to the SOCC and said that he wouldn't be coming into work today due to an "unexpected personal situation" that required he be home that day. The voice on the other end of the phone was more than perturbed in the reply, "Yeah, you and about half the force are calling in today to take care of the home front. I'll mark it down in the log and report it to the desk sergeant, who's busy putting out other brush fires right now." Joshua saw Ken's text and saw a reply all from Dustin as well:

Godspeed Ken and Terry. Hope you get this in time. Love you as well brother. Joshua, status?

Joshua felt his eyes well up, as he knew that unless the world started to mend very quickly, this might be the last time he ever got to speak with Ken on this side of heaven. Joshua replied:

Jeep w/ 5 pax, making all haste, sit not good in MD. Will be radio silent here after. Plz pray. Love you both brothers.

Joshua jogged back to the house. He knew that the Agency would likely do a "pull" on his phone when they figured out that he was AWOL, using tower registration data and network metrics to locate his phone and presumably him with it. In recognition of this unique "global adversary" with its finger in every pie, he pulled the battery out of his department-store TracFone and threw it away. (He had paid cash for it, and had activated it from an out-of-the-way pay phone, with no cameras around.) Next he propped the phone on a rock up against a tire on his Jeep so when he rolled out the phone would be demolished under the weight of their getaway vehicle, making him radio silent.

Malorie had the news on, and none of it was good. She helped get the boys dressed, and Joshua had breakfast on the table for them all to eat one last meal together at the LaCroix homestead before departing for Kentucky.

The mood was somber, and toward Martinsburg to the north, they could hear a distant gunshot punctuate the early morning tranquillity. Malorie spoke up. "I'm going to have the boys feed the animals; I think that the grownups need to talk about our plan."

Megan replied, "Good idea." She turned to the boys and said, "Jean, Leo, go feed the animals, we'll have breakfast ready for you when you get back—chop-chop."

In a moment of relative privacy, Joshua said, "I got a text from Ken and Terry last night—not good." Malorie and Megan could tell that Joshua was worried about his brother Ken in Chicago.

Megan said, "We'll just have to pray for the Lord's protection that we're doing what we should be doing and that His favor will rest upon us as we make this trip."

After they all took a turn and prayed together, Joshua started with the practical parts of the plan. "The way I see it is that any progress westward and southward is what we need. In a perfect world we could have left two days ago, but like they say, 'hindsight is twenty-twenty.'"

"What about being tracked?" Megan asked. "I still have the battery out of my phone from yesterday." She turned to Joshua. "If you got that text message, I'm guessing that you powered yours back on?"

Joshua cleared his throat. "Correct, I had to call in that I was not coming to work today, so I used my phone, saw that Ken wrote, and that Dustin responded, then replied all to say that we were mounting up. As you might have guessed, I purposely avoided being more specific than that." Joshua grabbed Megan's hand. (If they were going to have a disagreement, he wanted to start the habit of holding hands, because it is hard to lose your temper when you do that.)

Joshua continued, "As soon as I was finished I pulled the battery and put the phone under my tire so that when we roll I will be forever off the air."

"I understand," said Megan, and she looked at Malorie and said, "I'll do the same to my phone; I'm sure that Sprint will understand. What about you, Mal?"

"I rooted my Android phone a few months ago with a tin foil hat ROM that allows me to kill the cellular board and verifiably turn on or turn off the Wi-Fi card, leaving the device completely passive in true 'airplane mode.' I have a ton of survival, first-aid, and wild foraging apps and military field manuals on there that don't require a network connection. Personally, I think that with a twelve-volt DC charger that can be adapted to charge from a car battery if necessary, we're better off having that information along with us." Malorie may not have ever worked in the spook world, but she'd heard enough from her big sister to know that "one account, all of Google" was not your friend. Malorie put her phone back in her pocket and asked Joshua, "Do you have any GPS, Sirius, or XM installed on the Jeep?"

Joshua raised his eyebrows and said, "No, and I had a guy from my church go through and check to make sure that there were not any emitters on there. He works at the Agency, so he didn't think that I was weird."

Just then the boys came back in and sat down at the table for breakfast. After they had eaten and packed some coloring books and toys, Malorie shut off the gas and extinguished the pilot light on the stove, followed by turning off the well pump and draining the water in the line as best she could in a hurry. She knew that the bank or someone would eventually come for the house, but it was best not to make a bad situation worse due to neglect.

Joshua checked the weapons one last time and loaded them, with the adults holstering their pistols and positioning their long weapons next to them in the vehicle. Megan had remembered to grab some short bungee cords, which made it easy to secure the long weapons in such a manner that they could be easily presented. Megan let the boys run around to wear off some of their interminable energy before they were loaded up into the Jeep.

When you're forced to summarize an experience, it's typical to remember the first memory, the last memory, and likely any painful memories as well. The boys were distracted with getting to ride in a Jeep and unresponsive to Megan hugging them close to her for comfort. All she could think about was them. She thought of Jean toddling under the apple tree, and Leo carrying eggs in an old ice cream bucket up to the back porch grinning from ear to ear with pride. With one last look in the rearview mirror, Megan shed a tear as the Jeep rolled down the driveway, rendering two phones catastrophically destroyed. This would be a new life for all of them, in a world with nothing but the unknown ahead. Nostalgia and hesitation would likely be as deadly as the fires raging through Chicago or the strange, deadly new influenza strain in Charlotte. Joshua caught the gleam from the moisture in her eye in his rearview mirror and reached back to gently squeeze her calf between gear shifts.

As the sun started to paint the eastern sky orange they passed a gas station that had not been updated since the early seventies. Joshua was glad that he had wisely filled up with gas yesterday in Charles Town while the prices were still below seven dollars a gallon. There was a man sitting on a folding canvas camping chair in the back of a truck with a rusted cab; evidently the bed had rusted years before, as it had been replaced with a homemade welded frame and a deck made out of pressure-treated planks. He had a spray-painted plywood sign next to him that read:

Only Premium Gas
$7 $8 $10 per gallon
CASH ONLY.

There was a dog lying contentedly in the shade of the truck, and two much younger men with shotguns were also visible. Malorie noted that the power was still on, because through the garage door window you could see the red Coca-Cola illuminated sign from the vending machine, although the rest of the building was dark.

Malorie, like Joshua and Megan, had been operating on very little sleep and by this time was feeling punchy. She mused out loud, "You know, when you think about it, actually four dollars seems pretty cheap."

"Four dollars for what?" Joshua was not in any form to try to read her mind.

"Four dollars a gallon for gasoline, I mean before this 'Crunch' happened. People used to complain about the price of gas being high, but if you think about it we've traveled for miles already expending fuel that's almost priceless now. Think about it: If we were walking, then how far would we have gotten today? Maybe twenty miles if we were really moving, but not likely—not with two small kids in tow. So at four dollars a gallon for the five of us to be traveling down the road at thirty-five miles an hour seems like a bargain. Heck, forty-four dollars a gallon would seem like a bargain to me if I was one of those people stranded on the 495 D.C. Beltway right now."

"I can only imagine . . . that must be a massacre right about now," Megan groaned.

They slowly made progress down Route 3, keeping their eyes out for potentially adverse situations. Any lead time to spot a roadside ambush with roadblocks using trees or vehicles, malicious actors feigning a breakdown or injury, or really anything could spell disaster for them.

Joshua made eye contact with Megan in the rearview mirror and asked, "How are the boys doing?"

"Pretty tired, a lot of thumb sucking and not much movement. I would like to try to get them to pee when you find a good place to stop."

"Roger that."

Malorie said, "I can spell you and drive for a while if you like, Joshua."

"That may work out great; let's see about it when we stop."

As they clicked off the miles in a westerly direction, they noticed that people were generally moving about. It was uncommon to see a whole lot of work vehicles like landscaper trucks or plumbers' vans out on the roads. Most of the traffic consisted of overloaded cars. Joshua spotted one SUV with a clearly visible propane tank inside the enclosed cab, a disaster waiting to happen. Each small town was conducting itself differently in how it processed traffic. Some towns had a definite roadblock with either local law enforcement or sheriff's deputies stopping each vehicle asking questions about where they were coming from, their reason for travel, and their destination; and some towns were still oblivious to the enormous implications of the Crunch. Joshua usually did the talking when they were stopped at a checkpoint and had his badge at the ready—which usually took the anxiety level down for the law enforcement officer standing behind the B pillar.

Malorie was very cautious as she got the Jeep out on the highway. She kept her speed around fifty-five miles per hour on I-79 South. The afternoon sun was picking up all the hints of autumn as the light shone through the deciduous trees shedding their leaves for winter. Malorie said, "At our rate of speed, we should be in Charleston in forty-five minutes."

"Gotcha, I see our approximate location on our map. Wow, that's a lot of red brake lights up ahead, and I also see police lights past that—proceed with caution."

"Yeah, I am going to stay in the right lane with at least a car length in front of me so that I can jump out if need be," Malorie responded. "Last thing I want to do is be trapped in traffic and make us easy pickings for criminals looking to become Mad Max road looters."

Megan was looking around in all directions, then said with a puzzled voice, "You know, I hadn't thought of it until now, but I haven't seen a lot of semi-trucks with trailers; instead they're all disconnected, standing on the road shoulder. It seems like everyone is running bobtail. I wonder why?"

"I imagine that it has to do with the fact that a loaded semi only gets five or so miles to the gallon, but if they drop the trailer they can likely double that and increase their chances of getting home," Malorie replied.

"Speaking of, how are we doing for fuel?" Joshua asked from the passenger seat.

"Just over a quarter tank left," Malorie answered. "After we get through this mess ahead, let's find some gas. We can save the fuel we carried along with us for when we can't buy fuel at any price."

Joshua answered, "Good idea, looks like the West Virginia State Police are forcing everyone off at this exit." Joshua squinted to read the sign up ahead that identified the exit. "Exit 9. Well according to the map, this Exit 9 coming up is Elkview. And it looks like we don't have a choice; everyone is being forced to get off of the highway anyhow."

14

MUTUAL SELF-INTEREST

I have sworn upon the altar of God, eternal hostility against every form of tyranny over the mind of man.

—Thomas Jefferson

En Route Through West Virginia—October, the First Year

As they prepared to take the exit off Highway 79, Joshua was processing a lot of different information. No matter what the situation was, he knew he had to find solutions that wouldn't lead them into a trap. He didn't want to put them in that position if it could be avoided, not because they were incapable of defending themselves, but the five of them likely couldn't shoot, move, and communicate effectively if they became decisively engaged. "Looks like there's a Speedway gas station over there. Let's check that out. Malorie, be sure to look for a way out like a curb to clear or bushes to drive over for any line you pick to drive down. The last thing we want to do is drive into a shooting gallery that we can't get out of."

Megan, who had been passing out Goldfish crackers as a snack to the boys in the backseat, breathed a noticeable sigh of relief. "I'm glad that you said that, since I was thinking the same thing."

Malorie carefully circled wide past the Speedway to survey the area. A large group of cars seemed to be forming at the McDonald's and Bob Evans parking lots, with a few car horns sounding and people getting out of their vehicles to confront other drivers. The Speedway gas station had cones across the entrance, and a large piece of cardboard spray-painted with the words, NO POWER, NO GAS. Standing in the parking lot as an antilooting measure were five guys with long guns. Clearly, the expectation was that this situation could get ugly in a big hurry. Malorie drove past the gas station, turned the Jeep around, and pulled over. She then looked over her shoulder to address the group. "Seems like this whole area could get violent fast with the interstate shut down. No power, no food, no fuel—we need to figure something out quickly. I doubt most of these people in overloaded vehicles are as prepared as we are, but it's only a matter of time before they figure that out."

Joshua thought before he spoke and said, "That Speedway may still *have* gas to sell, but they aren't selling it because they don't have a way to get it out of the tanks in the ground. Lucky for them I'm with two very smart ladies who improvised a battery-operated pump for just such a situation. The question is, can we get close enough to ask them to allow us to pump fuel with our pump without seeming like a threat?"

"Joshua, if you walk up to them they are only going to see a fit guy with a holstered pistol and likely not hear what you have to say. If *I* walk up there with the pump in my hand and ask for the owner, they'll be less likely to perceive a woman as a threat. I think that I have the best chance of us actually finding out," Megan said. As she finished, a gray Chrysler sedan with the telltale lunging and sputtering sound of a car that is running out of fuel passed them and drifted to an odd angle as it coasted past them to the curb on the opposite side of the street.

"I can't say that I like sending you, but those guys don't seem like they want to get into any kind of a discussion about the gas, so I'll stay back here with the .270 to cover you if need be." Joshua swallowed hard. "Be careful. I noticed that there's a guy with a black rifle up on the roof. I love you."

Megan opened her door and then accessed the ammo can on the floorboard, removing the pump device that Malorie had fabricated for her. She then kissed the boys, said, "Mommy will be right back," and closed the door. She looked into the passenger window and smiled at Joshua and Malorie, then approached the men with the pump device in plain view. After a short conversation with the first man holding a shotgun, he pointed her to another man standing between the plastic-wrapped overpriced bundles of firewood and the ice-chest freezer. Megan confidently approached him and explained the situation. From behind the wheel of the Jeep, Malorie could notice the situation change after Megan spoke to the second man; she could see her gesture toward the Jeep and see him nod in approval. Then he started to shout something to the other men standing in the nearest entrance, gesturing wildly with his one hand while holding a lever gun in the other.

Megan's diplomacy had worked, and she waved to them in the Jeep, pointing to the cast-iron covers recessed into the cement in the rear of the Speedway parking lot. Joshua turned to the boys. "How are you guys doing back there?" An echoing "Good," came in stereo from the backseat, and Malorie slowly maneuvered the Jeep toward the fuel-access holes in the rear of the parking lot. She parked the Jeep so that it was facing generally toward the road, but so that she could easily clear the curb and make an exit through the adjacent back lot if need be. Joshua got out of the Jeep and met Megan by the man near the firewood and ice-chest freezer, noticing that Megan was relaxed and the man was obviously very happy. The man by the freezer spoke first and said, "Your lady here is very smart. I have fuel to sell, but I can't get to it. As you can see, the interstate is closed and things are going to get very ugly here soon."

Joshua answered, "We did notice the situation is potentially volatile here." He extended his hand. "My name is Joshua Kim."

The man with the badly pitted lever gun offered his hand and said, "I'm Ganesh Sansudeen. If you can pump the fuel out with your device, I can sell it to you at fifteen dollars per gallon. Of course, if you were willing to offer the pump in partial payment, then we could negotiate for a lower rate, say ten dollars per gallon. This gives you fuel at a lower price and me the opportunity to sell gasoline, something that would help us greatly right now."

Joshua sized up the offer and then prudently answered, "Ah, friend, you're mistaken if you think that I'm in charge here. Frankly, it's not *my* pump to sell. You'd have to ask this smart and beautiful woman right here. She's the owner of the pump."

Megan thought about the situation and the "savings" on fuel now versus what they might need to do in another situation tomorrow. "Mr. Sansudeen, I can appreciate your offer and it's a fair one on all accounts. However, we're traveling much farther west, our route is uncertain, civil order is deteriorating, and we can't say what the power situation will be at any other gas station on our way. This pump is our only means to access fuel in tanks below ground. Yet, I think that perhaps we can agree to do something to help the situation in your favor. I assume that you're running a cash-only business here today?"

Ganesh looked at her intently. "You are correct, ma'am."

Joshua was transfixed watching his fiancée negotiate this situation. It was clear that Megan was bargaining from a position of power. "Then we can pour fuel into our Jeep from the fuel jugs we have with us, then refill those jugs and be able to meter with a high degree of certainty how much fuel we are buying from you today. In trade, I cannot exchange my pump, but I would be happy to *rent* it to you so that you can fill your vehicle and then any jugs that you have available on hand. This would give you the opportunity to sell fixed quantities of gasoline to stranded travelers at a price that you set—fifteen dollars a gallon seems reasonable given how hard the commodity is to come by right now. In exchange for using my pump, we would be buying the fuel we take at nine dollars per gallon. Do we have a deal?"

Joshua showed his loyalty to Megan by maintaining a poker face as Ganesh stroked his chin and turned the offer over in his head. "We have a deal. How long are the leads on your pump?"

Megan had already thought of this and quickly responded, "Long enough to reach that pickup truck over there so as to not present the risk of starting a fire with fumes and an errant spark."

"You drive a hard bargain. Please fuel your Jeep from the cans that you have with you, as you said, then replenish the fuel that you need. I see that you have three five-gallon cans with you. As a separate agreement, would you sell me one of those *empty* jugs for thirty-five dollars? That's four gallons of fuel in trade for an empty jug. You see, I have thousands of gallons of fuel, but no way to get to it right now and precious few jugs to sell it in. Although, after seeing your pump, I intend to have one of my guys start building one right away if we're able to do so."

"Four gallons of fuel for an empty gas can?" Megan asked out loud to be sure that she understood, and Ganesh nodded his head in agreement. "Yes, we can agree on that."

Both Megan and Joshua shook hands with Ganesh. "Nice negotiating, there!" Joshua said as they walked away from Ganesh to the Jeep.

Joshua posted himself with his .270 rifle behind a small berm on the back edge of the parking lot. He had heard a lot of activity coming from the general direction of the McDonald's and Bob Evans across the street, and he wanted to identify threats before they became too proximal. Two of the men posted close to the road were turning away people regularly now, but Joshua wondered for how long people would take a polite "no" for an answer. With this many people stranded, someone was bound to get stupid. Having seen the whole transaction between his boss and Megan, one of the men employed by the gas station came over to Joshua.

Joshua knew that he would be coming to ask him what he was doing, so in the interest of brevity Joshua said, "I'm just here for overwatch while they fuel up the Jeep. We should be gone soon."

The man was in his midtwenties, with a short-cropped haircut and a good physique. He said, "Going where, exactly? Since you have Maryland plates I take it that you're not from here and that you probably haven't heard *why* the interstate is closed?"

Joshua had been moving from crisis to crisis since they exited the interstate, negotiated for fuel, and got themselves generally sorted out. He had uncharacteristically not thought of the next step from here. "You are correct, sir." Joshua remembered his manners and extended his right hand, "My name is Joshua Kim and I'm in need of information, please. We're headed west to Kentucky, if at all possible."

"Derrick Klaus. Nice to meet you, though I wish it were under better circumstances."

Joshua did not want to lose tactical awareness, so he posted himself with a 120-degree difference in field of view so that between the two of them they could at least keep an eye on the developing situation. "All of this chaos is nationwide, but the biggest news here in Charleston is the prison break last night," Klaus explained.

"Whoa, that's a big variable. How far from here?"

"It was the Mount Olive Correctional Complex, West Virginia's only maximum-security prison. It is less than forty miles from Charleston heading south and east as the crow flies. Although the prison houses less than a thousand inmates, they're the worst of the worst. The whole thing was clearly planned and likely an inside job. I would love to tell you that those thugs were on foot, but a group of them stole three buses, killed a bunch of guards, and likely had an arms cache supplied to them as well. All of that was reported across the ham network, not the news channels, mind you. They were not intent on raping and pillaging the common folk yet; instead they made a beeline for the state capitol building. By the time the authorities knew what was going on, they had two hundred violent criminals descending upon Charleston. The governor and the legislature fled and there simply weren't enough good guys with guns to quell the rebellion. Geography is your biggest obstacle right now, Joshua. The interstate freeways are blocked, and you're unfortunately on the wrong side of Charleston to be trying to flee westward."

"How long until your situation here becomes untenable?" Joshua asked.

Derrick never lost his cool; Joshua guessed he had some kind of military experience keeping him focused through all of this as he continued to scan his sector. "I think that we'll have a full-blown riot situation here in about ninety minutes or less, and I'm not expecting that there are any cops left to dispatch to this place."

To punctuate Derrick's comments a close gunshot was heard, followed by screaming from the other side of the Bob Evans. Joshua was following the briefing the best that he could, but realizing that they would need to leave soon, he asked, "Are we without any options?"

"I grew up around here, and the problem is that your Jeep is not amphibious. To get anywhere in West Virginia, you'll need to eventually cross water. If you head south and east toward Montgomery, West Virginia, then you're cut off from a viable route west anytime soon. I've been keeping tabs on the ham network through my friend Lou, who relays a summary to me every half hour or so. Lou is working up the road at the church with a community-organized roadblock. When the interstate was blocked, we didn't want people pouring into our neighborhoods, looking like refugees but intent on pillaging the good people that I grew up with."

Derrick pointed without looking to his right across Joshua's rifle. "If you head up Frame Road there, you'll run into the roadblock and not be able to get any farther west. However, if you like, I can radio to Lou and tell him to let the guards know your party is coming. They can let you through, and from there you can make your way to the Raymond City/Dunbar area. If that bridge isn't closed, then you might still be able to cross the river and then beat feet west and south from there to get to Kentucky."

Joshua assessed the whole situation before accepting Derrick's help.

"Now for your test of character and goodwill." Joshua looked puzzled. "Did you notice the Chrysler that sputtered to a stop past you where you were parked initially?" Joshua nodded. "That old lady is stuck; no fuel and no way to get it. I know that she lives over in the Raymond City area. The route west across the back roads is pretty complicated if you don't know it—but she does and could give you turn-by-turn directions. This isn't a must, but if I were you, I'd be sowing some good karma right now and take her with you to Raymond City. It's your choice and your risk to take her or not take her and lose precious time before that bridge potentially closes. I think that your ladies over there have that fueling mission wrapped up, so it's time to react most rick tick. I'll call Lou while you load up."

Joshua thanked Derrick and went over to the Jeep to brief Megan and Malorie on their options and the recent developments in Charleston. The sisters agreed that taking the grandmother was a good move. "I have to think that God would honor that," Megan said. "She can sit back here with one of the boys on her lap while you and Malorie continue to drive and keep your eyes open. I have a feeling that things are not going to calm down until we are well out of Charleston. I'll go talk to her; Joshua, you pay and ask Derrick how we signal the guys at the checkpoint."

Joshua hustled across the parking lot and thought, "She thinks of everything!" Derrick was walking toward him with the radio up to his mouth. Joshua said, "Derrick, I cannot thank you enough. My fiancée went to get the woman in the Chrysler; we can get her to Raymond City. What is our signal to Lou?"

"Good on ya, not everyone would have done that for her. Lou said to get a yellow plastic WET FLOOR sign and attach it to your front brush guard. That way they can wave you through from afar. The roadblock is layered, so to get past the first two points, then to the serpentine section, you have to advance to be recognized. Those boys up there are good shots, so proceed with caution. God bless."

Joshua thanked Derrick again and paid Ganesh in cash for the fuel, thanking him once more. He asked for a WET FLOOR sign for the checkpoint and Ganesh appeared back out in a moment with it and some duct tape. Joshua paid him an extra ten dollars for the sign and then got into the driver's side of the

Jeep. Malorie was partially standing in the Jeep, with one leg out, using the door for makeshift cover as much as possible in case she had to react quickly. The boys had been hunkered down in the bushes, but as Megan crossed the parking lot with her arm linked with the older woman's, Malorie called them, *"Viens ici!"* They were all loaded up as the last strip of duct tape was applied to the WET FLOOR sign. The Jeep pulled out of the parking lot, turned right, and then left up Frame Road. A short round of introductions and pleasantries were exchanged with Mrs. Townsend, their new passenger.

Joshua downshifted into second gear and slowly approached the first barrier, an old Pontiac station wagon from an era when Americans built cars that measured sheet metal in acres. The young man situated behind the engine block saw the WET FLOOR sign as a signal and waved them through, speaking into his radio.

Joshua slowly cleared the second barrier and was again waved ahead, then crept through the serpentine section up the hill toward Sandy Grove Missionary Baptist Church, where he was greeted by a young, overweight man holding an Icom radio. Malorie rolled down the window and the man said, "Hey, you must be Joshua; I'm Lou. I see that you took the extra passenger." Leaning over to talk to Mrs. Townsend, he said, "Ma'am, how are you?"

Mrs. Townsend answered, "I've been better, but thank you for all of your help. I was visiting my grandchildren in Sutton; now all I want is to get home. I haven't been able to get hold of my husband, Dale. The kids all insist that I carry this stupid cell phone, and it hasn't worked since about noon today."

"We noticed the same thing, but us hams are prepared for that!" Lou held up his Icom radio and then continued, "We are getting reports that the roads from here to Dunbar are passable, no significant reports of civil unrest. Keep that WET FLOOR sign on your brush guard; I can relay to other hams farther down to look out for you."

Joshua said, "Will do."

"How are you fixed for water?" Lou asked.

"We're good on water, food, and also fuel, thanks to some prudent planning by my sister back there," Malorie said.

"Once you cross the river you should be okay. Godspeed." He tapped the hood of the Jeep like some sergeant in a war movie, and they were once again making progress westward.

15

BYPASS

That's what happened under communism—and increasingly, it's happening in America. As Joseph Sobran put it: "Need" now means wanting someone else's money. "Greed" means wanting to keep your own. "Compassion" is when a politician arranges the transfer.

—John Stossel

En Route Through West Virginia— October, the First Year

The Jeep rolled slowly along winding roads. Malorie had already committed the next portion of the map to memory, so she knew to turn right at the intersection, as it was the most westerly option in the unfamiliar terrain.

Mrs. Townsend, or Beatrice as she preferred to be called, gave them exact directions on how to navigate to Nitro, West Virginia, where they would be looking for the Third Street Bridge. No one else in the Jeep could yet appreciate just how far out of the way they had had to go to circumnavigate Charleston, but it increasingly became clear just how providential it was that they'd met her. Beatrice explained that she was the wife of Pastor Dale Townsend of St. Paul Baptist church in St. Albans, and that he had been golf partners with Pastor Townsend since the two of them graduated seminary together more than forty years ago. "I never would have thought that law and order could diminish so quickly!" Megan let out a long, low whistle and nodded. "In all of my years in colaboring with Dale, we have been on dozens of mission trips and we have seen what happens when man decides not to live according to God's law and what a reckless experiment that is—but here in West Virginia? I'm sorry; I shouldn't talk this way in front of your boys."

Megan grasped her hand and said, "We appreciate you helping us, and your candor as well."

As Malorie threaded through the back roads, Beatrice engaged the children as only someone who has taught decades' worth of Sunday school could do. She was attentive as they explained the pages that they had colored and was even more pleased at the boys' recall of Scripture.

As they neared Nitro, there were noticeably more people and an equally high proportion of tension as well. Beatrice directed them toward the Third Street Bridge. They could see the cloudy sky at dusk reflecting orange back from the city that was engulfed with flames to the east. Traffic was thick, and they were not moving very fast, but at least they were moving. Malorie always made sure that she drove with at least one car length in front of her and a clear "out" in case she needed to do some evasive driving. Nearing the bridge they had an encounter with a local sheriff's deputy, who flagged them down to ask why they had a WET FLOOR sign on their front brush guard. Joshua, who spoke "cop," did all of the talking; he sheepishly grinned and said that he would remove it as soon as they crossed the bridge. Joshua took the opportunity to ask the deputy of any news on the other side of the river. "It's hard to say with all of the reports coming in. The interstate is shut down, and the through-town traffic is very dicey. We're getting reports of looting and even some break-ins."

Joshua knew that everyone else was getting impatient, so he kept the conversation brief and direct. "I think that we can avoid any retail areas just fine and steer clear of the looting, but are there any patterns to the break-ins? And what is the best route for us to get to Kentucky?"

Malorie kept her cool, nonchalantly smiling and nodding to defuse tension. The sheriff's deputy was getting noticeably concerned with the traffic lined up behind the Jeep, and he quickly responded, "None of the detectives have given any official statements, but the talk across the radio seems to be that people are fond of their social media street cred." Joshua looked puzzled as the sheriff's deputy continued, "I have yet to figure out why, but people who post all these pictures and links about guns seem to have pretty poor OPSEC, and some smart criminals must have been taking note before the power went out because they're making surgical strikes on those people now. Why people advertise about themselves like that is beyond me, but some folks sure are taking advantage of all of the geo-tagged photos now! We just don't have the manpower to stop it. Did you say that you're heading over the bridge?"

"Yes, we need to get Mrs. Townsend to the St. Paul Baptist Church parsonage just over the bridge. From there, we're looking to make it to Kentucky."

The deputy may have been young, but he had his senses honed to already know how many people were in the vehicle and a general description of each, so he looked directly at Beatrice Townsend and said, "Ma'am, there have been reports of gunfire from the apartment building behind your church—please be careful." He then shifted his gaze to Malorie and Joshua and said, "I would avoid any big roads. All routes into Charleston are closed due to the escalated criminal gang violence, making major highways going west pretty congested. I see that you have paper maps, good on ya, since the cellular service has been down most of the day. Keep moving. People are getting relieved of their lives and property if they hang out on the side of the road too long." The sheriff's deputy then stood up and tapped the hood of the Jeep and waved them on through the checkpoint, across the Kanawha River and over the bridge.

Malorie slowly let out the clutch. "Do they teach everyone the hood-tap maneuver around here, Mrs. Townsend?"

"It would appear so! The church is not too far up here on your right after you cross the bridge. Will you be on your way, or can you all come inside the parsonage and stay a while?"

Megan spoke up. "We would love to stay, but I'm afraid we will only have time for a bathroom break and then we must be moving on."

They reached the parsonage, and Joshua stayed with the Jeep while Malorie and Megan followed Mrs. Townsend inside with the boys. At this point, it was becoming less strange for Malorie to carry her sidearm and slung weapon with her wherever she went, but carrying it into someone's house would likely always be strange.

Megan cycled the boys through the bathroom, and Malorie had a moment to speak with Pastor Townsend about the deteriorating situation in the apartment building next door. Beatrice emerged from her well-stocked pantry with some late-season cabbage and kale. She then asked if she could give the boys some cookies from the batch that she baked before she left to see her grand-kids, to which Malorie smiled and answered, "We know better than to tell a grandparent what she can and cannot do with cookies."

Megan thanked the Townsends and left her sister to be the cool auntie and broker the cookie deal. She then went outside to relieve Joshua. Megan hugged Joshua while reflecting on the day's events. "It's already dark, and we only made it as far as Charleston—but given the current situation across the river we are very blessed to even have gotten this far."

Joshua replied, "Indeed, God has extended His grace to us in getting us here." Joshua looked her in those stunning blue eyes and said, "Watch your six out here, we'll be rolling very soon."

Joshua turned around to walk to the house with the empty water bottles in hand and Megan grabbed his sling across his back, spun him around, and kissed him, saying, "Hurry up in there. By the way, there's more where that came from."

16

THUNDER BAY

It's an edgy place. I mean, in the sense that it still hangs on out there like a rawhide flap of the old frontier, outposted from the swirl of mainstream America. The Upper Peninsula [of Michigan] is a hard place. A person has to want to hurt a lot to live there.

—John G. Mitchell, *Audubon* magazine, November 1981

Sault Ste. Marie International Bridge Plaza— October, the First Year

Once the Crunch started, Ray McGregor didn't waste any time leaving Michigan. He just settled up on the cost of the propane that he had used and said his good-byes to his hosts. Long experience with gooseneck trailers made hooking up his nineteen-foot Toy Hauler quick and easy. After testing his trailer lights, he was ready to roll. Even before he got on the highway, he turned on the pickup's radio. He immediately switched from his usual FM classical music station to WKNW, at 1400 AM. There, he heard a litany of bad news. This was it: *the Big One* that he and Phil had long talked about. The major whammy. The Great Reset. The end of the world as we know it. *Götterdämmerung*.

Ray's border crossing at Sault Ste. Marie International Bridge an hour and a half later was both slow and stressful. The bumper sticker on the RV immediately ahead of him was emblazoned with SAY YA HAY TO THE UP. He had a lot of time to look at it. Longer than he liked, since he was anxious to cross the border. There were thirty or more trucks, campers, and RVs ahead of his, and none of the usual perfunctory "flash and wave-through" transits going on. As he waited in the queue of vehicles ahead, Ray tried repeatedly to call his parents at their ranch in Canada and his sister in Florida, using his TracFone cell phones. None of the calls were going through. The only good news was that the toll for his pickup with a two-axle trailer was still pegged at six dollars, despite the raging inflation.

The border crossing at the international bridge was unusual in that it had a separate lower plaza for trucks, RVs, and anyone towing a trailer. Nearly everyone was stopped and questioned at length, and passports were closely scrutinized. Judging by the large number of vehicles directed to the return loop, it was obvious that the border was effectively closed to anyone except returning Canadians. The RV with Michigan plates ahead of him was allowed to pass, but he noticed that the man had passed a mixed bundle of U.S. and Canadian passports (of two noticeably different shades of blue) to the Border Services officer. Ray surmised that the man was a dual citizen or that he had a Canadian wife.

A series of signs posted by Canada Border Services Agency/Agence des Services Frontaliers du Canada, reading "Border Crossing Ahead," warned: ALL VEHICLES SUBJECT TO SEARCH and a more friendly: HAVE YOUR PASSPORT READY. When he reached the head of the queue, a young Border Services officer spent a long time looking through the pages of Ray's passport and scanning it. Ray had been accustomed to border checks taking less than two minutes. The officer quizzed Ray about firearms and Tasers, *twice*. In recent years, they had begun asking about the amount of cash he was carrying "in excess of one thousand dollars," but with the recent mass inflation, that question would have seemed laughable to most cross-border travelers.

When the questioning turned to his final destination, the officer seemed more relaxed and conversational. But then he asked a question that took Ray by surprise: "Do you have sufficient printed currency to buy fuel to reach your destination?" Ray promptly answered "Yes," but he realized how quickly the concept of cash had been inverted at the border, with the advent of the Crunch. Just a few months earlier, the officer would have been suspicious if Ray was carrying several thousand dollars. Now the officer needed assurances that Ray *had* a large enough wad of cash to see him home without being stranded. (Gas stations had suspended taking any payments with credit cards.)

The officer thumbed through the back of the passport, examining the entry and exit stamps. "It looks like you've been spending much more time in the States than you have in Canada, for the past two years."

Ray nodded, "Yeah. I've been researching a book on World War II aviators—doing a lot of interviews. I didn't bother with a work visa. As you can see, I've never exceeded six months for any stay."

This was the first time that Ray had ever had his vehicle thoroughly searched. Shining his flashlight around the interior of the trailer and seeing the chain saws and woodsplitter, the Border Services officer said, "You said that you were writing a book."

"Well I didn't say that a publisher was *paying* me to write a book. I've been writing it freelance, and I've got to eat, so I cut firewood."

"I see. Well, have a safe trip home to BC. Be very cautious, and keep your tank full. Gas is becoming hard to find."

Just north of the Canadian side of the city on Highway 17 (the Trans-Canada Highway) Ray crossed the boundary of Lake Superior Provincial Park. Watching the kilometer markers closely, he stopped at a pullout just past kilometer post 27. The spot was deserted, with only the occasional car passing by.

He pulled a folding entrenching tool out from behind his seat and his GPS receiver out of the glove box, and stowed both of them in a rucksack. After locking up his pickup and checking the tires on both the pickup and the trailer—as was his habit each time he stopped on long trips—he walked into the woods following a deer trail. About 120 yards in, he came to a large and familiar stump that had a distinctive protruding splinter that was left standing straight up where the first cut had met the felling cut. Backing up to the stump, he took nine paces south. This brought his feet directly in front of a pie-pan-diameter flat rock—one of just a few rocks that were within view, and the only one of its size. Flipping it over, he began to dig. Just a few inches down, his entrenching tool struck something that made a hollow sound. He pulled a plastic-wrapped ammo can out of the hole. Originally designed to hold flares, the twenty-inch-long steel can had been repainted with brown Rustoleum paint.

Peeling off the plastic, Ray was pleased to see that the can had acquired just a bit of surface rust in the fourteen months that had passed since he'd last inspected it. Opening the can, he found a plastic bag containing $640 in Canadian dollars. Beneath that was a translucent white plastic tube containing seventeen one-ounce silver Canadian Maple Leaf coins.

Wrapped in an oily rag and several layers of plastic bags was an Inglis Mk I* Hi-Power 9mm pistol. The gun's utilitarian gray phosphate finish was in fine shape, with no sign of corrosion.

He spent several minutes loading all of the magazines for the pistol with hollowpoint ammunition. He put all but one of them in their pouches. The last magazine—a twenty-rounder—was inserted into the pistol's grip. He loaded the chamber and, pointing the pistol into the woods, he gently lowered its rowell hammer (since it lacked a modern decocking lever) to quarter cock. He wrapped the pistol up again in the oily rag and tucked it in the large right outer pocket of his jacket. In the opposite pocket, he put a magazine pouch that held three loaded thirteen-round magazines. All of the other items went back into the ammo can, which he resealed. He tossed the plastic wrapping in the hole but kicked in just enough dirt to cover the plastic. He didn't bother to completely refill or camouflage the hole, because he didn't intend to return to it.

His grandfather had left the Inglis Hi-Power mostly unchanged from its wartime service configuration, except that its lanyard ring had been removed, its magazine safety taken off to lighten the trigger pull, and it had been retrofitted with checked rubber Pachmayr grips. Along with it were seven thirteen-round magazines, three twenty-round magazines, several magazine pouches, and a wooden buttstock with an attached leather holster. Both the gun and the magazines were unregistered and therefore considered contraband in Canada.

He reached Thunder Bay just after 2:00 P.M. By 2:10 he was parked across the street from the Royal Bank of Canada (RBC) branch on Hodder Avenue. The bank didn't close until 4:00 P.M., but there was a long line at the door. He switched into his other coat, which had a hood. After thirty-five chilly minutes he reached the door, where a security guard was enforcing a "one out, one in" policy to prevent overcrowding in the lobby.

Once he was finally inside, there was another long queue to reach the teller windows. His wait in that line lasted twenty minutes, where he overheard some irate customers attempting to withdraw more than the new thousand-dollar limit. "Today a thousand won't buy a shopping trolley full of groceries!" one man shouted.

When he finally reached a teller window, Ray first wrote a check for one thousand dollars, leaving just $126 remaining in his account. He was handed ten one-hundred-dollar Canadian bills. They were all the later post-2011 type, printed on a polymer paper. Then he exchanged the last of his U.S. currency into Canadian dollars. He was surprised to see that it now took nearly two U.S. dollars to buy one Canadian dollar.

Ray then asked to access his safe-deposit box. He was told that there would be at least a ten-minute wait, and that because of the current banking emergency, no bank accounts could be closed, and no deposit box rental agreements could be terminated. He explained, "I just need to get what's in my box."

At 3:30, after having his box rental card checked against his signature on his passport, he was ushered into the vault room. He handed his key to the custodian, a pimply-faced young man who looked no more than twenty years old. After both his key and the custodian key were turned, the tray of Ray's oversize deposit box was pulled out.

The custodian asked, "Would you like a booth?"

"No." Ray unlatched the box and swung the lid open. Inside was a black Conn brand trumpet case and nothing else. Ray pulled out the case and gave a nod.

As he put the box back into its slot, the custodian quipped, "Must be a valuable instrument."

Ray nodded. "Yes, it's quite precious to me."

When he got back to the truck, Ray placed the trumpet case in the passenger seat and changed back to his other jacket. The weight of the pistol and the loaded magazines was comforting.

When he had driven ten miles out of Thunder Bay on Highway 17, Ray pulled the pickup and trailer onto the off ramp for a disused provincial highway rest stop, open only in summer months. He looked around and could see no traffic in either direction.

He snapped open the latches on the trumpet case and lifted the lid. The top of the case was crammed full of green plastic twelve-gauge 000 buckshot shells. He began pulling these out and piling them on the truck seat. Beneath them were the two plastic-wrapped halves of a Winchester Model 12 take-down riot shotgun. The barrel had long before been shortened to nineteen inches. He pulled these halves out, and more shotshells tumbled down into the bottom of the case. (He had filled every available space in the case with extra shells.)

After taking another look up and down the road to ensure that he wasn't being observed, Ray removed the plastic wrapping and pulled the gun's maga-zine tube forward. He joined the two halves of the gun together and gave the fore end a half turn, connecting the barrel's and receiver's interrupted threads. Then he slid the magazine tube back into the receiver, gave it a twist, and popped the magazine retainer pin in place. The gun, now assembled, was a handy thirty-three inches long. Holding down the action release, he cycled the action three times to test it. It felt right, so he flipped the gun over and fully loaded the magazine, pumped the action, slid the safety button to the right, and added one more shell to top off the magazine. He draped a poncho over the gun to keep it out of plain sight. Ray let out a sigh of contentment, now feeling properly armed for his road trip west.

Driving around the northern periphery of Lake Superior was uneventful, aside from seeing one spectacular wreck, the victim of a lake-effect snow flurry the previous day, which had brought visibility down to just a couple of car lengths. An Audi had smashed into a guardrail and flipped over. As Ray drove by, a tow truck driver was rigging a line to attempt to extricate the car. Two RCMP officers were standing by, holding C8 carbines. That struck him as odd. Why was there any need to have rifles out at the scene of a car wreck? Had there already been looting this far from Detroit?

The drive west through Winnipeg, Regina, and Calgary was tiring but relatively uneventful. The news on the radio was disturbing. The looting was getting worse, and more widespread. Most of it was in the U.S. and in the east-ern provinces, but there were also disturbances in Edmonton and Calgary. For Ray, worst of all was the uncertainty about whether he'd be able to buy gasoline. The prospect of being stranded left him feeling tense. Where he was able to buy gas, he made sure that both his truck's tank and all of his six gas cans were completely full. He also topped off his motorcycle's gas tank and even the pair of two-gallon plastic gas cans for his chain saw. One service station charged thirty-five dollars per gallon, which he considered larcenous. But he paid the price without comment. His cash was rapidly dwindling.

After leaving Thunder Bay, he drove another three hundred miles, carefully choosing a camping spot where he'd be able to turn around with the trailer, but where the pickup and trailer were not visible from the highway. Rather than sleeping in the trailer, he slept back in the woods with both the shotgun and pistol in his heavy sleeping bag. The truck and trailer were just barely visible to him. He reasoned that if anyone spotted the truck and trailer, they probably wouldn't spot where he was sleeping.

He drove almost twelve hundred miles the next day. He repeated the same process for camping the next night and again he got only six hours of sleep. That left nearly a thousand miles for the final day of his drive.

Nearing Kamloops, he came upon four burned-out vehicles by the side of the road—two vans and two SUVs—that were so thoroughly shot full of holes that they had obviously been in a recent gun battle. There were no bodies and just a few badly burned remnants of baggage, so he assumed that the RCMP had hauled away the corpses. He didn't come to a full stop to take a close look, but the charred vehicles gave mute testimony to what had happened. The lack of crime scene tape left him troubled. He wondered out loud, "Have things changed that quickly?"

His final stop for gas was at 100 Mile House. He didn't have enough cash for all of it, but the attendant seemed content with taking eight silver dimes for the last four gallons of gasoline.

Although FM radio reception got increasingly spotty as he headed west, he was able to catch some news reports. Most of the large cities in the United States were in absolute chaos, and the collapse of the three U.S. power grids was anticipated by one expert. The key issue, he said, was the level of staffing at power plants. So many employees were in fear of leaving their homes because of the rioting that there wouldn't be enough staff to keep the nuclear power plants running within a few days. And the supply of coal at the coal-fired plants was reaching critical levels because the nation's rail network was imperiled by the widespread rioting.

17

DEEDS, NOT WORDS

But there will be no justice, there will be no government of the people, by the people, and for the people, as long as the government and its officials permit bribery in any form.

—John Jay Hooker

St. Albans, West Virginia—October, the First Year

Malorie had sat in the passenger seat, leaving the driver's seat open for Joshua to drive. She secured her folding-stock M1 Carbine and began finding the best westerly route out of town. Megan was buckling up the boys in the back, making conversation with them about their cookie fortune. While both Jean and Leo had been real troupers the whole day, she knew that this was major upheaval for them. Megan stroked their hair and gently applied the long-practiced craft of maternal interrogation to ensure that both boys were indeed okay.

Joshua said his good-byes and thank-yous to the Townsends, as they briskly closed the door, a distinctive sound of breaking glass ringing out from the apartment building behind the church. Joshua picked up a trot across the lawn and with one smooth motion climbed into the seat, secured his long rifle, started the Jeep, shifted into gear, and was off in the direction that Malorie was pointing. Malorie gave him immediate right and left directions as she correlated the map to the unfamiliar terrain they were driving through. Everyone could noticeably feel the difference in tension from being in the city to being on country roads.

Once they were passing farm country again Joshua said, "I feel pretty good to drive. Obviously we all heard what the sheriff's deputy said about stopping on the side of the road, so I think we need to head west and south as fast as we can." Malorie had stashed a couple of 5-hour ENERGY drinks in the glove box before they left Kearneysville that morning, and she offered one to Joshua, who accepted it. "Normally I don't drink these, but this is not a normal day—thank you."

"I don't think that we will see or even hear about normal for quite some time yet," Malorie said. "Okay, look for a right-hand turn coming up."

Megan, who was confined to the backseat, was starting to feel carsick. She opened the window a crack and tried to sing songs with the boys to take her mind off it. There were noticeably fewer cars on the back roads, and most of the houses that they passed by still had power. The moon was full and the air brisk as Joshua piloted the Jeep down the West Virginia back roads.

In Hamlin, West Virginia, there was a full-blown riot erupting at a local gas station. As Joshua looked to find an alternate route around the bad situation, he noted aloud that it was good that there were still cops responding to the scene. "I wish that I could think of an expedient way to cover those gas cans we have hanging off the back of the Jeep; they would make us a huge target if the wrong crowd spots them." Malorie asked if her sleeping bag would help, and Megan said that it would irreversibly smell like fuel forever.

The Jeep cleared Hamlin and Malorie was just briefing Joshua of his left turn onto Route 10 in West Hamlin when he interrupted her and said, "Whoa, there are road flares up ahead—everybody stay buckled up in case we need to turn around quickly or make an evasive maneuver off of the pavement. We don't know who the friendlies are here, and we don't want to drive into a trap."

There were houses on each side of the road with lights on inside, and just past the bridge in the town a delivery truck from the local lumberyard was blocking the roadway. Flanking the road on either side were a dozen or so men with hunting rifles and shotguns. Joshua didn't see any presence of the law there, but this didn't appear to be an officially sanctioned checkpoint. Joshua rolled the Jeep to a stop about 250 meters ahead of the action and left only the parking lights on. "Malorie, jump in the driver's seat and keep the Jeep running. Keep one hand on your shotgun and one on the wheel. Be prepared to get out of here in case I don't come back."

"Where are you going?" Megan asked from the backseat.

"I'm not going to drive us into a trap—we need information at arm's length. You staying here with the car while I walk up won't be as threatening to them, and I have no idea how triggering happy anyone is up there. If I'm detained and don't come back in thirty minutes, please leave and find another way around. I love you!" Joshua was moving quickly because the situation could change just as fast, and he didn't want to expose everyone by driving up into the fatal funnel. As the door closed, Megan cried out, "I love you, too!" She hugged the boys and rolled down both windows while loosening the bungee cord that retained her shotgun.

Joshua walked deliberately in the direction of the checkpoint and interlaced his fingers behind his head when he was a hundred meters out. The air was definitely cold, but he had kept his NSA Police service jacket unzipped so that they could see he was carrying a pistol. He hoped that the embroidered badge on his left jacket breast would at least give him some opportunity to speak with the person in charge. Malorie couldn't hear what was going on, but she could see three men approach Joshua as he neared the checkpoint, their weapons generally aimed at him. Joshua stopped and Malorie could tell that he was trying to say something. The three men escorted Joshua around the back of the truck and out of sight.

The next fifteen minutes were very tense, and Megan showed it on her countenance. Two of the three men who led Joshua out of sight rejoined the rest of the men at the checkpoint; no one seemed to be giving away anything by their conduct about what could be happening on the other side of the lumber truck.

What Malorie and Megan couldn't have known was that Joshua was being a very cool customer. When approached by the three men with guns, Joshua said, "My family and I in that Jeep request safe passage through your town to Route 10 South. We're on our way to see my brother in Kentucky. May I speak with whomever is in charge?"

The middle-aged, stocky man in a flannel shirt with a vinyl puffy vest zipped halfway up said, "Right this way." He reached out to grab Joshua's right arm to escort him behind the truck after noticing Joshua's pistol, keeping one hand on his rifle the whole time.

Joshua glanced at the truck, and other than the name of the lumberyard on the door, the GVWR, and the DOT number, he saw only a small vinyl graphic indicating a local chapter of the Knights of Columbus affiliation. Behind the truck he could see a small vendor's pop-up tent with three walls flapping in the breeze with the words KETTLE CORN written across the awning. Inside, a small group of older men stood around a kerosene heater trying to keep warm while a pair of Coleman camping lanterns illuminated the makeshift command post. Against the back wall was a table with a police scanner and a ham radio set being operated by an overweight woman. The man who had Joshua's arm addressed one of the men in the tent. "Mayor Simons, this officer approached the checkpoint and asked to speak with you."

The mayor was wearing a long tan wool coat with a crucifix pin on the lapel, earmuffs, and a plaid scarf. He was stamping his feet to keep warm and around the outside of his coat on his waist was a thick leather belt and a full-flap cavalry-style holster with what appeared to be a large-frame Ruger Blackhawk revolver inside. The mayor removed his right mitten, tucked it under his left arm, extended his hand, and said, "Mayor Lamar Simons. What brings you to West Hamlin today?"

"Mayor Simons, my family and I request safe passage through your town to take the junction south on Route 10. Sir, we are coming from Kearneysville, West Virginia, on our way to Kentucky to see my brother."

The mayor was distracted by an update from a fireman holding a Motorola radio in the tent, and turned to get a piece of paper off the desk behind him. "You may not know this, Officer, but the governor just declared martial law an hour ago. In his decree he gave local authorities"—the mayor was squinting to read the text—"the power to do what is 'reasonably necessary' to maintain law and order. Now, you no doubt came through Hamlin to get here; where were you before that?"

"Mayor Simons, by God's providence we were able to circumnavigate Charleston. No doubt you've been briefed on the events there today."

The mayor put his mitten back on his hand and stamped his feet as he talked. "Indeed, that's quite a death toll already, and the West Virginia National Guard is going door to door trying to contain the escaped convicts. The governor has left Charleston and is running the state remotely from a mobile command post."

"Sir, I know that you have no way to tell our party apart from anyone else coming down this road—it appears that your town straddles a key junction on these secondary roads. We simply want to get to my brother's house, near Danville, Kentucky."

"The Danville area, you said?" Joshua nodded. "Very well, how are you fixed for fuel?"

Although the general situation seemed calm enough, Joshua sensed that there was a fishing expedition being launched here rather than a benevolent mayor offering him fuel. It had been only forty-eight hours since he spoke with Dustin on the phone about "haves and have-nots," and Joshua realized that he needed to segue into another topic other than his resources. "We have a partial tank of fuel and empty cans on the back that we hope to be able to fill up at the next safe opportunity."

"Ah, that may be a while. By my order, none of the filling stations in town are selling any fuel—we need to ration what we have so that we don't end up like Hamlin. I'm short on police right now because all of mine have been dispatched there to restore order."

Joshua chose his words carefully now. "I did see that as we passed by; your men were doing a fine job and, in my opinion, should be commended."

Mayor Simons smiled. "In addition to being the mayor, I also own the local lumberyard. It may be a while yet before we start making deliveries again, so until then my truck stays parked there to regulate traffic." The fireman was speaking on his radio again, and the mayor was distracted by another aide in the tent. He took a six-inch-square piece of card stock off the table, picked up a pen, checked the time, and then signed the card. The mayor then held it by the corner and made a slight fanning motion as if he were cooling himself on a hot summer's day. Joshua picked up on the theatrics. All cops talk to each other about their experiences, and when he was on his one deployment to Al Udeid Air Base with the Air Force Security Forces he got an earful about how business was done outside of the First World. Joshua knew he was about to get asked for a bribe. "Now, this will cover you through West Hamlin, but West Virginia is a sizable piece of real estate. I know every mayor in this area between here and Kentucky. What's your plan to get past the other checkpoints if your luck runs out?"

Joshua realized that this had gone from fishing expedition to full-on quid pro quo and that there was a huge power differential here. One angry word from the mayor and they would all be detained, stripped of their belongings, and thrown into jail; there wouldn't be any habeas corpus anytime soon. Joshua remembered a missionary speaking about his ordeals in these bribe situations at his church in South America, where he had had little to leverage. Mayor Simons was understandably selling that which every government is in the business of selling: security. Joshua knew that he couldn't blame him; if every person were to give up fuel instead of taking it, then the town would be on the plus side just for straddling the key road junction. Joshua knew he had to strike decisively, and there were no extra-credit points for honesty. "My brother Dustin is a Catholic priest and I asked him to pray to Saint Christopher to give us safe travel. As you know, Charleston is under siege right now, yet God miraculously provided a way around for us. Dustin also has been burning a candle and keeping vigil for us to Saint Alban as we are refugees on our sojourn here. I expect that you have little use for cash right now and I do not have much to offer; we're merely trying to get through to Kentucky peacefully. I'll ask my brother Dustin to pray to Saint Francis of Assisi, the patron saint of merchants, to restore your lumberyard business tenfold. We place ourselves at your mercy, Mayor Simons. Surely the petitions of Saint Francis of Assisi are worth more than any material thing we have to offer you tonight."

The mayor handed the chit to Joshua and said, "Take this chit and give it to the guard at the gate when you approach with your vehicle. He'll allow you to pass and radio the guard on the checkpoint at the south end of town. Move smartly because you don't want them to start looking for you inside town limits—it won't end well for you. I'll have Captain Langus here coordinate with our radio operator to notify the other fire department captains in their respective command posts along your route to ensure that they know that you're coming."

Joshua smiled and said, "Thank you, Mayor Simons. Peace be with you."

Mayor Simons smiled and replied, "And also with you."

Joshua was escorted by the man in the vinyl puffy vest back to the checkpoint. He wasted no time, jogging toward the Jeep. Another car was lined up at the checkpoint now and Joshua could sense the tension rising among the guards and people waiting in the car. Malorie had wisely stayed with the Jeep. Joshua got in and promised to fill them in later as he told Malorie to approach the checkpoint with caution. Malorie noticed the car ahead being turned around, and the driver was angry as he roared past them. She proceeded forward by letting the Jeep advance in second gear at idle. Joshua turned to Malorie and said, "Give this chit to the guard; it should get us through."

With only the parking lights on, Malorie rolled to a stop by the guard and handed him the chit. The guard looked at it and said, "Maryland plates? We are redirecting all vehicles with out-of-state plates."

Joshua said, "We spoke with Mayor Simons, he granted us safe passage through town. Since we have women and children here we'll need to make a pit stop in town and Mayor Simons said that would be fine."

The guard looked incredulous and asked, "Mayor Simons said that?"

Malorie gave the man an Academy Award–winning shrug and a sly smile. Joshua replied, "If that man over there with the tan coat and the pistol is Mayor Simons, then yes."

As if on cue Joshua waved to Mayor Simons, who waved back. The guard said, "Okay, then. I'll take the chit and radio the checkpoint at the south end of town. You have thirty minutes to get there."

"Thank you," Joshua said as he handed ten .357 rounds to the guard, "Please see that these get to Mayor Simons from us."

When they cleared the command tent and came to the left-hand turn to pick up Route 10 South, Megan and Malorie both let out an enormous laugh. "I've only seen that work in *Dumb and Dumber*! I had no idea it would work in real life!"

Joshua, too, was chuckling, and said, "You don't even know the half of it; wait until Father Dustin Hodges hears about this."

Megan's face was perplexed. "You never mentioned that Dustin was a Catholic priest. I thought that he was a sheriff's deputy."

"He is a sheriff's deputy, but for our cover story Dustin *had to be* a Catholic priest in order for us to get through. I learned that technique from a missionary at my church. They never have much cash and can't pay out bribes to those who ask for one—so they hand them a tract and play on their religious sympathies by insisting that it is worth more than money."

Jean said, "I'm hungry, Mama."

Malorie answered, "We all are, buddy. And like Joshua told the guard"— she promptly elbowed Joshua—"Auntie Malorie has to pee."

The disarray of Hamlin contrasted sharply to West Hamlin. They noticed a distinct calm in the town. The steps that its citizens had taken kept the riffraff out of the town but would likely seal in their own native population of ne'er-do-wells. A patrol of four men walked briskly down the street with rifles at relaxed port arms, and Megan noticed that there were no women and children out, never a good sign.

Joshua suggested that they pull over at the local diner, and he stayed with the vehicle as the group went inside. The girls both had their pistols concealed and Joshua had them leave their carbines in the Jeep to avoid drawing attention. Joshua was never good at remaining idle and sorely wanted to take advantage of the stop to top off the tank, but he was sure that he was being watched.

Megan, Malorie, Jean, and Leo returned and got into the Jeep. Joshua discreetly told them about the fuel situation and they all agreed. As Joshua was just ready to walk inside Megan said, "Hey, check to see if our cheeseburgers are ready—I ordered them to go."

Joshua smirked and said, "I guess that means I'm paying?"

Megan answered, "Yes, that was about how I had it figured. If not, I'll gladly let you listen to the revolt that you'll have from the peasantry here in the backseat."

"Coming right up."

Joshua returned a few minutes later. He said that he was feeling awake and good to drive. There was something about having to talk your way past local corrupt politicians that markedly raised your blood pressure and adrenaline. Driving and eating takes a certain amount of skill. Driving a standard transmission, eating, and trying to not stand out as you pass through a well-organized town defense is something else entirely, and not for the faint of heart.

18

IN DEFENSE OF

Something happens when an individual owns his home or business. He or she will always invest more sweat, longer hours and greater creativity to develop and care for something he owns than he will for any government-inspired project supposedly engineered for the greater social good. . . . The desire to improve oneself and one's family's lot, to make life better for one's children, to strive for a higher standard of living, is universal and God-given. It is honorable. It is not greed.

—Rush Limbaugh, *The Limbaugh Letter*, 1993

Southwest of West Hamlin, West Virginia— October, the First Year

At subsequent checkpoints Joshua asked Malorie to do the talking, and she was able to get to the right person with a radio to confirm their bona fides. Mayor Simons wasn't exaggerating when he said that he knew all of the other mayors between West Hamlin and Kentucky. By the time they got to Wayne, West Virginia, they had somehow earned the code name "Pope Mobile," which one of the guards even wrote across the top of the windshield in yellow grease pencil to identify them. Functionally this moniker and Malorie's batting eyelashes got them through the checkpoints, but Joshua knew that God would be the judge of his transgressions in the final accounting. The necessity of Joshua's lie to Mayor Simons was the topic of rather heated discussion among the three adults when the boys napped. Malorie was grateful to be past that hurdle but was still perplexed and asked, "We prayed to God this morning at the homestead, which seems like a lifetime ago now, for His help to get us to Kentucky, and we have to break His law to jump through an administrative hoop?"

Joshua wasn't proud of what he had done, but there seemed to be little choice. "Okay, I can take your critique here—but what would you have done?"

"Well." Malorie swallowed hard before she continued. "Maybe he would've taken one of our guns in trade."

"True, Mal, but we'd run out of guns before we ran out of corrupt people looking to take them," Megan replied.

"No, I get that our resources aren't inexhaustible, but the rules are different right now under martial law," Malorie said.

"Why, exactly, should we follow these rules?" Joshua asked.

"Well, for starters they have guns—that seems to make it persuasive. Also, they are the governing authorities, which also makes it biblical according to Romans 13."

"True," Megan replied, "but those rules, having the teeth of law in our circumstance, are they just or unjust?"

"What does that matter? Are you taking his side on this?" Malorie asked her sister.

"I think that my thought process is pretty rational here, so I'll try to explain. Now, if a law is a law, what gives it power over people? If the answer is just guns and more of them, then all we need to do is get a whole lot of people with guns to agree with us and just declare the Constitution legal again. If it were that easy, then it would've been done by now. I'm talking about a battle of ideas here, not the profession of arms."

"Wait a minute, big sister." Malorie was no longer helping to watch the road for deer or other two-legged hazards; now she was facing Megan in the backseat. "What's right is right, and this is not situational ethics."

Joshua grew up in a boys' home and didn't have sisters, or he might have known never to get between them in an argument. "What if they demanded something more than a gun or food or fuel to pass through? What if they demanded one of you women or one of the boys? Do you think that human trafficking only happens somewhere else and not in America?"

"That's absurd!" Malorie retorted.

Joshua took a breath and calmly continued, "Perhaps it seems like a far reach right now, but this whole 'Crunch' is a permanent situation. There are multiple generations raised on the idea that government is an inexhaustible fountain of money. Did you see the president's 'Inequality Agenda'?"

"Yes, but what does that have to do with lying to the mayor?" Malorie was calmer now but was not giving any ground.

"This is what the Founding Fathers were fighting for—life and the sanctity of it. If I gave him a gun (that I bought fairly), then I'm giving him part of my life that I traded to earn money to buy that gun or food or fuel or whatever. The 'right' to demand money through taxation is legit, but the practice of corruptly taking from one to buy votes with another or to feather one's own nest is criminal and outside of the lawful purposes of government. Government is not there to be the guarantor that everyone gets theirs; that's not what Romans 13 was talking about. So whether taking money in the form of taxation or bribery—which is paramount to taking someone's life—or 'selling' the notion of security by getting people to trade their unalienable rights for such a notion is unjust. Governments are there to punish the guilty and to protect the innocent."

Malorie bit her lip and thought about that as Megan continued. "It's like the NSA. They want you to think that they're doing what's in their charter—to protect our national security by keeping our government's communications secure and by analyzing our adversaries' communications that are contrary to our national interests. This is not all that they concern themselves with now. After 9/11 they quietly added domestic communications to their charter, in the name of security, of course. But when the camel's nose is under the tent, you cannot convince him to stay out. They stood up the Cyber Security Service (CSS) to keep track of everything and everyone by archiving *everything* just in case they needed it later to find a correlation with 'retrospective searching.' Where in the Constitution do they get the right to do that? Technically it falls under U.S. Code Title 50, which was no doubt enlarged by the Patriot Act to serve their purposes."

"So the rules are not the rules, then? Is that what you're saying?" Malorie had her feet tucked up on the seat with her arms around her knees in full contemplation.

Joshua added, "Pretty much. Have you ever read either Runyan's book or Chuck Baldwin's book—both about Romans 13 and the Christian duty to oppose wicked rulers? And consider the guy who blew the whistle had to flee to Russia for protection. Think about that; he had to go to the former Soviet commies and get asylum from the U.S. in the land of the gulag to protect his and everyone else in America's right to free speech!" Joshua paused for effect. "If they get to make the rules, then they can move the target when it suits them—this is called positive law, something any libertarian can tell you about. However, when man agrees to follow God's rules, then the law no longer becomes an entity to itself; it has an anchor in God's character, which does not change. Me having to lie is wrong, and I'll stand before God for that. However, I deceived Mayor Simons because if I held my ground in the face of his corruption, I would have put us all at a much higher risk of getting stuck in the West Virginia wilderness, facing death by exposure."

"So you lied to save our collective hides, then?" Malorie had reconnected with her sarcasm.

"Joshua did what he did to preserve our lives," Megan said. "This is why we had to leave D.C. If we stayed, our life expectancy would be about as sure as the value of the dollar. As soon as the welfare checks stop cashing and the full faith and credit of the U.S. government is exposed to be the fraud that it is, we would be run like grist through the mill. Rome would be burning, but at least the inequality agenda would have reached its final populist conclusion—we would all be equally miserable.

"That's the dirty little secret of socialism, Mal." Megan had her hand on her sister's shoulder and gently squeezed it. "You must become what you hate to enforce the rules of equal distribution. It simply cannot and never will work. That is why God's model depends on productivity in conjunction with true Christian charity."

As they pulled up to Wayne, West Virginia, it was still early in the morning, and the sun was just starting to paint the horizon a pinkish orange hue. Malorie got out of the Jeep; she was getting good at dealing with the guards. The checkpoint was hastily set up near Wayne Veterans Memorial Park with "God Bless America" clearly displayed to indicate a bygone era of America. Megan had drifted asleep and Joshua thought, "America bless God!"

Malorie approached the checkpoint to the sound of a catcall that only she could hear over the idling engine. The exchange was taking longer than it should have with one rather large young man at the gate near the volunteer fire department. Joshua could only see what was happening from a moderate distance.

Malorie's body language showed that she was tense. The guard, who turned out to be a former star linebacker for the local high school football team, was easily a foot taller than Malorie. The other guards just stood there chiming in on what they'd like to do with such a pretty young lady. When he grabbed her arm, Joshua immediately got out of the Jeep and in his NCO voice said, "Hey, let her go, we don't mean you any trouble here." Megan awoke with a start and secured her carbine.

The guard, who seemed to be keeping warm by drinking Wild Turkey, let loose a long string of foul-mouthed words before issuing a challenge. "What do you plan on doing about it?" Joshua had the .270 out and resting in the V between the open door and the A pillar rather quickly, but not as quickly as some of the other guards were able to draw a bead on Joshua with their rifles.

The guard, in defiance of Joshua, reached to grab Malorie's left breast but had not accounted for the S&W revolver in her right hand. In a split second she had the muzzle of the revolver painfully buried in his copious double-chin fat. She said, "On your knees, punk!" His delayed reaction exceeded Malorie's patience so she kneed him in the groin. When he doubled over she grabbed the back of his collar and used his weight against him by simply pivoting and letting his inertia take him down to a fetal position, where he grabbed himself, screaming in pain.

Joshua shouted out, "Like I said, we don't want any trouble and you can avoid a lot of bloodshed by not getting stupid here like your friend."

The former linebacker yelled a vulgar insult. Malorie's only response was to pistol-whip him on top of the head, giving him something else to be concerned with other than his hurt pride.

The other guards caught on that Malorie was no one's plaything and acknowledged that they didn't want any trouble. Joshua got in the Jeep and pulled up to where Malorie stood. Megan timed opening the passenger door just as the Jeep passed her sister so that she could get in and they could drive off quickly.

"Are you okay?" Megan asked as she hugged her and the headrest at the same time.

Joshua was in third gear and accelerating past the park heading south on 37. Malorie was out of breath as she answered, "I'm fine, but it'll be a while before he lives that one down."

19

LPCs

Individuals receive, but they cannot send. They absorb, but they cannot share. They hear, but they do not speak. They see constant motion, but they do not move themselves. The "well-informed citizenry" is in danger of becoming the "well-amused audience."

—Al Gore, *The Assault on Reason*

Fort Gay, West Virginia—October, the First Year

The sky was a definite orange blaze now, and everyone was just glad that Malorie had gotten away relatively unscathed. Malorie looked at the map. "It seems like we should be getting to Fort Gay, West Virginia, at daybreak. That'll be where we cross over into Kentucky. From there it would only appear to be about 120 miles or so to Bradfordsville."

Megan stirred from the backseat and said, "Well, at this rate we could be there tonight perhaps?"

"If we can maintain this rate, then yes—but there's a lot to that 'if,'" replied Joshua.

The Jeep descended the small hill to the checkpoint at Fort Gay. The personnel at the checkpoint were mostly uniformed law enforcement, and Megan pointed out that there was one West Virginia State Police car parked off to the side. "The presence of cops must be good. I never want to go through a checkpoint like that last one again," Megan said.

Joshua said, "Without getting all *Terminator* on you four here, 'I'll be back!'"

Megan quipped, "Get to zee choppahr!" getting a laugh out of the boys while Joshua just rolled his eyes.

Joshua alighted from the Jeep and kept his coat unzipped and laced his hands behind his head as he approached his law enforcement brethren. He hoped that they'd notice his embroidered badge on his coat. The temperature had dropped significantly, and he was regretting not grabbing his gloves from the Jeep.

As Joshua approached he said, "Good morning. We're seeking to cross over into Kentucky to go see my . . ."

The local policeman on duty cut him off and said, "Ain't *no one* driving over into Kentucky anymore." The young cop seemed irritated from having to stay up too long on checkpoint duty. "The honorable governor of Kentucky has seen fit to block all motor traffic into or out of his state as of midnight last night, right about the time we lost utility power in town. They have two semis from the local Coca-Cola bottling plant in Louisa blocking the bridge and a Kentucky National Guard HMMWV with a fifty-cal, to make the point clear."

Joshua said, "Thank you, brother, I didn't know that. What about foot traffic?"

"Well, I would highly recommend that you not swim across to Kentucky right now. The temperature has dropped overnight and we're supposed to get a bunch of snow here in the next day or three. The *Farmer's Almanac* is predicting an early winter, too." Joshua nodded. He noticed that the cop seemed less irritated now and relaxed his arms. "As far as we know, people are still getting over on foot. Rumor has it there is a refugee camp starting up over at the Yatesville Lake State Park just west of Louisa, but I can't say what the conditions there would be like. You sure are a long way from Maryland; why aren't you with your force back there? Does that say 'NSA' on your service coat?"

"Long story, but we have a pressing need to get to my brother's house near Danville, Kentucky."

The cop nodded indifferently; he'd probably heard every sad story that there was to hear, and the Crunch had just begun. "Well, ain't none of my affair anyways. Danville, that's a good piece from here, 'specially on foot. Do you have little ones with you?"

"Two women and two children, plus me. Are we allowed to go into town to try to get supplies?" Joshua was trying to hide the panic in his voice over their lack of options.

"Maryland plates, huh? I suppose you have a Maryland driver's license, too? Does anyone with you have West Virginia identification on them?"

Joshua breathed deeply and said, "Both my fiancée and her sister do."

"I'll take your word for it, since you're a cop and all. But remember this, Fort Gay is a dead end—you can't go any farther in your vehicle. Y'all shouldn't bother going to the police station down by the river, either, to plead your case. They're turning folks away. As you probably know, if you made it this far, Charleston is up in flames and the governor of West Virginia is not going to take the time to hear from the Fort Gay mayor about how he should contact the governor of Kentucky on your behalf."

Joshua knew the drill and asked in a joking tone, "Someone already tried that?"

"Just as sure as I'm standing here." The cop cleared his throat and went on. "Any kind of supplies that you need are likely going to be sold out at the sports store—I would check the pawnshops."

Joshua said, "Thanks, brother," and turned around and walked to the Jeep.

A quick vote was taken on whether to go into Fort Gay. They decided that they had to get whatever supplies they could find and head west, especially with the bad weather approaching. The Jeep crossed through its last checkpoint and Joshua pulled into town, looking at the sign on the door of the diner, which read CLOSED. Ever the entrepreneurs, the local Boy Scout troop had a propane griddle set up in a parking lot between the auto parts store and the local feed store with a sign that read PANCAKES, ALL YOU CAN EAT $12.

"Twelve dollars seems wicked steep, but who knows when we're going to see hot food again in Kentucky," Malorie said.

"Okay, I'm open for ideas here, but hear me out first," Joshua began. He switched off the ignition and turned to look at both Megan and Malorie. "We're on foot from here on out, no doubt about it. I don't think that anyone is going to sell us a vehicle in Kentucky, gas will be wicked expensive or unobtainable, winter is supposedly coming soon, and we are due to get snow. The cop at the checkpoint said that there's a refugee camp over on the west side of Louisa in some park. I don't know about you, but I'm not keen on going there. I think it'll be a crime magnet where either of you or one of the boys could get abducted."

Megan was past overtired. "True, it could get positively *Grapes of Wrath* over there. We can't enter a situation where we're trapped and where one of us is separated from the group. We're simply too small a force to defend ourselves. And knowing the history of such camps, they'll probably disarm everyone coming in. Our primary mission is to stay warm, dry, and unseen. I don't think we'll be able to make much progress through the winter. If we find a place to stay overnight and then move westward only to find that there's nowhere for us to stay, then we'd be highly reluctant to backtrack to our previous camp."

"Great insight, Megan. I knew that you were the big sister for a reason." Megan flicked the back of her head as Malorie continued, "It would appear that we have to find a place and stay there through the winter—any chance that we can do that here in town? How about Louisa?"

Joshua winced and said, "I'm not certain that would work. Whoever was prepared enough prior to the Crunch to make it through the winter probably isn't open to the idea of adding five mouths to feed right now. Besides, we'd have to be very sure that the situation was safe and that people were not psycho or something, and you know what they say about beggars being choosers."

"Right," Megan said. "Taking on someone else's kids is going to be a hard sell." She squeezed the boys to let them know that she still loved them and continued. "So that leaves us headed somewhere on foot out of West Virginia toward Bradfordsville, but I'm under no illusion that we're going to be able to make it there in one multiday trek. I'd give us ten miles a day if we really pushed it, and that's not considering all of our stuff, either."

Joshua added, "The cop said don't bother with the sporting goods store because they were likely out of whatever we'd need. But he might have just been thinking of gloves, coats, ammunition, and freeze-dried Mountain House products. What we need is the ability to cover ground with our stuff on foot, like those game-cart contraptions."

"You mean like what you'd put a deer carcass on to pack out of the woods?" Malorie asked.

"Yes, exactly."

Megan tilted her head to one side and said, "I guess that just might work. We'd probably need more than one, though, no?"

"And if a batch of pancakes is already twelve dollars, then what is the world's most useful form of ground conveyance post-Crunch going to cost us?" Malorie asked.

"Just getting this far has increased our chances of survival," Joshua said. "Think for a moment how many people did not or will not be able to get past Charleston." The thought was sobering for everyone. "We'll have to see what we can trade the Jeep for. With the new restrictions, it's not going to help us reach our destination."

"Oh, Joshua! You couldn't bring yourself to do that, could you? What if we stayed here for a while, see if the laws change?" Megan asked with genuine concern.

"I'm not sure what other options, if any, we might have. Staying means certain misfortune. See what you have for cash between the two of you and take the boys to load up on pancakes; we're going to need the carbs. I'll go check out the town to see what is still out there between the pawnshops and the sporting goods store." The boys excitedly unbuckled their seat belts, eager to eat pancakes. "Malorie, can I borrow your Android so that I can take pictures of the Jeep?"

"Of course."

Joshua snapped a few pictures of the Jeep, especially under the hood, and then walked the family over to the Boy Scouts pancake fund-raiser. He found out where to find the sporting goods store and pawnshops from one of the parents. Turning to the ladies, he said, "Keep an eye on our stuff."

Joshua passed by a Food City grocery store that looked like it had been picked over rather well, a clear example of what happens when the Crunch meets just-in-time logistics. There was no resupply, and the store was down to nearly empty shelves in less than seventy-two hours.

Rounding the corner, Joshua came to the second pawnshop that the scout leader had mentioned and went inside. There was a pasty-faced teenager with pimples who was clearly a throwback to the grunge era, complete with an unbuttoned flannel shirt hanging over a Nirvana T-shirt. He was holding a shotgun at port arms, leaning up against a wall full of television sets; he nodded politely but was clearly all business. Joshua asked the man behind the counter, "Cash only?" and he nodded. "I need two game carts. Do you have any?"

"I have one that is about the size you would need for a doe, and a bigger one that will hold a big buck."

"What are you asking for the pair?"

The man behind the counter stood up. He had a small .380 pistol in the top pocket of his overalls and walked with a noticeable limp. He had a very round gut that made his silhouette look like two Solo cups stacked up rim to rim. He labored across the shop over to the room where the outdoor sporting goods stuff was kept. "The smaller one has two good tires, so I'll take three hundred dollars for that one." Joshua swallowed hard and tried not to appear shocked. "The bigger one needs a new tire, but we can get one off of the bicycles over there for you—I'll take just five hundred for it, on account of the tire."

"Eight hundred dollars for the pair, huh?" Joshua said. The man nodded. "Do you have any mess kits? How about green wool army surplus blankets?" Joshua asked.

"'Bout how many were you needin'?"

"Five blankets if you have them, and I could get by with three mess kits."

"I reckon that would bring us to eleven hundred U.S. dollars—this is my reserve stock, you understand, and I'm not expecting to be resupplied anytime soon."

Joshua maintained his poker face. "No, I get it. I might need a few other items, but are you willing to entertain an offer for a trade on that merchandise?"

"It depends on the trade. I am not taking *any* kind of electronics like TVs or Xboxes if that's what you had in mind."

"No, I'm looking to trade a modified Jeep that I rebuilt. I have the title document." Joshua pulled out the Android to display the photos, keeping one eye on the kid with the shotgun, who had crossed the floor to look over Joshua's shoulder at the pictures.

The kid spoke up with the savvy of someone who had grown up in a pawnshop and said, "Suppose you need to get on through to Kentucky and the bridge is closed now for vehicles." Joshua nodded, and the kid continued, "What if we say 'no'? Then you'll be stuck without the carts, blankets, and everything. Sounds like you're the one in the weaker position here. We may need to talk about this price some more."

Joshua assessed the situation dispassionately, took one look at the pimply-faced kid, and said, "True, I won't overestimate the strength of my position. I need the game carts to get to where I'm going, but you need to attract the girl of your dreams—this deal could help us both."

The old man laughed out loud and slapped the kid on the back as his shoulders dropped and he turned bright red. "Ha, how did you know that? Mister, I'll give you a forty-five-hundred-dollar store credit in exchange for the Jeep!"

Joshua hated to be so crass, but he simply could not get stuck without a way to transport what he and his family needed to get through the winter. Forty-five hundred dollars for the Jeep was a pittance, but he wasn't going to accept a stack of U.S. dollars, knowing their fate. Joshua replied, "Great, I'll bring my family back with the Jeep. There will surely be something that my fiancée needs to buy with the balance."

Joshua stuck to the main roads through town. It was already 9:00 A.M. and he was feeling pressed to get on the road heading west. He caught up to the girls, who had bargained to let the boys count as one person, allowing the three adults to load up on their fill of pancakes for forty-eight dollars.

Making full use of the time, Malorie had gotten a complete rundown from an Eagle Scout with an Order of the Arrow pin about the local lay of land, flora, fauna, and so on. She was not flirtatious, but she wasn't upset over the attention she was getting, either. The Eagle Scout spread out the Kentucky map and recommended that they head west for two days' walk to the Olympia State Forest, where the population density is low and there are a lot of caves to take shelter in for the winter. He told her which fishing lures would work to catch fish in the lake there and how to identify muskrat scat, and gave her many other useful tips—he was an encyclopedia on living outdoors, and he was sweet on Malorie. "I could come with you, you know—just as far as the state park if you like. It would take just two days to help you with all of your stuff. I could even show you some good caves. There are *lots* of caves there."

Malorie asked for a moment to think about it. She thought about the practicalities and the liabilities. Having an extra strong back to move supplies meant that getting the boys, the food, and the supplies they had to the state forest across unfamiliar land would be faster and safer. He returned with a quart-size bottle of real maple syrup from one of the pickup trucks and then said, "Take this, it has thousands of calories and you're gonna need them." In the end she politely thanked him for the syrup and the information but declined the offer of his assistance. She did send him away with a kiss on the cheek and a sincere "thank-you."

They loaded into the Jeep one last time. Joshua was solemn but knew that this was the right thing to do for the greater good. At the pawnshop, Megan went in to see if there was anything else that she wanted to buy with their credit. Joshua's only warning was, "No cast iron unless you plan on carrying it." Megan emerged with the two game carts, two spare tires and tubes for each cart, a small tube air pump, the blankets and mess kits, an e-tool, a thousand waterproof strike-on-anything matches, a twelve-by-twenty-four-foot tarp, a five-hundred-foot piece of paracord neatly wound up in a skein, a can of mink oil for their leather personnel carriers (LPCs), some extra bungee cords, a hatchet, a quality Henckels stainless steel kitchen knife, and two Olympia State Forest maps. She took the rest of the difference in pre-1965 "junk" silver U.S. dimes and quarters.

Out of the corner of her eye Megan peeked down the hall and saw a clothes dryer. She noticed that the kid was willing to deal, perhaps because she was an attractive woman or simply because he was very happy about his new Jeep.

"You know, you're getting a wicked good deal on that Jeep."

The kid smiled and started to blush, so she asked, "Say, would you trade my sister's toolbox full of tools here for that Gerber multitool, the flint-and-steel set, and that skinning knife with the gut hook?"

After eyeballing the high quality of the tools inside, he said, "Sure, that'd be fine, ma'am." The kid behind the counter completed the trade as the old man took a turn on guard duty by the front door.

"Kind of a strange request here, but would you let me empty the lint tray on your dryer? You know, so that I can have some tinder for my flint and steel." The kid shrugged, and Megan placed the keys to the Jeep on the counter and gave him the title, which Joshua had signed over. The old man countersigned it, and Megan came back from the dryer with the lint to shake hands.

When Megan had walked into the pawnshop, Joshua had remained outside and taken one one-tenth-ounce gold coin from his belt and put it in his pocket. He left Malorie to strip the Jeep of their stuff while he took Jean and Leo to the picked-over chain grocery store a few doors down.

It took half an hour to pack the carts. The girls would take turns pushing the smaller "doe" cart, while Joshua volunteered to push his "buck" cart the entire way. Since it was so cold, the cooked meat that Joshua had packed at the homestead was still deep chilled and fresh. Long weapons went on top, and everyone carried his bug-out bags on his back. The boys had small book-bag-type sacks to carry some water, socks, and a few small toys. Megan asked Joshua to pray for the next part of their journey. After the prayer, they set out on their LPCs over the Big Sandy River Bridge into Kentucky.

20

THE ZONE ONE GATE

On October 15, 1934, with Pan at the wheel ... we rattled
across the Canadian border.

From government officials, we ascertained that Tatla Lake,
five hundred miles north of Vancouver, was the northwestern
frontier of existing ranches. West of it lay the little-known
Anahim country, walled in on the north by the wild, unex-
plored Itcha and Algak ranges. Beyond the mountain barrier
lay our objective, the mysterious Indian taboo land on the
unmapped headwaters of the Blackwater River.

—Richmond P. Hobson, in *Grass Beyond the Mountains: Discovering
the Last Great Cattle Frontier on the North American Continent*

The McGregor Ranch, near Anahim Lake,
British Columbia—October, the First Year

As Claire McGregor was washing the dinner dishes, the Dakota Alert
driveway alarm announced, "Alert, zone one, alert, zone one." She
shouted to Alan excitedly, "Mercy! That could be Ray!"

They stepped out on the porch, hoping to see the familiar profile of Ray's
pickup and fifth-wheel trailer, but instead saw the shape of an unfamiliar
pickup truck with a camper shell. As the pickup neared the front porch, a
motion-sensing security floodlight snapped on.

Claire asked, "Who ... ?"

Alan hesitated with his hand resting on the porch rail, wondering whether he should step back inside for his elk rifle.

The unknown man waved, swung open his door, and declared, "Hi! I'm Phil Adams. I trust that Ray let you know that I'd be coming."

Alan nodded. "Yes, he told us. Come in, come in. Claire can warm you up some dinner."

As he climbed out of the pickup's cab Phil asked, "Is Ray here yet?"

Simultaneously, Alan and Claire replied, "No."

Arriving at the ranch in advance of Ray was awkward. Even though he had known Ray for more than a decade, Phil had never met Ray's parents face-to-face. And despite the barrage of dramatic news headlines, the whole concept of Phil's being there to help secure the ranch seemed odd—almost as if it was still in the realm of the hypothetical. It was, after all, a *very* remote ranch, and the nearest reports of civil unrest were in downtown Vancouver, British Columbia. That was 350 miles away, straight-line distance, or roughly 420 miles by sea and road, or 535 miles via the highways. Further complicating the situation, the telephone network was working only sporadically, and the McGregors hadn't heard from Ray in three days. Their daughters—one living in Florida and the other living in the Philippines—were also out of contact.

Outside of a narrow littoral that benefits from the moderating influence of the Pacific Ocean's thermal mass, northern British Columbia has a brutal climate. Upon leaving Bella Coola and driving east on Highway 20, the interior climate of British Columbia comes suddenly. The Chilcotin mountain range looms up, and without realizing it, you are entering a radically different climate zone. Nighttime temperatures during winter can reach a low of negative twenty-seven degrees Celsius. And daytime highs average right around freezing in January. The cool summers and cold winters in this region, classified as the "Montane Spruce Zone," result largely from its position in the rain shadow of the Coast Mountains and the high elevations. The low precipitation, dry air, and clear skies at night often create very frigid overnight temperatures.

The McGregor ranch was at a northern latitude where there were sixteen and a half hours of daylight at the summer solstice but only seven and a half hours at the winter solstice. The ranch was fairly close to the tiny hamlet of Anahim Lake, but the nearest good shopping and the nearest freight terminal were eighty-seven miles away in Bella Coola. To anyone outside the region, they used the shorthand of saying that their ranch was "near Bella Coola" because it took too long to explain that they were in the middle of nowhere. The ranch had 720 deeded acres with 410 acres of that in hay ground. (More than half of that had been muskeg swamp when the property was first staked in the 1930s, and then it had to be laboriously drained and cleared, originally with ditches dug by hand.) The property was off the grid, with a forty-two-year-old Lister diesel generator, and fourteen photovoltaic panels—which were useful for only nine months of each year.

The ranch house had been built in 1975, replacing the property's original homestead cabin. The house was 2,720 square feet, with four bedrooms. There was also a machine shop/shed, two large hay barns, a calving shed, an infrequently used guest cabin, and several corrals. In recent years, their income had come mainly from selling hay rather than cattle. Some of their hay was trucked to Bella Coola and then loaded on barges and shipped as far away as the Aleutian Islands.

The McGregors heated the ranch house with firewood. There was also an oil-fired backup heater that they used mainly when they had to be away from the ranch house in winter, to keep the pipes from freezing. The big Lister generator was also run on home heating oil, since they found that it burned the heating fuel just as well as diesel and was often less expensive. Their diesel and heating-oil fuel tanks had a combined volume of 2,600 gallons, and they were nearly full when the Crunch occurred. They also had a 250-gallon-capacity tank of unleaded gasoline, but it had only 180 gallons in it when Phil arrived.

A lot of the roads were unmarked, so driving directions were often based on highway kilometer markers. Typical directions would begin with something like: "You take the road going north from Marker 37 . . ." The off-highway road conditions ranged from fair to horrendous, with some notorious mud bogs in the spring and early summer. Surprisingly, some ranches were easier to access in the midwinter months, when the lakes and rivers were frozen, turning them into "snow machine" highways. Winter hospitality was legendary in the region. Because of the short daylight hours and long driving distances, a visit to another ranch was usually at least an overnight stay and might span a full week.

Seven miles from the ranch was the resort town of Anahim Lake, which had only two stores. One was called the Trading Store, but it wasn't much more than a glorified gas station minimart. The other was McLean Trading, which was a combination grocery store, hardware store, dry goods store, and butcher shop. They also sold fishing tackle and hunting licenses. The store had been run continuously since it was established by the Christensen family in 1898—originally in a much smaller building. At the time of the Crunch, it was three thousand square feet. The McLean family was celebrated for their willingness to "order in" just about anything that their customers requested, which ranged from books and canned ghee to canoes and snowmobiles. They generously made their loading dock available for locals to take delivery on an amazing assortment of trucked-in merchandise—everything from pianos to navy surplus generators, even if they hadn't been ordered through the store.

For most Anahim Lake locals, "going shopping" meant either a nearly two-hour drive (in good weather) west to the department stores in Bella Coola (population 625) or a three-hour drive southeast to Williams Lake (population 11,000).

In Bella Coola there was a Sears store, Moore's Organic Market and Nursery, Tru Hardware, the Alexander MacKenzie Comemorative Pharmacy, and a fairly well-stocked Consumers Co-op. But the nearest HBC (Hudson's Bay Company) and Walmart were in Williams Lake, which was a 206-mile drive from the ranch.

21

IN THE 1880S

Deyr fé,
deyja frændur,
deyr sjálfur ið sama.
Eg veit einn,
að aldrei deyr;
dómur um dauðan hvern.
(Translated:
Cattle die and kinsmen die,
thyself too soon must die,
but one thing never, I ween, will die,
the doom on each one dead.)

—*The Hávamál*, an Ancient Gnomic Norse Poem

The McGregor Ranch, near Anahim Lake, British Columbia—October, the First Year

Ray McGregor arrived at the ranch forty-three hours after Phil, looking exhausted. Everyone was greatly relieved to see him. After lots of hugs, Ray took off his coat and draped it over the porch rail, revealing his holstered pistol.

Alan chided his son, "I thought you still had your grandfather's pistol buried in a PVC pipe out next to the scrap-metal pile."

"I *did*, Dad, but I moved it a couple of years ago to a cache just north of the U.S. border. I just didn't tell you and Mom. I didn't want you fretting about it."

"Okay. No worries, son. Just glad to see you got back here safely."

The Crunch presented some immediate challenges for the McGregor ranch. Winter was fast approaching as the days grew shorter. Phil was amazed at how quickly the weather turned bitterly cold in the Chilcotins. After being acclimated to Seattle's fairly temperate drizzle, he found that the dry cold in the interior of British Columbia came as a shock. Nighttime lows in late October were around ten degrees Fahrenheit. By early November, they had their first subzero night. The Canadian radio stations reported temperatures in Celsius, so it took a while for Phil to get used to both the difference in the climate *and* the difference in the weather reporting.

The McGregors no longer had any prospect of being able to buy fuel. All of the gas stations in the region and even the propane distributors had recently sold out. They assumed that they wouldn't have enough fuel to run their Lister generator twelve hours a day, as they had been accustomed to do. In fact, running it just one day a week to do laundry might be too much. Nor could they run electric stock-tank heaters. As winter set in, they began a daily ritual of breaking up ice with sledgehammers.

A military immersion heater or a Japanese wood-fired hot-tub heater would have been ideal for this situation, but unfortunately they didn't have those, either. Claire suggested using a spare old rectangular wood stove they had stored in the machine shop to keep the main stock tank clear of ice. With the prospect of progressively colder nights and thicker ice ahead, they had to act soon.

To transfer the most heat from the stove into the stock tank, at least part of the flat top of the woodstove would have to be beneath the tank. The logical place to position it was at the end of the tank, where the ground sloped away. Obviously they would need to dig a hole, but the ground was already frozen solid to a depth of six inches. Rather than hoping for an unseasonal warm spell to thaw the soil, they simply operated the stove for twenty-four hours above the spot where they planned to dig, keeping the stove stoked continuously.

The excavation for the stove took longer than they thought, and it required considerable shoring with bricks and cinder blocks to provide access for loading wood, and enough of a slope to provide sufficient drainage for the inevitable snowmelts and rain.

Once the stove project was complete, the next task was erecting several new laundry clotheslines, both outdoors and in the sunroom on the south porch. Since they had no prospect of having their propane tank refilled, they went into extreme conservation mode—with just minimal use of the propane cooking range, and no use of the propane-fired clothes dryer.

The sunroom had once been quaint and decorous, and the place where Claire had often entertained friends for afternoon tea parties. She had always been adamant that muddy boots were banned from the room. But now the sunroom was decidedly utilitarian and crowded with clotheslines, a winter garden of salad greens in terra cotta pots on every available bit of floor space, and several solar battery chargers set up just inside the windows.

Laundry days were timed to coincide with the weekly and later biweekly running of "the light plant," as they called their generator. Those days were always a flurry of activity that started as soon as the generator was fired up. The laundry had already been sorted, and the dirtiest items had already been prewashed in the laundry sink. On those same days, they did any projects that required power tools.

At the ranch, it felt as if the pace of life was simply slowing down, and they were returning to the isolation of frontier ranching life from a century ago. The newspaper ceased operation and mail delivery was halted. The local CBC station went off the air. The landline phone stopped working. And even *if* they had been in a cellular coverage area—and they weren't—that service would have been unavailable as well. Nimpo Lake Internet—their local affiliate for Galaxy Broadband—ceased operation once the Galaxy satellite system went offline. (The satellite system required the continuous operation of ground segment stations.)

The shortage of gasoline and diesel meant that visits by neighbors and friends became infrequent and were now mostly medical or veterinary emergencies or involved problems with water systems. (Living a long way from town in times of fuel scarcity meant that neighbors had to depend on one another's help and expertise.) And suddenly, there were not enough horses to go around, and the asking prices for horses and saddles—all priced in terms of silver or barter goods—seemed astronomical.

Feeding the cattle required no power, and their water came from a shallow well that was serviced by a pump powered by their PV panels and their battery bank.

Hot water for the house had always been provided by a set of coils in the woodstove and a thermal siphon tank in the attic that had been nicknamed "the rumbler" many years before. They had a lot of books and had never become addicted to television. So, unlike many other families, the transition to Crunch living was not traumatic for the McGregors. (Alan had lived off-grid for most of his life, and Claire for all of her married life.)

Perhaps the greatest change for them was the overwhelming sense of being out of touch with the world beyond their fences. They missed getting regular local news. They missed being able to talk on the phone with their daughters in their far-flung locales. They realized that there was something special about being able to open a *fresh* newspaper, and the absence of that made them feel wistful. The new lack of citrus fruits and coffee was often mentioned. They also had to go back to the old standby of checking their barometer each day, since they no longer had access to regional weather forecasts.

The daytime AM radio reception at the ranch had always been poor, and their FM reception began only when they had driven halfway to Williams Lake, or in the other direction more than halfway to Bella Coola. (CBC Radio One in Prince George had a translator station in Bella Coola. Alan hated the CBC, invariably calling it "a bunch of socialist propaganda.") So for most of their years at the ranch, it was only in the evenings or during predawn milking sessions that they had good AM radio reception. (Alan had enjoyed listening to the news on KOMO at 1,000 KHz, a fifty-thousand-watt clear-channel station, in Seattle.) But now, even that was gone. Apart from Phil's shortwave radio—which Alan and Claire found difficult to hear clearly—their world had gone silent.

With their cow now back at the ranch full-time, they milked her twice a day. She had recently been bred by a Dexter bull and was due to calve again in the spring. For a city boy like Phil Adams, the cow-milking routine was a new experience. He eventually enjoyed taking his turn milking, although he never became as efficient as Claire. (She always seemed to get at least one more pint out of Tessa than Phil did at each milking.) At the ranch they drank their milk raw and simply filtered. When they ran out of paper filters for their funnel, they substituted cotton fabric squares, cut from new dish towels.

The cow produced more milk than the four of them could drink, and the skimmed cream made more butter than they could use, so the extra all went to five bantam hens that they obtained by bartering some extra salt blocks. The chickens were fed through the winter with milk, cream, and some oats from their cattle bins. The five hens were messy—inconsistently choosing odd places in the barn to roost each night—but the eggs that they produced were a blessing. Alan made plans to build a proper chicken coop in the coming spring or summer.

As recently as 2005, they had run up to six hundred cattle on the McGregor ranch, a number considered a "small operation" by local standards. Some of the ranches nearby controlled hundreds of thousands of acres of range pasture. But after their children had grown up and moved away, knowing the high cost of hiring ranch workers, they cut down to just twelve Coriander cows and heifers, and sixteen Coriander-Longhorn crosses (a mix of heifers and beef steers). They also had a Longhorn bull named Tex and Tessa, the Jersey milk cow, which were both often on loan to neighbors. In the two years before the Crunch, most of their income came from cutting hay. Because of Alan's numerous back surgeries, they switched to contracting out the hay cutting, keeping some of the round bales for winter feed for their own livestock. As the Crunch set in and fuel became scarce, the price of hay skyrocketed, even after being redenominated into silver coinage. A gallon of gasoline or diesel now sold for the equivalent of two or three days' wages for a laborer.

The Coriander-Longhorn crosses sold well, both before and after the Crunch. They were cold tolerant, making them a good breed for the region. They also knew how to use their horns, which meant they had a decent chance of fending off wolves, bears, and mountain lions—but they were by no means invulnerable. The Chilcotin Range had a notoriously dense population of predators.

After their children moved away Alan and Claire McGregor had stopped raising a vegetable garden. And while the larder was well stocked by local standards, aside from beef, they would be lacking many staple foods by the following spring.

They contacted a neighbor who was famous for her sprouting and traded a quarter of beef for an assortment of sprouting seeds and sprouting jar lids (stainless steel screens mounted in Mason jar lids).

As Phil, Alan, and Claire helped Ray unpack his pickup and trailer, a bit of a show-and-tell session began. Each item that they carried into the house or shop seemed to have a story behind it.

Once they had unloaded the trailer and parked it alongside his father's stock trailer, Ray planned to put his camper shell (which had been stored in the barn) back on his truck.

He had two almost identical Stihl chain saws, both with twenty-two-inch bars. One of the saws was stored in a factory orange plastic case, and the other was in a plywood box that Ray had constructed himself. For these saws he had a spare bar, a spare recoil starter assembly, and seventeen spare chains (although a few of them had been resharpened so many times that they were nearly worn out). He also had a lot of two-cycle fuel mixing oil and chain-bar lubricating oil in an odd assortment of containers—perhaps ten gallons in all. He had all of the usual safety equipment, including an integral helmet/earmuff/mesh face mask, and Kevlar safety chaps. He also had innumerable pairs of gloves, plastic wedges, files, tape measures, rolls of flagging tape in various colors, and other chain saw accoutrements, all stowed in a set of mesh bags mounted to the inside walls of the trailer.

The largest items in the trailer were his enduro motorcycle and a hydraulic woodsplitter. The motorcycle was a KTM 250 XC and had a two-stroke engine, so its gasoline had to be mixed. Ray had repainted the orange parts of the bike with brown truck bed liner paint three years earlier, but the rough-textured brown paint had held up remarkably well, with the original orange color appearing only in a few small spots. The KTM was considered street legal in both the U.S. and Canada, although he had let its registration lapse while he was in the United States.

The log splitter was a Swisher brand twenty-two-ton model with a Briggs and Stratton engine. One of the tires on the splitter had a chronic slow leak, but the machine was otherwise reliable and it cycled fairly quickly.

Ray spent a lot of time showing them his old-fashioned logging tools. Some of these had been acquired while he was living in Michigan, including a large assortment of axes, sledges, mauls, and wedges; a bark spud; a "Swede" bow saw and extra blades; and a pair of cant hooks for rolling and moving large logs.

Ray also had a well-stocked steel tool chest and a handmade plywood carry chest for his assortment of Ryobi eighteen-volt DC battery-powered tools. His father used the same brand, so they could share batteries.

In his pickup, there wasn't much to show for his "career" work as a historian, just two cardboard boxes, mostly containing back issues of history magazines. Claire was surprised to see that he had very few photocopied documents for his research; in recent years he'd used a scanner rather than make hard copies. All of his actual writings since high school fit on just one memory stick. He pulled out a compass and an altimeter that had been salvaged from a B-24 in a Kingman, Arizona, boneyard back in the 1950s.

Ray quickly recounted an inventory of his guns: In addition to a Remington Nylon 66 .22 rifle and a Winchester Model 70 .30-06 that he'd left at the ranch, Ray had the shotgun and the Inglis Hi-Power that he'd retrieved on his trip home. Phil was fascinated by the Inglis pistol. This was Canada's military-issue version of the venerable Browning P35 Hi-Power. Ray demonstrated how to attach and detach the shoulder stock, and the operation of its tangent rear sight, which was graduated out to an astoundingly optimistic five hundred meters.

At this point, Claire said, "I'll leave you to carry on with the Big Boy Toys, so that I can get dinner on the table. "

Laying out all of the ammo that he carried in from the pickup, plus the ammo that he'd left stored at the ranch, he counted fourteen ammo cans, more than half of which were filled with various shotgun shells.

As Ray was closing all of his ammo cans, Alan asked, "What about you, Phil? I guess we need to know what gear you have available to help us keep the place secure. I just saw you tote in your gun cases with hardly a word."

Phil nodded. "Yeah, I suppose you should know."

They walked down the hall to Phil's bedroom—which had once been occupied by Ray's sisters—and he opened the closet. The top shelf of the closet was sagging under the weight of the tidy phalanx of nineteen ammo cans.

He pulled out the two black plastic Pelican waterproof cases and set them on the bed. He flipped the latches on the smaller one and swung it open.

Alan let out a whistle and said, "That's enough to get Jean Chrétien rolling in his grave."

Resting in the gray foam of the gun case was a DPMS clone of the Colt M4 Carbine and one detached green plastic magazine.

"This one is semiautomatic only, and has a sixteen-inch barrel instead of the military-issue fourteen-and-a-half-inch barrel. But it's otherwise functionally much like the U.S. M4 or the Canadian C7."

Ray corrected him. "C8, Phil. The C7 is our service rifle, but the C8 is the carbine."

"Right. Thanks for the reminder."

Looking back down at the rifle case, Phil went on. "The scope on the Picatinny rail is a Trijicon TA01 with a 'donut of death' reticle. That's tritium-lit, so it's a day/night scope. I also have both a Bushnell red dot and a PVS-14 'Gen Three' night vision scope for it, packed in foam in one of the taller ammo cans. That scope can be used three ways: mounted on my M4, as a handheld monocular, or with a head mount. It may turn out to be the single most important piece of gear for securing the ranch."

Tapping the carbine's buttstock, Phil said, "I'm sure this is über illegal here in Canada, so I suppose we'd better find a good hiding place for it."

Ray chimed in, "The magazines, too. They're banned here, as well. We can't have anything larger than five rounds for a rifle, or ten rounds for a pistol."

"That law stinks. I've got about thirty-five spare magazines, ranging in capacity from five rounds to forty rounds. But a dozen of them are my designated 'go to war' magazines—just like that loaded one, there in the case: thirty-round PMAGs. I like the foliage-green ones."

He swung the first case closed, and then opened up the larger one. In it was a Savage Axis stainless steel bolt-action chambered in .223 with a 3–9X scope, a takedown stainless steel Ruger 10/22 rifle with standard sights, and a stainless steel Ruger Mark II .22 target pistol.

Alan clucked his tongue and said, "We'll have to make that Ruger .22 pistol disappear, too."

"Is that a .308?" Alan asked, pointing at the larger rifle.

"No. It's only a .223. Basically a varmint rifle, but it is insanely accurate. I suppose it would do for deer if I aim for the head."

"If you want to pot a deer, then you can borrow Claire's .243 Winchester. Her gun is a little Remington Model 7, about the size of that Savage."

Pointing up at the green-painted steel ammo cans, Phil said, "As for the ammo, there's quite a mix: 5.56mm, mostly ball, some match grade, about two hundred rounds of tracer, and a half dozen boxes of .223 Remington hollowpoint varmint loads that I can shoot in both my bolt action and my M4. But the 5.56mm NATO ammo I can shoot *only* in the M4 because of a mismatch in chamber dimensions, which can cause pressure problems in the bolt action. By the way, just the opposite is true in .308s, where you can shoot 7.62mm NATO in a .308 Winchester, but not vice versa."

Gesturing farther down the shelf, he said: "Then there's 9mm. You name it, and I've got it: ball, eight or nine different types of hollowpoints, some special low-lead ammo for indoor ranges, some tracers, and even one box of Arcane armor piercing. I also have two cans of .22 long rifle ammo, mostly hollowpoints."

After a moment, he added, "Oh, I also have one .50-caliber can there with some odd boxes of ammo that I've somehow accumulated over the years, for guns that I don't currently own. There's .45 ACP, .40 S&W, and some .22 Magnum, a couple of boxes of .30-30, and a box of .30-40 Krag. That ammo should all be good for bartering."

"Any .243 Winchester?" Alan asked.

"No."

"That's a pity, because we only have thirty-seven rounds of .243 on hand for Claire's rifle."

"And your deer rifle?" Phil asked.

"Mine's a .300 Winchester Magnum. That'll do for elk, moose, and caribou, as well. Thankfully, I have nearly fourteen boxes of cartridges for that. I once found it on sale at a hardware store in Lytton that was going out of business for just twenty-four dollars a box. So I bought every box that they had."

After a moment, Alan added, "We have several other guns here at the ranch, all off-registry: an Ithaca Model 37 pump shotgun, a Webley .455 revolver, two .22 bolt actions, a .22 Remington pump, a .300 Savage lever action, a Winchester .45-70 lever action, and even an old Snider .577 single-shot carbine that my grandfather brought over from Scotland. There's not much ammo on hand for most of those guns, I'm afraid."

"Perhaps we can do some trading with your neighbors."

"Possibly. But people have gotten very shy about discussing their guns in recent years. It's as if the Montreal crowd has muzzled the entire nation. Most people in Canada of course refuse to even consider registering or giving up their 'restricted' guns, but they certainly have become circumspect about mentioning any guns—of all categories—that they own in casual conversation."

Phil nodded in understanding. He turned and flipped the large case closed and then said, "Last, but not least."

He then reached up under his shirt to the small of his back and pulled out his SIG P228 pistol and pointed it at the ceiling.

Spiraling his wrist slightly, he said, "This shoots 9mm Parabellum—also called 9mm Luger—just like Ray's Hi-Power."

"Have you been carrying that all this time for the past three days?"

"Of course. I'd feel naked without it."

Alan laughed and said, "I didn't even get a glimpse of it, or have a *notion* that you were packing."

Phil smirked and said, "That's called effective concealed carry. The holster is a Milt Sparks Versa Max 2. This is the same holster that I carried every day as a CI agent. The spare magazine pouch is from a company called Mag-Holder. It lies horizontal, so it hardly shows."

Ray nodded, and said, "Nice."

He lifted his loose-fitting polo shirt to show them both the holster and the spare magazine pouch, and he reholstered the pistol with practiced precision.

Ray tilted his head and said, "All those ravening hordes from Seattle and Vancouver—not that many of them will ever make it this far."

Phil replied, "No, only the *most vicious* ones."

Alan asked, "Are you serious?"

"Dead serious. It will only be the really vicious looters who'll get this far north and west. Now, granted, the statistical chance of any looters making it out this far and then picking *this* particular ranch's little side road are pretty slim. However, the consequences if they do would be enormous. So I think from here on out, we keep every gun fully loaded at all times, and we should

each carry a rifle with us whenever we're outdoors. Ray and I both have concealment holsters for our pistols, so we'll carry those whenever we're doing
heavy chores where we can't carry a rifle. And that means whenever we hop
on a quad or drive a pickup. A rifle in a scabbard has got to be part of our routine *every* time."

Keeping guns handy yet out of sight required some creativity. Since they
had unregistered handguns and Phil's M4 at the ranch, those all had to be
kept hidden when not in use. Ray's Hi-Power pistol and magazines were hidden in the top of the antique oak expandable kitchen table. Reaching under
the table and pulling the lever that would normally be used to add wooden
leaves to the table revealed a compartment atop the table's central pedestal.

As a heavily armed illegal alien, Phil Adams presented a problem. A hiding
place was constructed for both him and his gear by converting his room's
four-and-a-half-foot by seven-foot walk-in garment closet into a hidden room.
The shelves in the closet were well-stocked with MREs and dozens of half-
gallon canning jars filled with water, as well as all of his guns and ammunition. Several more sturdy shelves of rough-cut lumber had to be added to
accommodate all of this.

The hidden room also had a night-light, a foam pad, and a sleeping bag. It
was even equipped with a small chemical toilet from the McGregors' camping trailer and a folding chair, in case he had to be there for an extended
period. Phil was also careful to leave his small assortment of books and military manuals in the closet, since many of them were marked with his name.
There was just enough room for Phil to lie out full length with his feet beside
the chemical toilet.

The twenty-nine-inch doorway to the closet was cleverly concealed by removing the trim molding and placing a tall, lightly stocked thirty-four-inch-
wide bookcase in front of it. Once inside, a pair of handles mounted at waist
level could be used to precisely position the bookcase. Then, nine steel brack-
ets screwed on the back side of the bookcase could be wedged in, using scrap
pieces of tapered wood roofing shingles. Once the shingle scraps were in
place, the bookcase had no gap or tilt, so it appeared to be built-in. And with
these wedges it would not move at all, even if subjected to very firm shoves.
Air circulation was provided by a small retrofitted vent to the attic. They
called his closet "The Ten Boom Room."

If the house were raided by authorities, the cover story would be that they had a dim-witted hired man named Phil Quincy—a Canadian citizen—but that he would be "out in the back acreage, working on fences," or alternatively, if there was snow on the ground, that he was "visiting a friend down at the lake."

It came as a logical conclusion that Phil would remain on the ranch at all times and that he should be ready to go into hiding on short notice. For any visiting neighbors, if Phil was spotted, then he was to play the role of a "slow" hired ranch worker with a speech impediment, who would wave and say little more than: "Hi, I'm Phil," and then wander away.

22

HUNGER

I am not fluent in the language of violence, but I can speak it well enough to get by in the parts of the world where it is spoken.

—Pope Benedict

Louisa, Kentucky—Late October, the First Year

As their small party of five with two carts merged into the crowd of foot traffic already walking across the bridge, Megan grabbed both boys by the hand and instructed them in French to stay very close to her and not let go of her hands for any reason. As they descended the bridge on the Kentucky side, they saw the Kentucky National Guard HMMWV with a Gore-Tex-clad soldier manning the crew in front of the two commandeered Coca-Cola trucks, just as the cop at the Fort Gay entry checkpoint had described it. The soldier on the Mod Deuce looked as though he was very cold and indifferent as he squinted in the morning light to see the approaching walkers. Joshua noticed—as did Megan—that there wasn't actually any ammunition belt hanging out of the .50-cal. It was simply a "show of force" measure.

Malorie kept the sense of direction in her head and successfully navigated them out of town on a westerly route past the Kentucky National Guard soldiers carrying their issued M16s without any magazines in their rifles. It seemed that the presence of the good guys was enough to keep law and order without having to actually risk life in this part of the world. There wasn't any power in the town, and although the streets were eerily deserted by day,

Joshua wondered how long you could keep thousands of hungry people from looting the shops under the cover of night.

Once they were on the other side of town, they stopped and adjusted their loads and drank some water. Malorie had her M1 Carbine across her lap as she sat down for a halt, as did Megan. They all discussed the importance of the Cooper situational awareness color code and one's ability to react to threats if one hesitates and/or is not paying attention. Their fluid SOP would be to pull out their long weapons at the halt with the exception of either Megan or Malorie—whoever wasn't pushing the cart—because she would already have her carbine at the ready. Joshua decided to keep his .270 rifle secured on the cart to not risk bumping the scope, which he had sited in for two hundred yards.

"By the way, thank you ladies for helping me to balance the cart so well back there on the West Virginia side. I'm doing okay with mine, how about you, Malorie?" Joshua asked.

"Mine seems to be riding well, thanks."

Megan suggested that they try to take a halt every hour if possible and rest for ten minutes so that they could maintain their endurance—especially with the little ones.

Malorie had her regional road map out and said, "I think if we stick to 32 at a good pace we can probably pick up Route 7 West tomorrow; that should take us to the Olympia State Forest by tomorrow evening."

Joshua craned his head over to Megan and said, "Can I please have the state forest map, beautiful?" She handed him the map and brushed his cheek.

He opened it up and as he looked at it he said, "Here's my thought process, but please let me know what you think. We should aim for the west side of the lake. Like this dovetail-shaped protrusion into the lake here. We'll have plenty of firewood and lots of access to water and fishing. This will also mean that we'll be over any major bridges, an obvious key choke point, after winter is over. Our strategy is not very complicated, but it is difficult—wait out the winter. Like you said, Megan, 'Stay warm, dry, and unseen.' We can't travel fast enough on the road to cover the 120-ish miles to Bradfordsville before winter, and it's not like we can get ahold of Dustin to come and pick us up, either." Megan and Malorie nodded in agreement.

"As cruel as it sounds, we'll have to let the starvation and cold of winter partially clear the way for us. Based on our dependency on cheap energy and given that winter is imminent, plus the fact that people typically only keep three days' worth of food in their house and the grocery stores operate on a just-in-time delivery system—I'd estimate that we'll lose about a third of the population before spring."

"Don't forget the roving criminal gangs, and people not getting their medicines," added Megan.

Joshua nodded. "With that said, we'll have less people between the state forest and Bradfordsville in the spring; however, the bad news is those that are left will be highly suspicious of road walkers."

"I agree," Megan said. "But I think that we should walk and talk so that we're making progress."

There were still a few vehicles on the road here and there, but not like what they had expected. There were other groups of road walkers as well, occasionally a family, but none of them seemed to be very well prepared. Joshua's party was wary whenever a stranger approached, and they kept their guns close at hand. Folks headed east would ask them about news out that way, whether they could cross over into West Virginia, if Louisa was peaceful, and so on. Likewise, the small group would try to ask for news to the west without giving up too many details of their own.

At a halt everyone would drink water and eat something, even if it was just three or four dehydrated carrot slices, in order to keep their energy up. Given their slower pace with the boys, the sixty minutes on- and ten minutes off-duty cycle worked out especially well for their mileage expectations. Since they were eating small bites here and there, they didn't need to take a long break for meals, either.

The group stopped to rest for the night before they reached the Route 7 junction. It was their first full day of walking and everyone was getting used to the hot spots on their feet. They all decided to move one hundred meters into the dense brush off the road to set up camp for the night. The carts were picked up and carried in through the first ten meters of thick roadside brush to avoid leaving any obvious sign of crushed brush that any unskilled tracker could follow. Since they didn't know who would be coming along the road, they also decided against having a fire that night. Jean and Leo heaped up a pad of leaves and pine needles about ten feet by twelve feet and six inches deep. Megan laid out the large tarp she'd bought at the pawnshop. Then she pulled out her smaller tarp, which was folded in half and zip-tied together on two sides, putting her sleeping bag inside that. Malorie did the same.

Jean and Leo would take turns sleeping with either Auntie Malorie or their mom on a given night, helping both of them to stay warm with each other's heat. Joshua put his sleeping bag in between theirs, and the other side of the tarp would fold over to keep them mostly dry should it start to rain or snow.

Sidearms were to stay either inside their sleeping bags or inside the fold of a sweatshirt acting as a pillow for ease of access. Likewise, long weapons would be between the sleeping bags to stay dry and not be out of arm's reach if they were to encounter robbers at night, a fear never far from the minds of the adults.

Since it had been days since the adults had slept, the group decided not to keep a watch that night, and with the exception of bio breaks in the middle of the night they all slept from complete exhaustion until daybreak.

Leo was the first to awake in the morning, when a squirrel dropped an acorn on the tarp. He had grown up on the homestead but had never slept under the stars before. In the still morning air, he just lay there snuggled up next to his auntie Malorie watching and pointing one little finger out of the sleeping bag at the squirrels racing up and down the tree. Not long after, Malorie awoke and noticed that her nephew was watching the squirrels. She kissed his head and smoothed his hair and couldn't help but think how incredibly hard the next few months would be for all of them, and how they were refugees in their own country.

The group broke camp and repacked the carts after a small breakfast. It was unspoken between the adults to not eat as much as they normally would so that the food supply would last longer for the boys. They would need more fuel for warmth and for growth, and it was their survival that served as the charter for this mission in the first place.

By late afternoon they had reached their destination in the state forest, but they still needed a place to shelter. Megan stayed with Jean and Leo to watch the carts, while Joshua and Malorie left on a recon patrol to find a suitable place to over-winter. Malorie had the map out and was speaking to Joshua on a hilltop overlooking the beautiful lake. "I heard you say that you liked this dovetail protrusion here sticking out into the lake? I think that we should check the south side of that ridge for a suitable cave to shelter in. This way we can maximize our solar exposure and not be as cold."

"Good idea, I like where your head is at."

Before long, they found a suitable cave that would prove to be very tight quarters, but would keep them dry and, they hoped, undetected by anyone passing through. They decided to drop their packs to lighten their load on the way back so that they could move quickly with Megan, Jean, and Leo before complete darkness. Malorie suggested that they just take what they needed from the carts and leave them cached well out of sight so that they could move faster and bed down before nightfall. Joshua replied, "Good idea. Megan, may I carry your pack? This way you can assist Malorie with the boys. I'll grab the tarps and extra blankets. I'm not sure about you, but I got cold last night."

"Not me," said Malorie. "I was too busy with all of the squirming going on in my sleeping bag!" as she reached out to tickle Leo, who squealed with laughter.

The next morning, everyone awoke and ate something. Megan wanted to start good habits, so she had the boys brush their teeth with the minimal amount of toothpaste immediately after breakfast, and then everyone gathered around and took turns reading a chapter of Scripture followed by prayer. It helped the morning feel more normal and familiar.

Megan and Joshua set out to retrieve the carts from their cache. It gave them a chance to sit, talk, and share their thoughts—something that they had not done since fleeing D.C.

"You know, Megan my love, the last time we got to sit and talk was at the Agency. It seems like a lifetime ago. I have to tell you, I really feel cheated by this whole Crunch."

"Really? How is that?"

"Well, I knew that I was falling in love with you, and of course I was thinking marriage, but it takes time to reach that decision, you know what I mean?"

"I do. As a matter of fact, I was in no hurry to get remarried. I was convinced that as soon as a guy found out that I had two sons, he would bolt. And even if he did stick around, who would walk me down the aisle now that my papa passed?" Megan traced a pattern in the forest floor between her feet with the stick she was holding. "That seems silly, doesn't it?"

"Not to me it doesn't. I want to hear your thoughts on marriage—I kinda like you." He elbowed her and she giggled. "Wow, when was the last time you laughed?"

"Just now!" She laughed again, then looked away as a whitetail deer bounded back into a thick clump of brush on the other side of the open glade. "When you came along and still wanted me despite of all of the turmoil in my life, I thought that I was getting that second opportunity to live life again. Then, after just six short months of a romance, we have this financial crisis and the whole stupid Crunch—it's just not fair. Why couldn't we just have had two years to be married? You could have taught the boys to ride bikes, I could've packed your lunch every day for work, and we could've gone for family hikes after church on Sundays—why all of this? Why now? How many couples come home to each other and don't say a word, each one taking dinner into a separate room to watch separate television shows and chat with separate friends on social media and sleep on separate sides of the bed? They wasted their days in peacetime, and they'll probably be the first to kill each other in the lean times of this Crunch. I just think that you and I could have done better together."

"I am with you now and if you'll have me, I plan on marrying you the first chance we get. And as for now, what would you say to an extended camping trip in the Olympia State Forest—no phones ringing, no high-side e-mail to check, no disgruntled ex-wives' club clicking their tongues around your cubicle space—how does that sound?"

Megan kissed Joshua. Then they got up, found their bearings, and located the carts. Getting the loaded carts up and over the rugged terrain was not easy and took most of the day. "This should make it more difficult for someone trying to pursue us, if it was this hard for us to get these carts up here," Megan said.

"Well, maybe, but someone doesn't need to bring very much with them to spell trouble for us up here."

When they returned to camp in the midafternoon, they were completely exhausted, but the weather had changed. The air was wet and almost warm, the kind of conditions that were familiar to Megan or anyone else who'd grown up in cold country as being a precursor to snow. "The snow should cover our tracks and give us a clean canvas to know if someone has been in our area. Also, it'll be easier to track game."

Malorie had Leo and Jean on leaf and pine needle detail. They eventually had quite a thick pad of brush down for everyone to sleep on. The cave had a narrow entrance, and they had to stoop to enter. It was a classic karst water-carved cave, but at some point the limestone formation had gone dry, leaving a chamber that varied between four feet and eight feet wide, with a gentle upward slope. The height varied between six and twelve feet, before sharply tapering at the back. The cave lacked fancy stalactites and stalagmites, but the boys still declared it "awesome."

They squeezed the deer carts into the back of the cave. There were spots wide enough for beds down the length of the cave, with enough room to walk by them. Joshua's bed spot was closest to the entrance, then came Malorie's, then Megan's, and finally the boys'. Megan and Malorie helped set up the quarters as best they could in the space they had. Once a blanket was rigged to cover the cave's entrance, they noticed that their body heat alone—when added to the sixty-two-degree ambient ground temperature—soon took the chill off the air in the cave.

Joshua set about improving the site in small ways, such as digging a slit trench for a solid-waste latrine, improvising an overwatch position, and making a range card for everyone's use.

"We're going to be here awhile, so we need to be able to defend it. It likely goes without saying, but our first defense is passive. That means that we remain unseen. We're too small a force to ward off anyone, and it won't take any time at all for the reports from our guns to alert anyone within earshot that there are people up here. People mean possible resources to exploit, which brings me back to the first thing that I said—passive defense."

Malorie added, "I can see a real need to go out for water, to forage for food, or to hunt. I'm assuming that our chief liabilities as far as protection would be the children. That being said, one adult is likely enough to stay here and take care of them and 'hold down the fort,' but if anyone needs to go out, they should have at least one adult with them."

"I like that idea," Megan said. "What about weapons?"

"Yeah, about that." Joshua took off his watch cap and scratched his head. "Handguns mandatory at all times—always within arm's reach. I'm fine with long weapons slung around your body, but definitely at the ready anytime you're leaving camp with another adult, like you said, Mal. I'm going to see what I can fashion out of some wood and 550 cord to put the .270 in the cave up off the ground so that it's accessible and out of the way. I think that your carbines are decent for close targets as are both of the shotguns; we'd only need to use these to defend ourselves, because if someone is out far enough that we would need the .270—"

Malorie finished his sentence, "Then we're to be quiet and unseen in a passive defense, right?"

"Exactly!" Joshua replied. "So for day-to-day storage, the .270 will be in the shelter out of the way. Besides, a shotgun is my preferred weapon anyway."

Megan said, "I'll do a thorough inventory of our food and set a rations schedule for us. We'll be dependent on fishing, foraging, and hunting for supplementing what we have. I can't think that we have anyone that we can trade with here, so we'll have to make what we have last." Joshua and Malorie nodded in agreement. "There must be houses around, so I think that we should probably set up deliberate two-person patrols to find out if there are others in our AO so that we can steer well clear of them. Anyone with a house nearby is likely going to be very keen on shooting first and asking questions later of anyone approaching their turf."

"Joshua, do you have much hunting experience?" Malorie asked.

"Truthfully, I don't. I have plenty of trigger time, so if a deer wants to hold the broadside pose I can hit it, but I know that there is more to woodscraft than that."

"Megan and I had lots of hunting experience with our papa, so I think that we should set out to hunt/patrol at least three days a week."

"Good idea, Mal," Megan said.

"We can move slowly, take notes, and report back on what, if anything, we see. And if, I mean when, we take a deer we can quarter it, hang it up, and pack it out in two trips."

"After we harvest the deer, we'll have to find a way to smoke it since we don't have nearly enough salt to cure the meat in order to preserve it. I'll start thinking of how we can do that." Malorie rubbed her fingertips across her eyes and said, "After our meat stock is good, we can certainly switch the patrol schedule around."

"I think that any two-person party leaving needs to leave a plan behind: where they're going, who's going with them, what's the intent, when they should be expected back, and what actions are to be taken if they don't return by that time. This will all be critical since I can't just take the boys with me to go get you or vice versa," Joshua said.

"I agree, let's do that," Megan said. "Also, we have all of our eggs in one basket here. What do you think about taking the bug-out bags and stashing them in another cave under a tarp covered with leaves? Perhaps taking the compact valuables as well as the junk silver, my AR-7, or ammo and cache that somewhere else, too? This way, if we do get hit here we can escape and evade without losing everything."

"I like it. It spreads out our attack liability," said Joshua.

"Since this is 'home' for a while, we need to set up a watch around the clock. This is going to mean a *lot* of boredom and downtime on watch. I don't mind taking the night shift provided that I can sleep during the day."

"I have an idea," said Malorie. "If everyone takes exactly eight hours with a small pass down at shift change then we'd be pretty much stuck on the same schedule all the time. But if we rotate seven hours or nine hours, then the watch will slowly change over time and no one person gets stuck."

"Hmm, Mal, that might just work," Megan said. "The other fourteen or eighteen hours could be divided up into sleeping or taking care of the camp, cooking, cleaning, looking after the boys, etcetera."

"But for us to really make the most of our time here, we'll need to hunt and do patrols as well. When it comes time to move in the spring, we'll be familiar with each other enough on the trail to cover the ground to Bradfordsville with the best possible chance of avoiding detection," Malorie said.

With the battery slowly running out of power on her phone, Malorie noted the date and devised a way to count tick marks to keep a written calendar on the cave wall so that they would not lose track of time. The group also took turns reading the survival guides out loud with the screen on the lowest brightness setting. They hoped that if everyone read them out loud, perhaps as much as 40 percent of the information could be recalled among the five of them.

23

SIGNALS COLLECTION

While we all benefit in some ways from modern technology, I do wonder what state our world would be in if we suddenly lost the electrical power necessary to keep our communications functioning. Would the younger generations know how to grow crops to feed a family? Would they know how to drop anchor and wait for the catch? Would they know how to survive by the sweat of the brow? New is good. Old is necessary.

—Reverend Billy Graham

Olympia State Forest, Kentucky—December, the First Year

The days continued to get shorter and the nights were colder. It was not common to see other people in the state forest, but when they did see anyone it was usually one or two people hunting for food.

The long times together in the cave off shift gave Megan and Joshua time to really talk about their spiritual, political, social, and any other kinds of beliefs they held. Joshua joked, "You know, maybe when this whole Crunch blows over, we can start a couples' wilderness retreat and do premarital counseling—this is great!" The large overlaps were comforting to Megan, and the points where they disagreed were not fundamental orthodox doctrine, so they could be mutually overlooked. Joshua was strict during watch, but on his off time he diligently worked to carve two wedding rings out of the core (or what would be called "quarter sawn" lumber) from an oak branch.

Jean would often go fishing with his auntie Malorie, and although it was not enough to subsist on, everyone was able to get his or her fill of sushi that winter. Leo and Jean were both becoming quite adept at finding edible plants, although they would stick to the ones that the group could positively identify, using the description from the survival apps on Malorie's phone until the battery ran out.

The three adults would train to stay in shape four times a week doing hill sprints and floor exercises. Each adult learned all the parts and the manual-of-arms for every individual firearm, in case someone had to pick up someone else's weapon to return fire. Jean and Leo were taught the parts of every firearm as well, but were strictly admonished not to touch one if it was loaded—and all weapons were assumed to be and were, in fact, loaded. The group slowly learned how to successfully move over terrain in two-person patrols, staying together and communicating with hand and arm signals. They knew that when they headed west in the spring they'd be traveling at night and sleeping during the day.

The winter had in fact come early, just as the farmer's almanac had predicted. One cold December morning while Megan and Malorie were out on a deer hunt, Megan left a plan with Joshua that they would head due west to recon the nearest road, gather any information possible, and see if there was still any vehicle traffic. Both Megan and Malorie kissed the boys and headed out to the west. With all of the cold and hunting pressure, it was hard for Megan and Malorie to get a shot at any game. Megan suggested that they make the most of their time and survey Clear Creek Road, which ran parallel to Route 211, to see if there was any traffic.

"You have to admit, this is boring, Megan."

"I freely admit that! I can think of better things I'd rather be doing than lying here on my stomach in the snow looking through Joshua's scope for signs of life."

Malorie asked, "Say, do you mind if I take a spell?"

Megan answered, "Be my guest. There is a patch of leaves over there that looks a little dry—I'll be right back."

Malorie scanned from south to north up and down the road. At that distance, she would not have been able to successfully pattern any deer by spotting the tracks through the snow, but she held out hope that she might at least see some movement along the narrow valley floor. As Malorie was just about to give up, she noticed what looked like a man sitting back against a tree along the east edge of the road.

"Pssssst, Megan! Psssssssst. Over here, I see a guy."

"I've seen one of them before, too."

"You're hilarious, you know that?" Malorie was not in the mood for humor. "He's sitting up against a tree right down there on the road."

Megan reached in the breast pocket of her jacket and got a pad and pencil. "Okay, let's take a SALT report: size, just the one guy?"

"It appears to be just him by himself, yes."

"Activity, what would you say that he's doing other than just sitting there?"

"Tough to tell; with these optics it looks really shadowy, but he has something in his hand that's flat, a book maybe? I'm really not sure, that would be mere conjecture on my part, but it looks like he also has some kind of handwritten sign on a piece of cardboard up against his leg."

"That would make sense if he was hitchhiking, but I can't imagine that there are too many vehicles looking to pick up people these days. Okay, I got that written down for activity. How about location? Still the east side of the Clear Creek Road?" Megan spread out the map of the state forest. "Can you point to it on the map here?"

"I would say right here, north of the junction of Leatherwood Road."

"Got it. Now the last is time, and I'll mark that at thirteen-forty-six. We can share this with Joshua later, but for now let's get back to our primary task; how about we stalk our way back to camp along the south side of this ridge here? We may be able to find a fat doe sunning herself."

"Sounds good to me. No four-wheeled or four-legged traffic to be seen here today—that guy down there does give me pause, though."

"I'm not so weirded out when it's a klick or more away and my boys are safely in the other direction."

"Gotcha. Okay, put your game face on; Papa would never let us get this chatty on a hunt—zip that lip, sis."

The McGregor Ranch, near Anahim Lake, British Columbia—Late October, the First Year

Phil soon worked into the routine at the McGregor ranch. With all liquid fuels now considered precious, a lot of their formerly mechanized tasks were laboriously performed by hand. So Ray and Phil's extra manpower were greatly appreciated. With the many chores—including lots of manure and sodden-straw shoveling—there was very little spare time available.

The precious free time that Phil did have in the evenings was spent listening to shortwave broadcasts on his Grundig G6 Aviator radio, trying to catch news reports. He was troubled that there were fewer and fewer stations operating each week, as the global economic collapse slashed the budgets of most stations, or as power grid failures took them down. But there were still many hams operating in the U.S. and Canada—some of whom had photovoltaic power systems—and he greatly enjoyed listening to their chatter. He even heard some radio amateurs in Japan and Siberia talking in English to hams in Alaska. With his training as an intelligence officer, Phil regularly took down detailed notes about what he heard.

Whenever he heard a callsign that began with a V or C, then he knew that it was a Canadian ham. A, K, N, or W prefix callsigns meant they were in the United States. The wealth of information that the hams imparted over the course of several months was amazing to Phil. But like all other raw intelligence, their reports ranged from reliable to wild speculation. Piecing together their reports, he was able to establish the severity of power outages and level of societal breakdown in most of the United States and Canada.

It became clear that the eastern United States had been the hardest hit. With its high population density, there simply were more mouths to feed than there was food, and the chaos was intense. He expected a massive die-off, especially in the frigid Northeast. Canada's large cities—particularly Toronto and Montreal—had enormous riots that had been quelled only with machine-gun fire. Alaska was completely isolated. Because it had long been dependent on air transport, there were thousands of deaths due to starvation and hypothermia. In Alaska's larger cities, there was even some cannibalism.

The McGregors were anxious to hear any news about the conditions of their daughters' locales in Tavares, Florida, and on Samar Island in the Philippines. The only concrete things that Phil heard about Florida and the Southeast were that the eastern power grid had gone down and *stayed* down, and that there was uncontrolled looting all along Florida's southern Atlantic coast from Coral Gables to Delray Beach. There was also continuous looting throughout the Tampa, Orlando, and Jacksonville metropolitan regions. He heard a secondhand report that the City of Ocala had barricaded itself and was fending off large bands of looters from Orlando. He hoped that Tavares, a slightly smaller town in the same region, had taken the same precautions.

Because they still deemed the threat of looter gangs minimal in the ranch's remote region, the McGregors didn't institute twenty-four-hour-a-day security, as they'd heard the families in Kamloops had done. They did take the precaution of doing some target shooting to confirm the point of aim for every rifle and pistol at the ranch—except for the old "flop top" single-shot .577 Snider carbine, for which they had only seven cartridges. Since neither Alan nor Claire had any military experience, Ray and Phil taught them the basics of patrolling, ambushes, and "fire and maneuver" team tactics. They did quite well, considering their age.

24

END IN MIND

By faith Noah, being warned of God of things not seen as yet, moved with fear, prepared an ark to the saving of his house; by the which he condemned the world, and became heir of the righteousness which is by faith.

—Hebrews 11:7 (KJV)

Olympia State Forest, Kentucky—Late December, the First Year

As the Crunch continued and society devolved, millions of average Americans were forced to go out and "forage" for food. The first targets were restaurants, stores, and food distribution warehouses. As the crisis deepened, not a few "foragers" transitioned to full-scale looting, taking the little that their neighbors had left. Next, they moved on to farms that were in close proximity to the cities. A few looters formed gangs that were highly mobile and well armed, ranging deeper and deeper into farmlands, running their vehicles on surreptitiously siphoned gasoline.

Once the envy of most nations, the United States quickly plummeted to conditions matching those of many Third World countries. Power failures were followed by municipal water supply failures, followed by major disruptions of food distribution, the collapse of law and order, fires, and full-scale looting. The last phase was a massive and desperate "Golden Horde" outmigration from all of the major cities, mostly on foot, as food supplies ran out. The loss of life was tremendous.

By late December, Joshua's little group had patrolled a sizable swath of the forest in their environs, and in that time they did not see very many people, nor did they see any snowplows on the roads, although there were tire tracks. They heard occasional rifle shots in the distance, usually just one or two shots. But on three different nights they heard firefights, with exchanges of gunfire that ranged from dozens to hundreds of shots. Clearly, someone was taking lives in addition to property. The closest firefight sounded like it was two or three miles away, an uncomfortably close distance.

When Megan and Malorie returned to the cave after the patrol out to Clear Creek Road, they reported that they had spotted more deer tracks and even fresh deer scat—but were unable to pack out any venison.

"I'm just glad that you were able to make it back safely," Joshua said. "The boys have been playing quietly most of the afternoon. When I went down to check on them earlier, Leo had fallen asleep."

Malorie slumped down to take the load off her feet and spoke first. "Megan and I did take a SALT report while we were out there. It was rather odd, so I'll let her tell it."

"Well, with a lead-in like that..." Megan smirked at her sister. Jean and Leo, who had decided to collectively sit on their mom's lap, giggled when Malorie returned fire by playfully sticking out her tongue. Megan continued, "We went west as far as Clear Creek Road on our hunt. We stopped to rest and observe on a hill overlooking the road. There were tire tracks, but no vehicles around. The odd thing was that Malorie spotted a man just sitting on the edge of the road by himself." Megan handed the scrap of paper holding the SALT report to Joshua to read over. "She observed him for a few minutes, but he just sat there. It appeared that he had some kind of cardboard sign with something written on it and something flat in his hand resting on his leg as he sat against the tree."

Joshua pondered what he had heard, and said, "It's only a matter of time until the fuel runs out, but I have to think that there will be more people tracking through these parts. We can't be the only ones to find out about the caves."

Megan spoke. "Good point, Joshua. I say that after the last of the snow melts off and at the last phase before a new moon we should leave here and continue west."

Malorie said, "That guy we found today makes me think that we might get discovered before then."

Joshua leaned over and grabbed a stick to draw on the ground, then said, "Take this as Clear Creek Road, and this as the lake over here to our east. We have no idea who or how many other people are out here, but if they didn't roll out of town supplied like we were, then most of them are not going to make it for very long."

Malorie looked down. "I hate that our survival chances depend so much on the demise of others."

"It bothers me, too, Mal, it really does," Joshua said.

As Malorie walked to the observation post, Joshua continued, "So the next patrol/hunt is not for two more days. We sure are burning up a lot of calories without having any meat to show for it. Can you pass the map to me?"

"Sure thing. I have to imagine that the hunting pressure is high on these deer and that they're making themselves scarce."

"So we've been checking out this swath of land here up to Clear Creek Road, right? Well, it looks like there is a pretty big section across that road over here before you get to Highway 211. I'm not much of a hunter, but perhaps I can go with Malorie. It appears to be about six miles one way, putting us there at midday if we set out early. And if we can't make it back in one day, we could set up overlooking Highway 211 and try to get some intelligence for what is going on."

"Right, but your best hunting opportunities are not going to be midday," Megan answered. "Game studies have shown that deer are actually active for feeding based on the rising and setting of the moon. Plus, don't you think that going to a patch of woods near a big road is dangerous? There would just be two of you—not enough of a force to mount an effective defense if you were spotted. "

"All good points, Megan. I guess that I just really want to know what is going on out there in the world! We still have a long way to go to get to Bradfordsville, and there just doesn't seem to be any way to get the info we need." After a few minutes he said, "Okay, tomorrow it's my turn to get water from the lake. I'll see what fish I can catch and perhaps a better idea will come to me." Megan nodded in agreement.

The next day Joshua grabbed his empty rucksack and eight quart-size Ziploc bags that the group had been using to collect water from Cave Run Lake. The most efficient way they had found was to fill up the bags with water and bring the water back to camp to filter through one of the one-quart-capacity Go Berkey travel water purifiers that they had with them. The second filter, along with their other small valuables, was in the cache that they made off site.

Joshua tried to fish but gave up after thirty minutes since staying out by the lake's edge meant more exposure and a higher chance of being discovered. He packed up the water, but as he ducked under a branch, one of the twigs caught the back of his rucksack and sent a shower of snow down on him, with some of it managing to find a path between his neck and collar. The cold, wet snow down his back made him take a knee to stop and shiver. He checked his watch. It was 10:37 A.M. on December 23. Before he could stand up he saw a glimpse of movement in his left periphery toward the lake. There, standing with her back half concealed behind a tree, was a yearling doe broadside. Joshua kept both eyes on the doe and when she twitched her nose and started to stamp and snort, Joshua raised his Remington 870 into position and established a firm position against the tree for support. The water sloshed in his backpack as he made his final adjustments and took the shotgun off safe. At this distance the 000 buckshot would spread out quite a bit, but he was not going to pass up the opportunity to bring meat back.

The doe was about to trot away when Joshua pulled the trigger. The report from the shotgun was loud, but it seemed deafening in the near-complete tranquillity of the state forest. The deer took off running toward the lake down a narrow trail. Joshua instinctively cycled the pump action on the shotgun to prepare to take a follow-up shot if need be. He examined the place where the deer was standing, and he saw some marks on the tree from where some of the shot had hit. Disappointed, he stood up and covered the last five minutes or so back to camp.

When Megan saw Joshua, she ran out to meet him. Everyone was so used to keeping their voices down that neither of them spoke until they were within normal voice distance. "Are you okay? We heard a shot."

Joshua looked down and said, "Yeah, that was me. I saw a skinny doe and took a shot at her, but she took off."

"Did you follow her?"

"No, are you supposed to?"

Megan giggled and said, "Did you see any blood?"

Joshua was still rather embarrassed as he responded, "I was sure that I hit her and even saw some shot marks on the tree she was standing behind. On the hunting shows the animals always seem to drop right there. I just don't get it."

Megan kissed him on the cheek. "Drop your pack and we'll go back and see if we can find blood and track her."

Joshua led Megan back to the place where he had shot the doe. Megan asked where he was when he made the shot, and he pointed across to the spot where he pulled the trigger. Megan drew a line and started to look for blood in the snow on the ground. "Joshua, come look." She pointed with a stick to the blood on the ground. "See the blood here? You definitely hit her."

"Somehow it all looks easier on TV." Joshua's eyes brightened and he said, "But if we have blood and some intermittent tracks through the patches of snow, then we can track her, right?"

Megan stood up, grabbed his hand, and said, "Yipper, right this way, Wingnut."

The snow was very sparse under the dense trees, but working together they were able to follow the doe's tracks, confirmed with small spots of blood. Eventually Megan found the animal in some thick brush near the water. She threw her arms around him and said, "Nice job! That's meat right there. I'll poke her with a long stick to make sure that she's dead, otherwise, you're liable to get kicked."

Megan confirmed that the doe was dead, and she then methodically showed Joshua how to open up the abdominal cavity and eviscerate the deer, saving the heart and the liver. She looked up at him and said, "It's tradition, you know." Joshua winced but was trying to be a good sport. He couldn't tell if she was pulling his leg or not.

Next she found a thick green branch that could be whittled down to a point on both ends to stick through the back leg between the bone and the tendon on the lower hock. Joshua had never done this before, but he was catching on, so he threw the rope over a sturdy branch. Megan lashed the two back legs to the green stick, which would have to do in place of a proper gambrel, then the two of them hoisted the deer up to working height. Megan started to take off the cape, but once Joshua saw how it was done he insisted on getting in there to help. Megan worked to cut off the doe's head while Joshua worked on removing the cape. She smiled and said, "You're lucky the doe is still warm; this is a real chore when the meat is cold!

"Tell you what, let's quarter this doe back at camp. It'll be good for the boys to see how it's done, and we can just tie the legs together and carry her out on a long pole between us," Megan said.

"Cool. Do you know how to do anything with this hide?" Joshua asked.

"Well, without salt it would be hard to preserve it, but if we scraped it really well we could likely roll it up and either use it for something or trade it. Let's put it in the lake with a bunch of rocks on top to keep it submerged in the water. That will soften everything up really well and we can come back for it in a few days. The meat and hair should scrape right off."

Megan and Joshua packed the deer out on a pole back to camp and returned midafternoon to cheers and high fives from Malorie, Jean, and Leo. "Merry Christmas, everyone!" Megan said. Malorie got to work with her knife alongside her sister, as there was still plenty to do with the deer carcass.

"We'll have to find a way to cook some of the meat and dry as much as we can," Joshua said.

"What if we dug another hole outside of camp and filled it with snow so that we could pack some of the meat in the snow—that should keep it from spoiling, with it as cold as it is," Megan suggested. "I remember Papa telling me about them having to do that sometimes when they were out at logging camp without refrigeration." In the end they roasted one front quarter in a pit, made jerky with the chest and flank meat, packed one hind quarter in snow, and hung up the other two quarters. Although they couldn't measure it exactly, they guessed the high temperature was only forty degrees during the day.

That night there was a lot of thanksgiving for their provisions as everyone had their fill of hot food for the first time in a long time. They made sure to stop themselves from overeating to prevent illness.

Joshua was on shift from the early hours of the morning through dawn when Megan came on duty to relieve him. "Good morning, beautiful. Listen, I've been thinking. Now that we have a store of meat, the pressure to conserve our supplies is a lot less immediate. I want to find out what is happening out there in the world. According to the tick marks on the wall, we checked out of the world two months ago, and for all we know, the government might not be the same government anymore."

"Okay," Megan replied.

Joshua waited for what seemed like a long time before saying anything. "I was hoping for more of your input."

"Tell me, are you thinking of the contingencies here? What happens if you get killed?"

"You're right. It sounds a lot more stupid hearing my idea repeated back to me. Our whole mission could fail." Joshua stood up and kissed Megan on the head and went back to the cave.

Megan spent the first part of her shift in silent prayer. Her thoughts raced from the great blessing of getting the venison, to her memories of walking out of the NSA the day before the Crunch, to meeting Joshua for the first time. Would he risk going alone to find answers? Could she bear that unknown? She was lost in thought, and didn't notice Malorie had walked up and sat down next to her.

"You have a friendly approaching." Malorie smirked as she nudged her elder sister.

"Yeah, some vigilant guard I am, huh?" Malorie smiled back and waited for Megan to say what was on her mind. "Joshua wants to ask somebody, anybody about news out there on the outside. He thinks that if he had more facts to parse he'd be able to make a better decision about our situation. I know he isn't arrogant enough to decide something unilaterally for our whole group, but we can't afford to lose him to an ambush or abduction."

"So my super-spook sister is asking me what I think about her fiancé going out for information about the state of our Union. Seems to me that the analyst in you would be chomping at the bit to get facts to parse, cross-examine, and assess."

"We're not talking about doing a Google search here, Mal."

"If Joshua was able to find out anything about the towns to our west, we'd know more about the ground we have yet to cover. Just because it's been quiet here in this little slice of the world doesn't mean that everyone else is sanguine with the world's lone superpower going offline. Heck, if you wanted to go with him, I'd hold down the fort here. You probably know how to ask more probing questions than I do."

Malorie got up and went back to the boys, who were asking her to play tag with them. Joshua returned with a blanket to keep Megan warm in the chilly morning air. She looked up at him and said, "Okay, you and I can go. Malorie can cover my shift. Since we're not stalking for game, we can move quickly and be back by dinner."

Joshua said, "Are you sure?"

"Yes, but I want to do this my way. If/when you see someone, you approach with your shotgun slung and your hands laced behind your head like when you went up to the West Hamlin checkpoint. I'll cover you with the .270. Keep in mind where I am, so that you don't get in the way of my shot if I need to neutralize a threat."

"A Marine and her rifle, it's a beautiful thing."

Megan and Joshua packed up some cooked venison and some dried apple rings, left their plan with Malorie for what to do if they were late in returning, said a prayer together as a group, and headed out around 0830 toward Clear Creek Road. They covered the distance in an hour and a half, setting up on a hill overlooking a long stretch of the road. They scouted any- and everything that they could possibly see through the scope.

Megan took the rifle after Joshua did a preliminary scan and said, "Okay, you're not going to believe this, but that same guy is just sitting there. He is really easy to miss, but look just to the left of that conifer with the twin top for a general bearing, and drop your view down to the roadside. You can just barely see him in the shadow. He is slouched up against a tree with some kind of cardboard sign and something flat on his lap."

"No way, let me see." Joshua took the rifle and saw the outline of a person, then looked at Megan and asked, "I'd say that it's about a klick away from here. Okay, how do you want to do this?"

"You know that we're showing our hand here, right?" Megan paused and Joshua nodded. "That being said, you won't have any cover once you're out in the open. So, if we set up so that I have clear line of sight and you stay to the left edge of the road, then I say that you proceed with caution."

Joshua and Megan took their time getting to the road's edge, always scanning their sector to make sure that they had accounted for all variables. Joshua spread out his poncho for Megan so that she would not get wet from staying for a prolonged time in the supported prone position. Without a rangefinder, it was up to Megan to judge the distance for elevation changes. "So, I can read what it says on his sign. It says, RELIGION?"

"This is getting weirder by the minute."

Joshua kissed Megan and said, "I'll be right back." Joshua stepped out with his shotgun slung behind his back and his hands laced behind his head. The man had been looking in their general direction, but when he saw Joshua emerge unexpectedly from the wood line, he wasn't startled or showing any signs of feeling threatened. He simply waved to Joshua, who proceeded forward with caution.

When Joshua was in shouting distance he said, "We mean you no harm, we're only looking for information."

The man sitting down said, "Come, sit, friend. I'm not armed, and I mean you no harm, either."

"If it's all the same to you, I'll just stand over here."

"That is fine, friend. My name is Aaron Wetherspoon. I'm pleased to meet you. I was praying that I would get to talk to someone today, and here you are."

"Indeed. You can say that we were praying for the same thing." Joshua stood at an awkward distance by the standard of most social mores, but the man didn't seem to mind. "My name is Joshua Kim. What can you tell us about current events? What is the state of the government? Do you know any information about towns to the west of here?"

"So you're looking to head west, you say? When was the last time you got any news? Do you have any idea what is happening in our land?"

"No, Aaron, I don't—we've been in hiding since the Crunch."

"I suspect that you scouted this area pretty well and that part of your 'we' is likely pulling overwatch right now?" Joshua nodded. "Very prudent of you. What if we went somewhere of your choosing to talk that made you less uncomfortable? How about you lead and I'll follow, and we can sit and parlay for a while—much has happened that you need to know about."

"Okay, Aaron. Let me run that past my overwatch—if all is fine I'll wave you over and we can find a place to sit and talk."

"Okay, that sounds fair."

As soon as Joshua was in speaking distance, Megan blurted out, "Did you find anything out?"

"Okay, so the guy's name is Aaron Wetherspoon."

Megan tried to be patient and said, "Okay, cool—you got the guy's name."

"He's really sharp, Megan; he picked up that I was nervous being out in the open, so he offered to go to a place of our choosing—say two hundred meters back in the woods, to talk. I didn't see any weapons and he said that he wasn't armed. Evidently much has been happening while we were off the radar." Megan checked the scope and confirmed that he had not moved. "You pick the place and we'll set up our meeting."

"Okay, wave him over. I'll find a spot well back into the wood line, probably at the base of the hill—look for me there. I haven't seen or heard anyone else out here, so we should be good. Who knows? This might be another divine appointment."

"'Tis the season," Joshua said as Megan sprang up and went to locate the meeting place. Joshua stepped out on the road to wave Aaron over to his location. Aaron was slow to get up, and he appeared to be unsteady on his feet as he crossed the three hundred or so meters to get to where Joshua was signaling.

"As a precaution, we're moving two hundred meters into the woods. Please join us there, Aaron. Again, we mean you no harm. We're simply looking for information."

"Very well, it may take me a while, but I'll get there, friend," Aaron said—he seemed as if he was wheezing as he spoke. Joshua assisted Aaron in making the trip off the pavement through the snowy wood line to the place that Megan had found, a spot covered in dry pine needles. Megan had set up the poncho as the location for their meeting.

"Aaron, this is my fiancée, Megan."

"Pleased . . . to meet you . . . ma'am." Aaron was taking long breaths as he spoke.

Megan was immediately disarmed by Aaron's apparently poor health, and she returned the pleasantries. "Aaron, we'll go first and let you catch your breath."

Joshua held his shotgun across his lap with one hand and held Megan's hand with the other as he spoke. "We're from the D.C. area and have made it this far, by God's grace. We were traveling by vehicle and making better progress, but we're on foot now and have chosen to over-winter here in the state forest on our way to Danville." Aaron nodded politely to show that he was following along, and Joshua continued cautiously, considering OPSEC. "We haven't gotten any news since we crossed the Kentucky state line and went into hiding. Our hope is that the awful chaos that we saw on our way here will have subsided by springtime."

"That's . . . a bit optimistic." Aaron chuckled between gasps for air.

Megan interjected, "Perhaps it is, but God has shown His providence so far. We have escaped danger, kept warm and dry, and up until now undiscovered as far as we can tell. However, we have many questions for you."

"My condition is worsening rapidly, which is why I came out here to die." Joshua and Megan sat up straighter upon hearing Aaron's admission. "I'm originally from Louisville." (He pronounced it "Lou'h-vull.") After taking an audible breath, he continued. "I went to Baylor and later was ordained a Baptist minister, after which I became a chaplain in the navy. One day I was setting my notes on the pulpit to conduct an evening service at Mayport, and I didn't have control over my own speech. Everything in my left peripheral vision and my right eye was blacked out, I lost my balance, and hit my head on the deck. I came to later when one of my parishioners, a corpsman, was standing over me. A few MRIs later and the docs told me that I had an inoperable diffuse grade-three brain tumor—an astrocytoma—and that I had cancer spreading into my lungs as well. My lead doctor advised me to get my affairs in order and only gave me eight or nine months to live. That was six months ago. You probably saw my sign that I was holding just now?"

Joshua and Megan politely nodded.

Aaron continued. "I came out here to die. I still have about nine months' worth of food, fuel, and both antiseizure and pain meds in my camp, which is very well hidden. I have a cousin who is with the Cleveland Federal Reserve Bank. Last Fourth of July, at a family reunion, I told him that I was terminal. He said, 'I have more bad news for you. So is the U.S. economy.' He said that there would be a financial crisis no later than November, and that it would probably take down the stock market, the dollar, and probably the power grids, and that I needed to find myself a bolt-hole. I remembered this park, and

I cashed out my IRA. Now I sit out on the road with that sign to talk with anyone who wants to talk about God. I share with them about Jesus."

"Pardon the interruption, but have you seen other people on these roads?" Megan asked.

"Yes, they're usually moving along on foot. That's how I've managed to stay informed about the state of things, by asking for any news of the wider world as people pass through. I see very few cars, though. I had just enough gas in my truck to make it here, so it's parked until the fuel starts flowing again, or the Second Coming happens, I suppose—but I don't expect to live to see either."

Aaron coughed into a handkerchief that had blood spots on it, and then he continued, "If you haven't been in civilization since the Crunch, then you probably don't know how bad it is out there. No gas, no electricity to speak of, wanton violence—I fear for anyone who is in a city. When the power went out and the trucks couldn't roll anymore, that is when things got really bad!"

"Would you care for some filtered water, Aaron?" Megan could see that he was having trouble swallowing. Aaron's hands shook badly as he took the canteen and poured water into his mouth, without touching the spout with his mouth, out of respect.

"Thank you," he said.

Joshua spoke to give Aaron a chance to catch his breath. "Please, tell us about the political situation out there. Do we still have law and order?"

"No. At least not *just* law, and if you're planning on staying in Kentucky, then know that you are now at ground zero. If you thought that D.C. was where power emanated from, then please allow me to amend your worldview. Last month a man named Maynard Hutchings by hook and by crook seized power at Fort Knox. Invoking the 'golden rule,' he then had his cronies pronounce him president pro tem, and he contacted the UN headquarters in Belgium." Joshua and Megan were shocked and sat there with their mouths open as Aaron continued, "Don't be alarmed if you see an increase in military troops running around here."

Joshua added, "We did see the Kentucky National Guard at the state line—that seemed odd."

Aaron looked equally shocked that they had been so insulated. "I'm not worried about good ol' boys from Kentucky. They're not going to loot and pillage their neighbors at gunpoint. No, for that you have to *import* troops."

"Wait a minute!" Megan was thoroughly agitated at this point, "You mean to tell me that we have foreign troops on U.S. soil?"

"Foreign troops at the behest of the new provisional government here, some of them in American uniforms—wearing the UN patch, of course." Aaron paused for effect. "You are in the middle of a civil war now, post–coup d'état. Fort Knox is the new capitol, and Kentucky is in the process of being 'pacified.' If you want to move west on foot, then I suggest getting smart on guerrilla tactics and covert movement. It's none of my business, but how many of you are there in your group?"

"Not enough to be a sizable assault force," Megan answered vaguely.

"I see," said Aaron.

Joshua knew that Megan was in a completely different mind-set at the moment, but he offered his next question. "Aaron, might I assume that you are still an ordained minister?" Aaron nodded.

Megan looked at Joshua as though he had just spoken Japanese as he continued, "Tomorrow is Christmas. Do you have plans?"

"My schedule seems to be open all day, shipmate," Aaron said.

"Chaplain, would you please marry us right here, tomorrow, say, at noon?" Joshua said as Megan—who was still enraged by the political situation— swung to the other end of the spectrum and tackled Joshua with a hug.

"I would be honored," Aaron said.

"Thank you! We need to get back to our group now, but we'll see you here tomorrow."

"Indeed, friend. Indeed."

Joshua and Megan shook hands with the chaplain, gathered up their poncho, and took a circular route back to their campsite with only a short pause for a tactically appropriate follow-up kiss.

25

PROMISES

It is painfully difficult to decide whether to abandon some of one's core values when they seem to be becoming incompatible with survival. At what point do we as individuals prefer to die than to compromise and live?

—Jared Diamond, *Collapse:
How Societies Choose to Fail or Succeed*

Olympia State Forest, Kentucky—Late December, the First Year

On Christmas Day, with Megan's sons and Malorie as witnesses, Joshua and Megan were married. Joshua made solemn vows to protect and provide for Megan, which under the circumstances had great significance. After the chaplain gave his blessing and invocation, he said: "I'd like to give you a wedding gift, but it comes with a price."

"What's that?"

"My gift will be the food, fuel, and cook gear that I have at my camp. In exchange I'd ask that you bury me. You see, back when I still had the strength, I dug my own grave."

He took a ragged breath, and then continued. "I want you to check on me, once every three days. One of these days, either I won't be in my usual spot, or you will see me dead here. The doctors tell me that the brain tumor will probably get me before the lung cancer, since the latter is growing more slowly.

They said that one day I'll have a grand mal seizure and then I'll go to be with the Lord. It will be that simple. Let me show you my camp."

He led them up a narrow trail into thick brush. The well-beaten trail led 150 yards to a steep, barren rock face, with a rivulet of water coming down a cleft. A rope was hanging down the rock, and they could see muddy scuff marks left by boots, leading up the first few feet of the rock.

Joshua was incredulous. "You climb up that?"

"No, this is where I get my water, and where I've left a false trail. I climbed up and rigged that hundred-foot guide rope back in late July—when I had the strength to do so. These days, I couldn't make it twenty feet up that slope."

He lifted his foot up and left a fresh mud streak on the rock. Then he turned back to his trail and led them down ten yards before turning sharply to the right, through a narrow gap in the brush. They noticed that he stepped carefully from rock to rock, so they did likewise. The tiny and circuitous trail, barely distinguishable, and with brush often scraping their clothes, led eighty feet back to a small clearing that had been hacked out of the brush, on a level spot. There, they saw two olive-green tents—a pup tent to sleep in and a larger one that was stacked full of food and gear containers. Beyond them was the hole that he had dug for his grave, which was five feet deep. He also showed them a small propane cookstove, and he had Joshua lift up a brown plastic tarp to reveal eleven propane tanks of the size typically used for home barbecues.

The chaplain said, "Six of these tanks are still full. I've tried to use the fuel very sparingly. When I jump off this mortal coil, everything here in my camp is for you folks. All you need to do is plant me over there. Let's pray about this."

Eighteen days later, Joshua took his regular check through his scope, just as he had done faithfully every day since getting married, regardless of the weather. This time Reverend Wetherspoon was not sitting in his usual spot.

Joshua very cautiously approached the chaplain's camp. Picking his way first around the meadow and then through the brush quietly took nearly an hour. He wanted to be sure that he wasn't walking into an ambush set by someone who had done harm to Wetherspoon. When the tents came into view, he found what he had expected: The chaplain was in his sleeping bag, clutching a Bible, at permanent peace.

Megan and Joshua buried him that afternoon, and said prayers for everyone that the chaplain had contacted in all of his years of ministry, praying that any of them who had not yet come to Christ would do so. They did not believe in prayers for the dead since they recognized that people could only be saved by faith in Christ, and that this transformation could take place only while someone was still alive. Of course they had assurance of Wetherspoon's own salvation.

They decided to leave the tents in place and to leave half of the food and fuel in situ. This would be their backup camp in case their cave was ever discovered by malefactors.

By harvesting three more deer—which were rapidly becoming less populous and more skittish—and by using the supplies left to them by the chaplain, they were providentially carried through the coldest months of winter. Wetherspoon had stocked up heavily on rice, beans, and oatmeal in five-gallon plastic buckets, as well as cans of stew, soup, chili, and various fruits and vegetables.

In the last week of February, they were down to the last two twenty-pound propane tanks, ten pounds of rice, and the last dozen cans of food. It would be the dark of the moon in three days. The nights were cold and clear, as a high-pressure system seemed to be building. The days were getting noticeably longer, and there was no more risk of snow. It was time to go.

26

REFUGE

All you need for happiness is a good gun, a good horse, and a good wife.

—Daniel Boone

Olympia State Forest, Kentucky—Late February, the Second Year

Joshua and Megan's little party loaded their deer carts even more heavily for the second leg of their journey. They now had the tents and some cooking utensils that had belonged to the chaplain. They would have liked to have brought the propane stove and the remaining cylinder of propane, but they were too heavy and bulky. They left those by the side of the road, in the hope that some wayfarer could use them.

They traveled only at night. With Jean and Leo in tow, they averaged four to six miles per night. It took them eighteen nights to reach Bradfordsville. They wanted to avoid the population centers of Lexington and Richmond, so they threaded their way on a more easterly route past the smaller towns of Mount Sterling, Clay City, Irvine, Winston, Speedwell, Berea, Cartersville, Lancaster, Stanford, and Chilton. The towns that had roadblocks either sent them on roundabout detours or escorted them through town, with stern warnings about coming back for handouts. At the roadblock north of Berea, Joshua resorted to a bribe of five silver dimes, to "pay for an escort." There was not yet any sign of the provisional government that they'd heard Reverend

Wetherspoon mention, but there was some talk of "the Fort Knox officials" at two of the roadblocks.

The roads were devoid of nighttime traffic, and they heard only a few cars and trucks go by, from their daytime bivouacs. They camped in brushy and heavily wooded areas. For security, their camps were exclusively "cold"— with no campfires. This was miserable, but they preferred living with soggy wool to being ambushed by looters who might be attracted to the smoke or the smell of cooking fires. Megan, Malorie, and Joshua slept in shifts each day, so that there would always be a sentry on duty. After a few days, little Leo and Jean became stalwart hikers, with progressively fewer complaints. Megan was very proud of them, and often praised them for their toughness. They arrived at the east end of Bradfordsville just after dawn.

Bradfordsville, Kentucky—March, the Second Year

The roadblock was a lot like the others that they had seen in Kentucky. A large hand-painted sign on a vertical four-by-eight-foot sheet of plywood proclaimed:

ID Check

Local

Traffic

Only!

Three men armed with rifles were standing at a sandbagged position next to a Case bulldozer and two large trailers that had been carefully positioned to slow traffic down to a serpentine crawl.

In front of the roadblock, they could see looping muddy tire tracks in the pavement, evidence that dozens of vehicles had been turned away. As they neared the roadblock, two of the sentries crouched down behind the sandbags, and the other stepped behind the bulldozer. One of them shouted, "Advance slowly and keep your hands where we can see them."

There were now the muzzles of three battle rifles pointed at Joshua's party. As he approached, Joshua mentally checked them off: an M4gery (or perhaps a real M4), an M1A, and a scarce HK Model 770.

Joshua said, "We are here at the invitation of Deputy Sheriff Dustin Hodges. He is an old friend of mine."

The roadblock sentries glanced at one another and one gave a nod, but the man who first hailed them pulled out a public service band radio from a belt pouch and said, "I'll have to check on that. Your name, sir?"

"Joshua Kim."

While they waited, Joshua and Megan sized up the roadblock. It was positioned on Highway 337, which was also known as Gravel Switch Road. The highway paralleled the North Rolling Fork River, which was now brown and churning, from recent rains. The roadblock was positioned to command the highway, the bridge, and the end of Wheeler Road to the north. The river was a natural barrier to the north, and the roadblockers had a clear view up a long straight stretch of the highway ahead of them—a great kill zone. There were also open fields to their right and across the river to their left, so there was little chance of their position being flanked.

Dustin arrived fifteen minutes later on horseback, wearing his sheriff's department SWAT BDUs. He was riding an unusually tall gray Appaloosa mare with a black nylon endurance riding saddle, and a leather scabbard holding a scoped bolt-action rifle.

As the mare's hooves clattered up to the roadblock on the asphalt pavement, Dustin exclaimed, "Hi, Joshua! If anyone was going to make it here, it would be you."

Dustin dismounted and gave Joshua a hug. Dustin said, "Sorry that I didn't bring my pickup, but we're still quite short on gas. One of you must be Megan." Introductions lasted the full twenty-minute walk to Dustin's house, as the horse was led by her reins. Dustin was pleased to hear that Joshua was married, and delighted to meet Megan, Malorie, and the boys. As they pushed the deer carts down the main street, Dustin explained that Bradfordsville was a simple farm town with just three hundred residents. It had been founded in 1777 by the Kentucky Longhunters as they established forts on the Rolling Fork River.

Dustin lived in a small house on an oversize lot at the west end of town. Even before they reached his house, Dustin mentioned that a young widow had just arrived in town and opened up a store selling vegetable seeds. "Her name is Sheila Randall. A very gutsy gal, if you ask me, to open up a store in the middle of all this chaos." From the tone of his voice, Malorie and Megan both immediately recognized that Dustin might have Sheila in mind for marriage.

Dustin's 1940s-vintage house was only eight hundred square feet, so clearly there was not enough room for Joshua's five-member party to "camp in" comfortably for more than a couple of nights, and "camping out" in the yard was precluded because the property's large backyard had recently been converted into a one-third-acre horse corral. The corral was surrounded by three strands of yellow "hot wire" nylon fabric tape. Oddly, this fence was electrified by a Parmak solar fence charger that sat *inside* Dustin's south-facing living room window. (The fence charger, he said, was now precious and almost irreplaceable, so he couldn't risk leaving it outside and having it stolen.) The constant "tick-tick-tick" sound of the charger took some time to get used to. And the presence of the charger and the electric fence required a lot of time to explain to Jean and Leo, with repeated "look, but don't touch" warnings. Naturally, the boys were fascinated by both the fence charger and the horse.

Dustin said that he had bought the horse, tack, fences, posts, and fence charger just as the Crunch was setting in. He explained, "I knew my life savings was about to melt away into oblivion, so I sank it all in the horse. She, along with all of her horsey accessories, cost me thirty-eight thousand dollars in cash, thirty ounces of silver in one-ounce silver rounds, and six hundred rounds of nine-milly. In retrospect, I'd say I got a good deal. And, since part of the deal was in the form of tangibles, I knew that the seller wouldn't get caught holding a bag of cash that would soon buy exactly squat. Oh, and the bonus is that I bought her already bred, so I should have a foal out of her in July."

With no other destination in mind—at least for the foreseeable future—Joshua asked about finding a house to rent. Dustin mentioned that there was a vacant house just two doors down. The elderly man who had lived there had died in January, from a diabetic coma for lack of insulin. The nearby vacant house was just one of three in town where there were no relatives living nearby, and currently there was no way to contact them. The town council had "emergency deputized" a local retired soils scientist to rent out the vacant houses and put the collected rents (denominated in pre-1965 silver coinage) in a special escrow box in the city hall's vault, once a month, under the over-sight of the city treasurer, acting as a "Guardian for the Property and Best Interest of Missing Heirs."

While the courts would surely have great trouble sorting all of this out later, it provided badly needed space for "relatives from the big city" (Joshua and his little group were not the only recent arrivals), and would keep every garden plot in town fully utilized. They soon learned that there were also al-ready plans to rip up many of the lawns in town and turn them into vegetable gardens in the coming weeks. For now, most of the residents of Bradfordsville were living on feed corn, venison, and alfalfa sprouts.

The eighteen-hundred-square-foot house on West Central Avenue was perfect for their needs, since it had a large, well-developed garden plot, three bedrooms, and a working fireplace insert that could burn either wood or coal. The house's oil-fired heater still had two-thirds of a full tank, which would get them through to spring, when they would have to get busy cutting and haul-ing firewood. Utilities were not an issue. The water was gravity-fed city water (currently at no charge), and neither the electricity nor the phone was working. The rent was set at two dollars per month in pre-1965 silver coin.

They moved their scant possessions into the house two days later. They were pleased to see that the owner had loved books, so there was plenty for them to read—except that Jean and Leo would have to plunge into books that were quite advanced for their age. The house was fully furnished, right down to linens and tableware. They all considered the availability of the house an act of divine providence.

Joshua was soon hired as a deputized roadblock guard, for twenty-five cents per day in silver coin. Malorie and Megan split a forty-hour job, doing records writing and filing for the Sheriff's Department's new substation in Bradfordsville's overbuilt storm shelter and community services building. The pay for their shared job was $1.50 per week.

Megan and Malorie met Sheila Randall in her sparsely stocked two-story general store, which had SEED LADY painted on the front windows. Her store seemed to be the only business that had been able to fully adapt to the rapidly changing marketplace. Instead of cobbling together multipliers for prices in the now almost completely destroyed U.S. dollar, she priced all of her

merchandise directly in pre-1965 silver coin. The only mathematical calcula-
tion came into play when someone wanted to pay in one-ounce (or frac-
tional) .999 fine silver trade coins or bars, or in gold.

Sheila had exotic good looks and wavy black hair, which she attributed to
her Creole ancestry. Although she could pass for white, her son was much
darker skinned and much more obviously African-American. Megan asked
Dustin if this would prove difficult for her, as a young widow in a rural
southern small town, but her store had been an immediate success. With the
economy in tatters, people desperately wanted to trade. And her starting
inventory—countless thousands of seeds in small paper packets—was quite
sought after. She had the right business mind-set, in the right place (a secure
small town), at the right time. And she had her son standing by with a shotgun
to back her up.

Megan and Malorie both became good friends of Sheila, in part because
they all spoke French. They spent many hours chatting in French and relished
comparing the peculiar differences between Canadian French and Louisiana
Creole French.

It wasn't long before Dustin was reassigned as a homicide and missing persons investigator. This proved to be a frustrating and largely fruitless job.
With the power grid and Internet down, he had no access to databases such as
NCIC, driver's licenses, and motor vehicle registration. Being thrown back to
nineteenth-century technology made it very difficult for Dustin to make
headway, and he had a mountain of open case files.

27

LA MAIN DE FER DANS UN GANT DE VELOURS

Part of your diversification strategy should be to have a farm or ranch somewhere far off the beaten track but which you can get to reasonably quickly and easily. Think of it as an insurance policy.... Even in America and Europe there could be moments of riot and rebellion when law and order temporarily completely breaks down.

—Barton Biggs, in *Wealth, War and Wisdom*

The McGregor Ranch, near Anahim Lake, British Columbia—the Second Year

The two years that followed the onset of the Crunch were fairly quiet. Everyone at the ranch got into a routine and stuck to it. Although there was some bartering with their neighbors, all other commerce essentially stopped. There was no point in wasting fuel to drive all the way to Bella Coola, because the few stores that were open had run out of merchandise and were reduced to bartering used goods, local produce (mostly from greenhouses), and locally caught fish.

After an initial die-off of 12 percent over the first winter, the population of British Columbia stabilized at 3.8 million. Most of the deaths resulted from chronic health conditions such as diabetes, kidney disease, and COPD. The suicide rate also jumped dramatically, as the threat of starvation loomed large for city dwellers. But actual deaths from starvation were fairly uncommon. Most British Columbians were able to revert to a self-sufficient lifestyle.

Greenhouses all over the country were quickly transitioned from growing flowers and decorative plants to growing vegetables. Windows from abandoned buildings were sought after for use in cold frames and greenhouses, as millions of Canadians sought to start gardening "under glass." Many farmers transitioned from monoculture to vegetable truck farming. Most of this work was labor-intensive, given the shortage of fuel. Refugees from the big cities provided much of the requisite labor, and quasi-feudal systems quickly developed.

The wave of property crimes committed by drug addicts, alcoholics, and the welfare class was manageable by authorities in rural western Canada, as long as the hydro power grid stayed up, so that burglar alarm systems still functioned and radio and phone communications would allow prompt dispatching of police. There was the gnawing fear that fuel and lubricants would run out before transnational commerce was restored. If that happened, then the collapse would become total—just as it had in Quebec and in most of the United States.

The world was a very different place, once the United States collapsed into chaos and its nuclear umbrella was suddenly missing.

The Chinese spent the first few years after the Crunch consolidating their position and gearing up for what would be a sequence of strategic national invasions. After quickly seizing Taiwan, they blockaded Japan, intending to gradually starve it into submission. Meanwhile, they used container ships converted into troop ships to invade Africa, starting with a foothold in Kenya and Tanzania. But first, on the absurd pretext of countering a concocted "terrorist plot," they used fifteen parachute-deployed medium-altitude neutron bombs in South Africa. These small neutron-optimized fusion bombs were dropped decisively: one on the capital city of Pretoria and almost simultaneous strikes on the key troop garrisons and air bases at Bloemfontein, Thaba Tshwane, Johannesburg, Durban, Kimberley, and Port Elizabeth. Then they followed up with successive neutron bomb strikes on Ladysmith, Langebaanweg, Lohatla, Makhado, Oudtshoorn, Overberg, Pietersburg, and Youngsfield. The PLA planners were so ploddingly methodical that these last eight bombs were dropped in alphabetical order, two per day, over the four following days.

Then, after their landings in east Africa, they began a systematic three-year campaign. This was nothing less than wholesale genocide, sweeping west and south across Africa, with conventional airstrikes, drone strikes, artillery, and massed mechanized infantry. It soon became obvious that they wanted to simply wipe out the inhabitants and that they were only there to plunder Africa's mineral wealth. The Chinese had brought with them their own miners, truck drivers, and locomotive crews. The sound of approaching Z-10 and Z-19 attack helicopters became dreaded throughout the African continent. Their fleet of drones was also feared. Their *Yilong* drone was a clone of the U.S. Predator UAV and the *Xianglong* was a clone of the U.S. Global Hawk.

Meanwhile, Indonesia took over Malaysia in an *anschluss*, and then proceeded to invade East Timor, Papua New Guinea, the Philippines, and northern Australia. There were many other wars that ignited globally, as long-held grudges and turf battles erupted, once Uncle Sam was no longer able to intervene.

Bradfordsville, Kentucky—July, the Second Year

While the eastern seaboard was still in the throes of a devastating influenza pandemic that caused huge loss of life, Dustin Hodges was called to the scene of a car fire and apparent homicide on Mannsville Road. Inside a torched 2009 Mercedes E350 sedan with no license plates, they found the charred remains of a man. By his dental work he appeared to be at least forty years old, and possibly as old as sixty. He wore eyeglasses. He could have been shot, but with the body so badly burned, it was hard to tell. (There were no bones with bullet marks, but most of the rib cage had been burned away, so it was hard to determine.) Inside the car, the only useful evidence he could find was an XD-40 pistol magazine near the body.

Outside the car, there were wrappers and other signs that several assorted boxes of food had been repackaged and hauled away. There was also a large footlocker containing more than two thousand driver's licenses and passports. Most of these were for Atlanta, Georgia, residents, although there were seventeen other states represented, as well as a few foreign passports. The majority of the IDs belonged to either college-age or elderly people. The coroner told Dustin that this would be consistent with influenza victims, since the highest number of deaths would be either in old people with weakened immune systems, or in young people who had suffered cytokine storm overreactions to the flu.

Dustin concluded that the driver was most likely a medical professional from Georgia who was driving west for some unknown reason and either ran out of fuel or had engine trouble, and then was waylaid by local bandits. Why he would be carrying such a large collection of IDs was a mystery.

With no communications available, and Atlanta in ashes, this case was baffling. The trunk was eventually dubbed "The Jonestown Footlocker" by the county sheriff, who remembered news accounts of a trunk filled with nine hundred passports, following the Jonestown, Guyana, murder and mass suicide incident in 1978. The trunk was placed in the Bradfordsville evidence room and largely forgotten.

Resistance to the provisional government grew slowly. At first, people were just happy to hear that grid power would be restored to Kentucky and southern Ohio, and that refineries would soon be operating. Then people started hearing stories of widespread corruption, incompetence, wholesale larceny, rapes, and other acts of savagery by out-of-control foreign "guest" troops. There were also dozens of cases of people who went "missing" in the dark of night.

Dustin, Joshua, Megan, and Malorie started to make plans for resistance in the region even before the decrees banning most firearms were issued by the ProvGov. Since Bradfordsville was relatively close to Fort Knox, they realized that they would have to be very cautious. They thought that covert sabotage would be the most effective use of their time, with only moderate risk.

Joshua started out by building a hidden compartment in his rental house to hold all of their guns and ammunition. This wall cache was put in the plumbing wall between the kitchen and bathroom, so that anyone searching with a metal detector would assume that it was plumbing pipes that were causing false returns. Then he helped Dustin build a similar cache in his house.

Realizing that their former positions with the NSA might give them a high profile with the ProvGov's nascent Gestapo, Megan and Joshua asked Dustin if he could somehow help them create fake IDs. Dustin spent several evenings looking through the mysterious Jonestown Footlocker. He ended up finding three Georgia driver's licenses that were good facial matches for Megan, Malorie, and Joshua. Megan would be Stacy Titus, age twenty-five; Malorie would be Carrie Lynn Peters, age twenty-three, and Joshua would be Joseph Kwok, age twenty-four. (Joshua thought this was ideal, since Kwok was a fairly common surname in both Korea and China.)

The ages on the false IDs were all too young, the body weights were all too high, and the eye color for Megan and the hair color for Malorie were both mismatches. But since the twenty-first century was the era of rapidly changing weight and hair color, and tinted contact lenses, those discrepancies could all be explained away.

In the same search, Dustin also found an ID that would be a good match for himself, if he grew a beard. The crucial thing was facial features, and for those, he had found quite good matches. As long as they memorized the details on their fake driver's licenses, they could get past at least cursory ID checks, such as roadblocks.

Because the IDs in the footlocker had never been cataloged, it would not be noticed that the four driver's licenses were missing. Since they were already known in Bradfordsville by their real names, Dustin suggested that they keep their false IDs hidden, just in case of any contingency.

Western Canada—February, the Third Year

Soon after the French arrived in each province, a decree went out that banned most firearms. Western Canada felt the impact of the Ottawa government's edicts much later than the eastern provinces. In their first few guns raids in Vancouver and Fort St. John, the RCMP took six officer casualties and netted just eight guns. So the RCMP suspended any future raids in British Columbia "for fear of officer safety."

The RCMP's failure to enforce the UN's gun ban made the UNPROFOR commanders furious. Despite some threats and posturing, they did nothing. They recognized that they needed the cooperation of the RCMP to successfully occupy western Canada, and that cooperation was marginal, at best. Although they had access to the same gun registration records, UN-PROFOR didn't even attempt to go door-to-door, searching for guns. They preferred to make proclamations and to send out notices. These public notices threatened the citizenry with long prison sentences, deportation, and even the death penalty for noncompliance.

The Canadian government had attempted to create a universal long-gun registry when the Firearms Act became law on December 5, 1995. However, it took until 1998 to develop a system to issue licenses and require buyers to register long guns. As originally enacted, by 2001 all gun owners were required to have a license and, by 2003, to register all of their rifles and shotguns. But there was massive noncompliance and loud complaints, especially in the western provinces.

The registry's database had some huge flaws. The consensus was that the registry was unworkable, that it had no impact on crime, and that it was outrageously expensive. (The administrative costs were estimated at $2.7 billion in 2012.) With the passage of bill C-19 in 2012 the registration scheme was abandoned, and the registry records were destroyed. So even if UNPROFOR was willing to take the casualties, they still would not have known where to find all of the guns in Canada.

The UNPROFOR occupation smothered every aspect of life in Canada. Most public meetings were banned. Any public protests were quickly broken up, and the leaders jailed. Freedom of speech and press were history. Government censors were in every newsroom. Amateur, CB, and marine band radios had to be turned in to the authorities. (After a public outcry, the marine band radio confiscation was almost immediately rescinded, for the safety of saltwater fishermen and crabbers.) While some dutifully turned in their radios, many of those turned in were nonfunctional transceivers with burned-out finals or other electronic problems, or they were earlier-generation spares. Nearly everyone retained their good gear but kept it hidden.

UNPROFOR had underestimated the growing resistance, characterizing the resisters as "bandits," "a few scattered anti-Francophone malcontents." They also misread the mood of the populace in western Canada. The citizens at first appeared happy to see "help from France" with the arrival of fuel tankers by road in Kamloops and by sea in Vancouver. But when infantry troop ships arrived at Vancouver and Prince Rupert, passive resistance began almost immediately. The French tried to use *le gant de velours* ("the velvet glove") approach at first, to cast themselves as the Nice Guys. But the passive resistance grew and soon morphed from vehicle sabotage to sniping.

UNPROFOR was slow to react, but when it eventually did, it came down with a fist of iron. Many of the French counterinsurgency tactics dated back to their experience in Algeria in the 1950s. As resistance grew, the French tactics became more brutal, with torture of prisoners becoming commonplace. Once the serious shooting started, the velvet glove was removed from the iron fist.

The French army had been freshly emboldened by massacring illegal aliens protesting in France, with impunity. Their Foreign Legion troops were used primarily to police Quebec, while the French-born soldiers were used in the other provinces, where English was the predominant language. These deployments both fit in with the UN's strategy of using unsympathetic troops to quell local uprisings.

28

BRUSSELS CHARADES

Calling it your job don't make it right, boss.

—Paul Newman, *Cool Hand Luke* (1967)

The McGregor Ranch, near Anahim Lake, British Columbia—May, the Third Year

The small meeting at the McGregors' house started with Phil recounting the chatter that he'd heard on the shortwave radio. In addition to Alan, Claire, Ray, and Phil, there was also Stan Leaman, a twenty-three-year-old bachelor from an adjoining ranch. Stan was a descendant of one of the earliest settlers of the region. Most of Stan's siblings had moved to Canada's oil sands region, following opportunities with the petroleum boom. So Stan had to hire laborers to help him operate his raw-milk dairy farm.

Stan rode up to the McGregor ranch house on his big gelding one afternoon and said to Alan, "If you're planning something to fight back against these UN clowns, then count me in."

The five of them formed an independent resistance cell that would later be known as Team Robinson. They chose the name in memory of the FOB in Afghanistan where Ray and Phil had first met each other. Their first formal meeting was in May, just after news came to them of some mass arrests in Edmonton. Stan arrived wearing his usual green-and-black-checkered flannel jacket. After Stan had joined them in the living room, Phil adopted a businesslike tone and said, "We obviously need to do something when

UNPROFOR arrives in British Columbia. But even *before* then, we need to train, organize—and of course cross-level equipment and ammunition. We need to cache a lot of gear. Not only will they be searching houses, but they're also going to lock down the towns *tight*, with checkpoints. So we need to gather intelligence, take stock of what we have available, and pre-position some gear so that we can use it to our best advantage.

"The vast unpopulated expanses in this part of British Columbia will give us a few advantages. It will be a huge area for UNPROFOR to control and patrol. Their forces will necessarily be spread thin. The muskeg regions are 'no go' country for nearly all of their vehicles. With our opponents on foot, we'll be fairly evenly matched, despite their firepower, communications, and night vision gear. And when we *do* engage them, the response time for them to receive any backup will be lengthy. That will give us time to beat feet, so that they'll have great difficulty in tracking us down."

Stan asked, "So what are you proposing?"

"I think that we can manage a few operations inside city limits—mostly very carefully targeted demolition and sabotage. Out in the boonies, we'll probably be doing ambushes on remote stretches of road, and perhaps engaging isolated detachments. In cold country like this, simply burning down their barracks in winter months will be quite effective—both logistically and to push down their morale.

"The UNPROFOR units will likely be moving in from the east via Highway 1, and by rail. Interdiction of these routes would be possible but likely limited to delaying actions by irregular forces; the prairies are awfully wide open. Any force with decent air superiority or armor will prevail conventionally. Once the French arrive to occupy the west, things will get more sporting. Securing the highways and rail lines through the Rockies and the coastal ranges will be much more difficult than pushing across prairie. Our country here is challenging terrain to operate in summer, and winter makes conventional operations extremely difficult.

"There are three main routes that they can come west on: south through Crowsnest Pass, in the center-west of Calgary on Highway 1, and farther northwest of Edmonton on the Yellowhead Highway."

Stan raised his hand and declared, "My family has a Mini-14, a SMLE .303

that was shortened, and a Browning A-Bolt, in .30-06 with a four-to-twelve-power variable scope. None of them have ever been registered. I don't even have a possession and acquisition license."

Ray laughed and said: "No PAL, but you're a pal of mine."

There were some groans in response to Ray's pun, and then he asked, "Ammo?"

Stan glanced upward and then said, "I've got about two hundred rounds for each gun. With the bolt actions, that's probably enough. But for the Ruger, laying down semiautomatic fire, that might only be enough for one lengthy firefight."

Phil nodded and said, "I can help you out with some 5.56 ammo for your Mini-14. I suppose I can spare at least three hundred rounds. But after our first few engagements, I have a feeling that 5.56 ammo won't be a problem, if we do our job right."

Stan chuckled, and said, "Yeah, I suppose that once they stop breathing, they cease to have any need for the ammunition in their pouches."

"Precisely."

Ray raised his hand and asked, "What about OPSEC?"

Phil cocked his head and shot back, "Ours, or theirs?"

"Ours."

Alan chimed in and said, "I've heard Ray talk about military operational security a few times over the years. It seems to me that our best OPSEC protection is absolutely no talk whatsoever about any of our activities or even of the *existence* of the cell to anyone, even if we *know* they'd be sympathetic. Leaderless resistance is most effective and impenetrable when the cells keep totally anonymous, and all of the members outwardly carry on with very mundane daily lives."

Claire asked, "Could we, or should we, expand our cell?"

Phil answered, "No, not unless the tactical situation on the ground dictates it. For now, I can't foresee fielding anything more than three or four people at a time for small raids, emplacing IEDs, and some sniping harassment. More people will just mean a larger signature, more chances of getting spotted, and more chances of a slipup or betrayal. And any group larger than three or four people in a vehicle or multiple vehicles convoying has 'resistance profile' written all over it. We want to operate in ways that don't attract suspicion."

Alan said firmly, "Agreed."

Claire asked, "How long do you think it'll take the resistance to drive them out of Canada?"

Alan answered, "It all depends on how quickly resistance builds—and a lot of that depends on the public perception of their tyranny. Perhaps as long as three, four, or five years."

"Nah. They're a bunch of cheese-eating surrender monkeys," Stan retorted.

Claire giggled, remembering that phrase from an episode of *The Simpsons*.

Phil turned to the couch, where Ray and Alan were seated and asked, "What about the RCMP?"

Alan replied, "I've been thinking a lot about that. Back in the east, the Gendarmerie Royale du Canada—the GRC—are nearly all quislings. Out here, we're policed by the RCMP's E Division, which covers all of BC except Vancouver. In E Division they're mostly good guys, but they have a reputation as rowdies who play by their own set of rules. The bottom line is that I predict that in a few months we'll be able to divide the RCMP in the western provinces into four categories:

"Category one will be all the RCMP officers who quit in disgust—but probably citing some fictitious ailment or some family crisis. They'll dutifully turn in their weapons, body armor, uniforms, and radios, and go home, feeling content that they 'did the right thing.' That may be a fairly sizable number. Perhaps forty percent of the force, at least in BC, Alberta, and up in the Yukon.

"Category two will be your real hard-core guys who wait for the right moment to either: a, abscond with as many weapons and as much body armor, ammo, and assorted gear as possible, and head for the hills and play Maquisards; or b, turn their weapons on the UNPROFOR while still in uniform, timing it so they can take several of the French bastards with them, before they get gunned down. But I think that this category will be very small—and nearly all of them will be unmarried RCMP officers, maybe one or two percent.

"Then there's category three, who will just go along with the program, by kidding themselves that they still represent a legitimate government, even if it means rounding up fellow Canadian citizens and putting them into forced labor. I'm afraid that might be as much as one-third of the force in the cities, and probably a smaller percentage out in the woods. It's almost always the freedom lovers who ask for the rural assignments.

"Lastly, there is category four. Those are the cops that are secretly *wanting* to resist, but who are blocked mentally from doing so, and always finding excuses that 'it's too soon,' or somehow intend to do subtle sabotage to the system, without getting caught. You know, like the old 'Hitler's Barber' comedy shtick."

"The *what?*" Stan asked.

"An old stand-up comedy routine by Woody Allen, from the 1960s. He played the part of Friedrich Schmeed, barber to Hitler and his general staff. After the war, he justifies his actions, claiming, 'Oh, but don't you see that I was always plotting against Der Führer, in my own small way. Once, toward the end of the war, I did contemplate loosening the Führer's neck-napkin and allowing some tiny hairs to get down his back, but at the last minute my nerve failed me.'"

29

UN ESSAIM

Why do you allow these men who are in power to rob you step by step, openly and in secret, of one domain of your rights after another, until one day nothing, nothing at all will be left but a mechanised state system presided over by criminals and drunks?

—*Die Weisse Rose* (The White Rose), Resistance Leaflet 3, 1942

The McGregor Ranch, near Anahim Lake, British Columbia—June, the Third Year

UNPROFOR swarmed into Canada's western provinces simultaneously from three directions: from British Columbia's western seaports, by road across the U.S. border, and by road from Ontario. Once they had control of the highways, they took over airports, seaports, and railroads. Because the rioting and looting had been less widespread than in the U.S., and the power grids suffered only limited interruption, reestablishing commerce went fairly quickly. The key ingredients were liquid fuels—gasoline, diesel, home heating oil, and propane—all of which had been disrupted by the Crunch.

UNPROFOR's strategy for western Canada could be summed up in the phrase: *Control the Roads.* Checkpoints, manned by mixed UN and RCMP contingents, were set up on all highways.

The parliament met in a marathon emergency session in response to the global financial crisis. By means of some back-channel maneuvering and building a fearmongering coalition, the new Canadian Le Gouvernement du Peuple ("People's Government," or LGP) took power. They promised to "restore law and order to the streets," and to "create order and fairness to the markets." The new prime minister was Pierre Ménard, a strongly pro-UN socialist/collectivist and dyed-in-the-wool statist. Even before trucks began rolling in with foodstuffs, the LGP took advantage of the stable power grid in most of Canada and launched Progressive Voice of Canada (a.k.a *Progressive Voix du Canada* or PVC), operating on the old CBC transmitters and using their old studios. Annoyingly, more than half of the broadcasts were in French. And even more annoying, the broadcasts were pablum propaganda: promising the world, and sprinkled with charming human interest stories about how the benevolent LGP was making everyone's lives beautiful. The truly laughable part of PVC was that it featured a lot of the same newscasters and radio show hosts who had been on CBC before the Crunch. Now they were dutifully parroting the LGP party line.

Alan McGregor said dryly, "Well, before I *suspected* they were a bunch of Bolsheviks, but now they've really come out of the closet, haven't they?"

Not to be outdone, Stan said, "The thing about *listening* to PVC is that it gives me the uncontrollable urge to go *dig up* my own PVC." (Stan still had his banned Mini-14 buried in a watertight length of eight-inch-diameter PVC water pipe, beneath his house.)

The one-dollar bill of the new LGP currency featured a portrait of an obscure 1950s French-Canadian socialist UN delegate with a distinctively round "moon" face. Because the old Canadian one-dollar coins had a picture of a swimming loon, and had been nicknamed the Looney, and then the bimetallic replacement one-dollar coin was nicknamed the Tooney, it was only natural that the new bill would be called the Mooney.

The citizenry was happy to see some commerce restored, but one of the immediate shocks was that their lifetime savings in the old dollars were now worth a pittance. With the exception of small change and the Looney and Tooney coins, the old dollar lost its full legal-tender status. The old paper dollars could be exchanged at banks for the new bills, but at a *one-hundred-to-one* ratio. Meanwhile, all deposits in bank accounts had two zeroes lopped off. In the case of the McGregors, their $81,220.52 balance at RBC became an

$812. 20 balance. The same thing happened to their Registered Retirement Saving Plan (RRSP)—an account similar to a 401(k) in the United States. The net effect was that they'd had 90 percent or more of their lifetime savings inflated away; and everyone implicitly *knew* that inflation was a hidden form of taxation. Somehow it was the government-enmeshed bankers, brokers, and bureaucrats who came out of it with a profit and a smile.

For the average workingman, the new economic order seemed strange. The new "living wage" was set at $1.20 new dollars a day. And while rents and groceries *seemed* less expensive with the shift of two decimal places under the new currency scheme, their real prices were actually higher. The most painful thing for farmers, ranchers, and commuters was that gasoline and diesel were both "fair market" priced at twenty-two cents per gallon. But when 62 percent of those prices was paying an "Economic Recovery Tax" levied by LGP, then everyone naturally asked, "How truly *fair* is this market?" Very few people could afford to pay five Moonies for a tank of gas.

About the only good news for the McGregors was that Alan's coin collection would now buy a lot of groceries, and that their property tax bill dropped two zeroes. But there was already talk of property reassessments. LGP began sticking its nose into many aspects of life by pegging wages and prices. All land transactions—even within families—had to be approved by a fairness monitor, and it was soon rumored that they didn't get out their approval rubber stamps until some cash (*"le pot de vin"*) was slipped to them.

Private transactions in gold and silver were officially banned. By law, any holders of bullion and miners could sell their refined metals to the government only at the "Free Trade and Fairness Balanced" official prices, which were quite detached from reality. Of course black market gold and silver transactions flourished, despite the government's threats of fines and lengthy prison sentences.

The bankers would still accept deposits of the 1962 to 1981 mint date Canadian nickels (which were 99 percent nickel) and both pre-2000 dimes and quarters (which had various compositions of silver and nickel, depending on their vintage) at face value. But nobody was surprised to see that once accepted, hardly any of those older coins were returned to circulation. Somehow, they just "disappeared." Only the later-issue copper and steel tokenlike coins were recirculating. Alan McGregor could see through this smoke-screen, so he held on to all of his pre-2000 coinage. He liked to say, "Gresham's law can never be repealed."

There wasn't much of it going on in the western provinces, but they heard on the shortwave that European investors were snapping up prime farmland in Ontario for a pittance, using their new euros. The new euro had a fixed exchange rate of 4.5 to 1 to the new Canadian dollar. This made a hectare of Canadian farmland worth only about 20 percent of the price of comparable land in Europe.

The LGP was clearly either firmly in league with the UN, or an outright puppet government. From their first few days in power, they requested the "temporary assistance" of UN military police and "technical experts." Not surprisingly, most of these UN troops dispatched to Canada were from France. (There were also smaller contingents from Holland, Chad, and Morocco.) The UN troops were under their own command structure, which was dubbed the United Nations Protection Force (UNPROFOR) Security Assistance Command.

Along with the LGP's much-heralded beneficence also came its new bureaucracy. It seemed as if Bloc Québécois had magically staged a coup. Every school that reopened had a French-speaking principal. These were snooty easterners with ubiquitous red maple leaf pins on their lapels and purses, a symbol that was fully co-opted by the new government and the *Agenda Nouveau*. By decree, all school students in the western provinces had two hours of French instruction daily, in a curriculum with a simplified vocabulary. Their goal was all too transparent: They wanted compliant "worker bees" who understood enough French so that they could understand orders, and a statist mind-set, so that they would accept orders unquestioningly.

Although news of it emerged slowly, there was a none-too-subtle long-term Francophone transition plan. Starting with the following academic year, all kindergartners would have 100 percent French instruction, and that mandate would advance one year, per year, so that after twelve years, all primary and high school students would gradually transition to French-only instruction. The obvious historical analogue to this mandatory language shift was in Alsace-Lorraine, where successive waves of invasion attempted to mandate public school instruction in German. In the case of western Canada, the shift in language would be more gradual.

Phil made a habit of saving recordings of shortwave broadcasts. To do this, he used an Olympus DS-50 compact digital recorder that he'd bought for his use as a DCS agent. But that had mainly sat unused in his glove box because of the SCIF rules on bringing in personal recording devices. Since the impedance of the radio's headphone matched that of the recorders' microphone input, all that he needed to make the recordings was a "male-to-male" ministereo plug cord.

To hook up the recorder to his shortwave, he used a Y headphone splitter and a "male-to-male" stereo miniplug cable. That way he could listen with his headphones and record at the same time.

In a meeting with his nascent resistance cell, Phil reported, "There's a ham radio guy I've heard who is using no callsign, but from his procedure he is obviously a ham. I gather that he is a Canadian, but he is now a refugee somewhere in Montana. He's displayed the cojones to repeatedly broadcast at twelve-point-something megahertz the planned deployments of UNPROFOR—their whole order of battle. If he and his OB documents are legit, then in western BC we'll soon be facing two French units . . ."

He paused to turn to some handwritten notes in his binder, and then read aloud: "'One brigade of *Infanterie de Marine* (IMa) from the *Troisième Régiment d'Infanterie de Marine (Troisième RIMa)* and a helicopter detachment of *Aviation Légère de l'Armée de Terre*, or ALAT.' Literally, that can be translated 'Light Aviation of the Land Army.'"

He closed the binder and continued, "On my laptop, I did some checking using my Wikipedia archive CD and I read that the *Troisième RIMa* has most recently been garrisoned in Vannes, a small city in western France. But the IMa's main responsibility for many decades has been policing brushfire wars in their former colonies, so these aren't just rear-echelon troops. Many of the NCOs in these units have probably seen combat in Afghanistan—with Task

Force Korrigan—and in Mali fighting the Tuaregs. So these guys won't be pushovers. Not on a par with the U.S. Marines, but still Marines. Tough guys. The ALAT troops are more technical, but they can rain down death from the air. They use Gazelle, Puma, and Eurocopter Tiger ground attack helicopters. I'm not sure which model that they plan to base in western Canada, but because of their great mobility and firepower, any of them will be significant threats.

"Supporting UNPROFOR will be some quisling elements of the RCMP. These guys will be loyal to Ménard. So they've got their own Maynard to idolize. How ironically coincidental.

"I should also mention that we'll be in a different situation than the resistance down in the States. They're doing their fighting in the midst of a *grid-down* collapse. But here, the hydro grids are up—although the economy is still a shambles—which will cause some peculiarities. For example, the UN garrison and motor pools will all be lit up with security vapor lights."

Alan interrupted, "We have to be careful about directing any fire on RCMP cars, because these are *local* cops, and we don't want the local populace turning against us. So I think that we should concentrate on sabotaging the RCMP's vehicles and radio towers. If we keep them immobile and incommunicado, then they won't be much of a theat. But if we start picking off Mounties, then we'll turn their relatives into UN loyalists."

The land units of the Canadian army—including reserve units—had all been disarmed and disbanded a year before, when UNPROFOR declared them "unreliable." Nearly all of their vehicles and weapons ended up in the hands of UNPROFOR—although two Princess Patricia's Canadian Light Infantry (PPCLI) and Lord Strathcona's Horse (LdSH) armories suffered "mysterious thefts" of *nearly all* of their small arms in the days just before the announced armory takeovers.

The French UNPROFOR troops were fiends for planting land mines in large quantity, and making intricate maps of where they had been planted, complete with GPS coordinates. But the region was so lightly populated that the majority of the inflicted casualties were on deer, and the main beneficiaries were bald eagles, ravens, and other scavengers.

Their favorite method was to use a land mine–planting machine to bury mines alongside roads. The placement of these mines was so regular (usually with mines spaced exactly four meters apart) and so obvious that the resistance soon learned how to dig them up and defuse them.

The resistance quickly learned—the hard way—to check for stacked mines, where a pressure-release mine was buried beneath a standard mine, to act as an antihandling device.

A resistance cottage industry was quickly established using a sheet metal brake and tin snips to make disarming clips for the mines. Disarming pins were usually just wire from paper clips. Hundreds of the plastic-bodied mines, of four different types (three antipersonnel and one antivehicular), were collected. Many of these were disassembled and their explosive charges and detonators were repurposed into homemade Claymore mines and various types of IEDs.

30

TOP CONDITION

Believe in your cause. The stronger your belief, the stronger your motivation and perseverance will be. You must know it in your heart that it is a worthwhile cause and that you are fighting the good fight. Whether it is the need to contribute or the belief in a greater good, for your buddy, for the team or for your country, find a reason that keeps your fire burning. You will need this fire when the times get tough. It will help you through when you are physically exhausted and mentally broken and you can only see far enough to take the next step.

—MSG Paul R. Howe, U.S. Army Retired, from *Leadership and Training for the Fight: A Few Thoughts on Leadership and Training from a Former Special Operations Soldier*

Whistler, British Columbia—Three Years Before the Crunch

The men had met by chance at the annual Ironman triathlon competition in Whistler, British Columbia. Their meeting had been precipitated by the mere sight of a red-and-white diver's flag sticker on the back of one of their bicycle helmets. Two of the men were from Vancouver, and two were from nearby Coquitlam. All four men were triathletes in their late twenties, and all four were recreational scuba divers. At the tail end of a thirty-minute session of swapping diving stories, they exchanged e-mail addresses and agreed to meet in a few weeks to dive "The Wall" at Ansell Point, near West Vancouver.

When they met for the dive, they learned of even more coincidences in their lives: All four men were conservatives and members of Methodist churches. Eventually, as the French invasion swept through Alberta, they formed a resistance cell that was part of the informal *Nous sommes la résistance* (NLR) umbrella organization.

The NLR got its start with aboriginal and mixed blood (*métis*) people in Quebec, but it soon spread throughout Canada by word of mouth. Since it was a leaderless movement, it was impossible for UNPROFOR and the Canadian puppet government to stop. Aside from some motivational and general guidance documents that were widely distributed nationwide, the NLR leadership exerted no control of local resistance groups and had no communication with them. In effect, NLR was a *philosophical* leadership for the resistance cells, rather than a command structure.

While the NLR's detached relationship and leaderless cells made it extremely difficult for UNPROFOR to penetrate the resistance, their lack of centralized control also became a weakness when resistance units occasionally showed poor judgment in picking individual targets, or failed to exercise fire discipline and caused collateral damage. Such acts tarnished the image of the entire resistance movement. On several occasions the occupational government was caught attempting to pin blame on resistance groups for massacres that they themselves had committed.

There was a huge variety of resistance cell structures and methodologies. This added to their unpredictability, which made locating and eliminating them difficult. The majority of the cells were dedicated to sabotage. Others had traditional infantry squad or even platoon structure, and could handle multiple tasks, including sabotage, demolition, raids, and ambushes. Some of the most successful Canadian resistance cells patterned their field organization on the USMC's Scout Sniper Team organizational concept. The teams ranged from four to six individuals. Unlike the Marines, they typically used *two* scoped bolt-action rifles instead of a machine gun and a sniper rifle. The heavy weapons carried by their two-man security elements varied widely, depending on the weapons that they were able to scavenge on the battlefield. The fifth man was usually a radio operator/rifleman, and the sixth man filled a variety of roles, ranging from RPV controller to demolitions man.

One of the first engagements between the NLR and UNPROFOR dismounted infantry was near Indian Head, Saskatchewan. The shooting started when six NLR fighters armed with scoped deer rifles engaged two squads of French infantry armed with FAMAS bullpups, across an open field. The resistance wisely opened fire at 570 yards. The French returned fire, but their 5.56 rifles lacked sufficient accuracy at that range. Instead of calling for fire support or a gunship, the French patrol leader attempted to outfire and outmaneuver their enemy. The end result was fourteen dead for UNPROFOR, and fourteen captured weapons. The NLR lost only one man in the extended firefight. This incident illustrated the mismatch in small arms. In essence the occupiers had three-hundred-yard-capable rifles, while the resistance had six-hundred-yard (or longer) range rifles.

In recent years, the preferred "budget" elk and caribou rifle in western Canada had been the Remington Model 770, chambered in .300 Winchester Magnum, with a twenty-four-inch barrel. These rifles could be found new, and factory-equipped with a 3–9x40 variable scope for less than $375, or less than $500 in the more weather-resistant stainless steel variant with camouflage stock. The scopes were already bore-sighted at the factory. One of these rifles, along with a few spare four-round detachable magazines was, effectively an "off the shelf" sniper rifle capable of six-hundred-plus-yard shots on man-size targets.

A significant part of the resistance war was a war of words. Individual NLR cells produced and distributed pamphlets on sabotage and resistance warfare. Among the most popular were a digest of the book *Total Resistance* by von Dach, and reprints of the OSS *Simple Sabotage Field Manual*, which had been declassified in 2008.

Through its publications, NLR also sought aid from sympathizers in Canada and the United States. Its most urgent needs were electric blasting caps, detonating cord (also known as det cord or Primacord), and rifle ammunition. Some of its specific requests for ammunition seemed odd or antiquated to residents of the United States, but these cartridges were still used regularly in Canada: .303 British, .300 Savage, .250-3000 Savage, .303 Savage, and .280 Ross.

31

STEEL SHIPS
AND IRON MEN

Military analysts pretty much agree Japan lost the war in the Pacific because they were playing chess while we were playing checkers. Overthinking all but guarantees failure. Engineers will tell you complexity increases as the square of the subsystems involved, or near enough, something survivalists should keep in mind when they attempt to replicate their 'normal' life. And no, being a nice, deserving person with good intentions won't make failure modes go away.

—Ol' Remus, *The Woodpile Report*

Vancouver, British Columbia—July, the Third Year

On July 7, the Kingsway resistance cell received an intelligence report that was marked "SAM Sensitive." These messages had sources and methods (SAMs) that if revealed could do great harm, for example, endangering the life of a confidential informant.

Their informant's report gave them details on the upcoming arrival of two French cargo ships operated by *La Compagnie Maritime Nantaise* (MN). The *MN Toucan* and *MN Colibri* were sister ships, with a gross weight of more than nineteen hundred tons each. These were commercial roll-on-roll-off (RO-RO) vessels, specifically designed for transporting vehicles. The ships had loaded at the HAROPA terminal at Le Havre fifteen weeks earlier and had transited the Panama Canal. They were both laden with a mixed cargo of twenty-five-ton *véhicule blindé de combat d'infanterie* (VBCI) wheeled APCs, fourteen-ton *véhicule de l'avant blindé* (VAVB or armored vanguard vehicle), and an assortment of military cargo trucks and Renault Sherpa 2 utility vehicles—the French equivalent of the U.S. military Humvee. Based on the recent experience of the resistance in Canada's eastern provinces, the VBCI "armored vehicle for infantry combat" was considered a key threat.

The two ships were standing in 170 feet of water in the Burke Channel, just a few miles from the port of Bella Coola. This inlet had been glacially carved during the Ice Age. Much like the fjords of Norway, Bella Coola Bay was surprisingly deep. Only the magnitude of its daily tides and its rough outer waters kept it from becoming a more significant seaport.

The ships were not yet anchored; their automatic station-keeping thrusters slaved to their GPS were holding within a few meters of their plotted location. The docking and unloading were scheduled for just after the regular midcoast BC ferry departed the ferry terminal at 9:45 P.M. The unloading was expected to take two full days.

Originally destined for Vancouver, the two ships had been diverted to Bella Coola when threat analysts from the French Directorate of Military Intelligence (*Direction du Renseignement Militaire* or DRM) decided that Port Metro Vancouver was too vulnerable to a mortar attack by demobilized Canadian Defense Force soldiers. Bella Coola, they reasoned, was a "safe backwater port."

The royal-blue-and-white-painted ships both had the enormous letters "MN" painted in white on their blue sides, so they were hard to miss. The ships were in good mechanical repair but were heavily streaked with rust.

As the town's small fishing fleet (now down to just four boats) motored out for the evening, the captain of one of the boats was careful to position his boat at the south side of the flotilla. Inside his boat, four divers were suited up and checking their gear. They crawled onto the boat's aft working deck, concealed by a stack of crab pots. A quarter mile before the boat came alongside the two French ships, the divers—now wearing dry suits—quickly slipped into the water.

They bobbed at the surface for a few minutes, to adjust the buoyancy of both the rubber bags containing the limpet mines and their own dive vests. At first the bags were too heavy and were dragging them down, but some squirts of air from their regulators into the bags soon brought them to neutral buoyancy. Then their dive vests gave them too much buoyancy, so they had to bleed air to get them back to neutral buoyancy. (This was the same procedure that they had used when adjusting the buoyancy of their camera and gear bags during sport dives.) They hadn't had the time to do a trial run with the limpet mine bags, and spending this much time on the surface now made them wish that they had.

They swam toward the ships at a depth of ten feet, welcoming the warmth from working their muscles in the chilly water. The leader popped his head above the surface for a moment to catch sight of the ships, then ducked back under and motioned with his arm, showing the others the correct bearing to follow. He held that position while the other three men consulted their wrist compasses and spun their outer bezels to set a rough azimuth for their directional arrows.

Swimming underwater to the ships and attaching the limpets was strenuous, but within the capabilities of the divers. Because they were nervous, they were all sucking air from their tanks faster than they would on a recreational dive. They each carried three limpet mines. All twelve mines already had their timers preset.

As they approached the ships, by prearrangement they diverged into two teams. The visibility was thirty feet, which was above average for the Burke Channel. One member of each team had to surface briefly to reestablish their bearings. Pressing on with only their wrist compasses to guide them, both teams had the enormous bulk of their target ships loom into sight after fifteen minutes of hard swimming. They had been told to attach the limpets at least six feet below the waterline. They opted for fifteen feet to reduce the chance that they might be spotted. The mines were magnetically attached directly over welded seams, at twenty-foot intervals. Each attachment made an audible clunking sound, and this worried the divers. Once the last mine was removed from each bag, they drained all of the remaining air and let them sink down into the depths.

Swimming under the keels of the ships, the two teams set their compasses for due north. They checked their compasses and wristwatches regularly. They were still anxious and going through their air supply quickly.

Two of their air tanks ran low when they were still two hundred yards from shore, so two of the divers had to clip into octopus rigs and share air, swimming side by side. Then they *all* ran low and one tank ran out completely. Their only option was to begin porpoising, surfacing once every twenty feet to breathe through their snorkels for the final eighty yards of their swim. They all reached the shore within seconds of each other and checked their watches.

There were still eleven minutes until the fireworks. Transitioning to just their cold-water neoprene booties, they rapidly walked uphill toward their planned rendezvous point, a location that was memorized but intentionally left unmarked on their maps.

Thirty seconds before the scheduled detonation they began to quietly but gleefully count down out loud in unison as they walked. At ten seconds before the detonation, they stopped at a clearing in the trees and looked back toward the bay. They sat down side by side and continued counting down, in their quiet chant. Right on schedule, they saw white gouts of foam jumping up the far sides of both ships. A few seconds later, they heard the dull thud of the simultaneous explosions. They sat, enthralled. They cupped their hands over their eyebrows, watching for signs of distress from the ships. Faintly, they heard some sort of klaxon. After two minutes, both ships had perceptibly begun to list on the sides where the limpets had been attached. And after five minutes, the ships were both listing at least forty degrees. Tony—their leader—said dryly, "They're done. Let's go." They resumed their hike, feeling invigorated. One of their local resistance contacts was waiting for them at the rendezvous point.

The four divers were all given the boots and bundles of clothes that had been handed off the day before. Their air tanks, regulators, masks, fins, weight belts, and other gear were buried in a large hole that their contact had dug earlier in the day. As they were refilling the hole, the four men downed Endurox liquid meal supplements—the same drink that they used after Ironman races. They had been saving their last few of these for a physically challenging day like this. Tony raised his in a toast and said, in a fake heavy French accent, "*Vive la resistance!*" and they all laughed.

They had timed their detonators for 9:45 P.M., just as the ferry was scheduled to depart, so that there would be no doubt that both ships would still be in deep water. The limpets were state of the art, from U.S. Navy UDT war reserve stocks, smuggled into Vancouver nearly a year in advance. The plastic-cased platter-shaped devices weighed seven pounds each and contained four and a half pounds of RDX explosive. (The magnets used for attachment took up most of the rest of their weight.) Their digital timers could be set to detonate up to 999 hours in advance.

When the limpets had first arrived, the logistics cell commander had questioned their potential use before setting them aside for terrestrial sabotage. But quite soon, they realized their intended maritime purpose. The limpet mines were smuggled to Bella Coola on a succession of fishing boat transits.

The team of divers was shuttled up to Bella Coola only forty-eight hours after intelligence of the planned RO-RO ship diversion was received. Their 620-mile drive took just over thirteen hours. The four men and all of their diving gear were crammed into an aging Dodge camper van. Their cover story was that they intended to conduct a series of hydropower dam inspection dives. Otherwise they had no justifiable excuse for the length of their journey or the presence of their dive gear. The only guns that they carried were two revolvers, both hidden behind a panel in the van. Luckily they encountered only one UNPROFOR roadblock, where they were simply waved through.

Their dive was carefully timed to coincide with the outgoing tide on their approach to the ships, twenty minutes of slack tide for their close approach and attaching the mines, and then the incoming tide to hasten their swim to shore.

After the sinking of the two ships, the four-man diving team had to go into hiding and wait two weeks before making their journey home to Vancouver. With dozens of roadblocks set up in the region, they had to make arrangements to get back to Vancouver by sea. This required the cooperation of five fishing boat skippers, who passed them "down the chain" to Campbell River, and finally Vancouver. In the aftermath, a rumor circulated that it was an American SEAL team that had sunk the ships.

After the sinking of the RO-RO ships, the occupation forces viciously clamped down on British Columbia. More checkpoints were established, and raids on suspected resistance safe houses increased. Most of these were the homes of innocent civilians with no connection to the resistance. Brutal acts of reprisal were carried out. Anyone who was a known scuba diver had his home searched, and dozens were arrested, interrogated, and even tortured.

The greatest fear of the resistance was the French helicopters. When paired with passive forward-looking infrared (FLIR) technology, they provided a formidable guerilla-hunting platform.

Whenever helicopters were heard, resistance fighters would quickly head under a tree canopy cover and don homemade equivalents of Raven Aerostar Nemesis suits. The Nemesis overgarments—nicknamed "Turkey Suits"—included a jacket, pants, hood, and face shield, all made with Mylar underneath uneven layers of fabric. The suits mimicked foliage and blocked the transmission of infrared heat signatures. (Emissivity is the value given to materials based on the ratio of heat emitted compared to a blackbody, on a scale from zero to one. A blackbody would have an emissivity of one and a perfect reflector would have a value of zero. Reflectivity is inversely related to emissivity and when added together their total should equal one for an opaque material.) The IR emissivity of Nemesis suits was between .80 and .82, which was close to that of vegetation, whereas human skin had an emissivity of .97, which was just below asphalt at .98.

The fighters who lacked Nemesis suits would cover themselves with heavy-duty olive-green space blankets, supplemented by a top layer of untreated green or brown cotton fabric. (Cotton, as a plant fiber, did a good job of mimicking vegetation.) When constructed, these blankets had all of their edges altered by trimming or by tucking and stitching, so that they did not present any straight lines or ninety-degree corners against the natural background.

Just by themselves, the cotton-covered commercial space blankets—which were silver Mylar on the inside and olive-green plastic on the outside—did a fair job of obscuring IR signatures. Without a distinctive human form, the covered resistance fighters would be invisible for the first twenty minutes. Then, as spots on the space blanket eventually warmed with the transmission of body heat, they would look like indistinct blobs that could not be distinguished from the heat signatures of wild game and range cattle. But if someone wrapped himself tightly in a space blanket, then a FLIR could detect a distinctive human outline in less than an hour. Eventually the NLR fighters learned to position branches to create an air space between their bodies and the blankets, so that the blankets would not be warmed above the ambient air temperature. (FLIRs could distinguish temperature differences as small as one-half of one degree.)

The other trick that they learned was to curl up into the fetal position, so that the distinctive outlines of their arms and legs were not obvious. One two-man sniper team even tried getting on their hands and knees whenever they heard a helicopter, hoping to resemble the heat signatures of bears. The resistance fighters appreciated the fact that there were so many wild game animals and so many cattle in British Columbia, providing a wealth of false targets for the FLIRs.

Bare faces and hands (with high IR emissivity) were a no-no. Gloves and face masks made of untreated cotton in earth-tone colors were de rigueur. (Since camouflage face paint had about the same emissivity as bare skin, it was ineffective in shielding from FLIRs.) The same rule applied for uncovered rifle barrels, plastic buttstocks, and handguards. These were all wrapped in two layers of earthy-tone burlap. Overcoming active IR was much more difficult than overcoming passive IR. Fortunately, few UNPROFOR soldiers used IR pointers or searchlights. Resistance units learned that standard cotton camouflage military uniforms (such as BDUs and Canadian DPMs) did not reflect much IR from an active source, but once they had been washed with modern detergents or starched, they became veritable IR beacons. The detergents with "brighteners" were the worst offenders, since they also gave cloth infrared brightness.

Preoperational IR clothing checks became part of the "inspections and rehearsals" SOP for resistance field units, both day and night. The fighters would first be observed with a starlight scope and given three "right face" commands. This was then repeated with the scope's IR spotlight turned on, and they would be "painted" up and down by the IR spotlight. Any clothing that failed the IR reflectivity test had to be discarded and put in a designated "decoy" duffel bag.

The overly IR-reflective clothes and hats from the decoy bag were later used to create fake resistance encampments, intended to lure UNPROFOR ground units and aircraft. "Scarecrows" constructed of branches wearing the reflective clothes were either proned out or stood up. Plastic milk jugs (with about the same IR emissivity as human skin) took the place of heads, and rubber examination gloves filled with soil stood in for hands. The scarecrows were topped with boonie hats or pile caps that had been washed in brightening detergent. When seen at a distance from a helicopter, the scarecrows were surprisingly effective, prompting the UNPROFOR helicopter crews to waste many thousands of rounds from their machine guns. They even credited one or more "confirmed kills" in some of these incidents. The ALAT was notorious for failing to follow up with ground action after aerial attacks.

The French made most of their *Reconnaissance et Interdiction* (REI) flights using their pair of Gazelles. These flights used a crew of three: pilot, copilot, and door gunner. They also could carry two "dismounts." Typically these would be a FN-MAG machine gunner and a sniper. They preferred to have the Gazelles operate as a pair for maximum effectiveness.

Following the loss of most of their APCs and trucks in the sinking of MN *Toucan* and MN *Colibri,* UNPROFOR systematically requisitioned civilian and corporately owned pickup trucks in British Columbia. Using Ministry of Transportation vehicle licensing abstracts, they searched for heavy-duty Ford and GMC pickups that were less than four years old and that were painted green or brown. Composite teams of RCMP officers and French Marines were sent to the registered addresses, carrying seizure paperwork printed in both French and English, and stacks of newly printed Canadian Provisional Government currency. Curiously, owners with French surnames never had their pickups requisitioned. These forays were more successful than their aborted attempts to disarm registered gun owners.

Owners of the pickups were forced at gunpoint to sign "voluntary" title release agreements and to sign receipts for the cash that they were handed. Once the pickups were driven back to the garrisons, they were spray-painted in flat camouflage patterns, and twelve-inch-tall "UN" stencils were applied to the doors, hoods, and tailgates in light blue paint.

The new war of resistance in Canada had some interesting aspects stemming from the U.S. border. In the early stages of the guerrilla war, American citizens were busy with a war of their own. After the corrupt U.S. ProvGov led by Maynard Hutchings and his cronies at Fort Knox, Kentucky, was overthrown, however, attention to the situation in Canada reached prominence. Inevitably, small arms, ammunition, and explosives began to cross the border, starting as a trickle, but eventually becoming a torrent. The Canadian Border Logistics and Training Volunteers (CBLTV) network sprang up and grew rapidly. The group, whose acronym was half-jokingly spoken as "cable TV," included thousands of U.S. citizens in border states and beyond.

The flow of arms to the resistance in Canada from the CBLTV did not go unnoticed. The Ménard government publicly chastised it as "the fiendish work of the CIA" when in fact nearly all of the materiel was donated and transported by private individuals. LGP soon announced a Land Purchase Plan for all privately held or tribally held land within ten kilometers of the U.S. border. This program was mandatory, and the forced resettlement all took place in a ninety-day span, starting in May. The only exception was incorporated areas, where towns and cities were in close proximity to the border.

This cordon sanitaire, also known as *une zone totalement dépeuplée*—was a ten-kilometer-wide strip that would be 100 percent depopulated. In this border zone UNPROFOR border guards could fire at will at anyone attempting to cross. The free-fire-zone policy was not publicly acknowledged at first, but warning signs were posted along its length, and eventually parts of it were planted with land mines, which killed deer with alarming regularity.

32

PUMAS AND GAZELLES

At the beginning of a 4th Generation civil war, everybody starts with a finite amount of ammunition. The ones who never run out are those who make every round count and thus are able to forage out the ammo pouches of the dead men who didn't. That's why marksmanship training matters.

—Mike Vanderboegh, *Sipsey Street Irregulars* blog

Williams Lake, British Columbia—August, the Third Year

Phil Adams was not surprised to learn that a detachment from the *Cinquième Régiment d'Hélicoptères de Combat* (part of the Fourth Brigade Aéromobile, or Fourth BAM) had established a helibase at the Williams Lake airport. They had brought in two types of helicopters, Pumas and Gazelles, both manufactured by Aérospatiale.

The larger SA 330 Pumas could carry up to sixteen troops, while the SA 342 Gazelles could carry only three. Phil considered these helicopters a key threat to the resistance, one that needed to be eliminated as soon as possible.

Lazy at heart, the UNPROFOR's local command foolishly set up its three roadblocks just five kilometers out of Williams Lake and didn't have any others until just outside Bella Coola to the west, Prince George to the north, and Kamloops to the southeast.

Driving his Ford F-250 pickup with a camper shell, Alan McGregor was able to drop off the three-man team just two miles before the roadblock. He then continued into town to buy supplies, as he did once every two months.

Canada's infrastructure had fared better than that in the United States, in part because the power grid was predominantly powered by hydroelectric power. There was still grid power up in much of Canada. Some stores were still open, but it was a scramble to find anything to buy. Alan and Claire were often disappointed on these trips. It wasn't until they learned to bring butchered sides of beef with them in their pickup that they got fully in tune with the barter networks in Bella Coola and Williams Lake.

The three raiders—Phil, Ray, and Stan—had opted to travel lightly armed, for the sake of speed on their planned exfiltration. Phil carried his M4gery with four extra magazines; Ray had his Inglis Hi-Power pistol with stock/holster and five extra magazines. Stan had a Ruger Mini-14 with four magazines. Stan and Phil also both carried .22 pistols in their packs. All three of their backpacks were bulging with glass cider jugs filled with napalm and padded with quilted poncho liners and their Nemesis suits. Each pack weighed nearly sixty pounds.

Although thermite would have been more compact and more effective, they opted for the expedience of simple Molotov cocktails, using gasoline. The gasoline was thickened with Styrofoam to the consistency of heavy syrup. Since they had used green Styrofoam pellets, the finished product had a light green tint.

Since there hadn't been resistance activity west of Edmonton other than the sinking of the RO-RO ships (an act blamed on "American commandos"), UNPROFOR's helibase at the Williams Lake Airport was lightly guarded and only three kilometers northeast of the town. From a timbered hill to the east, the raiders watched the routine for two days and nights, using binoculars and Phil's PVS-14 night vision monocular. A variety of tents and vehicle shelters housed the pilots, ground crew, and cooks. Their ALAT's light discipline was atrocious, with light blasting out each time a shelter door or a tent flap was opened. Their eight helicopters were parked in rows at eighty-meter intervals. Behind them was the unmistakable squat shape of a brown rubber fuel bladder—almost universally called a blivet. This one had a sixteen-kiloliter capacity. Next to it was a pair of fifty-five-gallon drums, standing upright.

During the first day that they watched, French soldiers used a commandeered bulldozer to methodically scrape the ground over a wide distance on
three sides to create a protective embankment around the fuel storage point.
They were obviously getting ready for a prolonged occupation. Taking his
turn with the binoculars and watching the bulldozer's work, Phil whispered,
"What do you want to bet that the next thing they'll do is bring in something
like Hesco bastions and make revetments for the helicopters?"

Even at 450 yards, Phil recognized the distinctive outline of the FAMAS
"bugle" 5.56mm bullpup carbines being carried by the French troops. By
2015, most of the French army had transitioned to the FÉLIN (Integrated Infantryman Equipment and Communications)—the French infantry combat
system of the 2000s. It combined a modified FAMAS rifle with a variety of
electronics, body armor, and pouches. The suite had an integral SPECTRA
helmet fitted with real-time positioning and information system, and with
starlight light-amplification technology. The power source was two rechargeable Li-ion batteries. The SPECTRA helmet was used by both French and
Canadian military units. In France, it was also known as the CGF Gallet
Combat Helmet.

The chronic supply shortages and breakdown of sophisticated electronics
repair facilities during the Crunch meant that the high-tech portion of the
FÉLIN gear was rendered useless. Without the communications, positioning, and night vision gear, all that they were left with was traditional "dumb"
helmets, body armor, and nonelectronic optical sights and "iron" sights for
their FAMAS carbines.

It soon became clear that there was only one pair of ALAT enlisted sentries posted each night in six-hour shifts, and that they walked the perimeter
in alternating half-hour rounds. Part of their patrols brought the two sentries
together at the far side of the airfield at regular intervals. There, they would
often take breaks to smoke cigarettes.

At just after 1:30 A.M., Phil and Stan waited until they saw the flare of cigarette lighters, which spoiled the sentries' natural night vision. The two sentries, both armed with FAMAS carbines, were sitting side-by-side, sharing
one pair of earbuds from a digital music player. They were singing along to a
French hip-hop song by Tiers Monde. Instinctively, the sentries faced toward
the airport's perimeter fence.

Wearing the masks from their Nemesis suits to conceal their faces from any security cameras, Phil and Stan quietly padded up behind the ALAT sentries and by prearrangement, shot them each ten times with .22 LR Ruger pistols loaded with target-grade standard velocity (subsonic) ammunition. The pistols had been fitted with empty two-liter soda-pop bottles duct-taped onto their muzzles, serving as ersatz suppressors. Each report was not much louder than a hardback book being slapped shut.

They continued just as they had rehearsed: They reloaded and flipped up the safety buttons on the pistols. Then they removed and stowed the pop-bottle silencers. It took a couple of minutes to clumsily pull off the FAMAS magazine pouches and detach the sling buckles from the lifeless bodies of the sentries. Slinging these extra guns and web gear made their heavy loads even heavier, but they weren't going to walk away from useful weapons.

They moved in, advancing on the rows of helicopters. There were three Pumas and five Gazelles. First they opened the fuel cells on each helicopter and opened their doors, which surprisingly were not locked. (They had brought a large hammer and a cold chisel in case they were.) Each of the raiders carried four one-gallon cider jugs.

They opened the caps on the jugs and poured the sticky napalm—about the consistency of honey—around the interior of the helicopters. They made a point of heavily coating the avionics panels—and poured traces to each fuel cell. With the cider jugs removed, there was now enough room for the FAMAS carbines in two of their packs. Their hands were shaking as they got those stowed, along with web gear and the Ruger pistols.

Their last task before igniting the napalm was rupturing the brown rubber fuel bladder so that it, too, would burn. Ray did this with a pocketknife, punching a hole at waist level and then giving it a short slash, sending a torrent of the fuel spurting out to form a rapidly widening puddle on the ground. Meanwhile, Phil walked up to the fifty-five-gallon drums and noted that they were labeled "110LL," which he knew was aviation gasoline. A crewman had left a bung wrench on top of one of the drums, which prompted Phil to whisper, "How convenient." He quickly removed the bungs from both drums, and with some effort, he tipped the drums onto their sides. Doing so made more noise than the pistol shots.

Phil and Stan simultaneously lit pairs of road flares. Ray opted out of this phase of the plan because he had splashed some JP4 on his hand and forearm when he'd slashed the fuel bladder open. Running in sprints with the flares, they quickly set ablaze all eight helicopters and the nearby JP4 fuel bladder.

They then began what would become a memorable escape. The flames lit up the entire airfield, making them feel exposed until they were through the gap they'd cut in the fence and well into the woods. After two minutes, they started to hear secondary explosions of the 20mm cannon ammunition on-board the Pumas cooking off. A minute later, the flames reached the fifty-five-gallon gas drums. They each exploded with a bright flash and a deep bang in rapid succession. The three men felt both exuberant and terrified. They paused to take off their Nemesis masks and stow them in their packs. These masks badly obscured their vision.

They alternately jogged, race-walked, and more deliberately walked until just after dawn. They ran due north for the first hour, then cut east for two hours, and then headed southeast. They found a particularly dense stand of timber on a steep side hill inside the Williams Indian Reservation, the nexus of the Secwepemc tribe. They carefully picked their way up the hill, doing their best to not leave any tracks. There was no level ground, but they found a large fallen tree that was lying transverse to the slope, so they sheltered behind it, keeping them from sliding or rolling as they slept. After their breathing got back to a normal cadence and they'd had some water, they donned their Nemesis suits, which were too hot to wear during heavy exertion, at least during summer months. (One of their nicknames was "Sauna Suits.")

Despite having been awake for nearly twenty-four hours, they had trouble falling asleep. As they lay prone behind the downed tree, Phil commented quietly, "You know, we didn't have to go to all the trouble of mixing up and lugging those jugs of napalm all the way there. If we'd only known that there was not just JP4 but also aviation gas there, all we would've needed to carry with us was some empty five-gallon buckets. A few buckets of gas thrown into each helicopter and it would have had about the same effect."

Ray chuckled and whispered, "We may be amateurs, but at least we're *effective* amateurs. You guys get some sleep. I'll take watch for the first three hours."

They were comforted by the lack of sound of any approaching helicopters. Phil suspected that the nearest functioning UNPROFOR helicopter was in

Kamloops, 290 kilometers away, or perhaps even in Vancouver, which was 540 kilometers. At midday, they faintly heard what they thought was a drone, but they never caught sight of it.

The raiders repeated the pattern of taking turns sleeping during the day and traveling quickly at night. They made a point of following small deer trails, or walking up creek beds, with the hope of throwing off any tracking dogs. The second night they walked eleven exhausting hours, changing directions often, eventually zigzagging to the southwest. They stopped for only a few minutes at a time, several times each night, for sips of water from their canteens. Still feeling edgy, they shouldered their rifles and disengaged their safeties whenever they heard a strange sound. This was often just a deer or a startled grouse.

At dawn they arrived at another hide campsite in deep timber. They were thoroughly exhausted. They took off their sodden boots and wrung out their socks. As usual, this would be a cold camp; they feared even a tiny campfire could be spotted by FLIR sensors. After waking in the afternoon they ate one IMP ration apiece, supplemented by some elk jerky.

Despite their exhaustion, they couldn't resist pulling the captured FAMAS F1 bullpup carbines out of their packs. The FAMAS was a curious design. It had a very long loop-top carry handle that resulted in the gun picking up the nickname "the bugle." FAMAS carbines were quite sturdy and had a good reputation for reliability.

Oddly, the carbines used a proprietary straight-bodied twenty-five-round magazine, while most other nations had adopted curved thirty-round magazines for their 5.56mm weapons. (Phil mentioned that the later FAMAS G2 model took the NATO standard thirty-round M16 magazines, but these guns were the earlier model, and their magazines did not interchange.)

The three of them took the time to practice loading and unloading the guns, the manipulation of their safeties, flipping open and closed their integral bipods, and switching the steel rear sights between their standard and low-light settings. Learning how to field strip the guns would have to wait for another day. Because Phil already owned a capable M4 Carbine it was decided by default that the two captured bullpups should go to Ray and Stan.

At one point they heard a single helicopter far in the distance. It never came within ten miles. A few minutes after the sound of the helicopter had faded away, only the intermittent rustling of a nearby bird could be heard. Ray whispered to the others, "I don't think the Frogs have a clue about our direction of travel, or which drainage we're in."

The others nodded in agreement. Stan said quietly, "The farther away we get, the larger the radius they need to search. Right now they are probably searching about a forty-mile circle. That's a *lot* of territory." After a pause, he added, "They must be pretty peeved."

Ray replied, "That's putting it mildly. They're probably swearing like sailors right now."

Then, sounding like joshing teenagers, the three men spent a few minutes trying to remember French swear words. They suppressed their laughter after reciting each of them. Somehow, the French soldiers in the movie *Monty Python and the Holy Grail* came up, and they started quoting the heavily French-accented taunts from atop the castle wall. Before he drifted off to sleep, Ray quoted, "Your mother was a hamster, and your father smells of elderberries!"

The next night they hiked another eleven hours, making slow progress bushwhacking over steep terrain, passing just north of Junction Sheep Range Provincial Park. Ray's GPS was helpful in choosing paths along contours where they could avoid steep canyons, but the going was still slow since they were avoiding established trails and roads.

Ray summed up their agreed approach to navigating: "If it's a trail that is big enough to be on a map, then that's not for us. That's just an invitation to get ambushed."

They continued through the night, roughly paralleling Highway 20. They had a couple of unnerving surprise encounters with moose crashing through the timber. One moose, uncertain of the direction it should head in the dark, trotted noisily past them, coming within ten feet, its hooves clattering on rocky ground. Phil was surprised how much noise the big animal made in comparison to deer, which were almost silent when they ran.

Just before dawn, after anxiously crossing the deserted highway in rushes, they reached their prearranged rendezvous point on the edge of the Anahim's Flat Indian Reserve. There, an elderly member of the Tsilhqot'in tribe named Thomas—a committed resistance fighter—had prepared lodging for two days and nights at a secluded hunting dugout cabin that was well stocked. These traditional earth-bermed cabins were called quiggly cabins, locally.

Thomas returned on the second day to tell them that the French forces were hopping mad and had been making reprisals in the town of Williams Lake.

The following day, Thomas came to tell them that their transport was ready. Before leaving the cabin, they donned the green masks from their Nemesis suits to conceal their faces. Thomas escorted them to an open-ended hay barn, where they and their gear were loaded into a four-by-four-by-eight-foot wooden crate that was in the center of an eighteen-wheel truck bed. The crate had dozens of one-inch-diameter ventilation holes bored through it, which created odd lighting for the three men once they were closed inside. A tractor then loaded the truck with large square bales. The bales, stacked four high, were strapped down, fully concealing the five exposed sides of the crate. They could just make out the sound of the tribe members, who laughed as they worked.

Two and a half hours later the truck stopped and they heard voices and another tractor starting up, to unload the hay bales. They were at a 140-ton capacity hay barn at the Squinas Indian Reserve Ranch, a few miles from Anahim Lake.

One of the Indians who was rolling up the tie-down straps that had just been removed tapped on the crate and asked, "You fellas still breathin'?"

Ray grunted in reply and swung the door on the crate open. He crawled out, cradling his Inglis Hi-Power and dragging his backpack. Phil and Stan followed him. They had their Nemesis face masks on again. One of the men there asked, "Why the masks? We're on the same side, you know."

Phil answered: "If you don't *know* who we are then you can't slip up, or be tortured into telling anyone, can you? That's just good operational security."

Another one of the men on the hay crew quipped, "Oh yeah. OPSEC. Secret agent stuff."

They thanked the hay crew and asked them to keep quiet about what they had just seen. Ray insisted, "Don't even tell your wives. Loose lips sink ships."

One of the tribe members said with a chortle, "They certainly did sink ships at Bella Coola. Blub, blub, blub."

The last few miles of their return trip to the McGregor ranch were quiet and uneventful. They walked at their now-accustomed intervals—five meters apart when under timber cover and ten to twelve meters apart when crossing open ground. They paused at the north corral and observed the ranch house with binoculars. There was no gap in the interval of clothes on the laundry lines, and the window curtains were all shut. If either of those had not been as they were, that would have signaled that there was trouble.

Details on the reprisals at Williams Lake reached the McGregor ranch via the rumor network: Two civilian employees at the Williams Lake airport had been tortured and then shot. The mayor had been tortured for two days, and then released without any explanation. Ten people of various ages were plucked off the streets of Williams Lake and interrogated for nineteen hours. They were all threatened with death and coerced by threats to their relatives. After it was apparent that none of them knew who was behind the helicopter sabotage, they were released. Most of them were physically unharmed, but all had undergone severe mental stress. One woman suffered permanent nerve damage in her hands because her handcuffs had been overtightened.

All eight helicopters were beyond repair. Only a few tail rotors and other tail section parts from three of the helicopters were useful for cannibalization. When replacement helicopters arrived for the squadron a week later— just *two* Gazelles—they were heavily guarded.

33

COLOR OF LAW

When plunder becomes a way of life for a group of men in a society, over the course of time they create for themselves a legal system that authorizes it and a moral code that glorifies it.

—Frédéric Bastiat

The McGregor Ranch, near Anahim Lake, British Columbia—August, the Third Year

On a Tuesday morning, three weeks after the helicopter sabotage raid, the McGregors were surprised to hear their Dakota Alert driveway alarm go off. A quick scan with binoculars showed Alan that there were at least four vehicles rapidly approaching. The one in the lead was a white RCMP Ford crew cab pickup with the usual red, yellow, white, and blue trim stripes.

"We have multiple vehicles due in *one* minute. Decision time!" Alan announced.

Ray said, "If we were suspects for the Williams Lake thing, then they wouldn't bother with the RCMP."

After just a moment, Ray made a snap decision. "Stealth mode!" he shouted.

Following their well-rehearsed procedure, Alan's elk rifle and Ray's shotgun were both quickly handed to Phil, and he was ushered into the Ten Boom Room closet. Within a few seconds, he was slapping the wedges into place. Claire straightened Phil's bed covers, and Ray hid Phil's shaving kit.

As Ray and his parents walked into the living room, they heard footsteps on the porch. There was a loud knock on the door. A man shouted, "RCMP. We have a writ. Open the door or we will enter by force."

Alan opened the door.

A portly RCMP sergeant with a holstered S&W 5946 and a clipboard said, "I have writ here, from UNPROFOR, formally requisitioning one Ford F-250 pickup, brown in color."

Alan said nervously, "I see."

"Sorry to put you to this trouble, but you'll be compensated very generously with nine hundred dollars in LGP currency. Do you have two keys for the vehicle?"

Alan handed over the keys, acting as if he was miffed. In reality he was greatly relieved, since he had expected to be killed or arrested.

34

SUSPICION

A caged canary is secure; but it is not free. It is easier for free men to resist terrorism from afar than tyranny from within.

—Pastor Chuck Baldwin

Bradfordsville, Kentucky—Late September, the Second Year

Dustin arrived at 3:00 P.M. on September 28, driving an old brown crew cab Chevy pickup with an extra-tall camper shell that Joshua had never seen before. It had CHEM-DRY CARPET CARE OF BOWLING GREEN painted on both sides, and a Chem-Dry logo painted on the back.

Obviously agitated, Dustin said, "Let's talk inside."

Immediately after the door had been closed, Dustin said, "A little bird told me that some MPs will be arriving in Bradfordsville sometime before noon tomorrow to put the bag on you and haul you to Fort Knox for questioning. Somehow, I don't know how, you ended up on *The List*."

Joshua, Megan, and Malorie were all wide-eyed.

As he handed Joshua an oversize Chevrolet logo key with door-lock remote buttons, he said, "I got a pickup from the county impound yard, which has rather lax paperwork. I picked it up during the lunch hour, and I didn't sign it out. There are no security cameras there. I'd already earmarked this one because it had belonged to some looters who were planted in the Calvary Cemetery, and because there is a signed title in the glove box. Anyway, the tank is nearly full, plus I put ten full Scepter cans of gas in the back end—courtesy of Maynard Hutchings. There is also a skinny unleaded Scepter spout and a lollipop fuel-can lid wrench."

Joshua nodded and sighed. "So no good-bye parties for us. We'll roll out of here before 0200. I'm going to miss you, Dustin."

Dustin gave Joshua a hug and said, "I'm going to miss you, too, bro. Give Ken and Terry my regards."

"Will do. Thank you for all your help."

Dustin bent down to shake hands with Leo and Jean, and said, "You boys are going on a big adventure with your mom, dad, and auntie Mal. Make me proud, and behave yourselves."

Leo said gravely, "We will, sir."

Dustin gave Malorie and Megan hugs, and then said, "Well, I'd better get back to the station before the shift change. I'll be praying for you. Don't blow OPSEC and try to contact me until Maynard Hutchings and his band of fools are in prison, where they belong."

As they backed the pickup up to the garage, Joshua said to Megan, "We need to act fast. Sheila's store closes in less than one hour."

Joshua unloaded all of the gas cans into the garage while Megan and Malorie gathered all of the items that they had accumulated in the past seven months that they wouldn't need or couldn't carry on their upcoming trip. They loaded everything in the pickup, including a push lawn mower, a hibachi barbecue, a shovel, a hoe, a spading fork, a stiff-tined garden rake, a leaf rake, a wheelbarrow, a pressure canner, three cases of canning jars, two bicycles, a wood-splitting maul, some clothes and shoes that Jean had outgrown, two boxes of books, a wooden clothes-drying rack, a washtub, a washboard, and a four-gallon earthenware crock.

Megan and Joshua went to the store while Malorie stayed at home with the boys and continued to pack. She also pulled the guns, ammo, magazines, and false IDs out of the wall cache.

Joshua pulled the pickup up in front of the store at 4:52 P.M. They were relieved to see that Sheila had not yet closed the store. When they walked in, she was behind the counter working on her ledger. There was no one else in the store. Megan knew that Sheila was a resistance sympathizer, so she was direct. She said, "We've been told that we're under suspicion, so we've got to get out of Dodge City tonight."

Sheila nodded.

Megan asked, "Can we trade our heavier possessions for seeds and other compact, lighter-weight trade goods?"

"Yes, but it'll have to be at a discount. You see, by taking trades like that, I'll be violating one of the cardinal rules of barter, which is, 'Don't trade hard for soft.'"

Megan gave Sheila a puzzled look.

"Okay, let me explain," Shelia said. "In barter, if what you're offering in a trade is a compact, durable item that is in short supply, or something that is otherwise highly valued, then a savvy barterer doesn't make the mistake of trading it away for items that are less durable or less desirable. That is trading hard for soft. Otherwise, at the end of the day, your counterpart will be going home with the better goods than you. The only exception to this rule would be if your counterpart is willing to trade a much greater quantity of his items and you know that you have a ready market for them. A corollary to this rule is that 'it's better to trade your bulky for his compact.' Or, as one old gun show dealer I met said, 'Don't never trade away handguns for rifles or shotguns.'"

Megan said, "Okay. Understood. I'm willing to trade at a deep discount."

"Go ahead and bring in what you have to trade."

As Joshua started to unload the back of the pickup, Sheila flipped around the sign on the front door from OPEN to CLOSED.

With three of them working, the pile of tools and other barter items rapidly grew in the middle of the store's sales floor.

Sheila sized it up and said, "Okay, this is better than I had expected. We can negotiate swaps for each item individually, or we can expedite things by just calling all of this a $5.25 silver coin purchase credit."

Megan said, "I vote for expediting things." Joshua nodded in agreement. Megan stepped forward to shake Sheila's hand, and said firmly, "Deal."

To use their purchase credit, they settled on eight AA rechargeable Sanyo Eneloop batteries, a 12V DC AA battery charger with a cigarette lighter plug, two cans of dark brown spray paint, a large roll of masking tape, a U.S. road atlas, and a box of fifty .22 LR cartridges. Together, those purchases came to $4.75 in silver coin. They used the rest of their purchase credit on some packets of nonhybrid carrot, squash, lettuce, and celery seeds. These were all varieties that would grow well in northern climates.

Once they were back at the house, they packed everything that they had originally brought with them to Bradfordsville, including the deer carts, in case they might have to abandon the pickup at some point and continue on foot.

As Megan and Joshua filled all of their canteens and laid out items to pack by the door that connected the living room to the garage, Malorie checked out the pickup and took it on a short test drive.

She returned and started looking under the hood. Meanwhile, Joshua used some 409 spray cleaner and rags to carefully wash the portions of the door panels that had the painted advertising text and logos. He then neatly masked off rectangles around them, backed with scrap paper left over from Jean and Leo's homeschooling, to protect from overspray. Two coats of paint, with a twenty-five-minute delay between the first and second coats, made the Chem-Dry logos and the area code 270-prefix phone numbers disappear. The rectangles were a full shade darker than the rest of the truck, but at least the truck now looked much less distinctive. Once the paint was dry, Joshua peeled off the masking tape and scrap paper and put them in a paper bag, along with the empty spray-paint cans. Megan was about to toss this in the trash can, when Joshua snatched it away, and said, "We can't leave clues like that around for the MPs." He stowed the bag next to the gas cans in the bed of the pickup.

As they positioned a sheet of scrap cardboard over the two rows of gas cans, Malorie rattled off a report on her inspection of the pickup. "There's no time to drop the transmission pan, but the color of the transmission fluid on the dipstick looks decent, and it shifts smoothly. The oil was one quart low, and with a hundred and ninety-two thousand miles on the clock, I suspect that it's starting to burn some oil. The oil didn't look dark. The tires are in fair shape and their pressure was fine except the left rear, which I brought up with the hand pump. The engine compression seems decent, and the serpentine belt should be good for several thousand more miles. The body is in fair shape but the rear wheel wells are rusted out. The shocks are iffy, but with the load we'll be carrying, they should suffice. The gas gauge reads seven-eighths full, if that can be trusted. I checked the owner's manual, and that shows this rig has a twenty-eight-gallon tank. Conservatively assuming fifteen miles per gallon on the highway, that gives us a four-hundred-twenty-mile range. Those five-gallon cans will provide another seven hundred fifty miles. *Not bad.* The power steering fluid is a bit on the dark side, but the power-steering pump it-self doesn't sound noisy. No noise from the water pump, either. There is a little slop in the steering wheel, but it'll do. The brakes seem firm, and while I'd pre-fer to pull the hubs to do an inspection, there's not enough time. The battery has full cells, but the terminals look a little snowy. Hoses look good and feel supple, but you never know with a vehicle that's been parked for a long time. In summary, I'd say that whoever owned this pickup must've taken pretty good care of it—at least mechanically. Too bad that it isn't four-wheel drive, but beggars can't be choosers."

Joshua and Malorie took one last look around the house while Megan wrote a note to their landlord. At the last minute, Malorie tossed in the tire pump, alongside the deer carts. They left at 11:30 P.M., just after saying prayers and bedding down Jean and Leo in sleeping bags in the back of the crew cab. Leo asked, "We're going on an adventure, aren't we, Mommy?"

Megan stroked his hair and answered, "Yes, we are. It's time to go to sleep now."

Picking a route that would avoid UNPROFOR checkpoints, they headed west on Highway 733 to Elizabethtown. As he drove, Joshua started simulat-ing interrogations of Megan and Malorie on the details of their Georgia driv-er's licenses, to be sure that they still had the details memorized. They did the same for him. Joshua cut north to Owensboro. From there, they took a suc-cession of small highways through Henderson, Waverly, and Morganfield. Since they had mainly been walking for the past six months, their progress seemed lightning fast. Near 3:30 A.M., they crossed the Ohio River into Indi-ana. They stopped on a side road to refuel. Six hours and another refueling later, they were in Havana, Illinois. There, they found one gas station that was open. Spending almost all of their ProvGov Blue Bucks, they refilled the tank and all of the gas cans.

Leaving Havana, they ran into a UNPROFOR roadblock. There was just a cursory ID check, where they handed the bored MPs their "inherited" Geor-gia driver's licenses. Megan offered a story about how they had been promised work at a food-processing plant in western Illinois. There were lots of people moving long distances within UNPROFOR territory to find work, so this sounded plausible to the sentry. They were greatly relieved that they weren't searched (since their guns were hard to hide), and that their IDs were not

scanned—as UNPROFOR had started to do in Kentucky. (They didn't want
to end up in a database.)

It took all of them a couple of hours to calm down from the tension of the
roadblock stop. Megan later asked Joshua about his impressions of the incident. He said, "My mind was mainly on reminding myself not to take chest
shots, since they were wearing Interceptor Body Armor. My mind got caught
in a loop: 'They're wearing IBA, so aim for the ocular window…'"

At the same time that they were pulling away from that checkpoint, an
MRAP pulled up in front of their former house in Bradfordsville, Kentucky. A
team of German Bundeswehr soldiers armed with G36 rifles and carrying a
battering ram trotted to the door. Finding the door unlocked, they rushed in
to find the house deserted. The officer in charge called in the two *Soldats* who
had been covering the rear of the house. Disgusted with finding their prey
missing, the officer snorted, "*Ekelhaft.*"

They found an envelope on the kitchen table, addressed to the landlord.
Inside was four dollars in pre-1965 half dollars and a handwritten note that
read:

> Dear Mr. Combs,
>   We were called away on short notice to attend to my
> grandmother in South Carolina, who is ill. Enclosed
> you will find our house lease money for October and
> November. If we have not returned by November 30,
> then you can assume that we will not be returning
> and you can rent the house to someone else.
>   Thanks, and God Bless, Megan Kim

Joshua's party continued to switch drivers once every two or three hours as
they zigzagged west and slightly north, on smaller highways. At 1:15 P.M. in
Osceola, Iowa, they made inquiries about how to avoid UNPROFOR checkpoints around Omaha, doing their best to sound casual. They were told to
cross into Nebraska on Highway 138.

There was gas available in Osceola, but the station took only silver in payment. They again completely refueled and also bought two quarts of oil, since the engine was obviously burning some. They crossed into Nebraska at 4:30 P. M., feeling exhausted. Even sleeping in shifts, fatigue was catching up to them. They stopped at the parking lot of the abandoned Tecumseh Country Club to make sandwiches and to get some sleep.

Megan, Malorie, and the boys squeezed into the back of the pickup after pulling out the deer carts and the tent bags so that there'd be room to sleep in the camper shell. The Scepter cans sealed exceptionally well, so there was just a faint aroma of gasoline. Joshua did his best to sleep in the pickup's rear seat, but it was too short for him and had some uncomfortable bumps. He awoke at 3:00 A.M. with a backache. He spent some time stretching his back before waking the others. Using his flashlight, Joshua checked the radiator, the radiator hoses, and the serpentine belt. Then he checked the tires with a pressure gauge. They had everything reloaded and were back on the road within ten minutes.

Eight hours later, with Malorie doing most of the driving across the broad prairie expanses of Nebraska, they arrived in the town of Gering, just south of Scottsbluff, across the river. There was gas available at a station in Gering, but the price there was forty cents in silver per gallon—twice as much as they had paid farther east.

In Gering, they got confirmation that a point twenty miles west of Scottsbluff was still the farthest western outpost of UN troops. Beyond the Wyoming state line, they would be outside UNPROFOR-controlled territory. It would also mean that they probably wouldn't be able to buy gasoline. They were warned of a large UNPROFOR contingent in Scottsbluff and at the state line on Highway 26. However, a state line crossing point on the much smaller Highway 88—only a dozen miles south—was said to be unguarded.

They said some prayers asking for protection before turning west on Highway 88. The crossing was indeed unguarded, and Joshua breathed a sigh of relief. They stopped short of La Grange, Wyoming, to make sandwiches, using the last of their bread and some peanut butter that was made in Oklahoma under the post-Crunch trade name of "Glop." Over lunch, they scrutinized the Rand McNally road atlas and did some mileage calculations.

The more direct route would have taken them through Casper, Billings,

Butte, and Missoula. Taking that route, they might make it all the way to Bovill, Idaho, with the fuel that they had available. But on that route, there were recent reports of heavy looter activity, and gangs controlling several cities and highways.

The alternate route—about 140 miles longer—would take them looping south, though Idaho's "Banana Belt." They would pass through Jackson, Wyoming; Rexburg, Idaho; and then through Pocatello, Twin Falls, Boise, Lewiston, and Moscow, Idaho.

Joshua said, "Okay, from here on, we set the cruise control at just thirty-five miles per hour, for maximum gas mileage. We took a huge risk rushing out of UNPROFOR territory the way that we did. From now on we'll plan on logging just two hundred fifty miles a day. We go slower, and move much more cautiously. We've successfully escaped the clutches of Maynard Hutchings, so we can relax a bit. Proverbs twenty-eight teaches us rightly that only the wicked flee when no one pursues."

35

THE NEW HIGHWAY PATROL

I foresee that man will resign himself each day to new abominations, and soon that only bandits and soldiers will be left.

—Jorge Luis Borges

Dubois, Wyoming—Early November, the Second Year

Their progress driving through Wyoming was good until they reached the town of Dubois. The roadblock there was very cleverly and covertly constructed. It was where Highway 26 passed through the city streets at the south end of Dubois. At the corner of South First Street and East Ramshorn Street, the highway made a sharp turn to the west at a stoplight that had been retrofitted with a stop sign.

As Joshua slowed and neared the stop sign, someone forward and to the left of his truck shouted, "Out of state!"

Horizontal half-inch steel barricade cables were simultaneously raised to a height of thirty inches ahead of them, to the left, right, and behind them, all within seconds. These cables were jerked up and pulled taut by teenagers spinning hand-cranked windlasses. Men swarmed out of buildings on both sides of the street. Joshua pivoted his head left and right to see that nine men had rifles of various vintages pointed at the cab of the truck.

A young man with a scraggly beard approached closer than the others, with a shouldered SKS rifle. He had it pointed at Joshua's head. He shouted, "Shut it down!"

Joshua did as he was ordered.

Four more men appeared, three armed with ARs, and one with a Saiga-12 shotgun. A dozen teenagers, some of them armed, soon followed.

A gray-haired pudgy man holding an AR-10 and wearing a camouflage hunting jacket walked out of a nearby café. He ordered, "Hands on the dashboard and the backs of the seats, all of you! Driver, roll down your window."

Joshua cranked the window down immediately.

They could now hear the man more clearly. "I'm Elder Josiah Wilson, and I'm in charge here. We cannot have hordes of easterners coming into our county."

Joshua shook his head and said in a calm voice, "We're not a 'horde.' As you can see, there are only *five* of us—and two are small children. We are God-fearing and law-abiding folks, and we're just passing through your county on our way to live with a friend of mine up in northern Idaho, up near Moscow."

"You are vagrants with no visible means of support."

"I'm no vagrant. I am a *traveler*, exercising my right of way. Now, if you'll be so kind as to drop that cable to my left."

Wilson said, "You're not going anywhere until after we've exacted our road tax and fine for vagrancy."

The man with the SKS approached and pressed the muzzle of the rifle into Joshua's temple, and ordered, "Flip that key forward, just one click. If you *start* that engine, I'll shoot all of you."

Joshua did as he was ordered. Then he put his right hand back on the dash.

The man glanced down at the gas gauge and shouted over his shoulder, "They've got a quarter tank."

Joshua said, "I don't believe this. I'm not—"

Wilson, looking angry, yelled, "No, no! You *are* going to pay the county a fine and tax consisting of any fuel that you have in cans. You may keep what is in your gas tank. Then you can decide whether you will press on, beyond the confines of Fremont County, or if you want to turn around and head back from whence you came."

After a pause, Wilson ordered: "Search the vehicle."

Six men swarmed the back of the truck. There were gleeful shouts when they dropped the tailgate and saw the ten Scepter fuel cans. In just a few minutes, they had removed all of the cans, the spout, and the lid wrench.

Wilson said consolingly, "We haven't molested any of your other belongings. We're civilized here."

The man with the SKS pulled out a blue slip of paper and placed it on the dashboard between Joshua's hands.

Wilson explained, "That is a pass, good for twenty-four hours. It'll get you through the roadblocks on either side of Jackson Hole and all the way to the Idaho state line. You may proceed, but don't stop anywhere in Fremont County. Once you've left Fremont County, you may not return, or you will be shot on sight. Have I made myself clear?"

"Perfectly."

Wilson said snidely, "Have a nice day. You are free to go."

The cable to the left was dropped, and Joshua started the engine.

After the pickup had cleared the barrier, Joshua asked, "Did you see any badges?"

Megan answered, "No. But what difference would that make in times like this? They've got the ultimate revenue scheme."

Joshua, still livid, asked, "How many of them did you count?"

Megan answered, "There were at least twenty-two of them."

Joshua shook his head and said, "If I was by myself, I'd sneak back there and wax as many of them as I could."

"But you're *not* traveling by yourself," Megan chided. "You can't take on a whole town. We have the boys to look after. We certainly can't do that if we're dead."

When they were ten miles south of Driggs, Idaho, with Megan driving, the engine blew a head gasket and noticeably lost compression. The fuel gauge was pointed near E.

Malorie said dryly, "Do you suppose this is God's second way of telling us that we need to start walking?"

Megan pressed on, wanting to squeeze another few miles out of their gas tank. With the fuel tank exhausted, the engine hesitated and finally died

---

when they were two miles south of Driggs. Megan turned the wheel and coasted to park the pickup on the shoulder of the highway.

They reorganized their load onto the two deer carts. Malorie checked the tire inflation on the carts and found two tires were a few pounds low, so she topped them off with the hand pump. With the extra canned food that they'd brought from the house, this was by far the most that they had ever loaded on the deer carts. The heavy carts, along with backpacks that were quite full, made for slow going. Even Leo and Jean carried small loads in their rucksacks.

The afternoon was cold, and the dark sky threatened snow. They started walking, singing hymns to raise their sprits.

Driggs was an interesting town. For many years it had been considered the poor man's version of Jackson Hole. Like Jackson, it had a wonderful view of the Grand Teton peaks—but as seen from the west side, rather than the east. The town was unpretentious and had only the basic amenities. Not surprisingly, most of the businesses were closed.

One of the few open businesses was a Big R farm and ranch supply store. The cavernous store was unheated and now had a pitifully small inventory. It obviously was in the process of becoming a secondhand goods store.

While Malorie watched the boys and guarded the carts, Megan and Joshua went in and struck up a conversation with a sales clerk, who was dressed in heavily insulated mechanic's coveralls, gloves, and a fluorescent orange pile cap.

Hearing of their plight, the clerk said, "Those bastards in Dubois have been doing that ever since the Crunch. And the deputy sheriff and city council in Jackson are complicit, since they get a percentage of the gasoline. The County Board of Supervisors and the sheriff up in Lander claim that they can't do anything about the organized highway robbery down in Dubois. The sheriff's deputies in Dubois and Jackson have officially been fired, but they're still wearing their uniforms and badges. The police in Jackson haven't done anything about it, either. They're also still on the job, and also on the take. It's a lot like back when the federal government used to hand out free cheese. Nobody speaks up about it when they get a piece of the action."

Megan noted that the clerk pronounced Dubois "Dew-Boyce," rather than the French style, and that made her cringe.

The man continued, "You've got to understand that Fremont County is about the size of Vermont, but it isn't unified. Mormons control some of the towns. Here in Driggs, like in the rest of southern Idaho, the majority of us are Latter-day Saints, but we respect other people's property and the law. I'd say that's true for the majority of Mormons. But just like with any other group, there are a few bad apples. In Dubois they started out just trying to defend their town from outsiders, but they pretty quickly slipped into their gasoline banditry. It is basically no different from what national governments do, on a grander scale, even in normal times. They systematically rob you, but they call it a tax, and they have the police to back them up."

Megan asked, "So folks are law-abiding here?"

"Yes, indeed. You will find that Driggs is a world apart from Dubois. There's a famous retired actress who is the mayor here. She now has the nickname Mayor Furiosa. But that's kind of a joke since she believes in constitutional government."

Joshua asked, "With winter coming on, there's no way that we can make it all the way to northern Idaho on foot. Is there anywhere near here where we could find work?"

"What are your skills?"

"I'm a former Air Force security cop and NSA security officer, my wife is a former Marine and NSA intelligence analyst, and her sister was a millwright and mechanic."

"Do you folks know how to shoot?"

"Yes, quite well."

"Well, there are some big ranches up the valley that might need a mechanic and a security guard or two."

"Where should we ask?"

"Up in Alta. That's about six miles east of here. There are a lot of wealthy ranchers and retirees up that way. But for tonight, I can put you folks up at my house. I wouldn't want you camping out in weather like this."

The small town of Alta was just across the Wyoming state line. Alta was preferred by some of the more wealthy residents of the Teton Valley because Wyoming had no personal income tax. Many of these families had been preparedness-minded before the Crunch, and hence were well stocked.

They learned that there was only one church in Alta: St. Francis of the Tetons Episcopal Church. An Adventist church used the same building on Saturdays. (People from around Alta who were of other religious affiliations attended various churches in Driggs, up until gasoline became unavailable.)

The elevation in Alta was 6,400 feet, making it a slightly colder, snowier climate than Driggs, which was at 6,100 feet. Driggs had a population of 1,675, while Alta had just under 400. Driggs was the county seat of Teton County, Idaho, while Alta, Wyoming, was ostensibly still policed by the Fremont County Sheriff's Department. With the deep rift between Lander, Wyoming (the county seat), and the outlying sheriff's offices in Jackson and Dubois, the residents of Alta considered themselves self-policing. As one resident put it, "We're a libertarian enclave, sort of like Galt's Gulch." If a Fremont County Sheriff's Department vehicle were to drive through Alta, Joshua surmised it would probably be engaged with rifle fire.

There seemed to be very little commerce going on in Alta. There was a sign up in one disused parking lot that read, FARMERS MARKET & SWAP MEET 10:00 A.M. TO DARK ON SATURDAYS. But that wasn't much help since it was Tuesday, so they made inquiries at the Alta Branch Library. The librarian suggested that they look for work at the Sommers ranch, which was less than three miles north of town. The librarian said, "They've lost two of their sons so they're short-handed."

The walk to the Sommers ranch was memorable. The ranch was on Alta North Road. It started to snow as they trudged down the road. They began praying aloud as they walked. There was a burst of sunlight just before they reached the mailbox. They decided that it would be Megan who would approach the ranch house alone, since she was the savviest negotiator. They didn't want to alarm the residents by arriving as a group. While the others waited at the mailbox, Megan walked up the house, which was nine hundred yards away.

A woman named Tracy Sommers answered the knock on the door. Megan and Tracy spoke with each other for ten minutes through the intercom before Tracy opened the door, with a big Colt Anaconda .44 Magnum in her hand. Ron Sommers was behind her, holding an M2 Carbine. Their conversation continued through the open door as it started to snow again.

It was not until after they had made eye contact, and after Megan had spoken the magic words *former Marine*, that she was invited inside. They talked for another twenty minutes before Tracy said, "Your husband, sister, and sons must be freezing their tails off. Go fetch them."

The deer carts were soon dripping dry in the garage, and Joshua's party was warming themselves near the Sommerses' big Hearthstone Equinox wood-stove.

The Sommerses were in their late fifties. They had one adopted grandson who was living at home. His name was Chad, and he was nine years old. (Their estranged daughter, who was a drug addict living in Dallas, Texas, had dropped off the roly-poly grandson with them six years earlier, and they had not heard from her since. Chad formally became their ward just before the Crunch.) Ron Sommers tearfully described how one of his two sons had died of a burst appendix at age twenty-six, six months after the Crunch. His other son had never returned from college at Norwich University, Vermont, where he was in his junior year. With no word from him, he was presumed dead.

As they continued talking, Chad brought out a plastic tote bin and was quietly building Legos with Leo and Jean. Tracy apologized for not having any coffee or sugar, but she did have some tea bags. She brought out mugs to fill with hot water from the teapot that was constantly on the woodstove.

Oddly, there was no formal interview or job offer for Joshua's party. Their three-hour conversation with the Sommerses just gradually shifted toward their new responsibilities at the ranch and what bedrooms they would be sleeping in. They were hired.

The ranch was a 320-acre rectangular half section. They raised registered Black Angus. They had no bull of their own (they had used artificial insemi-nation for breeding before the Crunch), but they now had the use of a loaner Angus bull from the other side of Driggs to cover their twenty-five cows, in exchange for one weaned calf per year—with steer calves and heifers in alter-nating years. Although it would have been better to have their own unrelated bull to ensure that every cow was bred, they lacked a bullpen. Building a bull-pen was on Ron's lengthy to-do list.

Ron was a former Marine Corps 3002 ground supply officer, who after leaving the service worked agricultural credit and later in investment bank-ing. Their move to the ranch in 2011 was the fulfillment of a lifelong dream.

The Sommerses' ranch house sat on a bench that had been cut on a shallow slope. The main barn sat on another terrace slightly above and beyond it, and the open-sided hay barn, beyond that. The elevation of the ranch was 6,420 feet at the west end, and nearly 7,000 feet at the heavily timbered east end. They had sixty acres of cultivated hay ground, and the rest was in pasture and timber.

West of the house was a six-hundred-square-foot hand-built greenhouse that had been constructed over a framework that was originally designed for a small pole barn. Ron called their greenhouse the Monstrosity. Ron had built it just after the Crunch began, using dozens of used windows that had come from condemned buildings—mostly old trailer houses. The roof was covered in corrugated translucent roofing plastic. The west, east, and south walls of the building were covered in an odd assortment of old window units with various-color frames. Very few of the window panes matched and they were pieced together like a quilt work, with four-by-fours and scraps of corrugated translucent roofing plastic in between. Only the north wall of the greenhouse was solid and insulated. The greenhouse was drafty and leaked badly whenever the snow and ice melted, but it had kept them well fed since the Crunch. Tracy kept the greenhouse garden going year-round. A rusty old woodstove in the center of the greenhouse was kept burning continuously from November to April of each year.

The water for the house and barn was gravity fed. The only electricity was provided by a pair of fifty-five-watt PV panels, which charged a bank of eight golf-cart batteries, cabled together series-parallel in a system that Ron had crafted after the Crunch. Because it had no proper charge controller, the system had to be watched closely in the summer months to prevent overcharging the batteries and boiling off their distilled water. This battery bank was used primarily for charging smaller batteries, powering the intercom, and charging Ron's assortment of DeWalt power tools. It also provided power for intermittent use of their CB radio, which was their only link to the outside world.

The Sommers ranch would be Joshua, Megan, Malorie, and the boys' home for the next one and a half years. With the ProvGov stretching its tentacles westward, they started to feel as if they were living the lives of NOC clandestine agents. Their false IDs were flimsy, since they had no other documentation. Once UNPROFOR troops passed through Driggs for the first time,

Megan explained their situation to Ron Sommers, and he was sympathetic. It was decided that henceforth, only Ron or Tracy would make trips into Alta or Driggs.

Their two summers at the ranch were frenetically busy with moving cattle, hay cutting, wood cutting, constructing a henhouse, building a bullpen (with stout cedar posts buried at three-foot intervals), and gardening. Joshua's party more than earned their keep all through the year. Their main security problems at the ranch were four-legged, rather than two-legged. Their war with the mountain lions, bears, coyotes, and wolves was endless. With the help of Joshua, Megan, and Malorie, only two calves were lost to predators, and none were lost to rustlers.

36

HOOFING IT

We have the illusion of freedom only because so few ever try to exercise it. Try it sometime. Try to save your home from the highway crowd, or to work a trade without the approval of the goons, or to open a little business without a permit, or to grow a crop without a quota, or educate your child the way you want to, or to not have a child. We all have the freedom of a balloon floating in a pin factory.

—Karl Hess

Alta, Wyoming—April, the Fourth Year

In early April, Tracy had heard that UNPROFOR Homeland Security investigators were asking questions around Driggs, making lists of "anyone suspicious." According to Rumor Control, this included anyone with a military service record, anyone who refused to accept ProvGov currency for payments, anyone who had made disparaging comments about the ProvGov, and anyone who was not originally local to the area. Though Megan matched all these criteria, the last category concerned her most.

Megan, Joshua, and Malorie decided that it was time to leave the Sommers ranch, and with the snow off, the timing was good. They had been able to help Ron with some of the most intense work for two summers, so they felt that they had contributed enough labor to justify their upkeep.

On the day of their departure, they had their deer carts packed much more efficiently than when they had arrived. Over the past seventeen months, they had systematically acquired an assortment of gear that was better suited to cross-country travel than what they had arrived with. They also had three carts now—one for each adult. All three carts had been spray-painted in flat green and brown blotches. The heavy canvas tents that they'd inherited from the chaplain had been replaced with a pair of forest-green Fjällräven Singi lightweight nylon three-season backpacking tents. These Swedish-made tents were well used but of very good quality. Ostensibly two-man tents, they had just enough room for the five of them to sleep comfortably. The same retired backpacker in Driggs sold them several small waterproof dry bags to protect their gear from the elements.

Joshua's party had also upgraded to better-quality sleeping bags for the boys, lighter-weight cooking gear, and four army surplus green foam sleeping pads that Joshua trimmed to match the interior profile of the tents. Their food was mostly beef jerky and freeze-dried Mountain House backpacking foods that they had bought at great expense with some of their pre-1965 silver coins. Anticipating a diet that was heavy on meat, they laid in a supply of Metamucil powder and an acidophilus-blend probiotic powder to maintain digestive regularity.

The boys had new broken-in boots instead of tennis shoes, and everyone had olive-green or woodland-camouflage ponchos.

After making their good-byes to the Sommerses, they headed out on the morning of April 10. The boys were crying. They were going to miss Chad. Their life at the Sommers ranch had hardened them in some ways but softened them in others. They were physically much stronger, given the exertions of wood felling, bucking, hauling, splitting, and stacking as well as hauling hay. (Nearly everyone in the region had switched back to small bales, since they didn't require the use of tractors.) But they had become accustomed to regular meals and sleeping in warm beds. Roughing it out on the road would be much different and their mental stress level would be much higher.

Their progress through Idaho was slow. They made it to Driggs the first day, but then transitioned to night travel for the sake of stealth. (They were traveling armed, and not only were most of their guns in the ProvGov's banned categories, none of them were registered.) Their intended route through the Banana Belt and up Highway 95 was 685 miles. After reaching the outskirts of Rexburg and averaging only 4.5 miles a night for the first week, Megan "did the math" and realized that their trip would probably take them five months if it was all done on foot.

Their modus operandi was to sleep during the day in brushy or wooded areas, cook their "breakfast" at dusk, and then be on the road by full dark. From Rexburg all the way to Payette, they were in open, arid country. Since the power grid had gone down, much of this erstwhile farming country had reverted to desert and had become largely depopulated. They looked forward to seeing windmills as their associated stock-watering tanks were often their only source of water after being filtered.

They became experts at dodging off the highway whenever they saw approaching headlights. This happened infrequently, since southern Idaho had just recently been occupied by UNPROFOR troops and fuel was still scarce. Whenever they saw headlights, they just assumed that it would be a UN vehicle. During the day, while the others slept, Joshua would often hunt rabbits and birds with a folding slingshot. He even became adept at stunning or killing trout with large pebbles from the slingshot, once he learned how to aim low, to compensate for the refraction of the water. Starting in Rexburg, they were also able to buy food to resupply their party, paying in silver dimes and quarters.

By May 7, they reached the strange town of Arco. The cliffs behind the town were painted with huge, gaudy, two-digit numbers representing high school class years. It was now nearly a ghost town. The most difficult stretch of their trip was the forty-three miles between Arco and Carey, since it took them through the dusty Craters of the Moon National Monument. They averaged seven miles per night, and found water only once, at Lava Lake. They rested, fished, and filtered water there for two days.

On May 14 they passed by Carey, and were able to refill their canteens again at Carey Lake and at the Little Wood River. From there on, water was less of a concern since they passed by water sources nearly every night. Often, however, the water had an alkaline taste even after being filtered. On June 10 they reached the outskirts of Mountain Home, Idaho. Because of an obvious UN troop concentration in both the city and the adjoining Air Force base, they took a circuitous route, via Mountain Home Reservoir. They slept in abandoned houses each day and averaged only two miles of travel each night.

The daytime heat was becoming oppressive and they longed to get into the mountains.

They cut between Nampa and Meridian, Idaho, on small farm roads. Here, the population density was higher, but the people were friendly and generous, even though they had obviously been suffering since the Crunch. Most of the families here were Mormon. Rather than staying on Highway 95, they took Highway 55 north from the town of Eagle. It was here that they heard their first resistance firefights in Idaho. One of these was within a mile of them, and a few stray tracer rounds from UNPROFOR machine guns passed over their heads. Jean and Leo seemed more excited than frightened. The adults, in contrast, felt exposed and outgunned.

They quickly climbed into cooler, more timbered country, which was how they had always imagined Idaho would be. It was 155 miles from Mountain Home to the former ski resort town of McCall. On the way, they passed through the derelict sawmill town of Cascade, which still had mountains of sawn logs.

On July 12, they made it to McCall and camped just one hundred yards from Payette Lake. There, they were surprised to witness a drunken contingent of Belgian troops partying by the lake, teaching themselves how to water ski. They were using a pair of stolen ski boats that they had brought back to life with UN-supplied 94-octane gasoline.

The next ninety miles, which brought them back onto Highway 95, en route to Grangeville, took them through some scenic mountainous ranching country and forest lands. On July 20, Joshua shot a young cow elk with his .270 rifle. They rested for the next four days, gorging themselves on elk steak and making as much jerky as they could carry.

Then they dropped down into arid country alongside the Little Salmon River. Except for the town of Riggins—which was the farthest northern point of UNPROFOR occupation—the population density was very light, and there was no sign of UN troops except for a couple of daytime convoys.

A local, who was a former whitewater rafting guide, warned them to avoid a UN roadblock that was at the north end of Riggins. He advised them of the route they should take, and drew them a tracing of a Forest Service map. They would have to turn off on Big Salmon Road and take a long detour. This squiggly route, which took them through abandoned Salmon Hot Springs and then up the mountainous gravel Salmon-Grangeville Road (on NF-263 and NF-2630), had not been maintained since before the Crunch. Because of landslides and downed timber, the road was just barely passable in spots with their game carts, and would have been impassable for anything else except perhaps dirt bikes. The detour took them two grueling nights and fifteen hundred feet of elevation change, but ironically it deposited them back on Highway 95, less than a mile north of Riggins.

They now could make better speed, but they still traveled only at night, for fear of bandits or being strafed by UNPROFOR helicopters, which had been seen as far north as White Bird.

On August 20 they passed through White Bird and started up a long, steep grade to the Camas Prairie, skirting around the town of Grangeville.

There were several buildings near Grangeville that were blackened ruins. They didn't stay to ask if the buildings had been burned by looters or by a long-ranging UNPROFOR gunship. They just avoided getting close to the town and moved through the area as quickly as possible.

After transiting the Nez Perce Indian Reservation, they dropped down to the city of Lewiston. They ended up taking the dozens of switchbacks on the Old Lewiston Grade to avoid any vehicles on Highway 95. Once at the top of the grade, they entered into the rolling Palouse Hills country. Although mostly cleared and cultivated, the region offered lots of shady forested canyons, where they could lay up each day. Once up on the prairie, there was a maze of small farm roads that they could take toward Bovill.

By September 5 they were in the hamlet of Blaine. Finally, on September 9, they reached Bovill. There, a man with the local CB network contacted Todd Gray's ranch. Ken Layton came to pick them up in Jeff Trasel's pickup truck, towing a box trailer.

There were lots of hugs. The carts and backpacks were quickly loaded on the trailer. Riding with Ken in the cab of the pickup, Joshua and Megan sat with their rifles between their legs. Malorie sat in the bed of the pickup holding on to the boys. She was joyously singing them an old French Canadian sea shanty.

When they approached the lane from the county road that led to Todd

Gray's house, Ken said, "I love you like a brother, but I've got to warn you that things are *crowded* here. So crowded, in fact, that there's already talk of splitting the group and putting half of us down at Kevin Lendel's ranch, which is just a few miles down the road. Until that happens, things will be very cramped.

"Since UNPROFOR is already in southern Idaho and central Montana, we expect them to move in to northern Idaho next year, and things may get dicey. In fact, Todd made the mistake of speaking up and identifying himself publicly, when a UN spokesman came to give a speech at the Moscow-Pullman airport a few months ago. So when the Blue Helmets *do* arrive—and that could be as soon as this autumn—we may be at the top of their hit list. Todd and Mary are thinking that we may have to bug out. Now, don't get me wrong, from a self-sufficiency standpoint, this is a great region to live in. I just don't think that it'll remain safe for you here at Todd's ranch for very long."

Joshua asked, "So what do you recommend, Ken?"

"I'll make some inquiries, but I think that one of the big cattle ranches around St. Maries might be looking for a team like yours. You will, of course, have my strong recommendation, plus the letter of recommendation you're carrying from that rancher you worked for near Driggs."

Joshua sighed, and then said, "We're going to have to pray about this and talk it over. We all have skills, and we want to help fight the ProvGov, but we have the safety of little Leo and Jean to consider."

Ken said, "I'll leave it up to you. Working at a ranch is probably the best option since you have your kids with you. But if you have enough precious metals to support yourself for a while, then maybe you'll want to go and get involved with one of the militias that are forming. They're popping up all over the region. I'm sure that they could use the help of folks with a background in intel gathering and analysis."

They slept in the living room of Todd and Mary's house just one night. They stayed up late, sharing stories of their adventures and testifying of God's providence and protection. They caught up on events in different parts of the United States as they had played out during the Crunch and its aftermath.

The next morning, they awoke early. Joshua, Megan, and Malorie prayed together. Over breakfast, Joshua talked with Ken. Joshua said, "We reached a conclusion. We've decided that God has protected us thus far, so we need to continue to trust in him. So we think that we should get involved with one of the new resistance groups in the region. For the sake of the boys, we need to keep a fairly low profile. We'd like you to make the introductions, but please do so under our assumed names from the very beginning."

Ken nodded, and said, "You got it, brother."

37

BLENDING IN

Thou art my hiding place; thou shalt preserve me from trouble; thou shalt compass me about with songs of deliverance. Selah.

—Psalm 32:7 (KJV)

Moscow, Idaho—September, the Fourth Year

Joshua rented a house on Harden Road, on the northwest side of Moscow, just north of the University of Idaho campus. As a college town, Moscow had been depopulated following the Crunch, and only now was it getting back to its earlier population level. There were plenty of rental houses and apartments available. They also started attending Christ Church, which met nearby on Baker Street.

The Moscow Maquis already had eighteen members. With Ken Layton and Todd Gray vouching for their bona fides, Joshua, Megan, and Malorie were recruited to form a new cell within the organization—one that specialized in intelligence analysis. Their new cell and its location would be known only to the two key leaders of the Maquis, and they would be identified only by their first names during their interactions. For the sake of OPSEC, the Moscow Maquis leaders habitually referred to Joshua's small cell as "the intelligence guys in Spokane."

The local economy was starting to recover and there were even hopes of reopening the university, but the threat of invasion by UNPROFOR loomed on the horizon. To have enough silver to live on, Joshua, Megan, and Malorie

shared a twenty-four-hour-a-day job as "receptionist/concealed-carry security guard" at the front desk of Christ Church. They each took an eight-hour
shift. The job paid $1.20 a day, which was just enough for them to live on.
Though they had to deal with many issues as receptionists (mainly referring
refugees to sources of aid), there were also lots of quiet hours at the desk, time
Joshua devoted to gathering intelligence about ProvGov activities and UN
troop movements. Malorie took the day shift so Megan could homeschool the
boys, Megan took swing shift, and Joshua took the graveyard shift.

Their new living arrangement worked well through the winter. They settled into a steady work routine. Thanks to Malorie's skills as a mechanic, they
even set aside a little more silver.

Moscow, Idaho—October, the Fourth Year

The Moscow-Pullman region was immediately thrown into turmoil when the
UNPROFOR armored column appeared. As usual, UNPROFOR began with
flowery promises, but eventually delivered tyranny.

In response, Joshua's cell went completely underground. They quit their
receptionist jobs and began full-time intel analysis. With the Maquis now
paying their rent and delivering them groceries once a week, Megan and
Joshua decided to set up their own higher-level Tactical Operations Center,
or TOC.

Instead of just setting up another collection or analysis cell attached to an
individual militia, Megan and Joshua decided on the brigade-level TOC concept for several reasons. First was Megan's recent military expertise, both in
uniform and as an NSA contractor. She had spent a lot of time working in a
tactical TOC and knew that she could set one up herself if she ever had to.
There were not many other intelligence analysts in the region with her expertise. Second, the other intelligence cells attached to the Maquis and other militias were usually busy collecting raw intelligence and had few analytical
skills or resources. Third, and most important, since the Moscow Maquis was
currently the largest and most active militia in the area, these other intelligence cells needed someone to provide intelligence synchronization. "The
intel people in Spokane" could battle-track the big picture for the entire

region and then create intelligence reports, situational map templates, and so on, to brief the two Maquis leaders. And they wanted to fulfill the intelligence requirements (IRs) that these militia leaders had for their region as close to real time as possible.

Joshua was chosen as the contact to sell this arrangement to the other militias' intelligence cells (some of which consisted of only one person, a collector). Joshua's intention was to get the other cells to routinely report events and incidents as they occurred. In return, the other cells were encouraged to make their own Requests for Intel (RFIs) to Megan, Joshua, and Malorie. The other cells could also rely on them for "reachback" support, meaning research and analysis of particular weapons systems, vehicles, order of battle (OB), UN deployment schedules, or anything else that the other cells needed to know. This also included providing training to the other cells, in areas such as SALUTE format reporting, military symbology, and battle tracking. For OPSEC, Joshua spoke only with the actual intel people involved in "training the trainer" mode. This way the intel cells could then train the rest of the members within their own militias.

There was already an incredible "unity of effort" within the resistance, an advantage of most insurgencies. Many military schools (the U.S. Army, in particular) teach the concepts of unity of effort, unity of command, and so forth. However, in reality, these concepts tend to go in one ear and out the other, particularly with occupying military forces that are engaged in counterinsurgency warfare.

A majority of the other intelligence cells were actually relieved that a centrally organized intelligence effort was now taking place. This added to the perception that the resistance was getting bigger and better. Just the word circulating of "the Spokane Intelligence Center" was a huge morale boost within the resistance in the region.

The first two weeks of setting up their TOC were rough going. Since they lived in a small rental house in the middle of a suburb, they needed to establish where the TOC was going to be located within the house itself. After briefly considering one of the bedrooms, they decided on the small dining area attached to the kitchen. Things needed to be as compact as possible to fit map boards and several netbook computers for report writing and maintaining an event log, along with a printer.

Next, they had administrative OPSEC issues. They needed to operate under maximum light and noise discipline. All blinds and drapes around the TOC were closed, with blankets taped to the window frames, and reinforced with black, heavy-duty plastic garbage bags duct-taped over the top. For a final yet important touch, they installed a "lightlock" around the back door of their house, which used the same principle as an airlock on a spacecraft or submarine, except for light instead of air.

They had one of the Maquis members test their light discipline one evening, using a captured PVS-14 night vision monocular to look for any light leaks that might be seen by someone with well-adjusted natural night vision, or through another night vision device. The lightlock was not perfect for concealing all trace amounts of light, but being located in town, it did not need to be.

They also had thermal signature considerations. Despite the fact that most houses used woodstoves all through the winter, they did not want to glow like a Christmas tree to any airborne thermal imaging systems at odd hours of the night. Heat was kept to a minimum since the bodies, radios, and computers created their own residual amounts of heat.

For noise discipline, the blankets over the insides of the windows worked well, though they also covered the linoleum floor of the dining area with throw rugs to absorb noise. This had the added benefit of providing heat insulation.

For message traffic, they encouraged the other cells to make a series of written SALUTE reports using USB thumb drives. They were to leave them at a dead drop inside a plastic play "fort" in the backyard of an abandoned house down the street. The dead drop was checked early each morning by Jean and Leo, who regularly rode their bicycles in the neighborhood.

Last but not least was access to the TOC. Since it sat in the middle of the house, they did not entertain guests. No one saying that they were a "militia member" could just enter the house. The only people permitted inside the TOC were the two Moscow Maquis leaders, and then only to receive briefings (or debriefs) by Megan, Joshua, or Malorie.

They encouraged the other cells to include as much detail as possible in their SALUTE reports and not to worry about redundancy within a report, such as mentioning equipment, or weapons, a second time. This made for more accurate reporting, they explained.

They also taught the other cells to "filter" or review and rewrite these reports, if necessary, rather than just sending lots of small, separate SALUTE reports. For instance, an analyst at a cell might receive a bunch of small, separate SALUTE reports coming to them from several different militia members, all seeing the same thing. This filtering would not only make Joshua, Megan, and Malorie's jobs easier, it would provide better OPSEC, in limiting unnecessary message traffic.

Before they could get the TOC up and running, they focused on putting together their own situational templates (SITTEMPS) that would display all current information on events in the region.

A SITTEMP tells anyone looking at it, through military symbology, what is currently taking place on the ground. These were maps, attached to a board behind them, with clear acetate overlays placed on top of the map, with all three parts securely connected to one another using duct tape. Megan would have killed for some decent 1:50,000-scale military grid-reference system maps and a good map board to hang them on. However, all they could come up with were regular road atlases, some USGS maps, and some U.S. Forest Service maps of the national forests in the region. For the map boards, they used simple four-by-eight-foot sheets of half-inch plywood. Because of the limited quality and availability of maps, they maintained several separate SITTEMPS in different map scales.

Young Jean and Leo helped out as couriers, but because of their age, they mainly observed the daily routine at the TOC, read books, and quietly played with their toys. The map board became such a fascination for them that Joshua constructed a two-by-three-foot toy map board for them using Megan's old Virginia Beach Quadrangle map and a sheet of acetate. This kept the boys from being tempted to doodle on the TOC's working map boards.

Before the Crunch, as a prepper, Megan had been aware of an online mapping service called MyTopo.com. She had once looked at the website, but had never used it herself. It was a powerful resource, allowing people to take a "snapshot" of any place on earth, where they could choose whether they wanted a map in longitude/latitude, or in the global UTGM military grid-reference system. Their maps were also offered with lamination, meaning that users could still draw or stick symbology directly on them in the event that no transparent overlay material was available.

The symbology used in a SITTEMP was basically the same as that found in the old Avalon Hill war simulation board games that were sold in toy stores. This was one of the reasons Megan enjoyed the tactical side of intelligence analysis. In her training, that was basically what a map exercise (MAPEX) was: an elaborate war board game. With symbology that represented units, movement, actions, situations, and unit boundaries, a person skilled in reading a SITTEMP could read this information like words on a page. That, after all, had always been Megan's personal standard.

Megan had brought her old military map bag with her that she had carried since her days at the Navy and Marine Corps Intelligence Training Center (NMITC). She wouldn't have been much of an analyst if she hadn't. In it were several military map-reading protractors in 1:50,000 and 1:100,000 scale. There was a variety of fine-point permanent ink pens in various colors, Vis-à-Vis brand temporary markers, and a small felt pen that was filled with alcohol for erasing, a set of military symbol stencils, and a folded 1:50,000-scale military map of the Virginia Beach area that she had been allowed to keep after her Advanced Individual Training (AIT). There was also a DVD that had been prepared for each student, containing PDFs of various Army and Marine Corps manuals, such as *Intelligence Preparation of the Battlefield* (IPB), and *TOC Operations*. Megan also had a stack of transparent, single-sheet document protectors. She had been taught how to use these to make "mini" SITTEMPS, using a single-page photocopy of a map, or anything else that was on one sheet of paper, inserted. By stapling other empty document protectors on top of the one holding the map, one could make a product of multiple overlays, depicting avenues of approach, hydrology (rivers, lakes, and streams), restrictive terrain, and obstacles.

One thing that Megan *was* able to acquire was a spare copy of Army FM 101-5-1 (Marine Corps MCRP 5-2A): *Operational Terms and Graphics*. A copy had been given to her by Jeff Trasel, of the Northwest Militia. He told her that he had picked up several copies from an Army surplus store in Sandpoint, Idaho, that he jokingly called Grogan's War Surplus. Each copy still had its price tag of $2.49, from before the Crunch.

Megan thought this manual was a godsend. While she had this manual and others saved as PDFs on her DVD, this hard copy was invaluable. It was funny that an Army surplus store in the local area would have them available for a pittance. The date on the FM was 1997, but the symbology was what she was most interested in, and that had not changed over the years. It included all of the symbols for low-intensity conflict–type events, such as drive-by shootings, vandalism, graffiti, "drug vehicles," and refugees. This would serve as an invaluable hard reference, particularly if the resistance captured any UNPROFOR operations or intelligence products, since all of the other "formerly NATO" countries used the same symbology.

Given the nature of their work, and their vulnerability, they kept a thirty-gallon galvanized steel trash can in one corner of the TOC, with a one-quart motor oil container filled with gasoline hanging at the top. In the event that they were raided or faced any other emergency that would compromise them, they wanted a rapid way of destroying as much data, documents, thumb drives, and laptops as possible.

As Megan put it, "If the house goes up in the process—oh well. That will destroy even more evidence."

One day at the TOC in late October was particularly eventful and stressful. Reports arrived on USB thumb drives, but there were more than twice as many as usual. (There had been ambushes conducted the day before by both the Bovill Blue Blaze Irregulars and the Moscow Maquis.)

As she began opening the files on the USB sticks, Megan began muttering. "Here's *another* one that reads just like a 'What I did on my summer vacation' essay. Why can't they follow our instructions on using SALUTE format?" she exclaimed.

"Beggars can't be choosers," Malorie replied from the kitchen. "We're lucky to get the resistance groups to report directly to us at all. And we sure can't jack them up about it. They aren't in our chain of command. And what are we gonna do—threaten to dock their pay?"

Megan laughed and said, "You're right; half of nothing is still nothing."

As usual, Megan put each separate report in the Message Traffic Log spreadsheet, which was an ongoing document saved on one of their netbook computers. It mentioned in much-abbreviated form what had been reported.

Next, she started plotting the gist of the reports, one by one, onto the Moscow Region–Current SITTEMP overlay of the main map board. Megan had developed a way of using a computer printer to print symbology onto clear plastic sheets, with the event information next to that symbol. In this way, anyone visually analyzing the SITTEMP could see the map's terrain information through most of the printed material. Needless to say, the UN forces were marked in red, and any symbology marking a militia unit or action was marked in blue. Due to the limited number of reports that came in on most days, the symbols were left on the SITTEMP boards indefinitely, unless they started to crowd each other out. In that event, the oldest plotted information was removed first.

Malorie could hear Megan's frustration level as she worked. "I just spent twenty minutes digesting this and then when I go to plot it, I discovered that it was the same event, as seen from the opposite direction by a different unit, except that I now have *conflicting* reports on the type of German vehicles that were engaged. Were they six-wheeled TPz Fuchs or were they eight-wheeled GTK Boxers? Arrrgh!"

Malorie laughed. "That's why they pay you the *big* bucks as a hotshot analyst, sis."

"Twice nothing is still nothing," Megan shot back.

Moments later, they heard the sound of an approaching helicopter, and then the unmistakable chugging sound of a 30mm cannon. Then they heard the cannon shells impacting close by—close enough to rattle their windows.

Malorie pulled back the curtain of the kitchen window just far enough to see that a farmhouse a quarter mile north of them had been hit and was engulfed in flames.

Megan gasped. "Must be retaliation for yesterday's ambushes."

Joshua, who had been awakened by the explosions, stepped out of the bedroom wearing a pair of sweatpants and his body armor over his T-shirt. He glanced out the window and asked, "Any idea whose house that is, or should I say *was*?"

Megan shook her head.

Malorie whispered so that Jean and Leo wouldn't hear her from the other bedroom, "Sweet Lord, that could have been *us* if *we* had been identified as 'the suspect dwelling.'"

As Megan got back to work at the map board, her hands were shaking.

As one shift ended and another started, Joshua, Megan, and Malorie would brief one another on what had transpired during the previous eight-hour shift. Normally, this would take no longer than a few minutes. Megan usually took the crucial day shift, Malorie was swing shift, and Joshua took nights. Most of these later shifts were dedicated to radio watch, monitoring shortwave and CB traffic as well as scanning the public service bands.

Occasionally, the two Moscow Maquis leaders (or just one of them) would arrive at the TOC unannounced. They would invite them into the living room and set up the map boards with their respective SITTEMPs. Joshua, Megan, or Malorie would then brief the current situation, describing significant events and current UN force operations, and answer any questions or concerns that the leaders had.

In between periods of handling message traffic and plotting on the SITTEMPs, the three of them would write intelligence summaries, do OB and target vulnerability studies, conduct after-action damage assessment, and coordinate and synchronize all of the other intelligence activities for the Maquis. Their parent organization soon numbered fifty-five members in six distinct cells (three operational and three support) that had little contact except for a few combined operations.

Though there were many close calls, Joshua's cell was never detected. Their intelligence products proved crucial as the resistance war heated up in the western United States, though by this time the ProvGov was already nearing collapse. In essence, they had attempted to conquer too much territory too quickly and had spread their forces too thinly.

In northern Idaho, Todd Gray's Northwest Militia fled to a remote valley to use as a new base of operations. Todd stayed behind to demolish his own house with remote-controlled mines and firebombs, just as the empty house was being raided by German troops. Todd's group spent one winter encamped in the national forest and conducted numerous raids and ambushes.

They also used captured nerve gas canisters on an UNPROFOR barracks and at an UNPROFOR staff meeting. Very rapidly, the occupiers were losing ground to a well-armed citizen resistance in the inland northwest.

Shortly after the bombing of UNPROFOR's regional headquarters in Spokane by the Keane Team resistance group, there was a local surrender. In early July, there was a nationwide capitulation of the Maynard Hutchings government, and a withdrawal of UNPROFOR troops began.

As the new Restoration of Constitutional Government (RCG) administration was being formed, Joshua, Megan, and Malorie went back to their previous work as receptionists at the church. Things were getting back to normal in the region. The power grid was back up continuously, and a new currency that was truly "redeemable on demand in silver" was being issued. But there was a huge unresolved issue that pressed on everyone's minds: Canada.

38

PACKING IT IN

SEND A GUN TO DEFEND A BRITISH HOME. British civilians, faced with threat of invasion, desperately need arms for defense of their homes. THE AMERICAN COMMITTEE FOR DEFENSE OF BRITISH HOMES has organized to collect gifts of PISTOLS—RIFLES—REVOLVERS—SHOTGUNS—BINOCULARS from American civilians who wish to answer the call and aid in defense of British homes. The arms are being shipped, with the consent of the British Government, to CIVILIAN COMMITTEE FOR PROTECTION OF HOMES, BIRMINGHAM, ENGLAND.

—From a full-page advertisement in *American Rifleman* magazine, November 1940

The Gray Ranch, Bovill, Idaho—July, the Fifth Year

Only days after the UNPROFOR capitulation in the United States, Ken Layton, Todd Gray, Mike Nelson, and Jeff Trasel volunteered to make a series of CBLTV logistics excursions to Canada. For his part of the supply effort, Joshua donated two of his deer carts to Todd's group.

Following the suggestions that they'd heard on the shortwave, Todd had packed both of the camouflage-painted carts half full of rolls of detonating cord, a few magazines (M16, FAL, and HK G3—all freshly loaded and wrapped in plastic), and an assortment of ammunition calibers that included 7.62x39, 5.56mm NATO, .303 British, .300 Savage, .30-30, .270

Winchester, .308, .30-06, 9mm Parabellum, .45 ACP, and twelve-gauge buck-shot. Any of the ammo that was not already in sealed plastic battle packs was carefully wrapped in sealed plastic bags. On top of this, he packed each cart heaping full of blasting caps in padded boxes. Some of this padding was woodland pattern BDU camouflage pants and shirts, which they assumed the resistance could also use.

The loads were secured with scrap pieces of camouflage netting, attached with paracord and plastic cable ties.

For their own defense on the trips, Todd's team decided to carry guns that they had captured from UNPROFOR and then leave them with the local resistance before returning to the U.S. These rifles were all captured AK-74s. Coming home, they would be traveling only lightly armed, with just one gun for each man: a FN P90 bullpup, a Steyr AUG bullpup, and two Colt M1911 pistols.

Their first CBLTV trip to Canada began on August 20, and they were back home by August 24. Their first crossing was east of Lick Mountain, which was north of the town of Yaak, Montana. There, the Yaak River Road looped within three miles of the Canadian border. By prior arrangement, they simply dropped off their cargo at a prearranged set of GPS coordinates just across the border. They hastily cached the pile of parcels with cut fir boughs.

Their second trip, which began on August 27, was nearly identical except that their crossing was on the west side of Lick Mountain.

Their third trip, in early September, was a shorter drive, but a longer walk. They parked at the Good Grief store, 2.5 miles short of the then closed Eastport border crossing station. From there, they had a strenuous hike for ten miles up Canuck Basin Road, which was impassable to vehicles. A half mile beyond the border fence (three strands of barbless wire, which had previously been cut) they came within one hundred yards of the southern terminus of Hawkins Canuck Road. Waiting for them there was a man named Chet—their NLR contact. He thanked them profusely for the two previous deliveries as well this latest one. He presented each of them with a keepsake Canadian silver dime and declared them members of the NLR.

Chet stayed to talk with them for two hours, describing his perspective on the current situation in British Columbia, the NLR's current logistics and technical needs, and some ways that people in the United States might be able to help with the Cause. He was convinced that the U.S. could do more to apply diplomatic pressure on the UN to withdraw their troops. He also questioned why the CIA wasn't involved. On this note, he said, "It shouldn't just be volunteers footing the bill."

Providentially, all three trips were without incident except for one sprained ankle on the last return trip. (Jeff Trasel rode the last mile back to his pickup in a deer cart.) On all three trips—each with four hundred pounds of materiel—they were able to fill some specific requests that had been relayed from resistance cell leaders. These requests included a replacement magazine for a SMLE Mk. III rifle, some CR123 batteries, and ammunition in some oddball calibers including .25-35, .307 Winchester, .38-55, .30 Remington, .30 Herrett, and .221 Fireball.

Filling the special requests took some coordination via the CB radio relay network. (The phone network was still down, but the CB network covered from Grangeville, Idaho, northward and stretched into eastern Washington and western Montana.) Much of this ammunition had been custom handloaded.

Though they had planned to make additional trips into Canada, news of construction of a cordon sanitaire and uncertainty about just where it might be land-mined gave them pause. Instead they sent their gathered ammo and gear to Jerry Hatcher in Bonners Ferry, Idaho. Jerry was a former Alaska bush pilot who had volunteered to make some daring solo low-level night flights into Canada in his Cessna 180, an airplane equipped with oversize tundra tires. He landed in remote farm fields near Wynndel, High River, and Taber, British Columbia. In all, he made eleven flights, ferrying between 350 and 420 pounds of cargo per flight depending on the distance to his landing fields. On three occasions, he also flew out wounded resistance fighters to the United States for medical treatment.

39

INGRESS

Any single man must judge for himself whether circumstances warrant obedience or resistance to the commands of the civil magistrate; we are all qualified, entitled, and morally obliged to evaluate the conduct of our rulers. This political judgment, moreover, is not simply or primarily a right, but like self-preservation, a duty to God. As such it is a judgment that men cannot part with according to the God of Nature. It is the first and foremost of our inalienable rights without which we can preserve no other.

—John Locke

Moscow, Idaho—September, the Fifth Year

Ken Layton and Kevin Lendel came to visit Joshua's house on a Sunday afternoon in mid-September. Soon after he arrived, Ken had a question for Megan and Malorie. He asked, "I know that you two grew up speaking French. Do either of you know how to translate written French, like technical or military documents?"

Megan answered, "I assume this is about your NLR friends who are fighting the French forces up in Canada. Technical translation would be Malorie's department. She is more fluent in French than I am, and she used to work part-time as a technical translator."

Malorie nodded. "For translating technical things, yes, but military things might be a stretch since I don't know anything about the French army, their order of battle, or their command and staff structure. After all of the fighting here, I know a lot more about the German and Belgian land forces than I do the French. Do you have the document that needs to be translated? I assume that it's a captured document."

Ken said, "A little more complicated than that. My resistance contact up in BC mentioned that they're looking for a French translator on site with a small intelligence unit of some sort to translate captured French documents and military manuals."

Malorie blinked. Her mind was racing. She asked, "*Go* there? So how soon do they need this translator?"

Ken answered, "Yesterday. Are you up for it?"

Malorie and Megan were transported to Todd and Mary Gray's ranch in a captured Krauss-Maffei Wegmann light truck. Todd and most of his group were there to help. They had all brought some gear to donate. They already had Malorie's gear and clothes spread across the floor of the living room. As she was segregating items into piles, Malorie asked, "So what does a girl pack for a trip like this?"

Kevin Lendel suggested sarcastically, "How about a stainless Walther PPK, a little sack of cut one-carat diamonds, some knockout drops, a couple of lipsticks, and a Gerber Mark II fighting knife?"

Ken groaned. "This isn't a 007 trip. It's more like going off to a university or going to work on some intense corporate research project—but, ah, you should be ready to rough it out in the boonies, just in case."

Working together, they tore apart Malorie's pack and dry bag, and then re-packed them, now including many items donated from the occupants of both Kevin's house and Todd's house.

In the end, her load was heavy on cold-weather clothes and light on weap-onry. The pack contained her M1 Carbine, eight spare loaded magazines (six of them were fifteen-rounders), a rifle-cleaning kit, two bandoleers of .30 car-bine ammunition, a Cold Steel Voyager XL tanto pocketknife, a fairly com-plete outdoor survival kit with a waterproof match case and a magnesium fire starter, an olive-drab space blanket, two SureFire compact flashlights, some trioxane fuel bars, eleven MRE entrees, and several pairs of socks. There were lots of other practical items like a Bible, thirty-one dollars' worth of 1950s and 1960s Canadian silver coinage, a pair of Yaktrax ice creepers, four legal pads, an assortment of pens, a pair of rubber-armored Hensoldt Wetzlar Dienstglas 8x30 binoculars (that Kevin had liberated from a captured German officer), a folding stereo viewer for analyzing aerial photos (also recently liberated), and an eight-by-ten-inch Fresnel lens page magnifier.

On short notice they were able to locate a copy of the Routledge *French Technical Dictionary*, per Malorie's request. It was a gift to the resistance effort by a professor at Washington State University. Adding the dictionary to Malorie's pack brought its weight to nearly thirty-five pounds. The dry bag held the overflow of cold-weather clothing and her sleeping bag. That was another twenty-two pounds.

While she was packing, Malorie mentioned that she considered it ironic that she—as a mechanic and millwright—would take on the responsibility of intelligence analysis, when it was her sister, Megan, who had the more formal training in the craft of intelligence. (All of Malorie's intel experience had been OJT.) But she reasoned that the resistance mainly needed her skills as a linguist.

With the boys to raise, Megan's place was clearly at home, but Malorie was willing and able to get involved.

Her weapon was the same M1 Carbine with a replica M1A1 paratrooper folding stock that she had carried since she left Virginia. She had realized from the beginning that it was an underpowered gun. However, it was compact, lightweight, and most important, she was confident and competent shooting it. Malorie was warned by fellow shooters that the carbine shot a pipsqueak pistol-class .30 caliber cartridge that was not a reliable man stopper. But at the time it was all that she could afford and find available from a private-party seller. (Her first choice had been a folding stock Kel-Tec SU-16B .223, but the only ones that she could find were being sold by licensed dealers—and she detested filling out Federal Form 4473s.)

Although she was offered the gift of an "only dropped once" AK-74 by Terry, Malorie thought that the stress of learning to handle, shoot, and field strip another rifle would be one stress too many to add to her already long list. (Her anxiety meter was already pegging, and her departure was in less than twenty-four hours.)

Megan assumed that seeing Malorie board the plane would be too stressful for Jean and Leo, so Malorie made her good-byes at the Gray ranch. Megan told the boys that "Auntie Malorie is going to work on a map board in Canada." The sisters did their best to appear cheerful and upbeat. Later, Megan let Joshua know her concerns. "Mal is very important to me and the boys. I'll be praying for her safety, several times a day."

When Ken and Malorie arrived at the hangar in Jeff Trasel's pickup, Jerry Hatcher was adjusting cargo tie-down straps and preflighting the plane. A year earlier, the underside of the plane had been spray-painted dark gray and the upper surfaces were painted a mottled green camouflage, giving it a very serious, warlike look. The oversize tires were specifically designed for rough field landings.

Jerry was a slender, balding man of just under average height. Ken and Malorie handed the backpack and dry bag to him. As they did, Ken said, "We were told that we needed to be precise about weight. Together, these weigh in at fifty-seven pounds."

Jerry nodded and stowed Mal's gear behind the passenger seat. (The rear passenger seats had been removed, and that area was already crowded with a row of ammo cans beneath duffel bags of various colors.) Jerry turned toward Mal, asking, "How much do you weigh?"

"About one twenty-two. Figure probably another five pounds for my clothes and boots, to be safe."

Jerry punched some numbers into a JavaScript Weight and Balance calculator program on his iPad. The program was tailored specifically for the Cessna 180G model.

Mal looked interested in what he was doing, so Jerry explained the screen. "You see here that a 180G has fifty-five gallons of fuel capacity, which equates to three hundred thirty pounds. But tonight will be a short trip, so we are flying with just one hundred forty-five pounds of fuel. Here we've got weight, arm, and moment for each section of the aircraft. And this is the CG."

Malorie said, "I understand center of gravity, but 'arm' and 'moment' are Greek to me."

"It's a little complicated and hard to explain. Moment—which is a measure of the tendency of a force to cause a body to rotate about an axis—is calculated by multiplying the weight of an object by its arm. The main thing for us to be concerned with is this little red crosshair in the fat red circle. If it goes outside of this green envelope grid, then we might fall out of the sky, which would not be good. As you can see, at two thousand five hundred forty-five, we are definitely pushing the envelope, since the maximum takeoff weight is two thousand five hundred fifty pounds. So I'll plan on an extra-long takeoff roll. The weight also pushes our safe maneuvering speed up to one hundred and six miles per hour. With just me in the plane, that will drop to just ninety-six. The stall speed with the flaps extended is, of course, much lower."

Malorie asked, "I've always wondered what 'pushing the envelope' meant. Now I know. Cool. And I'll just skip on getting a grasp on arm and moment. So maneuvering speed is different than stall speed?"

"Yes, higher. But suffice it to say the heavier the plane is, the higher the stall speed, and the lighter the plane, the lower the stall speed. We'll be staying above the stall speed, which is why we have to calculate where that is, especially during takeoff and landing. It will also vary depending on altitude, temperature, and humidity of the air. I won't go into the difference it makes whether we are looking at true airspeed versus indicated airspeed for this explanation, but it also matters where the power levers are and how many g's are on the aircraft. Confused? That's why we have performance charts."

Not noticing that Malorie's eyes were glazing over, Jerry went on, pointing again at the screen. "Now that I've added in the weight of you and your gear, you can see we're still just barely inside the envelope. We'll drop down farther into the green once I burn off some of the fuel en route, as it will lower the weight and shift the CG in our favor. And of course my return trip will be 'easy breezy.'"

Malorie nodded. They were scheduled to leave just after sunset.

Ken gave her a hug, and said, "*Bon chance*, and kick some UNPROFOR butt."

As she was about to board the Cessna, Malorie balked for a moment. The enormity of what she was about to do struck her. She took a deep breath and whispered to herself, "I'm just going to trust God's providence on this."

She stepped up into her seat quickly, but then fumbled with the unfamiliar seat belt arrangement.

Jerry noticed her nervousness and asked, "So, ahh, is this your first time in a light plane, or just your first time flying into occupied territory where you'll face *summary execution,* if you're captured?"

That broke the ice, and Malorie burst out laughing. She was still chuckling when she finally got the odd seat belt buckle latched.

Jerry said, "Don't worry, I'll talk you through everything that I'm doing. Fact is, as a former instructor pilot, I have a tendency to talk to myself. I've flown this same route before, entirely on instruments, in much worse weather than this, and on softer fields. This is a very solid and trustworthy aircraft. It was built in 1964, but it's been well maintained. As for me, my model year was 1968 and I've logged almost thirty-eight hundred hours of flying."

Jerry put on a dark blue baseball cap with an Alaska Aces hockey team logo, showing a ferocious polar bear taking a swipe. He handed her a pair of pale green Clark headphones with a boom mike, and said, "You can put these on once I start the engine. Press this button here to talk. But don't push that button, or you'll be broadcasting on the radio. Not good, under the present circumstances."

After strapping himself in, but before starting the engine, Jerry mounted his GPS receiver in its cradle and turned it on. He immediately dialed down the brightness of the color screen.

He explained, "This is my cheater. It's a top-of-the-line Garmin Aera Model 795. I paid fifteen hundred dollars for it a year before the Schumer hit the fan. Now that the GPS ground stations are back online, the accuracy and full coverage of the GPS constellation has been restored, so we no longer have to fly by the seat of our pants. I've programmed in waypoints for our entire route—in three dimensions—plus four alternate exfiltration routes."

He tapped the screen to give a different view and continued. "This thing is sweet. The most important thing is that it gives me pop-up alerts with plenty of warning, based on altitude and heading. Basically, it won't let me screw up and fly into a mountain."

Malorie laughed nervously. "That's reassuring," she said.

It was full dark when they took off, and they were across the Canadian border in just a few minutes.

Jerry punched the intercom button and said, "Ever since the Frogs grounded most private plane flights in Canada south of fifty-three degrees latitude, whenever someone hears a plane, people just *assume* that every plane they hear is a UNPROFOR flight."

After a few minutes of maneuvering at full throttle, Jerry pulled the throttle rod back and adjusted the trim wheel.

Looking straight ahead and regularly glancing down at his instruments, he said, "Okay, the field ahead is a hay field that has had its final cutting of the season harvested and all of the bales have been hauled out. So that's about as good a grass strip as you're going to find anywhere. It is a one-hundred-sixty-acre field, so that's plenty long. The nearest power line is a half mile east. To be covert, I'm going to delay turning on my landing lights until the last minute, but I'll need them just to make sure there are no hay bales or a tractor sitting there. That could be a VBT."

"What's a VBT?"

"A Very Bad Thing."

As he turned toward the field and lowered the plane's flaps fully, he started speaking more quickly. "Airspeed eighty-five, three-fifty AGL. We're looking good, lined up on final. Now, I don't like to dawdle once I'm on the ground. I don't plan to be down for more than about two minutes. I won't be shutting the engine down, so whatever you do, do *not* walk *forward* of the wing, or you'll get the proverbial mouthful of propeller. Once you see me unbuckle, you do the same, and jump out. You can help me unload everything. We'll unload everything on *your* side of the aircraft. Then sit right down on the pile of gear and close your eyes tight, because when I throttle up to turn around, the prop wash is going to kick up a lot of dust. Understood?"

"Understood."

Jerry made adjustments to his controls as he spoke, interspersing his description of instrument readings. "There are friendlies scheduled to be waiting. Airspeed seventy, about one-ten AGL. Looking good. If someone drives up with their headlights off, then relax, that'll be your friendlies. Airspeed fifty-eight, sixty AGL. But if you see headlights, then grab your pack and beat feet for the nearest timber."

"Okay."

What happened next was a blur. She felt the plane bounce and then touch down solidly. Jerry pulled back the throttle sharply, and he visibly braced his shoulders back against his seat as he stood on the brake pedals. The plane

slowed very rapidly. Even before it came to a full stop, he turned off his landing lights. They were out of their doors quickly and Jerry ran behind the tail
and joined Mal, who was already unloading gear. Even idling, the prop wash
was strong. It felt like standing in a twenty-five-mile-per-hour wind. The pile
of gear grew rapidly, ten feet to the right of Malorie's door. Then Jerry shouted,
with a wave: "Last one. God bless you!"

Jerry ran around behind the tail again and jumped back in the plane. He
throttled the plane up in a roar, executed a tight 180-degree turn, and took off,
this time with no landing lights. Suddenly it was quiet, except for a dog barking in the distance. The air felt chilly. Malorie pulled her backpack out of the
pile and opened its top flap. She snaked out the carbine and laid it across her
knees. After refastening the pack's top flap, she reached into a cargo pocket of
her pants and pulled out a fifteen-round magazine for her carbine. She slapped
it in place, gave the magazine a tug to ensure that it was latched, and then
chambered a round. The clank of the slide operating seemed uncomfortably
loud. She reached down to confirm that the gun's rotary safety was pointed
down to the six-o'clock position. She waited. Only then did she notice that her
hands were shaking. A few moments later, Malorie could hear a vehicle approaching. She was relieved to see that its headlights were off.

Malorie was sitting at the kitchen table of a farmhouse. A woman with
graying wavy hair and a face ravaged by too many years in the sun sat across
from her.

The woman said, "I can get *you* up there, and I can arrange to smuggle that
carbine there, but I don't think I can necessarily get both you *and* it there at
exactly the same time."

"Are you worried about checkpoints?"

The woman nodded. "Yes. There'll be several of them. They don't ask for ID
except for whoever is driving, but they often search vehicles. We'll have to
send that gun and all the ammo, and any other items that might be hard to explain, via the courier network."

Malorie nodded and her host continued, "It's ten hours of driving. At the
checkpoints, all you have to do is lay on the charm, and chat them up a bit in
French. They love to hear anyone out west who speaks fluent French, and they

always assume that French speakers are Ménard loyalists. Just don't overdo it on the charm, or they'll start thinking of you as a potential date rape."

"Oh, great."

The woman glanced at her wristwatch and carried on. "Our cover will be that we are midwives, driving a long distance to attend a twin birth."

"So how do we carry that off?"

"I really *am* a midwife, so I can answer all of their questions, and I'll have all my usual home delivery kit with me. I've learned to say in rudimentary French, '*Je suis une sage-femme*' and '*Je suis pressé*.' Saying I'm a midwife and that I'm in a hurry usually does the trick."

"And what if they question *me*?"

"You're an apprentice midwife, so you won't be expected to know a lot. Right?"

They were stopped at seven checkpoints between Wynndel and Williams Lake, and their car was searched at two of them. At the checkpoint near Kamloops, one of the military policemen mentioned that Malorie's olive-green Kelty backpack looked "too military." He began unpacking it, methodically building a pile of clothes from the pack on the trunk lid of the car.

Malorie had stood silently, smiling. She now laughed disarmingly, and asked in perfect French: "And my panties? Do they also look too military?'

The soldier blushed and said, "*Donc, vous parlez français!*"

"Of course. As every good loyalist should."

The soldier began repacking the clothes, looking embarrassed.

After they had driven well past the roadblock, the midwife began laughing. Malorie kept giggling for several more minutes.

It was Claire McGregor who was waiting to meet Malorie at the Hudson's Bay Company store parking lot. Switching Malorie's pack and dry bag between car trunks took just a minute. The midwife left with a wave.

"How was your drive, Miss LaCroix?"

"Gorgeous scenery. It was just stunning. Lots of elk, and there were bighorn sheep. I'd never seen those in person before."

"Any problem with the internal security checks?"

She turned to Claire, put on a smile, fluttered her eyelids, and said, "*Pas de problème.*"

Claire laughed and replied, "Feminine wiles beat brute force every time." They talked nonstop all the way to the ranch. Claire reminded Malorie of her aunt Helen. Very soon, Malorie knew that she would feel comfortable at Claire's ranch house.

40

JE NE SAIS QUOI

Who can find a virtuous woman? For her price [is] far above rubies. The heart of her husband doth safely trust in her, so that he shall have no need of spoil. She will do him good and not evil all the days of her life. She seeketh wool, and flax, and worketh willingly with her hands.

—Proverbs 31:10–13 (KJV)

The McGregor Ranch, near Anahim Lake, British Columbia—Late September, the Fifth Year

Malorie settled in quickly at the McGregor ranch. For her privacy, she displaced Phil from his bedroom and Phil began sleeping on a folding futon on the floor of Ray's room. Meanwhile, Malorie's bedroom doubled as the intel analysis and translation office. A boom lamp was set up over the desk, for the days that they ran the generator. On all other days, light was provided by a pair of Aladdin mantle kerosene lamps.

On her first full day at the ranch, Malorie gave Phil a briefing on her recent intelligence analysis experience and described how she had done French technical translation.

Then Phil said, "Rather than fill you in on our operations here, first I have a mental exercise for you. I want you to watch this movie along with Ray and his parents."

He handed her a DVD of the World War II movie *Defiance* with Daniel Craig, and said, "You can watch this on our laptop tonight, which we occasionally power from the McGregors' battery bank. I want you to watch it very carefully. There will be a quiz in the morning."

"Okay. Can I take notes?"

"No. This is a memory exercise."

The next morning, he quizzed her in detail, for thirty-five minutes. She thought that she did fairly well in answering his questions. Then he said, "Now what I want you to do is watch the movie *again*—by yourself, with *total concentration*. This time I want you to just ignore the story, the music, and the foreground action. You are going to watch for all of the subtleties in the *background*: colors, shapes, sounds, vehicle types, clothing textures, type of footwear, body language, flora, fauna, cartridge casings, wear and tear on objects, architecture, temporal incongruities, et cetera—everything *except* what the characters are saying and doing."

"Okay."

Three hours later, over lunch, Phil quizzed her again. He started by asking, "How do you feel?"

"Exhausted!"

Phil grinned and said, "Good, very good. That means you did the viewing in the right frame of mind."

Malorie exclaimed, "That was an amazing exercise!"

"I thought that you'd like that. By the way, you can do that watching *any* movie—even a romantic comedy. That was a trick taught me by a colleague from MI5, in England. Oh, and I should mention that two other variants of the exercise are to turn the sound down completely, or to flip the laptop screen nearly closed or dim the screen and concentrate on just the audio. I've watched the same movies four times using these exercises, and it is amazing what you learn to pick up, each way."

Mal and Phil were always careful to pull out no more than three or four file folders at a time, just in case all of the "intel boxes" had to disappear into the closet in a hurry. (The plan was for both Phil and Malorie to hide in the closet in case of a search.)

Because of the huge backlog of captured documents, Malorie initially worked ten to eleven hours per day, sorting through documents and translating them. Phil was usually with her for most of the day, explaining the military jargon, acronyms, and intelligence terminology. The documents had already been roughly sorted by date, but beyond that they were a jumble. After they had been reorganized and sorted in neatly labeled manila folders, they filled four boxes. Each folder was labeled by subject and also had its tab color-coded blue, yellow, or red to designate low-, medium-, or high-intelligence-value material.

Most of the documents were not fully translated. With 90 percent of the documents she would simply staple on a "gist" summary page. Only the most important documents were translated word for word. Later, when she had more time, she worked back through a lot of the gisted documents and wrote more detailed summaries. As winter set in and the pace of work slowed, she shifted her attention to captured and pilfered technical manuals. The highest priorities were manuals for radios and small arms.

They used Phil's laptop to write summaries of key intelligence that would be useful if broadcast. These were transferred to memory stick and then sent via the courier network to Washington, where they were read over the air by ham radio operators and relayed to the newly reemerging U.S. mass media. Intelligence on specific targets that needed to be kept secret until after a resistance strike was carried via couriers to the communities within striking distance, where resistance cells were already in place. (Another intelligence cell in Vancouver had been doing the same since the first few months of the resistance war. This was the cell that had coordinated the sinking of the MN *Toucan* and MN *Colibri*, in the single-most effective resistance action of the war. It had inspired the formation of dozens of resistance cells.)

Malorie got along well with everyone at the ranch. She and Claire were soon like a mother and daughter. Malorie enjoyed hearing the McGregors' Canadian idioms. To the McGregors, a couch was a "Chesterfield," a colored pencil was a "pencil crayon," a table napkin was a "serviette," tennis shoes were "runners," a parking garage was a "parkade," a fire station was a "fire hall," and a restroom was a "washroom."

Phil, Ray, and Stan were all immediately attracted to Malorie, for both her looks and her abilities. When Claire mentioned them staring at her, Malorie joked, "Of course they're interested. I could be plug ugly and they'd be interested. I'm the only single female in an eight-mile radius."

Malorie soon gravitated to Phil, but she did not make her interest clear immediately. Malorie found Phil to be a delightful coworker. Despite the stress of the heavy workload, Phil always maintained a good sense of humor. (Phil worked for eleven hours a day doing intel analysis, in addition to his ranch chores.) They shared the same faith in Christ, with an "all grace" outlook on salvation. She loved hearing his stories about Afghanistan and some of his more recent adventures with DCS Task Group Tall Oak. When the subject of his childhood came up, Phil said, "I suppose I had a very regimented upbringing, compared to most kids. It was very Russian."

"Russian?"

"Yes. The family's original paternal name was Adamski. My grandfather shortened it to Adams when he became a naturalized citizen. His parents—my great-grandparents—escaped the Russian Revolution and subsequent civil war by traveling across Siberia to the city of Harbin, where there was a large Russian colony. My great-grandfather worked there for the Trans-Siberian Railroad."

Malorie seemed fascinated. "Tell me more."

"Okay, here's the condensed version of how my folks got to the States: Both of my grandparents on my father's side grew up in Harbin and came to the States separately. My grandmother left Harbin for Seattle to attend the University of Washington before World War II. After my grandfather got a master's degree in electrical engineering in Harbin he went to Shanghai and somehow got a job in Australia, where he worked at the Mount Isa mine, with the ultimate goal of coming to the United States to marry my grandmother. He was in Sydney for the weekend when the Japanese attacked Pearl Harbor. The next day, he went to the U.S. embassy to try to join the U.S. Navy. But when he was there, he ran into a Merchant Marine captain who needed someone to fix a turbine since his ship's engineer was in the hospital with a hot appendix. My grandfather fixed the turbine and stayed on the ship, leaving all of his clothes and books behind in Mount Isa. He spent the rest of the war in the Merchant Marines."

Phil continued, "While he was on leave on the West Coast in 1945 he married my grandmother. Then, years later when they were established in California, they ransomed my great-grandparents from the communists and brought them to the States, so my dad got to grow up with both sets of his grandparents living in a cottage on the San Francisco peninsula. So a lot of my grandfather's and great-grandfather's personalities rubbed off on my dad, which then rubbed off on me. The last of my grandparents died when I was ten years old, but a lot of their stories are quite well remembered, and a lot of their attitudes are firmly entrenched in me. They had a strong Christian faith and a deep distrust of totalitarianism—and, in fact, of most other 'isms.'"

On Malorie's third day at the ranch, it was wash day. Ray went out to start the Lister generator set, but it wasn't long before he shut it back down and came into the house, looking glum. He kicked off his mud boots and walked to the kitchen table. He said, "We have a problem, ladies and gents: The engine is turning just fine, but the generator is not."

"Uh-oh," Alan said.

Alan, Phil, Malorie, and Ray all walked out to the generator shed together. Ray brought a rag and a flashlight.

Examining the generator set, they could see nothing outwardly wrong, other than its usual small and chronic oil leaks. It was Malorie who spotted some metal filings beneath the coupling that joined the engine shaft to the generator shaft. "Hey, look here: Looks like it ate a Woodruff."

Phil, who only had rudimentary mechanical knowledge, asked, "What's that?"

Malorie pointed the tips of her index fingers together to illustrate. "The two shafts come together end to end, like this. A Woodruff spline keeps them aligned, and this coupling sleeve holds the spline in place, and the coupling is in turn held in place with these big Allen-head screws."

After a pause, she went on. "I'll need a set of Allen wrenches—they look like three-sixteenths—but it could be a size smaller or larger, or possibly even metric. Oh, and I'll also need some sort of degreaser, preferably in a spray can."

Ray nodded. "The Allen wrench you need is right here." He pointed to a wooden tray of maintenance tools that had been power-screwed to the wall of the shed.

Alan offered, "I used to have to tighten those Allen screws once every few months, but then I got wise and stared using green Loctite so that they don't drift."

"I'll be right back with a spray can of carburetor cleaner," Ray said.

While Phil held the flashlight, Malorie deftly loosened the Allen screws. Just as Ray stepped back into the shed with a spray can, Malorie slid the sleeve aside and chuckled.

She said, "I knew this thing was old, but I didn't know it was *this* old. This thing is pre-Woodruff."

"Meaning what, Mal?" Ray asked.

"Meaning it is not a square Woodruff key that got eaten. It's a *taper* key, which is what they used before Woodruffs became commonplace. That means that finding or making a replacement key will be a lot more difficult."

She went on to explain. "The good news is that keys are made from mild steel, with parallel sides and base. The top face of the key has a slight taper of just a one- or two-in-a-hundred ratio, which allows you to fit it into a keyway, followed by a rapid take-up of the slack in the hole, by the taper."

"So you're saying that you have to fabricate a replacement for a part that you've never seen, because we only have a few fragments," Ray said.

"That's right. I don't suppose you have a dial micrometer?"

"No," Alan answered glumly.

"But I'll bet the Leaman ranch has one that we can borrow," Ray offered.

Mal looked up. "Also ask if they have a tube of some machinist's Prussian blue. It's also called blue dykem."

Ninety minutes later, Ray roared back to the ranch on his KLR motorcycle. He shouted, "Got 'em!"

After spraying all of the parts with degreaser, Malorie used the projecting tips of the calipers to measure the keyways on the shafts and coupling in several places, and took notes.

"Not only do I have to account for some taper, but the keyway also shows some wear, even though it was obviously harder steel than the spline. So to compensate, I'm going to have to taper the new key in two different axes."

She made the new taper key from a standard seven-sixteenths-inch threaded steel bolt. She wisely left the head of the bolt in place for most of the steps so that she'd have that to clamp firmly into Alan's bench vise. An Aladdin mantle lap was fetched and set up for light to work by.

Malorie explained as she started: "Normally I'd use a milling machine or even just an abrasive cutoff wheel to work this down to the rough dimension, but of course we're without power, so we'll use the old-fashioned method. Namely, hand files and plenty of sweat."

The four of them took turns filing flats on four sides of the bolt shaft. After one hour and fifteen minutes, they were close to the requisite rough dimensions, and Malorie started measuring with the calipers more and more frequently. After nearly two hours of work, Malorie was doing all of the filing and all of the calipering as the three men stood back and watched. She let the work piece cool for a few minutes as she took a sip of water. Then she loosened the vise and dropped the workpiece into a rag.

"Time for a sanity check," she declared.

After carrying the roughed taper key and the "mike" to the generator shed, she did a test fitting. She nodded. "I just wanted to make sure that I was visualizing the taper correctly in both axes."

After taking another measurement, she carried her work back to the vise in Alan's shop.

She continued with more filing, now much more deliberately, and taking regular measurements.

Next, she sawed off the head of the bolt with a hacksaw and cleaned up that rough end with a bastard file.

Over the next hour, she took three more trips back and forth to the generator shed between filing sessions. She now used the tube of blue dykem to mark the taper key so that when she did test fittings, contact with the high spots would become apparent.

The finished taper key was tapered not only from top to bottom, but also along its length to compensate for the worn keyway.

Installing the key took just a few light taps of a brass hammer. The coupling went on with ease. It was a perfect fit. The Allen screws were again cemented with green Loctite—a special formulation that was designed to break loose, when needed. (Standard clear cyanoacrylate glue was unforgiving and all too permanent, for machine screws.)

Wash day began several hours late, but Malorie's mechanical skills had saved the day. Describing the repair later to Claire, Alan commented, "It was like watching one of the Dutch Masters do an oil painting. That job would have taken me two or three days. We're very lucky that Malorie came here when she did. Great timing."

Claire replied, "I don't believe in happenstance. I believe in divine appointments. God brought Malorie to us for more than one reason. All of those reasons will become clear to us, with time."

That evening, as they were washing and drying the dinner dishes, Phil said to Malorie, "You really amaze me. You've got a lot of hidden talents. Mechanical ability like yours is a rarity in men, and a great rarity in women."

She blushed slightly, and replied, "I'm sure you have hidden talents, too. I notice that you've hardly mentioned what you did when you were working in counterintelligence."

"Most of that doesn't have much relevance to our work here. In fact, my knowledge of things like order of battle and terrain analysis date back to when I took my Officer Basic Course rather than my later work in CI."

"But I'm sure you have some great stories to tell about your cloak-and-dagger days."

"Nah. It was mostly just pushing paper."

41

IN A PAST LIFE

The secret of happiness is freedom, and the secret of freedom
is courage.

—Thucydides

Seattle, Washington—June, Three Years
Before the Crunch

Phil Adams hoped that the Iranian hadn't spotted him. If he had, then he
might as well as pull the plug on the day's surveillance.

Phil was fortunate to still be in the loop. Most of his contemporaries
disappeared into anonymous and mundane civilian life after their assignments ended and their clearances lapsed. But Phil had made the transition
from active-duty military intelligence (MI) into intel contracting almost ef-
fortlessly, thanks to the longevity of Task Group Tall Oak, an ongoing DIA
(and later DCS) program with proven success. Their specialty was industrial
counterintelligence, but to some extent they were capable of "all source" intelligence gathering and analysis.

Phil was a contract case officer specializing in offensive counterintelligence based in the smallest of the five Task Group Tall Oak offices on the
West Coast, Tall Oak–Washington. When he mentioned his role to his sister,
she said, "Wow, that sounds glamorous." He quickly explained to her that it
was actually a lot of hard work, and much of it involved boring report writing.
As was typical in the counterintelligence world, it took hundreds of hours of

work to generate a lead, and only a few leads panned out to be solid cases to follow. Their victories were few and infrequent, but each one was relished. Catching a foreign agent red-handed felt very rewarding, but since they were usually operating in the U.S. under diplomatic cover, their immunity protected them from prosecution. They would simply be declared persona non grata, and told that it was time for them to go home. Getting a foreign agent declared persona non grata (PNG or "Ping," in CI slang) was considered a feather in the cap of any CI agent.

The man Phil was observing now was with the Iranian Ministry of Intelligence and Security (MOIS). For days, they had been trying to catch him in the act of visiting a dead-drop microcache location. The MOIS, also known as VEVAK (*Vezarat-e Ettela'at va Amniyat-e Keshvar*), had agents who were some of the CIA's most challenging opponents. The VEVAK was an outgrowth of the Shah Pahlavi–era SAVAK, and it was widely known that SAVAK got their training from the CIA and the Israeli Mossad during the 1960s. So the tradecraft employed by the Iranian MOIS was excellent.

The MOIS agent stepped into his car with diplomatic plates, and then spent several minutes combing his hair, trimming his fingernails, and checking for specks of food between his teeth using the car's rearview mirror. Finally, he popped a breath mint in his mouth before starting the car's engine.

Phil chuckled. This was *not* the behavior of a man who was afraid of being followed. No, this was the behavior of a man headed to a date. Phil started the engine of his own car and pulled out to follow. He trailed ten car lengths back. Using his hands-free microphone, he radioed in on the DCS Task Group Tall Oak secure network: "Subject in view, and rolling west on East Denny Way. Now crossing Twenty-fifth Avenue. No worries."

A minute later, Phil heard a tone on his earpiece, indicating that someone had joined the secure "chat."

Clarence Tang gave his usual "Hul-low there, guys" intro and then said, "I've got a situation. Mr. Lo, my former subject and now *suspect* at the Chinese consulate, just got a so-called secure e-mail asking for a meeting at 'the usual place' at noon. Based on his previous movements, I think that means the Main Post Office. Can any of you be there with your badges and credentials before noon?"

Phil chimed in, "I can definitely be there. Let's say we meet on the roof of the Republic parking garage—the Cobb Garage—on Union Street, at 1140 hours. I think it's the closest one to the post office."

"Sounds good. I'll brief you and show you photos of my two subjects."

Clarence was there waiting, as expected, sitting in his silver "High-Speed Pursuit" Honda Hybrid, which was often the butt of jokes at the office.

Phil parked nearby and walked over to the Honda. As he slipped into the passenger seat, he could immediately see that Clarence was agitated.

"This could be *it*, Phil. A face-to-face between Mr. Lo and his corporate mole with Boeing, an engineer named Robert Chan."

He flipped open his laptop, keyed in a passphrase, and navigated to a file designated "T.O. Case 121—UCAS Follow-On."

Clarence continued. "What the Chinese are after is some stealth technology from a UAV that is under development by Boeing." He deftly clicked the computer's track pad and opened two street-surveillance photos, side-by-side. Pointing, he said, "This is the inscrutable Mr. Lo, and this is Bob Chan. If we catch them passing data, we can arrest Chan, but Lo is beyond our reach since he has diplomatic immunity."

"But we can Ping him right out of the country."

"Right!" Tang replied excitedly. "And I brought two body cams to *nail* their assets."

"Perfect."

Phil was wearing black jeans, a polo shirt, and a tan windbreaker. He put the camera recorder in the jacket's inside pocket. The camera's tiny lens and microphone head were then pinned directly through the jacket to the recorder lead. The four needle-sharp pins on the back of the camera head served to both hold the camera firmly in place and pass the video and audio signals to the recorder leads. The lens and microphone head were built into a small enameled Ecology pin, effectively camouflaging it to casual observers.

Clarence did the same with an identical camera through his gray Aéropostale hoodie jacket. He glanced at his wristwatch nervously, and said, "Showtime."

After stuffing his laptop into a rucksack and locking the car, they headed to the stairs in a trot. Two minutes later, they entered the Seattle Main Post

Office (also known as the Midtown Post Office) through separate entrances. After scanning the lobby and the queue at the service counter, Phil took on the role of "indecisive shopper" at the rack of postal service shipping boxes, tote bags, and collectibles. Meanwhile, Clarence got in the long noon-hour line of customers approaching the service counter.

Two minutes later, at 11:57, Mr. Lo arrived. He was wearing polished shoes, dark pants, and a black raincoat. He pulled some junk mail out of a trash receptacle and pretended to study mail-order catalogues.

At exactly noon, Robert Chan walked into the crowded lobby. He walked over to the tall table where Mr. Lo was standing and began picking through the clear acrylic rack of postal forms, eventually grabbing a green-and-white customs declaration form. Meanwhile, Mr. Lo pulled a fat envelope from his pocket and laid it on the table. Chan palmed the envelope and slid it into his oversize iPad man purse. Getting a subtle high sign from Phil, Clarence left the line and walked toward the table in time to see Bob Chan reach into his pocket and pull out a wrapped stick of chewing gum. He laid it on the counter. As soon as Mr. Lo's hand touched the gum stick, Clarence shouted, "Federal agents—you're under arrest!" Both he and Phil quickly rushed the two suspects, putting them both in armlocks and shoving their chests into the table. In the scuffle, the stick of gum was flicked to the floor.

After both men were handcuffed, Phil snatched the wrapped piece of gum from the floor. On camera, he unwrapped it, revealing that it contained a miniature SIM card, resting in a rectangular notch cut out of the gum stick.

"Gotcha," he exclaimed triumphantly.

Lo protested, "I am a member of the People's Republic of China consular staff. I have a diplomatic passport. You cannot detain me."

Again on camera, Phil searched Lo's pockets, stopping when he found his passport. He slowly passed each page of it in front of his body cam. Then he said, "With apologies for the inconvenience from the United States government, you are free to go, Mr. Lo."

As Phil keyed Lo's handcuffs open, Clarence added, "But *you*, Mr. Chan, have an appointment with a federal magistrate."

Lo made a hasty retreat out the door. Robert Chan whimpered and started to cry.

The bulging envelope contained fifty thousand dollars in hundred-dollar bills—a figure that was confirmed in three separate supervised counts at the FBI office, where they took Chan for his initial processing. Phil had no reluctance handing the cash over to the FBI, but then their agents wanted to copy the data from the SIM card. Phil put his foot down, citing Title 10, and said forthrightly that this was a DOD investigation, a DOD arrest, and that because the arrest had been made on federal property (the post office), technically there wasn't even any need for the FBI to be involved. It didn't take long for the feebees to relent. They settled for photographs of the SIM card, the partial stick of gum, and the wrappers. But there was still chain-of-custody paperwork to fill out—and it was unusual that the SIM card (with gum wrappers) and cash had different destinations. That, too, caused a little confusion. With the FBI, "following protocol" was an art form, and unusual situations like these ruffled their feathers.

Offices of DCS Task Group Tall Oak, Joint Base Lewis-McChord, Washington—June, Three Years Before the Crunch

Very few of the subjects of Tall Oak CI investigations were in the nonofficial cover (NOC) category or clandestine agents. But with sufficient evidence, the Americans whom the foreign agents had used as assets *could* be prosecuted, or more often than not, turned. Turning an asset into a double agent was difficult, complicated, and stressful, particularly for the assets. As a handler, Phil spent much of his time trying to distinguish fact from fiction. A lot of his work required him to develop a level of trust with "assets" who had already proven themselves to be *entirely* untrustworthy to the other side.

Phil worked at Joint Base Lewis-McChord. The nearest town was DuPont, a small bedroom community. More than half of its residents were Fort Lewis officers and NCOs who lived off-post. Phil's apartment was in DuPont, not because he particularly liked the town, but because he disliked long commutes in traffic. The four-apartment building had two floors, and his modest two-bedroom apartment was on the second floor.

The DIA's counterintelligence (CI) agents could do some things inside the United States that the CIA couldn't. Under the National Security Acts of 1947 and 1949 the CIA was barred from domestic intelligence gathering. Ironically, the Tall Oak intelligence reports went "up the pipe" to the CIA just as if they had been produced by CIA agents. Phil didn't mind being a surrogate for the CIA, especially if he was a *well-paid* surrogate. And his work didn't pose any ethical dilemmas. The subjects of his investigations were nearly all foreign nationals who were trying to steal American secrets—most often industrial secrets.

In 2012, a reorganization within the DIA created the Defense Clandestine Service (DCS). To the Tall Oak staff, the change mostly meant a change of business cards and stationery. Tall Oak shifted from a DIA "Project" to a DCS "Task Group." (Tall Oak was never a separate compartment, but now its name could be spoken outside DIA circles.)

The DCS had an emphasis on languages and gave hiring preference to agents with language proficiency. They sought people who spoke Arabic, Russian, Chinese, Korean, Farsi, Pashto, Urdu, Dari, Hindi, Turkish, Tajik, Spanish, French, German, and Portuguese, but it was an open secret that the main emphasis of the DCS was watching China and Iran.

Phil's officemates were Brian Norton (an electronics wizard), Clarence Tang (a Chinese linguist), and Scott Paulsen (a Russian linguist). The section chief was Hal Jensen, a crusty old vet who had been with the DIA's Counterintelligence Field Activity (CIFA) for eight years before it was rolled into DCS. With no path to career advancement unless he moved, he described himself as "a GG-13 for life." At sixty-three, he had long been eligible to collect his twenty-year military pension and could have already collected a DOD civilian pension as well. But he was waiting to turn sixty-five, so that he could "triple dip" and collect Social Security, too. (He had also accumulated forty-plus quarters in the Social Security system.) For his planned retirement, he had a cabin waiting for him near St. Maries, Idaho. Jensen was fond of saying, "I'm delaying my retirement just to keep you contractors honest, and of course for the great coffee."

Even though they spoke different languages, Clarence and Scott were buddies, since they were both prior service 98G MOS Army Intelligence linguist NCOs. They had both attended the Defense Language Institute (DLI) in Monterey, California, at the same time, and they had both transitioned to the DCS when they were E6s. The 98Gs (or "Golfs," as they called themselves) tended to be clannish and were some of the Army's most highly educated NCOs. A surprising number of them had master's degrees in foreign languages *before* joining the army. And until recruiting policies changed in 2011, a few of them were age-waivered to be able to enlist after their thirty-fifth birthday.

Phil and Hal became friends quickly, even though they had been born thirty years apart. Their bond was rooted in the fact that they both got their start in tactical SIGINT (officer specialty code thirty-five career-tracked) and had eventually migrated into the CI/HUMINT field.

The offices for DCS Task Group Tall Oak–Washington were inside one of the three Stryker Brigade headquarters at Fort Lewis. Three of the U.S. Army's seven Stryker Brigades were based at JBLM. The brigade headquarters building was the ideal place for the Tall Oak Section to hide its SCIF (spoken "skiff") in plain sight. It was already classified as a "U.S.-Controlled Facility," so that made SCIF accreditation easier. The Tall Oak staff could walk in and out of the building at any hour of the day or night in civilian clothes without arousing any suspicion.

The Tall Oak–Washington outer office measured only ten feet by ten feet and had just one small desk, a coat rack, a wall-mounted set of horizontal cubby shelves, and a pistol-clearing tube. Its main purpose was to shield the SCIF inner door from the view of casual passersby in the hall. The outer door was solid core oak and had a cipher lock. The outer office was their nondiscussion area, where classified discussions were not authorized because it lacked adequate sound attenuation.

Between the outer office and the SCIF itself was a six-by-six-foot security vestibule. This vestibule was monitored with a closed-circuit television camera and was controlled by an electronic latch release with a loud buzzer during the day, and by a second cipher lock with a distinct combination after hours. Then came the heavy steel vault door itself.

Behind the proverbial "Green Door," the SCIF was a drab, windowless space that felt claustrophobic despite the high ceiling. The only large adornments were two large maps—a world map and a map of the Pacific Northwest—mounted on foam-core backings. There were two OPSEC reminder posters, a DCS core values poster, and a DCS mission statement poster. The office's only decorative ficus tree with plastic leaves looked comically out of place. Years before Phil arrived, some wag had taped a sign reading, DO NOT OVER-WATER onto its trunk.

The SCIF was permeated with the smell of coffee but also had a faint smell of tobacco, which came from Hal Jensen's clothes. (He still grumbled about being forced to smoke outdoors.) The SCIF was not a quiet place. There was the constant hum of the fluorescent light fixture ballasts and the whir of more than a dozen muffin fans, which were cooling the many computers. The other noise source in the SCIF was the constant soft rushing sound of the DIAM-mandated white-noise generators, made by a company called Florida Sound Masking. This system was designed to foil any potential eavesdropping.

The SCIF's Comm Center was dominated by a three-sided ring of eight-foot tables. Atop these tables were six computer monitors, two large tabletop printers, a document scanner, a Defense Red Switch Network (DRSN) telephone, and a STU-III secure telephone with an attached speakerphone. The six prominently labeled monitors each had a specific communications and data retrieval function: JWICS, DCS WAN, SIPRNet, Tall Oak LAN/Operations Net, READOUT Multi-Net, and NSANet. Because Tall Oak was a "multiple INTs" shop, it had better connectivity than many U.S. Army command headquarters.

Emanations security was an obsession in the American intelligence community in part because they had exploited emanations so thoroughly in East Germany in the 1960s. Recognizing their own vulnerability, TEMPEST teams did regular sweeps of all SCIFs, using a strange-looking assortment of spectrum analyzers with specialized antennas.

Adjoining the Comm Center was a 230-square-foot conference room containing a long oak table topped by a large triskelion-shaped Polycom speakerphone. A twenty-four-inch flat-panel monitor with integral camera was mounted on the partition wall that divided the conference room from the Comm Center. This recent addition was an encrypted video system that could be linked directly to the other Tall Oak offices or to a Defense

Intelligence Operations Coordination Center (DIOCC) Workroom in the Defense Intelligence Analysis Center (DIAC) at Joint Base Anacostia-Bolling (JBAB) in Washington, D.C.

The other four Tall Oak offices on the West Coast covered San Diego, Los Angeles, the San Francisco Bay area, and Portland. The largest of these was in Sunnyvale, California, and had been nicknamed the Beehive, both because it had a staff of thirty-five people and a constant stream of visitors flying in from DIAC, and for its large number of agents who had been raised in Mormon families.

Unlike the smaller Washington office, the Sunnyvale Tall Oak office was considered a Continuous Operation, with a SCIF operated twenty-four hours a day. It was located in a large, nondescript one-story office building with a sign vaguely identifying it as Williams Design Group. The front lobby had the familiar "California Corporate" look, but just to the right of the front desk was a heavy door that led to a Honeywell Man Trap entrance. Beyond that was a three-way hall intersection that led to the nonsecure offices on the right and left, and to the SCIF, directly ahead. The core of the Sunnyvale building was a forty-five-hundred-square-foot windowless SCIF, which included an open-storage workroom.

Silicon Valley was a major target for foreign industrial espionage. The Beehive was located just a mile from Apple Computer's recently completed main headquarters building, "The One Ring." The Sunnyvale staff enjoyed warm weather and blue skies but also suffered a lot of traffic snarls. Their FBI counterparts were located nine miles away in Campbell, California. Nine miles was considered a just barely comfortable distance. The Beehive wanted to keep relations between their respective operations "courteous but distinct and geographically detached." Privately, they considered the FBI's CI agents a posse of bumbling buffoons.

Similarly, the Tall Oak–Washington staff at JBLM was happy to have the nearest FBI office thirty-eight miles away, on Third Avenue in downtown Seattle. Ironically, the Tall Oakers actually had much more cooperative working relationships with the U.S. Diplomatic Security Service (DSS) and the Canadian Security Intelligence Service (CSIS), in Burnaby, British Columbia. As Phil put it, "At least the Canadians know how to keep their mouths shut." On many occasions, they had proven themselves worthy of mutual respect.

Tall Oakers worked in plainclothes and investigated national security crimes and violations of the UCMJ, within U.S. military CI jurisdiction. But unlike their active-duty army "Strat" CI counterparts, the Tall Oakers had more of a focus on industrial espionage. Their "cover" story at JBLM was that they exclusively did purely preventive work like SAEDA briefings. But in actuality, their lives were a bit more exciting, but only occasionally dangerous.

The acronym *CI/HUMINT* was often spoken in the same breath, but the two roles were actually distinct. The old saying in the Army intelligence community was, "If you want to try to do some Agent 007 stuff, then go HUMINT. But if you want to try to *catch* people who are trying to do 007 stuff, then go CI." The rule was that a HUMINTer couldn't do investigations and a CI special agent couldn't do interrogations. With Task Group Tall Oak, Washington, that distinction was blurred, since some of their taskings were HUMINT (rather than CI), and the Tall Oakers did indeed interrogate turned assets.

The leeway in Tall Oak's mission came by virtue of both their specific taskings and the fact that they were *contractors*, selectively operating under either Title 50 or Title 10, as needed. (Title 50 was the portion of the U.S. Code that governed the legal authority of the CIA, NSA, and NRO, whereas Title 10 governed and authorized the Armed Forces.) It also helped that their chain of command jumped directly to DIA headquarters at JBAB in Washington, D.C., rather than being under the control of a regional Army command.

The Tall Oak staff was supplemented by nine part-time contractors. The part-timers all held at least secret-level clearances but only two of them had top secret clearance and SCI access. These "ad hocs" were used primarily for stakeout surveillance and maintenance of stakeout video cameras. Most of them had prior service as NCOs in the Military Intelligence or Civil Affairs branches. Just one of them was a former MP who had only a few months of CID experience, but he was recruited because he had a lot of combat experience in Afghanistan, and because he spoke some Arabic and Pashto without the benefit of any formal training.

The ad hocs lived in a tenuous netherworld. In some weeks they might not work at all, but in others they could work as many as seventy hours. They were paid well (on an hourly basis, at forty dollars per hour), but the job carried no benefits, and it had a few risks. One of the reasons that the ad hocs were at risk was that they were not allowed to carry badges and credentials. In a few instances, this led to some dangerous unintended confrontations with local law enforcement and, on one occasion, with FBI agents.

While they were careful to schedule most of their arrests in conjunction with the FBI, the majority of their "street" time was entirely under Tall Oak tasking, with no coordination with the FBI, and only minimal supervision from DIA headquarters. They had hardly any contact with the CIA, save for a few instances where "handoff" was required when tracking the movement of suspects into Canada. This also meant liaison with the Canadian CSIS, whom the Tall Oakers referred to as "The Burnaby Boys."

They even had a bit of interplay with local police departments—most notably the DuPont, Washington, Police Department. The liaison with police departments was mainly to coordinate arrest and search warrants, which were normally exercised by the FBI.

The agents all carried compact SIG P228 pistols, designated the M11 by the military. But they used Winchester Ranger STX 9mm hollowpoint ammunition. Even after the DCS transition, their office still bought commercial off-the-shelf (COTS) ammo. Once, that nearly cost them an inspection "gig" when an inspector *thought* that he knew a regulation that didn't exist.

For his personal use Phil bought a used, mechanically identical pistol at a gun show. Other than being made of stainless steel and having tritium night sights, it was almost identical to his issued SIG. He also bought four twenty-round factory SIG magazines to carry for his backup magazines, at his own expense. (For his quarterly shooting "quals," he used only the standard-issue thirteen-round magazines.)

Phil's position at Tall Oak was a sure means of escape from the endless merry-go-round of deployments to Southwest Asia. Although still officially in a U.S. Army Reserve Control Group, his "position in the national security interest" with Tall Oak meant that he could not be recalled to active duty for anything short of World War III.

42

MILK RUN

The necessity of procuring good intelligence is apparent and need not be further urged.

—General George Washington, then commanding the Continental Army, July 26, 1777

The McGregor Ranch, near Anahim Lake, British Columbia—Late September, the Fifth Year

The second week after Malorie arrived at the McGregor ranch, they had another raid drill. The first one had been called during breakfast, and it was both comical and slow, since they had to make two sets of tableware disappear. But this drill, which was held at 11:00 A.M., was a lightning-fast and well-orchestrated success. Malorie, Phil, the intel cardboard boxes, and the guns were closed up in the closet very quickly.

Just after Phil had emplaced the wedges "by Braille," Malorie reached out and took his hand in the darkness. A few moments later they were silently holding both of each other's hands. Then they were kissing.

Ray spoke toward the bookcase in a loud voice. "Okay, all clear. We set a new record: forty-three seconds. You can pull the wedges."

There was no response.

Ray repeated, now shouting, "I *said*, you can pull the wedges now!"

Malorie shouted, "Give us a minute. We're busy kissing."

Ray shook his head and muttered, "Well, I guess the best man won."

Phil and Malorie were married two days later. Phil explained that they'd put their relationship "on a wartime footing, with none of the usual engagement pretensions." The ceremony was conducted at the home of a retired Wesleyan minister who lived near Anahim Lake. All six of them (including Stan Leaman) squeezed into Phil's crew cab pickup for the short drive.

Running the intelligence analysis cell violated one of the basic tenets of the NLR movement: The cell had *connections* to some other cells, and hence the risk of their detection and location by counterguerrilla units was much higher. They recognized, however, that unless a few cells were willing to gather and analyze intelligence, the NLR would be far less effective. Following instructions that were frequently mentioned on shortwave radio and distributed along with resistance pamphlets, several NLR cells, such as Team Robinson, compiled intelligence spot reports in SALUTE format, detailing "The Five Ws."

One of the flyers read:

Resistance Fighters:
Your Battlefield Intelligence Is Crucial!

The intelligence that you provide will help win the war against our occupiers.

Please **do not** courier hard copies! (They are easier to find in a search, and can carry fingerprints or DNA traces.) Instead, put it on an unmarked USB memory stick ("thumb drive") with the date of your report included in the file name and then use hand sanitizer or oil to wipe off your fingerprints. (After that, handle the USB sticks only with gloves.)

How to send intelligence reports: Use SALUTE or 5Ws formats:

S

Size (Platoon? Battalion? # of vehicles, # of persons.)

A

Activity (Convoy, checkpoint, patrol, cordon, training, interrogation, relocating/evacuating citizens, etc.)

L

Location (GPS/grid coord, address, road name/#, direction, proximity to landmarks, nearest town, etc.)

U

Unit (Domestic/foreign, police, military, branch, guard/reserve, unit designation, civ supt, volunteer, uniform, vehicle stenciled bumper numbers or license plate numbers, etc.)

T

Time & Duration (Time/date group: Yr mo date 24-hr-time e.g., 20131117 0930 Mtn/Pcfc/Zulu/etc.)

E

Equipment (Weapons, equipment, supplies, vehicles, armor, etc.)

Who

(Who are you [code name]? Did you witness this yourself? Who did? Is this person credible/reliable? Who did you speak with? Who told you this? Did you get his/her contact information?)

What

(What happened? What did you see? What did you hear? What did they say to you? What was the end result? [CREATE A TIMELINE, in chronological sequence].)

Where

(Same as L [Location] in the SALUTE report. Where did this happen/is this located? What direction? Location of first and last observation? Be as precise as possible.)

When

(Same as T [Time] in the SALUTE report. Time/date and duration.)

Why

(Explanation given for activity [yours & theirs], if any. Why were you there and why did you have access to this event/information? [Passerby, observed, participated, solicited, coerced, detained, etc.])

How/How Many

(How do you know? How did they treat you? How did you re-act? How were they carrying out this activity? How many people, trucks, tents, crates, trailers, antennas, backpacks, etc.)

All files should be in standard formats, such as .doc, .rtf, .jpg, or .wav.

Lastly, <u>without compromising sources and methods or your own identity</u>, give an honest written summary of the *reliability* of your source and rate it on a scale of 1 to 10.

INCLUDE DOCUMENTATION: Photos, sketches, maps, copies of documents, videos, audio interviews, radio intercepts, or interview transcripts/notes. **SCAN THEM** and put them on the USB stick with a related file name and matching dates. Each piece of documentation should be accompanied by a description with basic 5Ws/How (or SALUTE) information. Audio files should be in .WAV file format.

Working together, with God's Providence,
Victory is inevitable
Death to the New World Order.
***They* are on the run, and *we* are on the march!**
We are the Resistance! NLR!!!

It was Stan's dairy that allowed courier drop-offs and deliveries to the McGregor ranch without much chance of being noticed, even if the courier was followed. The McGregors owned their own producing dairy cow, but the milk delivery truck would still stop five days a week and exchange a full bottle of cream for an empty bottle that was left in their oversize mailbox. Hidden beneath the mailbox, a small sheetmetal box had been constructed by Ray. This spring-loaded box, only seven millimeters deep, allowed the delivery truck driver to surreptitiously drop off and pick up USB memory sticks. The tray would hold up to eleven sticks.

43

FERTILE CRESCENT

Never tell people how to do things. Tell them what to do and they will surprise you with their ingenuity.

—General George S. Patton

British Columbia—October, the Fifth Year

The resistance war in British Columbia continued, with UNPROFOR steadily losing troops and equipment. Replacements were sporadic and never brought the units back to full strength. Morale of the French troops was deteriorating. Their road patrols became less frequent, more heavily armed, and more likely to be aborted, with an early return to base (RTB). There were very few nighttime patrols. Increasingly, the ALAT and IMa troops stayed bottled up in their compounds, and their helicopter flights became less frequent.

The few convoys that ventured out were always escorted by an APC or two or more technical trucks—pickup trucks with pedestal-mounted machine guns. Ambushing the UNPROFOR convoys was a challenge at first, but eventually the resistance cells became quite adept.

Rather than the traditional L-shaped ambush formation, the resistance adopted a crescent-shaped ambush perpendicular to a road, usually in places where the ambushers had the advantage of commanding terrain. Putting troops only on the short leg of the L and claymore mines on the long leg of the L made it easier for the ambushers to withdraw in an orderly fashion. Some of the resistance cells were large, so they could field fifteen-man ambush teams.

Many of their ambushes were devastating, and so complete that they were able to advance into the kill zone and quickly scavenge weapons and ammunition from the dead UNPROFOR troops. Most of the ambushes, however, were conducted in classic guerrilla style—a method that minimized casualties among the ambushers: pounce and retreat.

Team Robinson, with just five field fighters (and sometimes only four, depending on Alan's intermittent back problems), preferred deliberate crescent ambushes, using plenty of carefully positioned improvised claymores, which were detonated simultaneously. They used "breadpan claymores," a popular design that they heard had been developed in Idaho. Theirs used explosives salvaged from French land mines instead of dynamite.

Malorie was exhilarated by her first ambush, but seeing two running men fall after aiming her M1 Carbine at them and squeezing the trigger had a strong effect on her. It was the knowledge that she *personally* had snuffed out their lights that bothered her. To just be "someone shooting" in an ambush was one thing, but to see two of her particular targets go down, and one of them kicking after he fell, was troubling. The images of them falling plagued her dreams for weeks. Gradually, she became more inured to it, but in a way she was never the same person again. She was now a killer, but she still had a Christian conscience.

The resistance ambushes became so successful that UNPROFOR had to adopt the tactic of sending out any unarmored vehicles *only* in convoys, with a three-vehicle minimum.

Because steel cable was so ubiquitous in logging country, the resistance cells often used it to block roads at ambush sites to prevent their targets from "blowing through" an ambush.

After several weeks of recon and ambush patrols, Malorie had switched to using a captured FAMAS carbine.

44

TAKING OUT THE TRASH

I believe that being despised by the despicable is as good as
being admired by the admirable.

—Kurt Hoffman, in his *Armed & Safe* blog

Williams Lake, British Columbia—
April, the Sixth Year

Terrence Billy was an enrolled member of the Secwepemc. He had been
born into the T'exelc band and held a band card. He grew up on the Soda
Creek Reserve near Williams Lake. He liked his job with the Central
Cariboo Landfill. The job was a paid thirty-two hours a week (plus some overtime in snowy weather), had benefits, and wasn't stressful. Four days of each
week he drove the truck on regular routes. When the Crunch came, he was
"made redundant," but he had expected that. Not only was the money inflated
horribly, but everyone expected diesel fuel to become scarce. Just before he
was laid off, all of the litter cans, household rolling trash bins (called "Schaefer
Carts" in most of British Columbia), and Dumpsters were collected, hauled
to the transfer station, and stored in neat rows. It was announced that the old
landfill off Frizzi Road would be available for use, but that all families and
businesses would have to haul their own trash. Rather than using precious
fuel to haul it, most of the locals started burning their trash in rusty open-
topped fifty-five-gallon steel drums.

After his layoff, Terrence got by with hunting, fishing, and gathering bitter-
root, cattail root, Siberian miner's lettuce, bilberries, and huckleberries. He

traded the extra meat and hucks for other things he needed, such as salt and soap. He slipped into the Old Way fairly comfortably.

When the French arrived, they brought with them the new money and a steady stream of fuel tankers. The oil was produced north of Edmonton and refined on Refinery Row, east of Edmonton. The fuel and new "blue back" currency got the economy going again. Within just a few days after the gas and diesel tankers began runs to the coast, Terrence Billy got his old job back. But now it was just twenty hours a week and had no health benefits.

Like many others, he had a deep resentment of UNPROFOR, because he'd heard how they were treating some First Nations girls, turning them into sex slaves and keeping them locked up. One of those girls, his seventeen-year-old cousin named Katie, was kidnapped out of his own band. He heard that she and the others were being held in a hotel that had been converted into a brothel-prison. The former hotel was euphemistically called a *centre d'interrogation*. Terrence was also angry that public gatherings had been banned, which meant that there would be no more Secwepemc gatherings. He considered the UN's ban an affront to his culture.

UNPROFOR soon took over the Williams Lake campus of Thompson Rivers University (TRU) on Western Avenue to use as their regional head-quarters. This base covered the administrative region that stretched from the 100 Mile House to the south, Quesnel to the north, and Bella Coola to the west. The main building of the junior college—a brick structure with a graceful arched front and five pillars—had been completed in 2007. Because of the cold climate, nearly all of the college functions were integrated into that one building, with a gymnasium at the west end; offices, classrooms, labs, and a library in the center; and a cafeteria, computer lab, and trades class shops in the east end. Because it was a commuter campus, there were no dormitories.

Once the French army took over the TRU campus, there was a lot more garbage to haul. Several of the classrooms were converted into barracks rooms, and some of the faculty offices became bedrooms for officers. The cafeteria got a pair of large cooking ranges, and there were several new refrigerators and freezers installed. These appliances had been torn out of the Culinary Arts building at the TRU Kamloops campus. Trash pickups were scheduled for Tuesdays and Fridays instead of just once a week, and there were now four Dumpsters instead of two.

Terrence's brother, John, was a fishing buddy of Stan Leaman. Before the Crunch, they often fished the Upper Dean River together. They were happy to get together and just fish with traditional spin-casting gear—without all the fancy equipment and snootiness of the local fly fishermen. Stan liked the Secwepemc (also known as the Shuswap) people. They were honest and unpretentious. And a lot of them, like John, were great fishermen and hunters.

When John and Stan were doing some ice fishing on Anahim Lake in early February, John mentioned to Stan that Terrence was looking for a way to get even with the French. So while denying any involvement of his own, Stan very discreetly replied that he had a friend who was with the resistance who was "a privacy freak," and that he would be willing to meet Terrence only if he could wear a mask to the meeting. Through John, Stan scheduled a meeting with Terrence the following Saturday near Chilanko Forks, at a trailhead.

The trailhead was less than a quarter mile from the Chilanko Forks General Store. When Terrence arrived at the trail junction, he was fifteen minutes early. He sat down on a large cedar stump and rolled a cigarette. Just as he was about to light it, he heard a voice from close behind him. "State your name."

Startled, Terrence jumped up and turned around. He said, "I'm Terrence. Are you the guy?"

A voice that seemed quite close answered, "Yes, I'm the man you're supposed to meet."

Terrence Billy was confused because he couldn't determine where the voice was coming from. Then the bush fifteen feet in front of him started to move.

Ray McGregor emerged. He was wearing a shredded burlap ghillie suit, which he had borrowed from Phil.

Terrence laughed and said, "I guess I should call you 'Mr. Tree.'"

"That name will work just fine, sir."

As he walked forward, Ray said, "*Weyt-k,*" the Secwepemc word for hello.

"*Weyt-k,*" Terrence echoed back.

They now stood just two paces apart. Terrence couldn't see Ray's face through the ghillie suit's green-mottled face net. Ray said, "I'm not of the First

Nations. In fact I'm of Scots-Irish extraction, but I have respect for your people. I understand that you don't like the French and their evil deeds."

"You understand correctly. Fact is, you could say that I hate their guts. I want to make war on them."

"I heard about your cousin Katie. The UNPROFOR soldiers are world-class sicko bastards."

After a pause, Ray asked, "Are you willing to use a dump truck to deliver an explosive device somewhere? You'd set a timer and walk away."

"Skookum. Sign me up."

"Now, *wait*. You have to realize that this will be a *very big* device, so there could be collateral damage, and that after you do this, you definitely won't be able to show your face in town. You may have to hide out for *years*, or perhaps go into exile down in the States. So do you have someplace to go, and a good network with your band that can keep you supplied?"

"Yeah. My uncle has a cabin way back in the woods, outside of Dugan Lake, that he lets me use. It's a 'hike-in' cabin. You take a trail in off Horsefly Road. That cabin was grandfather-claused when the provincial forest service got set up. But a few years back, they made my uncle mad when they told him that he couldn't build a road to it. They had a hearing at the Forest Headquarters office. He told them, 'I'm an old man and getting crippled, and you tell me I can't build a road to my own cabin. You are disgraceful persons.' Anyway, he promised me the cabin after he dies. I can stay there, and I have lots of cousins that can bring me grub."

"Then I guess we can work together. But you are never to know my name— except as 'Mr. Tree'—or see my face."

Terrence laughed again, and said, "You NLR guys sure have a flair for drama."

Ray snorted and said, "Pardon my elaborate precautions. Oh, and by the way, you can call *yourself* NLR now, too. *We are* the resistance."

The truck was a 2012 Peterbilt New Way front-end loader Dumpster rig, with a forty-yard capacity. It was painted white with Central Cariboo logos on the sides. It had a Cummins 320 horsepower engine and a hauling capacity of fifteen tons, with a twenty-ton front axle and forty-six-ton tandem rear axles. The Mammoth brand front-end loader had been factory installed. Since the truck was fairly new, the forks were the only part of the truck that looked rusty and well-worn.

To gain the use of the truck, all that Terrence had to do was loosen a hydraulic line coupling slightly, just before he finished his route on Friday. The tremendous pressure generated by the hydraulic pump quickly made a mess of that side of the truck, spraying red hydraulic fluid around copiously behind the cab. When he got back to the transfer station, Terrence pointed to the truck and told his manager: "We got a leaky hose, just like the off truck used to get. I can drop it off at Haynes Machinery tonight, and they'll have someone drop me back here so I can get my car. They can fabricate a new hose for it since they're open on Saturdays. Do we have an account with them?"

"Yeah, we've got an open account," his manager replied.

Terrence gave an exaggerated nod. "Okay, no sweat, boss. I'll handle everything and head out from their shop directly to my route on Monday morning. And don't worry, I won't try to log overtime."

His manager snorted. "What overtime? The UN contract says no overtime will be paid, *period*."

Terrence parked the truck at a prearranged position, a quarter mile short of Haynes Machinery, and left the key under the floor mat. Before he walked away, he used a wrench to retighten the loose hydraulic line.

The truck never went to Haynes Machinery. Instead, at eleven o'clock that night, wearing a ski mask, Phil Adams climbed into the truck and drove it to a large shop with an RV door near the end of Western Avenue. The property had been abandoned after the owners had driven their diesel pusher RV to Montana, just as the Crunch began. Once the truck had been backed into the cavernous shop, they rolled down the door and got to work.

The explosives had been stockpiled in the shop for several months. They were stacked on pallets and covered with tarps. Packing the truck with explosives took Phil, Ray, and Stan nearly twenty-one hours, in three successive seven-hour sessions, over the course of Friday, Saturday, and Sunday nights. Stan did most of the positioning of the explosives, while Phil and Ray used a pair of dollies and a large Radio Flyer child's wagon for the many trips back and forth from the explosives pile. Nearly every item got a wrap of PETN detonating cord to ensure that they'd all explode simultaneously. They included every explosive that they could find: hundreds of recovered land mines (with their detonators removed), some mining gelignite, as well as a few dud French artillery shells, which were handled very gingerly and wedged in nose-upward. By the end of the third night, Stan's back was going into spasm.

In all, they estimated that there was ten tons on board, and even after deducting the weight of the artillery shell casings and land mine housings, there were *at least* eight tons of various high explosives.

At 10:15 on Monday morning, Terrence drove the Central Cariboo Dumpster truck to the front gate of the UN headquarters building, right on schedule. The gate guard recognized both the truck and Terrence's face and waved him through.

One Dumpster was located at a door on the north side of the building, just east of the round Gathering Place Building, which after the UN took over the campus became jokingly known by the French as the Sex and Drugs Building. This Dumpster was near the auto shop. The nearest door was marked: DOOR 5.5 (SHOP). Two other Dumpsters were located at the southeast corner of the building near Door 7. But unlike those, Door 5.5 was outside the field of vision of the gate guards.

Terrence simply backed the truck up to Door 5.5 alongside the Dumpster, using the truck's rearview camera to get the truck within a foot of the overhang. Leaving the engine running, he pulled the fuse igniter and then immediately hopped out of the cab and reached back in to jab the joystick to make it sound as if the truck was lifting a Dumpster, as usual. He ran in a sprint to the north fence. A dozen snips with a small pair of bolt cutters made a gap in the rear fence big enough for him to slip through. In his haste, he tore the shoulder of his jacket. Terrence was soon up and running.

The senior gate guard—a *caporal* with four years of service—grew impatient. He wondered why the garbage truck had not returned to the front of the building to empty the other two Dumpsters. He muttered, "*Où êtes-vous, Macaca?*"

Macaca was an epithet originally used by the French colonials to disparage the natives in the Congo, but more recently it had been applied to the aboriginals in Canada. The guard surmised that the driver was smoking a cigarette. He picked up his radio handset and hesitated. Finally, he pressed the handset's talk bar and hailed the security office in the building.

At that moment a massive explosion leveled the building, leaving just one part of the west wall standing. A sixteen-foot-deep crater marked the spot where the dump truck had been parked. The adjoining round Gathering Place Building was also destroyed. Because that building was partially earth-bermed, it left a large circular crater next to the smaller, oval bomb-blast crater. The explosion killed everyone in both buildings. It also seriously injured the gate guards and ruptured their eardrums.

The shock wave from the explosion threw Terrence off balance and made him stumble to his knees, even though he was more than 450 yards away. Looking back, he could see that the explosion was sending fragments in all directions, and it had raised a huge reddish cloud of smoke and dust. The red hue of the dust had been created by pulverized bricks. The blast wave shattered house windows in a quarter-mile radius and set off car alarms even farther out. The sound of the explosion was heard as far away as the hamlet of Riske Creek.

Terrence regained his footing and began running. It sounded as if every dog in town was barking or howling. Nearby, he heard emergency service vehicle sirens wailing. He started to sing an old Salish fight chant as he ran. His getaway vehicle was his rusting old Ford Escort, now outfitted with stolen license plates. It was parked a kilometer away at the junction of Highway 97 and Dixon Road.

Terrence quickly got on the highway and past the reservation to make the turn to Dugan Lake before any new roadblocks were set up. A woman from his band was waiting right where she promised she would be. As she got in the car, she exclaimed, "Wow, I could hear that ka-boom from here! Was that really all the way down at the TRU campus?"

Terrence nodded and said with a laugh, "Yep. Big explosion!"

Ten minutes later, he stopped three hundred meters short of the trail to his uncle's cabin and pulled his backpack and a duffel bag out of the trunk of the car. He handed the middle-aged woman the car key.

Terrence said, "Take bad care of my car for me, okay?"

"Okay. *Pútucw!*" (Good-bye.)

———

The scene around the headquarters was chaotic. Aside from the gate guards, the firefighters didn't find any survivors, only bodies in the rubble. And close to the north door, where the truck had exploded, they found only *parts* of bodies. The unofficial casualty count was 207, but it was eventually arrived at by taking the full unit rosters and deducting the number of soldiers and airmen who were at the airport or at outlying posts. Among the dead were the French brigade commander and his entire staff.

In the following five days, UNPROFOR patrols and checkpoints began hand swabbing anyone they contacted. Anyone who tested positive for explosives—and false positives were commonplace—was subjected to arrest and lengthy interrogation. It was already well established that false positives were created by soaps and hand lotions containing glycerin. Traces of fertilizer and cleaning products also gave false positives for nitrates. Two elderly residents who took nitroglycerin pills for angina also had their hands test positive. There were summary executions of five men, all aboriginal, who were suspected of conspiracy in the bombing. Two of these men had failed hand-swab tests. Only one of them was a close friend of Terrence, and none of them had anything to do with the bombing.

Terrence later learned that his small house on Proctor Street had been searched very thoroughly by a composite team of RCMP and UNPROFOR officers. They even removed many Sheetrock wall panels. The yard was scanned with a metal detector and dug up in several places, but the investigators found nothing. The UNPROFOR officer in charge then ordered the house burned. Since it was a rental, Terrence's landlord was not pleased.

Two weeks later, Terrence sent identical handwritten letters via courier to the editors of both the Kamloops and Prince George newspapers (there was no longer a newspaper published in Williams Lake). The letters read:

> Dear Editor:
> By now, you've heard that I drove the truck that carried the load of explosives to the UN HQ at the TRU Campus. Yes, I done it. I am not ashamed of what I done. Those basterds deserved it. We blew them

up with their own land-mines and artilary shells.
Serves them right! They are rapists, thiefs, and
murderers.

But I do want to say that I am sorry for all the
broken windows and the upset dogs, in town. (I hear
they barked for two days.)

Most Sincerely,
Terrence Billy, Of The Secwepemc People

UNPROFOR's censors refused to let the letters be published.

Terrence Billy was killed in a gunfight with an UNPROFOR patrol two months later, in which Terrence killed two French soldiers and wounded two others. Ironically, they never identified his body, even though he had been the prime suspect in the bombing and his photograph had been circulated widely. Following the gunfight, his body was intentionally burned in a house on Stanchfield Road near the hamlet of Miocene.

The French often found it easier for their troops to burn buildings than to haul bodies. So they systematically burned any house from which "bandit" gunfire had originated. This sent a strong message to the locals. In Fort St. James, resistance was so strong that the French army massacred more than five hundred mostly unarmed people (of a population of seventeen hundred) and burned every building in the town. Years later, when he eventually went on trial, the brigade commander lamented, "That was our Philippeville," referring to a dark day in Algerian history.

45

LE DERNIER COMBAT

One of the most dangerous errors is that civilization is automatically bound to increase and spread. The lesson of history is the opposite; civilization is a rarity, attained with difficulty and easily lost. The normal state of humanity is barbarism, just as the normal surface of the planet is salt water. Land looms large in our imagination and civilization in history books, only because sea and savagery are to us less interesting.

—C. S. Lewis

Williams Lake, British Columbia—April, the Sixth Year

In the aftermath of the UNPROFOR headquarters bombing, it was learned that most of the casualties had been support and service-support troops. These were mostly pencil-pushing clerks, paymasters, bakers, supply NCOs, mechanics, and various technicians. There were also two French Directorate of Military Intelligence (*Direction du Reseignement Militaire* or DRM) agents in the building. Those in the French contingent who survived did so by virtue of being out "on the line" when the bombing happened. These were nearly all regular combat troops. The survivors reacted with predictable ferocity. Their new battle cry was: *"Leurs têtes vont rouler"*—their heads will roll.

All of their old smiles and feigned civility were gone. The UNPROFOR *troupes de ligne* were now quick on the trigger and had zero tolerance for insolence. There were more checkpoints, more searches, more raids, more arrests, and much more torture. If anyone had doubted it before, British Columbia was now clearly under the iron heel of military occupation. They even stopped cleaning up their messes, allowing ravens to police the battlefield.

The strong resistance in the western provinces—highlighted by the Williams Lake headquarters bombing—was well publicized in the east, and consequently the level of UNPROFOR brutality was stepped up nationwide.

UNPROFOR's heightened oppression had a surprising effect: Instead of making people cower, it brought out their courage. French patrols could now expect to be sniped at wherever they went. Any UNPROFOR or RCMP vehicle left unattended would soon be firebombed or at least have its tires slashed. NLR and MOLON LABE! graffiti was spray-painted and penned almost everywhere imaginable.

Nearly everyone felt that there would soon be a general uprising, but that subtle breaking point had not yet been reached.

46

THE TRAP

Shortly before World War I, the German Kaiser was the guest of the Swiss government to observe military maneuvers. The Kaiser asked a Swiss militiaman: "You are 500,000 and you shoot well, but if we attack with 1,000,000 men what will you do?" The soldier replied: "We will shoot twice and go home."

—Historian Stephen Halbrook, as quoted by Bill Buppert
in *ZeroGov: Limited Government, Unicorns and
Other Mythological Creatures*

The McGregor Ranch, near Anahim Lake, British Columbia—May, the Sixth Year

The continuing threat of UNPROFOR's two remaining Gazelle helicopters based at Williams Lake weighed heavily on the minds of the McGregor resistance cell. The helicopters patrolled regularly, and they often engaged at any sign of activity. In several instances, woodcutters and fishermen were strafed without provocation. The FLIR sensors that they carried had been given the menacing nickname "The Eye of Sauron" throughout Canada, making helicopters greatly feared by the resistance.

Since the Gazelles sat in hardened revetments, they were invulnerable to small-arms fire. The helibase was also heavily guarded and lit with infrared floodlights. A Pilatus PC-12 patrol airplane that belonged to the RCMP at the same airport had been covertly sabotaged with a time-delay firebomb—apparently set by another resistance cell or a solo—but there had been no other successful hits in recent weeks. The Team Robinson cell spent many hours brainstorming ideas—everything from fabricating mortars to adulterating the base's deliveries of JP4 fuel. In early May, news leaked out from the airport that one of the two Gazelle helicopters at Williams Lake was grounded with engine trouble.

It was finally Phil Adams who came up with a workable plan to eliminate the remaining helicopter. Phil had spent hours poring over topographical maps, comparing them with a set of aerial photos that had been pilfered from the unoccupied BC assessment office. Much of the region was a sea of trees, dotted with occasional clearings—either angular clear-cuts or more oblong openings from lightning-sparked timber fires.

When scanning through an aerial map of the area five miles east of Nimpo Lake, Phil spotted one small clearing that was the only open ground within a one-mile radius. If they were going to have a good chance of isolating the helicopter anywhere, then this would be it. By comparing some distinctive curves of a stream bottom, he correlated the aerial photo to the topo map and was pleased to see that the opening was at the edge of a plateau, with a steep descent on one side.

He tapped on the map with a forefinger and said to himself, "Perfect."

That afternoon he brought the map and aerial photo to present his plan to Ray and Alan, who had just come in from doing some fence work. They sat down across the kitchen table wearing their socks. (Claire was strict about allowing muddy boots in the house.)

Phil began, "I think I've found a way to ambush the last functional ALAT Gazelle at the helibase. If we present them with a target that they can't engage effectively from the air, they'll probably want to insert airmobile troops or an artillery forward observer. But we've seen that the ALATs certainly don't like fast roping."

"*Mauviettes!*" Ray blurted out.

"Yep, they're wimps. Operationally, they've demonstrated that they prefer to pop into open LZs and land briefly or just hover for a few seconds to drop off troops."

Ray jumped in. "So we create an attractive target and make them want to use a nearby LZ on a promontory terrain feature that we already have covered."

"So how do we then take out the helicopter? With IEDs?" Alan asked.

"Much simpler than that: We use five-eighth-inch steel cable. There's *miles* of it available, with all of the old logging operations around here. A steel cable in the main rotor will ruin your whole day."

Ray shook his head and chided, "So we string a cable over an opening. Even if we were to paint the cable to make it blend in, depending on the lighting, they'd probably spot the cable and divert at the last minute."

Phil pointed his forefinger toward the floor and said, "Not if the cable is hidden in the grass."

Ray cocked his head. "What? How's that going to work?"

"I'll explain it all to you when we hike out there for a recon."

Rigging the LZ for helicopter ambush took some time, but the terrain was advantageous, from the size of the trees to the steep drop-off just east of the clearing. One end of the cable was attached with three cable clamps in a row, twenty-four feet up a large cedar tree on the northwest edge of the opening. The cable was left slack, so that it touched the ground at the base of the tree. It was then threaded as deeply as possible through the knee-high grass, diagonally across the middle of the oblong seventy-yard-wide opening. At the southeast side of the opening there was a large cottonwood tree with a wide fork twenty-five feet off the ground. The cable was tossed over that fork, but again left slack on the side that faced the opening. The far end of the cable was carefully aligned through the trees to a large, dying western larch tree at the edge of the drop-off.

Now came the tricky part. Using a girth strap and a pair of tree-topper's climbing spikes, Ray quickly climbed thirty-five feet up the larch, hoping that the tree wasn't rotten at the core.

Watching him climb so deftly, Phil said, "Hey, that's pretty slick. You climb with a purpose."

Ray shouted back, "Just a Jedi trick that I learned from my cousin Obi-Wan."

Phil laughed. Ray often joked about the actor Ewan McGregor, who shared their surname. He kidded about the actor being a first cousin, when he was more likely a fiftieth cousin.

Trailing from his belt was fifty feet of parachute cord. Once he'd reached the desired height, he reset his boot spikes solidly and leaned back in the strap. He felt solid, but the situation still made him nervous. Climbing a dying tree that might be rotted or hollowed out by wood ants was a dicey proposition.

He shouted down to Phil, "Okay, tie on the cable with a sheet bend and a half hitch!"

"Ummm . . . okay. What's a sheet bend?"

"You're such a rear-echelon pogue. Just use four or five half-hitches, and then stand well clear in case you screw up, so you don't put your eye out."

"Okay."

Pulling up the paracord hand over hand, Ray pulled up the free end of the cable. After untying the paracord, he flung the cable around the tree. He misjudged the length required, so he had to adjust and try twice more before he was able to grab the free end. When he finally did, the needlelike frayed end of the cable filament drew blood from the meat of his hand. (He wasn't wearing gloves because he would soon be working with the nuts on the cable clamps.) Ray visibly winced.

Phil shouted up from the ground, "Ooh, that's gotta hurt."

"Yeah, thanks for the sympathy, pal."

He pulled up the slack in the cable so there was just a slight sag in the portion that ran back to the big tree fork. Pinching the cable back on itself took the full strength of one hand, and he knew that positioning the first cable clamp and its pair of nuts would require the use of two more hands, leaving him one hand short. He had come prepared with some plastic cable ties. Pulling one of the ties tightly gave just enough tension to free up his left hand so that he could position the cable clamps. Even so, it was tricky and exhausting. He dropped two of the hexagonal nuts in the process, but fortunately he had brought spares. By the time he was done torqueing down the pair of Nylock nuts on the third cable clamp, sweat was dripping off the end of his nose.

He put the socket wrench back in his tool-belt bag, and shouted, "Okay. Done here. Coming down."

When he reached the ground, Ray said, "Okay. The North Woods Lumber-jack phase is done. Now it's your turn, Mr. Gee Whiz Explosives Expert."

Phil shook his head and said, "I'm no expert, but I think I can fake it."

Phil had already sized up the tree. It was leaning slightly downhill, which was good. Rather than attaching the explosives at the base, he opted to position them six feet up the trunk. Here, the girth of the trunk was 30 percent smaller.

The explosives they had were not ideal for the job—he would have preferred to use C4 plastic explosives—but the dynamite sticks would suffice. Phil started out by reexamining the sticks of DuPont dynamite. They were the 80 percent variety, with diatomaceous earth filler, and brown cases and red warning labels. He checked them for any signs of weeping or leaking. The cases looked dry, and that made him feel less tense.

Phil spent a few minutes whittling a stick to a fine point, smaller than a pencil. He used this to drill transverse holes in the middle of eight of the dynamite sticks. Next, he dug a claw hammer and a handful of eight-penny nails out of his pack. Walking to the uphill side of the tree, he sighted upward and aligned a nail with the cable that was stretched back toward the opening. He reached up, and standing on his backpack, he drove a nail into the trunk at a forty-five-degree angle, at nearly nine feet off the ground. The head of the nail was angled upward.

Then he walked around the tree and did his best to estimate the counterpoint of the nail that he had just driven. He used a nail point to scratch a vertical mark, six feet off the ground. He drove the nail in at that spot with just a couple of light taps of the hammer. Then he stood back to size up the positions of the two nails. He walked around the tree twice, at a distance of five paces. He judged the angle at which the tree was leaning again. Not satisfied with the position of the lower nail, he repositioned it upward four inches and two inches to the right. Then he repeated his inspection walk. Finally, he drove the second nail straight into the tree trunk, leaving just one inch exposed.

He said softly, "This'll be the center point of the lower charge."

Ray gulped and said, "Whatever you say. You're the expert." After a pause, he added, "Is this something scientific, or is this all seat-of-your-pants Kentucky windage I'm witnessing?"

Phil palmed the side of the tree twice as he answered. "A little of both,

I reckon. A lot of it will depend on just how solid the core of this tree is. I'll try to err on the side of caution, and this old boy being more stout than he looks."

He knelt and carefully threaded the end of a twenty-foot length of green parachute cord through the holes that bisected all six of the dynamite sticks. He then positioned them vertically in a flat bundle, straddling the lower nail.

"I'll hold these in place, with each of them flat against the trunk, while you give it a couple of wraps around the trunk."

Ray did as he was asked. Once the line was loosely around the tree trunk, he asked, "How tight?"

"Tight enough so that they won't budge, but not so tight that the paracord digs into the cases. I'll let you know."

Ray applied tension to the paracord as Phil watched.

Phil nodded and said, "That's good. Tie it off."

Phil then began wrapping detonating cord at a forty-five-degree angle around the trunk of the tree with the high end looped around the uphill nail and the low end of the coil passing over the sticks of dynamite. In all, he applied twelve concentric wraps of the explosive-filled detonating cord. His goal was to have the det cord cut a deep gash around the tree while simultaneously collapsing the downhill-rear side of the trunk, by means of the larger dynamite charge.

They spent another twenty minutes camouflaging their handiwork with slabs of bark (attached with commo wire) and festoons of light green old man's beard moss.

As they worked, Phil said, "You know, with tamping, we could get by with only half this much dynamite."

"Yeah, but with the charge that far up the tree, and it being on the downhill side, it would take a great big long brace to hold a box or maybe a burlap sack of tamping mud, and the sight of that would be all too obvious from the air."

"I agree."

The final step in the process was using the sharpened stick to puncture the ends of two of the dynamite sticks, and then insert a pair of electric blasting caps. Their wires were secured with plastic cable ties in place of the traditional tied girth hitches. Although these were wires connected in parallel to a piece of commo wire, they were left shunted for safety.

The commo wire was carefully routed around the small meadow and led up to an observer's position twenty-five yards east of the opening. Here, by looking straight down the length of the cable, the observer could determine the precise moment to explosively fell the larch. They were confident that the falling tree would hoist the "chopper stopper" cable to full height in just a couple of seconds.

47

THE CHEESE

Remember not only to say the right thing in the right place,
but far more difficult still, to leave unsaid the wrong thing at
the tempting moment.

—Benjamin Franklin

Near Nimpo Lake, British Columbia—May, the Sixth Year

After some discussion, it was decided that the key observer's position should be an earth-covered trench to provide thermal shielding, thus countering any use of FLIRs. They also decided to bury the commo wire just a few inches under the ground. Then two more trenches with overhead cover were constructed—one for Alan at the east edge of the opening, and one for Phil at the north end. Each of these took the four men a full day to construct and camouflage.

The "cheese" for their trap was a smoky campfire. Stan, who was the fastest runner of the three, had both the hazardous and tedious task of keeping the campfire going and walking back and forth to the cable ambush site, doing his best not to leave a trail. His hide, ninety feet north of the east end of the cable, was the only vertical entrenchment. It had a unique tablelike top cover with a waterproofed sod covering that afforded him a view of both the landing zone opening and the smoke plume from the bait camp.

Once they had the entrenchments and the "cheese" camp set up, they had

Malorie translate and transcribe a short handwritten note composed by
Claire. The original had read:

> Messieurs,
>   I am a proud loyalist. I have a reliable report that
> there is a bandit training camp being built about five
> kilometers to the northeast of Nimpo Lake. I trust that
> you will find this information useful. Amitiés.
>   —Giselle

The note, in a sealed envelope, was passed to a gate guard at the new Williams Lake UNPROFOR Headquarters (the old Service BC building on Bor-
land Street) by an eleven-year-old boy on a bicycle.

The Gazelle arrived the following afternoon. The pilot wasted no time and
began orbiting the bait camp, which was in heavy timber six hundred yards
northeast of the cable ambush opening. Predictably, as the Gazelle orbited
in a counterclockwise direction, the door gunner poured four hundred
rounds of 7.62 into the vicinity of the base of the smoke plume at the "*fromage
camp.*"

The Gazelle then swung into an even wider orbit and headed for the opening that Team Robinson had rigged. Phil waited until the helicopter slowed
and its skids were about to touch ground. The cable was about eight feet ahead
of the helicopter's nose. With a diameter of thirty-three feet, six inches, the
rotor disc made for a big target.

Phil whispered to himself, "Perfect," and twisted the handle on the ten-cap
blasting machine. The explosives at the base of the big larch tree went off with
a loud bang, and the tree fell. Before the Gazelle pilot could react, the cable
snapped up out of the grass just as planned. In an instant, the cable caught in
the rotor, the helicopter spun violently, and the three fiberglass composite rotor blades were sheared off. Two men were thrown out, and the fuselage
pitched violently over on its side. The helicopter's fuselage thrashed around
violently on the ground like a gored beast, and it spun 270 degrees before

coming to a halt. The stubs of the rotors, now hitting the ground, were further shortened as the rotor mast shuddered to a stop amid a cloud of dust, dirt clods, and tufts of grass.

One four-foot-long shard from one of the helicopter rotor blades came bouncing across the meadow directly toward Phil's hide. Though it passed harmlessly overhead, it made Phil gasp. If the shard had flown a few feet lower, his fate would have been much different.

Either the pilot had shut down the Turbomeca turbine engine, or some automatic safety feature triggered a shutdown, because it soon was quiet enough for the ambushers to hear shouts from inside the Gazelle's fuselage.

There were four ALAT personnel still onboard. The two others who had been thrown free in the crash were not moving. One of them was clearly dead—since the top half of his body was fifteen feet away from his pelvis and legs.

The fuselage was lying on its side. The shorn rotor mast had stopped spinning. A wisp of smelly white smoke was coming from the engine compartment, apparently from leaking oil that had reached something hot. The door gun's muzzle was pointed straight upward. After more shouting from inside the helicopter, the pilot, copilot, and door gunner all crawled out in rapid succession. They were apparently not badly injured in the crash. The pilot and copilot started shooting wildly at the tree line with PA-50 9mm pistols. Meanwhile, the door gunner was reaching up, attempting to detach his FN-MAG-58 light machine gun from the mount.

Phil had a good angle on the pilot, and Alan had line of sight to the copilot and door gunner. With deliberate neck shots, all three of the men were shot down and bleeding out in less than twenty seconds.

The ambushers quickly advanced on the downed helicopter, firing coup de grâce head shots once they were within forty feet. Inside, they found another crewman dead, apparently from a broken neck. His weapon was a FAMAS bullpup, but it had a bent barrel and a broken stock. They decided to bring it with them to use for spare parts.

Phil exclaimed, "Hoo boy! This is better than a box of Cracker Jacks. I always wanted an M240, and here's a MAG-58, which is almost identical."

He detached the machine gun from its dogleg mount and examined it.

Except for a scraped flash hider and a gouge in the pistol grip, the MAG had survived the crash intact. Once it was detached, it could be fired from its bipod. The door mount included a four-hundred-round ammo box of linked ammunition, but the gun could also be operated from a teaser belt and a Bulldog two-hundred-round camouflage nylon shoulder bag that they also found onboard. In addition to the four hundred linked rounds in the ammo can and the two hundred linked rounds in the Bulldog bag, there were one thousand rounds of ammo in narrow, brown-painted European-style two-hundred-round ammo cans. All of the ammo was FN-made 7.62mm NATO, a four-to-one alternating mix of ball ammo and tracers.

Ray warned, "Okay, the clock is ticking. We need to strip anything useful off this bird, burn it, and get out of here before they send anyone to investigate."

They worked quickly. There wasn't any time to remove the Gazelle's built-in avionics. They did strip a notebook and a callsign/frequency card from a clear pocket that was built into the pilot's flight suit, just above his knee. They also took a satchel that held a sectional aeronautical chart and a notebook. The loose belt of ammo for the door gun, ammo cans, six extra FAMAS magazines, the two pistols, and the broken FAMAS carbine were all distributed and stowed in their backpacks. Almost as an afterthought, Alan pulled out the helicopter's plastic first-aid chest and stuffed it into his own pack, along with one of the two-hundred-round ammo cans. Phil carried the twenty-eight-pound MAG and the Bulldog bag. Since he was also carrying his M4, his combined load was almost eighty pounds.

They walked thirty-five yards to the tree line at the north end of the opening. Phil got down prone and pulled back the cartridge from the loose end of the MAG's teaser belt and clipped on the first cartridge from the Bulldog bag. He fired two short bursts from the MAG into the Gazelle's fuel tanks. The tracer bullets (interspersed every fifth round on the belt) soon set the fuel ablaze.

A year before the Crunch, Phil had the chance to buy a nearly new semi-auto version of the M240 light machine gun, made by Ohio Ordnance Works, but he had balked at the eleven-thousand-dollar price tag. In retrospect, when the purchasing power of his savings dropped to nearly nothing and the value of an M240 soared to an incalculable level, he wished that he had bought it.

Now, with the capture of the MAG, he felt redeemed from his previous mistake.

Alan shouted, "As they often say in the French army: 'Nous devons fuir!'"

They did just that. They ran away, heading into the dense timber to the north. They didn't slow down until an hour and a half later, when they had covered five miles of rough ground.

48

EFFRONDREMENT

All tyrannies rule through fraud and force, but once the fraud is exposed they must rely exclusively on force.

—George Orwell

The McGregor Ranch, near Anahim Lake, British Columbia—June, the Sixth Year

The day of the collective disgust arrived, at last. It came immediately after a pronouncement on Progressive Voice of Canada that all residents age six years and older would have to enroll in a National Identity Card program. These new smart cards, with an embedded microchip, would be used both for identification and as a cashless debit card that would be required for all transactions over three dollars. After the announced forty-five-day enrollment period, cash transactions would be banned, as would mere possession of the old paper currency or any gold or silver bullion. All would be criminal offenses.

A rapid turn of events for the Ménard government followed. There were large street rallies in cities throughout Canada protesting the National Identity Card scheme. The crowds were ordered to disperse, but they stood their ground. Then some RCMP officers crossed the line and joined them. This proved to be a key psychological turning point. The crowds of protestors grew larger. In some cities, as the UNPROFOR troops grew weary of the standoff, they began using tear gas. But this only strengthened the resolve of the protestors.

Most of the mass protests were filmed, mainly with smartphones. Then, via satellite Internet connections that had recently been reestablished, these videos were aired on U.S. television networks. News spread that the handwriting was on the wall for the Ménard regime, which had recently been derided as "The Mauviette Union" by detractors.

The UNPROFOR troops were ordered to retreat to their garrisons. The protests then shifted from town and city squares to the perimeters of the garrisons. The citizenry created a twenty-four-hour "perimeter around their perimeter." Sensing that the scales had shifted, Ménard and his entourage panicked and fled to France on a midnight flight. Once word leaked out about this Airbus A380 flight, it was all over for both the LGP and UNPROFOR.

The UNPROFOR command in Ottawa quickly agreed to demobilization and a rapid withdrawal from Canada. Calls for war crimes trials were outnumbered by a majority (mainly in Quebec and Ontario) who favored a general amnesty and "Peace and Reconciliation" commission hearings. It took two months for most of the UNPROFOR combat troops to leave the country, and it would be six months before all of the support troops were withdrawn.

After the Ménard government's capitulation, there was not much cheering in the streets. Most Canadians simply wanted to get their lives back in order. The French minefields began to be cleared, but it was estimated that even with the meticulous emplacement maps available, the process would take five years. Commerce across the U.S. border was slowly restored, and Canadian factories gradually resumed operations. Food and fuel came first, to meet a pent-up demand. A free-floating exchange rate with the gold-backed U.S. dollar was established, and then quickly rescinded after the new Canadian dollar plummeted. The precious metals redeemable U.S. dollar very quickly became the de facto currency in Canada, as many sellers had begun refusing to take payment in Mooneys.

The citizenry fell into three categories: those who had collaborated with the Ménard government, a small minority who had actively resisted, and a majority who—though they sympathized with the resistance—had stood by and done nothing. They earned the new label "The Mundanes." The collective guilt for several years of inaction weighed heavily on the nation. Inevitably, many collaborators fled the country. But most collaborators stayed—facing humiliation but not prosecution.

49

BEIJING CHARADES

The first rule of unrestricted warfare is that there are no
rules, with nothing forbidden.

—From the treatise "Unrestricted Warfare" by Colonel Qiao
Liang and Colonel Wang Xiangsui,
People's Liberation Army (PLA) of China

The McGregor Ranch, near Anahim Lake, British Columbia—November, the Sixth Year

Three years after the liberation of the U.S. was declared and one year after the liberation of Canada, there was some startling news: Chinese ships were landing troops in Canada via the seaports of Vancouver, Bella Coola, Bella Bella, and Prince Rupert. Meanwhile, Chinese troops of the People's Liberation Army (PLA) were landing at airports in Kelowna, Edmonton, Calgary, Kamloops, and Saskatoon. Wave after wave of troops arrived before any organized resistance could be mounted.

The Chinese had the audacity to call themselves a "UN" force and fly UN blue flags. They did so because the original UN resolution that had authorized peacekeeping troops in Canada was poorly worded and open-ended. The declaration stated, "Any nation with a full UN delegation that is willing to send troops may do so, using their organic transport capability."

So now the UN was in a strange position: "UN troops" were again invading western Canada. But, in their classic debating-society style, the UN General Assembly adopted a "wait-and-see" posture, rather than condemning the

Chinese incursion. Some of the delegations reasoned that if the invasion was not immediately countered by the U.S. there might be international trade advantages in allowing the Chinese to stay.

Phil reacted to the news. "The sheer numbers are daunting. While the French had attempted to control western Canada with just a few brigades, the Chinese are pouring in corps-size formations. By the way, the Chinese use the term *brigade* to designate what most other armies would call a 'division,' and what they call a 'division' most other armies would call a 'corps.' In their mechanized infantry brigade table of organization, for example, there are four thousand soldiers.

"As near as I can determine, there is a full mechanized infantry brigade controlling a fifty-kilometer-wide swath stretching from Bella Coola to Williams Lake. Each brigade has four battalions of mechanized infantry, one battalion of tanks, one artillery battalion, one communication battalion, and one engineer battalion. Oh, I should mention that there are two different flavors of PLA mechanized infantry: one with tracked equipment and the other with wheeled equipment. And it is obvious that the one that they are garrisoning here is the wheeled variety.

"Now, assuming that they are using their published post-2006 TO&E, then within the mechanized infantry battalions, there are three companies, with three platoons per company. Each company has thirteen infantry fighting vehicles (with four per platoon) plus one command vehicle. Now, the artillery brigade has seventy-two PLZ89 122mm self-propelled guns, and their tank battalion has ninety-nine Type 96 main battle tanks.

"So, *not even counting the tanks*, we're talking about a total of 156 APCs in just our sector. That means we're facing more *armored* APCs on the ground than the French had fielded vehicles of *all* descriptions—of which half were merely stolen pickup trucks that were turned into technicals. Add to that another ninety-nine tanks? That is a Schumer-load of armor."

He paused to let his words sink in, and then continued. "The bottom line is that we simply *cannot* fight the Chinese the same way we fought the first UNPROFOR."

Alan said, "I think they plan to treat Canada just as they have much of Africa, as a colonial strip mine. They want all of our mineral wealth, and they want our timber. Why else would they be here in force?"

The PLA timed their invasion of Canada for the period just after UNPROFOR's capitulation, but before a Canadian Defense Force could be reestablished. China recognized that it was in a nuclear stalemate with the United States. Both nations had nukes, but both were reluctant to use them for fear of escalation to a full-scale exchange. The Beijing government, therefore, felt that they could get away with invading western Canada. Their plan was to seize all of the provinces from Saskatchewan westward, and then bargain for permanent occupation and a peace settlement with the Toronto government.

As one well-known political and international affairs blogger put it, "So the Chinese position is simple: 'We take western Canada and keep it for our own. And if you play nice, then we promise not to nuke you.'"

When the Chinese arrived in western Canada, they had expected a level of resistance similar to what they had encountered in Africa, but they were in for a rude surprise. Not only did the resistance cells that had fought the French UNPROFOR troops have plenty of experience, but they were now very well equipped, with large quantities of captured weapons, ammunition, and night vision gear. Much of that gear was widely distributed in homes, farms, and ranches. (After the French had surrendered, the new status symbol for Canadian ranchers was to have a captured UN armored vehicle in their machine sheds, alongside their tractors.)

The Chinese had few friends waiting for them in Canada. They were almost universally despised. Even the majority of the large Chinese immigrant population hated them, since the PLA represented everything that the immigrants had left behind when they fled China.

Six weeks after the Chinese arrived, Malorie had switched from carrying her FAMAS to a captured Chinese 5.8mm carbine. Her new weapon was a QBZ-95 (Type 95 automatic rifle). Like the FAMAS, this was a bullpup-style carbine manufactured by Norinco. It shot the Chinese 5.8x42mm cartridge, which, up until the Crunch, was only rarely exported, and only for military contracts.

The PLA's experience in invading Africa had helped ready them for their planned Canadian invasion. They had become accustomed to operating with a long logistics "tail," ranging over long distances with limited resupply. The majority of their tanks, APCs, and trucks were retrofitted with trundle racks to hold fuel cans, giving their vehicles "longer legs." While this increased their vulnerability, the longer-range capability was a must. And, since Canada was viewed by Chinese strategic planners as a vast, underpopulated expanse, it was decided that all of the vehicles sent to Canada should be similarly outfitted for long range. (The PLA borrowed the aviation term "radius of action" in their ground-combat doctrinal treatises.)

50

BLINDING FLASH

I believe that liberty is the only genuinely valuable thing
that men have invented, at least in the field of government, in
a thousand years. I believe that it is better to be free than to be
not free, even when the former is dangerous and the latter
safe. I believe that the finest qualities of man can flourish only
in free air—that progress made under the shadow of the policeman's club is false progress, and of no permanent value. I
believe that any man who takes the liberty of another into his
keeping is bound to become a tyrant, and that any man who
yields up his liberty, in however slight the measure, is bound
to become a slave.

—H. L. Mencken

United States Phil Bucklew Naval Special Warfare
Center (NSWC), Naval Amphibious Base Coronado,
California—July, the Eleventh Year

The air-conditioning unit was not working, but as was the tradition in the
U.S. Navy, adverse environmental conditions were not an excuse to
cancel or reschedule training. Rather, they were considered "an opportunity to excel." It was ninety-five degrees Fahrenheit in the classroom. The
video that they were watching was on improvised explosives and incendiary
devices. A lot of the Basic Underwater Demolition/SEAL (BUD/S) students
were not paying close attention to the film. They were now in the final days of
phase three (land warfare) of their twenty-four-week course and feeling

confident that they would beat the odds, graduate from the course, and go on to a SEAL team assignment. Many of the students were slumped in their chairs, daydreaming about cold bottles of beer. As Petty Officer Third Class (PO3) Jordan Foster was watching the video, his mind began to wander. He thought about his cousins in Regina, Saskatchewan, and he pondered their situation living first under the French Army occupation, and now under the Chinese Army occupation. He wondered how they might be fighting back. As the training film was showing a time-delay thermite incendiary device, an idea popped into Jordan's head. He sat bolt upright in his chair, and a scatological expression escaped his lips. He stood up and walked briskly to the door. His instructor had been standing in the back of the classroom, doing his best to stay awake. Noticing the petty officer's odd behavior, he followed him out the door, close behind. Once they were outside, the bright sunlight made them both blink.

"What's the matter, trainee? You know, it's not too late to disqual you and send you back to the fleet. Can't take the heat, pogue? Attitude problem?"

"No, sir! With your permission, I need to diagram something for you."

Jordan pulled a notebook and pen from the breast pocket of his utilities. He began sketching a long, cylindrical object.

Jordan described it as he drew. "Sir, this may not be an original idea, but I believe that its potential application may be. Here we have a hermetically sealed cylinder, say, forty millimeters in diameter and about a half meter long. A full pound of thermite is in the bottom two-thirds of it, a time-delay electronic timer just above that, and a spring-loaded sleeve at the top end."

The instructor removed his BUDS baseball cap briefly to wipe his brow. He asked, "What the flying fig is this all about, trainee?"

"Canada, sir. Reliberating Canada!"

51

PROJECT JORDAN

For by wise counsel thou shalt make thy war: and in multitude of counsellors [there is] safety.

—Proverbs 24:6 (KJV)

United States Phil Bucklew Naval Special Warfare Center (NSWC), Naval Amphibious Base Coronado, California—July, the Eleventh Year

Two hours after PO3 Jordan Foster had his flash of brilliance, his invention diagram was reviewed by a UDT lieutenant commander staff officer with SEAL Team Seven, also at NAB Coronado. Recognizing its potential utility, he wasted no time and picked up a STU phone to call one of his old classmates, who was now a paramilitary operations officer with the CIA Special Activities Division (SAD)—the action arm of the National Clandestine Service, in Virginia.

Three days later, "Project Jordan" went into formal planning. The first prototype "Pogo Stick" was built one month later and was approved for final design review and production soon after, under a classified Presidential Decision Document (PDD) finding. It was decided early on that the devices would be built with all-commercial off-the-shelf components so as to be untraceable. Ironically, their PROM timer chips had all been manufactured in China before the Crunch. The key component in the thermite igniters had also originally been made in China but was marketed by the Estes Rockets company as model rocket engine "Solar Igniters." Full-scale production began in

October, and the production run of eight thousand units was completed in
January.

The Pogo Sticks began arriving in Canada in February. Some were
parachute-dropped by B2 stealth bombers while others were infiltrated by
land or sea in civilian craft. In one case, they were transported via hermetically sealed containers on the Multi-Mission Platform on a stealthy U.S. Navy
nuclear Seawolf-class submarine.

The Pogo Stick incendiary devices were all timed to burn at 1212 hours on
December 12—nearly a year after their manufacture. They were not pro-
grammable. To enable them, the upper sleeve needed to be depressed by one
inch (or more). If the sleeve was left fully extended, they wouldn't function.
Alternatively, the spring could be removed from the sleeve cap, so that the
sticks became armed without being under tension. They couldn't be more
simple or foolproof.

They were designed to fit in a standard twenty-liter Chinese "Big Mouth"
plastic fuel can. These ubiquitous cans were used for gasoline, diesel fuel, and
kerosene. They were quite similar in design to the Scepter cans widely used by
the U.S. and Canadian militaries.

Prototype tests had shown that if a Pogo Stick was placed in a fuel can
filled with diesel, when the timer went off a stream of molten thermite would
quickly burn through the bottom of the can and still have the exothermal energy to burn through fourteen millimeters of plate steel beneath. Then, depending on the width of the air gap, up to twelve liters of flaming diesel fuel
would follow down the hole that had been cut by the burning thermite. Alternatively, if a Pogo Stick was placed in a fuel can filled with gasoline, there
would be a flaming explosion with a twenty-foot-diameter fireball.

Inserting a Pogo Stick took just a few seconds. Because they were spring-
loaded and because there were internal tapers on the top and bottom of the
fuel cans, the top of a Pogo would automatically wedge itself into the far corner of a can, where it could not be seen through the open spout hole.

The Chinese did not trust Canadians around their vehicles (for fear of sabotage), but it had become the norm in the lengthy occupation to send out all
of their empty fuel cans to commercial fuel stations for refilling. Because the
Pogo Sticks would be inserted incrementally, there would be no way of knowing whether any particular can had already been rigged. So a discreet stripe

drawn with a felt-tip marker underneath the triple carry handles on the cans was devised.

Although not all of the commercial fuel contractors were "in the loop" and supplied with Pogo Sticks, more than 60 percent of them were. Between March and August, the resistance rigged the majority of fuel cans in most of the Chinese-held Canadian provinces and territories. Always well regimented, the PLA had a policy of rotating their stocks of stored fuel, so that it would not go bad in storage, and this policy was enforced quite stringently in Canada, partly as an "antisabotage measure." As a result, even though it was more laborious, their SOP was to always use gas in cans *first* before filling vehicle tanks directly from pumps. This meant that eventually the resistance would get their hands on nearly every Chinese fuel can in many regions.

Then, in September, the resistance had a major coup. In the Northwest Territories, a part of Canada where Pogo Sticks had become available only late in the game, three boxcars full of brand-new empty fuel cans were received from China, all with yellow cap straps—designating them for use with diesel fuel. With the impetus of a kickback payment from a fuel contractor, the regional logistics coordinator was convinced that the new cans should be distributed *full* of fuel. This gave the contract operator the chance to insert Pogo Sticks in every one of those fuel cans.

52

TIEBREAKER

Most people can't think, most of the remainder won't think,
the small fraction who do think mostly can't do it very well.
The extremely tiny fraction who think regularly, accurately,
creatively, and without self-delusion—in the long run, these
are the only people who count.

—Robert A. Heinlein

Prince George, British Columbia—September, the Eleventh Year

The first wave of China's invasion had largely ignored the importance of the Canadian rail network. But in the second wave, the Chinese clearly planned to use the railroads extensively to "vigorously extract" Canada's mineral and timber resources. Some key mineral resources were the zinc, lead, copper, and molybdenum mines in British Columbia and the base-metals mines of Ontario, the Yukon Territory, and British Columbia. With many decades of reserves, the Leduc oil fields and the more recently exploited oil sands in Alberta were also considered strategic. Saskatchewan also held uranium and the world's largest deposits of potash. The gold mines in northern Saskatchewan and British Columbia were considered plum prizes, especially the extremely rich Eskay Creek gold-silver mine. The former Nickel Plate gold mine in British Columbia was reopened. There was also diamond ore to be exploited up in the Northwest Territories and Nunavut.

Although Canada had no bauxite reserves, the Chinese had plans to expand

British Columbia's aluminum industry, to take advantage of the region's plentiful hydro power. The bauxite ore would be hauled by ship from their newly seized mines in Guinea and brought across the Pacific to Vancouver.

Because China and Canada used the same standard "1435" rail gauge— 1,435mm (or four feet, eight and a half inches)—their rolling stock was mostly compatible. (Their car couplings and brake hose fittings were different, but they had brought plenty of adapters.) Within the first week of the Chinese invasion, Chinese rail speeder trucks were seen operating. A few weeks later, there were Chinese-built switch engines and flatcars in operation that came in through the Port of Vancouver, which was accessible by railcar ferry ships. The PLA commandeered all of the railroad rolling stock that was within their reach.

The hundreds of miles of rail lines that connected Jasper to Prince Rupert and Jasper to Vancouver were repeatedly severed by the resistance. Both the Canadian Pacific Railway (CPR) and Canadian National (CN) rail lines were broken, often for days or weeks at a time. Harassing fire on the crew responding to the first break changed everything. They insisted on having security posted before they would go out for another repair. This added several days to all subsequent repairs, since PLA forces had to be sent out in advance to set up a security perimeter.

Most of the rail breaks were made on curved sections of tracks, over trestles, and on grades to make repairs more difficult. Explosives and thermite were used sparingly in destroying tracks. The resistance found that "borrowed" Cat D8 or Komatsu D155 bulldozer could do the same work, leaving their initially small supply of donated, improvised, and stolen explosives and incendiaries for more important uses—primarily for targets that were under active guard.

The resistance also had hopes of derailing trains, but modern rail-signaling technology often prevented this. Electrical continuity checks detected breaks in the rail miles in advance of approaching trains. The resistance cells learned to overcome this technology in two different ways. First, if they blew up tracks immediately in front of a train on a curve, there was no way that a train could come to an immediate stop. (Stopping distances for laden trains at full speed were measured in *miles*, not feet.) Second, they learned to use heavy-gauge electric cable to "splice" circuit continuity, so that if a section of rail was loosened, it would still show a complete circuit.

Inevitably, the industrious Chinese began repairing the rails nearly as quickly as the scattered resistance cells could break them. The war against the rails had reached a stalemate. While the resistance succeeded in *degrading* the efficient use of the railroads, they could not quite *deny* them to the Chinese.

Alan McGregor, who was an avid reader of U.S. Civil War and American frontier books, came up with an invention that would almost permanently deprive the Chinese use of one long stretch of railroad from Prince George to the outskirts of Vanderhoof. His brilliant idea, "The Claw," was based on accounts that he had read of the Union army's destruction of Confederate railroad lines.

They chose the section of track that meandered west from Prince George through the mountains because it was a single track. With no redundancy in this segment, destroying just one track would completely deny the PLA the use of that route.

Guyot Railway and Engine Maintenance, Ltd., was a family-run business that had been in operation since 1939. They mainly did railway maintenance, but they were also set up for engine and railcar repairs. Their long rectangular shop had two sets of rails running straight through it.

The centerpiece of the shop in Prince George was a 180-ton-capacity overhead rail-mounted crane that straddled the inside of the building. Most frequently it was used for lifting railcars off their four-wheel and six-wheel bogies (also called trucks) so that the undercarriages could be repaired or replaced. Up until the Crunch, the big crane had been used to lift entire engine and motor units out of diesel-electric locomotives. After the Crunch, however, with currency fluctuations, erratic train scheduling changes, and uncertain payments from CN Rail, the Guyot company had laid off most of its work crew. Under their new contract with the Chinese, they didn't do much more than track repairs, minor engine repairs, lower-level (but still heavy) railcar repairs, and putting on four-hundred-pound car adapters.

Unlike most European nations, which had long since converted to the use of concrete railroad ties, Canada's western railroads still used wooden ties quite extensively. In Canada there were typically three thousand wooden ties per mile of track. Alan preferred to use the British Empire term *sleepers* instead of *ties*.

Even without the weight box, the Claw weighed nearly two tons. It had originally been a piece of open-pit mining equipment called an Alternate Drag—a cable-dragged rock ripper used by a coal mine operator for the times when their excavations hit a layer of hard shale. Its cross section was much like that of a traditional farming plow, but scaled up by a factor of four. The blade was twelve feet long, six feet tall, thirty-eight inches wide at the rear, and just two inches wide at the front.

The Claw's plow blade was expertly recontoured into an axelike blade and a notch to tailor it for cutting railroad ties at a precise depth below the wheels. The new tie-cutting notch was reinforced with dozens of successive rows of TIG welds. Honing the Claw's notch and point took nearly seven hours and burned up fourteen abrasive cut-off wheels in the process. This was followed by flame hardening, quenching it with water from a hose, and then annealing it with a second application of heat from a torch.

The Claw was attached to a double set of six-wheel trucks that had been salvaged from both ends of a scrapped intermodal well car. Atop this was a massive framework holding the Claw, and above that was welded a deep C-shaped metal box, which held twenty-seven tons of assorted scrap steel that had been laboriously hauled from the Guyot shop scrap pile. This enormous weight was designed to keep the wheels from jumping off the tracks once the Claw dug in. Their hope was that despite the tremendous vertical and lateral forces generated by the Claw, the great weight of the twelve-wheeled apparatus would keep the wheels on the tracks.

The Claw could be raised only by a pair of hydraulic pistons that had originally been mounted on a Case IH LRZ 150 front-end loader tractor. The pistons were simplistically set up for "one-time use"—meaning that they could be raised only using an off-board hydraulic pump at the railway shop.

They backed a coupled trio of SD70M-2 engines into the shop. These engines still had mostly Canadian crews but per PLA orders there was always at least one armed guard on each train that was "in motion." (The guards usually came in pairs.) Once the engines were turned over to the shop for repairs, they were "out of sight, out of mind," and left unguarded.

Like the rest of CN's rolling stock, these three engines had been commandeered by the Chinese in the first few weeks of the invasion and crudely re-painted in PLA colors (black with red trim) with a PLA logo on the front, the ubiquitous "Eight One" (in *hanzi* logogram characters).

The three train engines had all come into the Guyot shop over the course of the four preceding days on various repair pretenses that had been faked by resistance operatives. (The PLA rail transport coordinator had been lulled into the habit of taking all repair paperwork at face value.) One of the three work orders read: "Replace Broken Turbo-Entabulator."

The three engines were the SD70M-2 model, a powerful DC traction engine that had been built from 2005 up until the Crunch and widely used. Canadian National had 190 of them. They were all equipped with the 16-710G3C-T2 prime mover, which was rated at 3,200 kilowatts, which equated to 4,300 horsepower, generating 113,100 pound-feet of continuous tractive effort, and 163,000 pound-feet of starting effort.

The resistance consulted two structural engineers to calculate the energy needed to break up the ties. Their final estimate was that it would require around 250,000 pound-feet of force on level ground, which meant they'd need the combined power of three locomotive engines.

The most complicated part of the planned rail sabotage operation was not constructing the Claw itself. Rather, it was making all of the arrangements to spirit away the Guyot employees and their families, finding them jobs under assumed names where they could be put in hiding for the duration of the conflict. At the same time that the Claw apparatus started ripping its way west, all five of the Guyot employees and their families were on a bus headed east to Calgary.

Just before the planned midnight departure of the engines, Alan met with Larry Guyot. The two men prayed. The three engines pulled out of the Guyot shop on the dedicated spur line to the main line, heading west. Just past the switch, Larry gave Alan his final directions. He then jogged back to the workshop.

Alan watched his wristwatch carefully. At exactly two minutes past midnight, he gave two toots of the engine's air horn and advanced the slaved trio of engines to full throttle. The dead-man's vigilance alert system as well as the dead-man's foot pedal had already been fully bypassed by one of the Guyot employees. Alan quickly walked forward to the engine's front steps.

When the engines reached what felt like five miles an hour, Ray hit the release lever for the hydraulics. As soon as he saw that the Claw was dropping, he immediately hopped off the Claw assembly's small forward platform and tumbled to the ground beside the tracks.

After gouging the top of the ties for the first thirty feet, the Claw finally bit down and caught beneath the ties. It immediately began loudly snapping the ties, one after another, with ferocity. They were amazed to see that instead of slowing down, the trio of engines continued to accelerate. The noise was tremendous.

As the engines approached seven miles an hour, Alan leaped from the bottom step of the front stairs of the forwardmost engine and rolled down the ballast. He banged his right knee in the process. Just as the old man regained his feet, the Claw came ripping past him, sending shards of creosote-impregnated tie wood and a spray of ballast rocks painfully against his legs.

His son walked up to him and they stood side-by-side, watching the destruction of the tracks ahead of them in the moonlight and listening to the cacophony of the uneven rending and snapping of ties. It sounded like an enormous deck of cards being shuffled. All of this was accompanied by the roar of the three engines. As the ballast rocks were shattered and struck each other, they threw off a strange blue-green brisance that formed a halo-like glow around the Claw. The Claw itself had already heated up so much that it started throwing sparks as well.

As the noisy contraption drew farther away, Ray shook his father's hand and shouted, "Well, Dad, you've really done it this time. You are the Master of Disaster."

Back at the Guyot shop building, there was the sound of rending steel and the whine and clanking of the overhead crane that had just destroyed its own undercarriage and one corner of the building.

Ray supported Alan McGregor as he hobbled back to where the Claw had first dug in. The gash between the rails behind them was tremendous. Both rails were tipped up at a thirty-degree angle, and chunks of broken ties stuck up at odd angles. They were startled to see that at the transition between the undisturbed ties and those that had been broken, the rails were each literally twisted outward almost forty-five degrees.

Stan's pickup came up alongside them on the wayside service road. Stan shouted, "Hop in, guys! If we stay here, we'll be in a world of hurt."

Alan slowly reached the door of the truck, and Ray helped him get in.

In the aftermath, the distance that The Claw had traveled amazed everyone. Even their most optimistic predictions were for the destruction of ten to fifteen miles of track before it either fell apart or came off the rails. But the contraption continued, ripping up tracks relentlessly. From a distance it looked like an enormous zipper had been opened. After reaching a speed of twenty-seven miles per hour on level ground, the apparatus slowed to just twelve miles per hour on some of the steepest grades. With the tremendous power of the engines, the Claw still motored on, mile after mile. Finally, after ripping up the track for almost fifty-eight miles, the growing heat and cumulative fatigue of the steel in the Claw became too great. Now glowing deep orange along its full length and bright yellow at its notch, the Claw finally sheared away, leaving the lower portion embedded in the ballast.

The three engines picked up speed after that. By the time they passed through Vanderhoof, they were going sixty miles per hour. Two miles west, the trio was up to 105 miles per hour and ran off the rails when they came to a sharp left-hand curve, just past the Highway 27 overcrossing. All three engines and the Claw assembly came to rest in a surprisingly neat row. It was only after the engines had tipped over that mercury safety switches triggered relays to shut down the electric motors and diesel engine units.

When the first PLA officers arrived at the scene of the wreck, they found that the broad top rim of the Claw's counterweight box had been emblazoned with raised beads from an arc welder. They read NLR! on both sides, BEWARE THE CRAW! on the forward rim, and DEFILE YOUR ANCESTORS TO THE EIGHTEENTH GENERATION on the back rim.

In the aftermath of the Claw's track sabotage, it was estimated that 57.8 miles of track were rendered useless and that 173,400 ties had been snapped in half. Most of the rail was badly bent—particularly on curves—so that it could not be reused. Since nearly all of the rail had been welded together, it would have to be cut into sections before it could be removed and replaced.

The enormous length of unzipped track was the most beautiful mess that Alan McGregor had ever seen.

The escape of the Guyot shop families was nerve-racking, but successful. In the hours preceding the Claw's track sabotage, the employees spent several hours destroying the big lathes and the shop's other heavy equipment with cutting torches. Then all of them except Larry went home to their families to prepare for their imminent departure.

They had already rigged the crane to self-destruct. The crane had tremendous lifting force available. It was fairly simple to pay out all two hundred feet of cable, loop three wraps of the end of the cable around the crane's own T-shaped wheeled undercarriage, and then connect the snatch block to the I-beam post at the northwest corner of the building.

The original plan was to somehow replace the crane's momentary on-off switch with a continuously on switch. But since the combined skills in the shop were more mechanical than electrical, they opted instead for the expedient of fabricating a clamp that would hold the green Lift button fully depressed.

As soon as Larry Guyot heard Alan toot the train's horn, he triggered the crane Lift button, affixing it in the fully depressed position with the clamp fixture. The slow, high-torque crane began pulling in the nearly two hundred feet of slack cable as Larry ran for his car. He had already accelerated his Dodge to forty-five miles per hour and was a half mile down the road when the cable finally pulled taut. The gantry crane then folded itself in half and collapsed the front of the building. When the snatch block reached the motor housing, the tremendous force of the motor snapped the steel cable. The stub end of the cable in the cable housing made a loud "thunk" once every four seconds, until the motor was finally turned off by the first fireman to arrive at the crumpled building.

The charter bus was idling and had its door open when Larry pulled up. They heard a siren in the distance. He jumped out of his Dodge and leaped aboard the bus, and it started to roll forward even before the hydraulic door had completely closed. Larry's brother was at the wheel of the bus. He was wearing an N95 respirator.

Larry's wife, wearing a nurse's uniform and also wearing an N95 respirator, gave him a hug. The families cheered as the bus rolled out toward the Yellowhead Highway.

They carried with them two forged letters that were designed to get them past PLA checkpoints on their intended route. The first letter was an official-looking document that certified that the passengers onboard the bus were residents of Olway (just west of Prince George) who were quarantined H7N9 influenza patients being transported to an infectious disease ward at the seven-hundred-bed Foothills Medical Centre, in Calgary.

Just as they hoped, the mere sight of the mask-wearing nurse and the words *influenza* and *quarantine* were enough to get the guards at two highway checkpoints to quickly wave the bus through.

From Prince George the bus drove six hours southeast to the Highway 11 junction. Once they were there, the respirators and the nurse's uniforms were hidden, and the second letter was readied. They stopped briefly to switch the license plates on the bus.

They continued, carrying a forged RCMP letter identifying them as wedding guests from the vicinity of Eckville traveling to the town of Smoky Lake (north of Edmonton) to attend a wedding. (Weddings were one of the few exceptions to PLA's "no public gatherings" rule but required official travel documents.) This letter successfully bluffed them through three more checkpoints.

At 4:30 P.M. local time they reached their actual destination, Fort McMurray, in the heart of Alberta's Athabasca oil sands region. They had been on the road for fifteen and a half hours and were near the end of the bus's one-thousand-mile driving range. Seven cars, vans, and pickups were waiting to shuttle the Guyot families to their new homes and jobs, under assumed names, at the Suncor Mine. The mine was part of the recently reemerging oil industry in Alberta. The Suncor operation was already back up to twenty thousand barrels of production per day, with plans for much larger production in the months to come. (Back before the Crunch, Suncor's Mackay River plant had produced thirty-four thousand barrels per day, and had plans to eventually produce three times that much. In anticipation, there had been a lot of "spec" housing built, which now was mostly vacant. The Guyot families ended up in these houses.)

After their baggage had been unpacked, the bus was immediately driven by a resistance man to the Suncor Fort Hills mine, where it was parked next to an enormous overburden pile. There, the conveyor belt arm was shifted temporarily to direct the flow over the top of the bus. They ran the conveyor for three hours, burying the bus under thirty feet of overburden soil and rock. The bus was never seen again.

DRM investigators quickly made the link from the Guyot shop to the "quarantine bus" described by the *Sécurité Routière* sentries, but they lost track of it from there. Their fruitless search for the saboteur families centered on Calgary.

The FM radio network—which had recently been renamed People's Voice of Canadian Liberation (PVCL)—downplayed the severity of the rail sabotage, referring to it only as "a temporary railway disruption, west of Prince George."

Larry worked under the name Larry Gwinn for many years, eventually reaching middle management with Suncor. His role in the Claw sabotage plot was not publicized until after his death in 2047.

53

NI HAO

When written in Chinese, the word "crisis" is composed of two characters—one represents danger, and one represents opportunity.

—John F. Kennedy, "Convocation of United Negro College Fund"

Forty-eight Miles East of Bella Coola, British Columbia—November, the Eleventh Year

Alan and Claire borrowed Ray's pickup to go buy supplies in Bella Coola. They were hoping to spend some of their Chinese Occupation Scrip before it lost much more of its value to inflation. (Since the Chinese arrived, the new currency had already lost 70 percent of its value.)

The pickup hit a patch of black ice in a shady stretch of road and spun out. There was no damage, but it ended up perpendicular to the road, nose down in the borrow-pit ditch on the right side of the road. The slope of the ditch was quite steep. Alan put the pickup in four-wheel drive before attempting to back up, but the tires immediately cut through the thin crust of frost into the soft mud beneath. Experience told him that continuing his attempt to drive out would only dig his wheels in deeper, so he shut down the engine.

Alan said resignedly, "Prepare for a long, chilly wait, my dear."

He stepped out of the cab and messily made his way up out of the muddy ditch. Now standing at the back of the truck, Alan lifted the camper shell's glass and then flipped down the tailgate. He could see that Ray carried his usual oiled twenty-five-foot tow chain in a plastic box strapped with a bungee cord in the front end of the pickup bed. Along with it was a well-worn rectangular laundry detergent bucket filled with traction sand, an axe, a come-along, a short D-handle shovel, a hank of rope, a folded tarp, and a sheepherder's jack. All of this gear was neatly secured by bungee cords. Seeing this assortment of gear made Alan smile. His son was prudent and methodical, just like him. He had raised him well.

Alan's boots were a muddy mess, so he stretched out prone to reach down to the tow-chain box. Pulling the heavy box with him as he inched his way back up and out of the pickup bed strained his back. He muttered to himself, "Here we go again."

Alan often reinjured his back, and recovery from each injury could last weeks; each episode began with two or three days of his back muscles in painful spasm. Taking valerian root helped reduce the muscle spasms and magnesium pills helped limit the inflammation. But each injury tested his patience; he was a man who didn't like to slow the pace of his daily chores. Alan carefully set the tow-chain box on the lip of the icy road, careful not to further injure his back. He leaned back in on the lip of the open tailgate and waited.

Claire cranked down her window slightly and asked, "Are you all right?"

"Not exactly. I tweaked my back again. Getting old really stinks, you know that?"

Claire rolled up her window and began to hum the tune to the gospel song "This World Is Not My Home."

Alan wondered how long he would have to wait until someone with a stout vehicle would come by and help tow them out. He reached into his coat's front snap pockets and pulled out his camouflage hunting gloves and his green pile cap. After donning them, he let out a sigh.

The sun's direct rays were beginning to strike the pickup. It was a cold morning, but the fog was beginning to lift. The landscape now lacked its recent autumn beauty. The aspens had lost their leaves, and the western larches had lost their needles. The dense fir trees on both sides of the highway still looked beautiful, wearing a coat of frost. Where the sun was hitting them, mist was rising from their boughs. He concluded that it was a still a scenic place to be stuck in a ditch.

A few minutes later, he heard a low rumbling accompanied by a higher supercharger whine from the east. Soon it became distinct: the sound of numerous vehicles in a convoy. In another minute, they came into sight. It was a convoy of four Norinco Type 92 wheeled six-by-six APCs followed by a canvas-topped Dongfeng 2.5-ton troop truck.

Alan shouted to Claire, "A Chinese patrol. What do you want to bet they'll just wave and offer us no help whatsoever?"

Claire rolled down her window slightly and shouted back, "What if they search us?"

"They won't find diddly-squat. But don't be surprised if they rough us up. You know they've been pretty brutal with folks they've encountered outside of city limits recently. So be ready for that."

She shouted back one of her favorite sayings: "We have nothing to fear in this world. This world is not our home."

The convoy slowed to less than twenty miles an hour. Once they were within one hundred yards, Alan began to wave, flagging them down.

Mistaking the McGregors' spun-out truck as a ploy for a road ambush, the PLA's first lieutenant in the lead APC ordered a herringbone deployment using his radio handset. Once the APCs had splayed out, he shouted, "Attack!"

The gunners on the first three vehicles opened fire with four machine guns—a type 67 (7.62x54r) and three Type 77 heavy machine guns (12.7mm DShK variants). After shooting Alan and shredding the pickup, the gunners on all four APCs engaged the tree line on both sides of the road with seven machine guns, mostly with fire from the Type 77s. By chance, one of the 12.7mm rounds detonated an old French land mine. This excited the gunners, and they fired even more frenziedly. The young second lieutenant commander in the second APC in the column even ordered his 25mm main gun to open fire where the mine had gone off. Finally, the convoy commander ordered a cease-fire using both his radio and his APC's public address loudspeaker.

The PLA later logged the incident as a "thwarted ambush, with PLA prevailing. Two insurgents killed. No PLA casualties or damage." They also dispatched an Explosive Ordnance Disposal (EOD) team to map the land mines. The Chinese usually just mapped French minefields, rather than going to the trouble of disarming and removing them.

The Chinese did not bother to collect Alan's and Claire's bodies, or to tow away Ray's pickup truck. They simply dragged Alan's body to the side of the road and rolled it down the borrow-ditch slope. Stan Leaman's father discovered the scene several hours later and relayed the sad news to Ray. It was Ray, Phil, and Malorie who came to collect the bodies. By the time they arrived, a pair of gray jays was already pecking at Alan's body and ravens were starting to congregate nearby. Ray shouted and scared off the birds. Then he sat down near his father's body and sobbed.

They had brought several tarps to help them collect the bodies. Phil fought back tears as he wrapped up Claire's lifeless figure. Malorie helped him carry it up from the pickup. The corpse was placed in the back of Phil's pickup. By then, Ray had regained some of his composure, and he helped them wrap up his father's corpse in several rolls of a twelve-by-twenty blue tarp. After the three of them carried Alan's shrouded corpse to rest alongside that of his wife, Ray said to Phil, "Please see what you can salvage from my truck. I don't want to look in the cab."

The interior of the pickup was drenched with blood and the truck was thoroughly riddled with holes. All four tires and the spare had been punctured. All that they could salvage was the Hi-Lift Jack and the axe from the back end of the truck. The shovel's blade and handle had both been penetrated by 12.7mm bullets. From the glove box, they got a handful of road maps and a flashlight. They also took the tow chain, which was still in its box by the side of the road, surprisingly untouched by bullets.

The ravens had flown off, but the gray jays lingered, hopping around in a nearby larch tree. The birds seemed curious about what Ray and the others were doing.

As Phil was stowing the salvaged gear, Malorie asked, "What kind of birds are those?"

Phil answered, "They're called gray jays. They're in the crow family."

In a surprising moment of clarity, Ray added, "Around here, we call them whiskey jacks. That's an Anglicized corruption of their original Algonquin name, *Wisakedjak*. He was the Trickster in their mythology—a lot like Loki was to the Norse. To the First Nations, *Wisakedjak* was the one responsible for the Great Flood." Ray's cheeks were streaked with tears, and his face showed profound sadness.

Ray's pickup had not caught fire in the attack, even though its gas tank had been punctured by the Chinese machine-gun fire. The vehicle still reeked of gasoline. Just one tossed road flare was all it took to set the pickup ablaze. As they watched the pickup burn, Ray picked up a few pieces of the Chinese .30 and .50 caliber brass from the highway. The brass had "CN," "101," and "CNIC" head stamps. He tucked the brass in his coat pocket.

"Evidence. Also made in China," he said.

Ray decided to bury his parents' bodies side-by-side on the knoll behind the ranch house. They were still wrapped in the blue tarps. As they dug the shared grave, Ray mentioned that it was on this same small hillock where his great-grandfather Samuel McGregor had pitched his tent, when he first staked claim to the ranch in 1913.

They read some psalms and said prayers. Then they refilled the grave and said another prayer. Phil helped Ray construct a matching pair of crosses for the grave the next morning.

Almost immediately after the deaths of Alan and Claire, Ray and the rest of Team Robinson decided to do some combined operations with another local resistance group that Stan had met. The unnamed group had eight members and had been responsible for several sniping incidents and repeated sabotage of PLA vehicles from Anahim Lake all the way to Bella Coola. Their trademark was a time-delay vehicular incendiary device that used a machine-rolled 100mm cigarette as a time-delay fuse.

What started out as a cooperative agreement eventually turned into a merger. While Phil and Malorie would still be in charge of intelligence analysis, Ray went on to lead the combined group, which had assumed the name Team Robinson.

Fighting the Chinese turned out to be much more difficult than fighting the French. Because they had so many more armored vehicles, IED-initiated ambushes were far less decisive. This meant that there were fewer opportunities to capture weapons, and that ambushes often ended with the ambushers fleeing for their lives into the forest, as their fire was returned by damaged but still partly functional APCs. Because they wanted to minimize track wear, the Chinese tanks rarely left their garrisons. Even if they did, few resistance units would attack them while they were manned and in motion. Nearly all of the Chinese tanks destroyed by the resistance were sabotaged while they were parked and unattended.

The first Chinese weapon that Team Robinson "inherited" was a QSZ-92 Services Pistol ("Type 92 handgun") that was stripped from the body of a uniformed Chinese junior officer. This young man was foolish enough to drive an EQ2050 East Wind (a Chinese Humvee equivalent) into the town of Anahim Lake by himself. Perhaps he was looking for romance. Three shots from Ray's FAMAS ended his military career and his life.

Fearing that the vehicle was equipped with a hidden transponder, Ray left it where it was. But Ray did get the pistol, a full-flap holster, two spare fifteen-round magazines, a magazine pouch, and the officer's wallet. He also grabbed a Chinese e-tool entrenching tool, which was superior to the U.S. and Canadian models.

The QSZ-92 Services Pistol, designed and made by Norinco, shot the diminutive 5.8x21 cartridge. Ray described the gun as "China's idea of how to make an FN Five-Seven."

54

THICKER THAN WATER

I heard my country calling, away across the sea,
Across the waste of waters she calls and calls to me.
Her sword is girded at her side, her helmet on her head,
And round her feet are lying the dying and the dead.
I hear the noise of battle, the thunder of her guns,
I haste to thee my mother, a son among thy sons.

—From "I Vow to Thee, My Country," a British patriotic hymn, based
on a poem by Sir Cecil Spring-Rice, set to a theme from Gustav
Holst's "Jupiter," a movement in *The Planets* suite

Tavares, Florida—March, the Eleventh Year

The Jeffordses arrived in a chartered Super Osprey amphibian plane. The plane touched down on Lake Dora and taxied to the city of Tavares Seaplane Base. The breezy day made the water choppy. The Altmillers were waiting for them. Janelle Altmiller and Rhiannon Jeffords had arranged this meeting, primarily to discuss their parents in British Columbia. The sisters were worried that they had been out of contact for so long.

Lance Altmiller was now twenty-two years old. He had found part-time work in the local thrift store, moving and sorting boxes of donated household goods. He still lived in his parents' home. Sarah Jeffords was eighteen, and had recently begun arguing with her mother about wearing eye makeup. She now spoke with an acquired Australian accent.

The Jeffordses were home in America, to stay.

The first thing that Rhiannon said when she saw her sister was, "Uggggh. You got old."

Janelle replied, "You've got wrinkles too, sis."

"Well, we can count our blessings. At least you never got fat, and I got skinny and I stayed that way. And we all have our health."

Janelle nodded. "Yes, God is good."

Unloading their luggage took a while, and was tricky, even with the amphibian plane tied up to the pier. The swells caused the plane to oscillate, making for hesitant footing at the cargo door. The Jeffordses had brought seven suitcases, two Pelican pistol cases, and four Kolpin long gun cases. The six people and luggage were a tight squeeze in the two vehicles that the Altmillers had driven to the seaplane base.

The conversations on the short drive to the Altmillers' home focused on the Jeffordses' lengthy flights on an Airbus A380 and a Boeing 747-8 to Miami, and then the charter in the smaller amphibian to Tavares. The men were in one vehicle, and the ladies in the other.

When they reached the house, they were ushered in by the day guard. Their housekeeper, Elena, already had lunch ready for them. The Habana sandwiches and mojito salad were served with coffee and iced tea.

Over lunch, the conversation soon turned to their family in British Columbia. Jake said emphatically, "There's been outright resistance in Canada. Almost everyone has wanted the foreign troops out for *years*."

"I've already been praying about this. I suppose we'll have to do something about Canada," Peter said.

"Do you suggest that we support the resistance or *join* it?" Jake asked.

Peter sighed. "If not now, then when? And if not us, then who?"

"I agree," Rhiannon said.

"I think we're all in agreement that we need to take action," Jake said. "So let's summarize: The first wave of invasion, the French, was pushed out after a few years, but the second wave, the Chinese PLA with a bunch of technocrats in tow, came in force, and they're practically *terraforming* the place. They have the nerve to call themselves UN forces as well. They're expanding mines and building a whole new city from scratch, east of Vancouver—between Surrey and Abbotsford—that's been nicknamed New Shanghai. It is laid out in a grid of streets that will connect Surrey and Abbotsford. It's huge."

"We know the essentials of what the Chinese are now doing, but we're out of touch with Mom and Dad," Janelle said. "I only got one message relayed via ham radio from Mom and Dad shortly after the French capitulated, but before the Chinese landed."

She passed a handwritten transcription to Rhiannon and Peter. Rhiannon read it aloud, twice:

"Greetings! Good riddance to the French. We were with the NLR, as was Ray, his friend Phil, and Phil's wife. We will be rebuilding our herd. We are all healthy here. Can you come up to visit after things go back to normal?—A & C McG."

"Well, obviously the Chinese occupation changed everything, after that was written," Rhiannon said. "Their occupation has gone on for five years."

Jake jumped in. "The Chinese have a news blackout about their occupation of western Canada. The happenings up there are sketchy—just a few things that the news media hear from border crossers. The Ottawa government is sitting on their hands, endlessly parlaying with the Chinese about the details of the border between the former Saskatchewan and Manitoba, when they *should* be demanding an immediate withdrawal.

"Meanwhile, since there is a nuclear stalemate between the U.S. and China, the RCG is only providing some covert aid. It is analogous to what they did to support the mujahideen in Afghanistan, back when the Soviets were there in the 1980s. That means no direct military support, no air support. Nothing."

"So we have no way of knowing the current situation for Mom and Dad," Janelle said. "Ray is there. They mentioned plans to build the cattle herd back up. But what is really going on? Are they still healthy? Do they need help getting out of the country? Or do they need help fighting the Chinese? It's not even clear whether there is a functioning local economy. We really won't know until we get up there to see what we can do to help."

Peter gave Jacob a look and they both nodded. Then Peter said, "I suggest that Jake and I infiltrate British Columbia by ourselves, and then after we get there and fully ascertain—"

"No way!" Janelle interrupted. "Alan and Claire are *our* parents, not yours. It sounds all noble and chivalrous of you, but Rhi and I are both very good shooters and we know our way around those woods a lot better than you do."

In the end, they decided that the Jeffordses would leave their daughter, Sarah, at the recently reopened Lake Mary Prep School, and that she would spend her summers "house sitting" with Elena and working as a sales clerk at the Altmillers' hardware store. Meanwhile, the Altmillers would leave their son, Lance, in the care of Elena. Lance—who had the intellect of a five-year-old—needed constant supervision. The store would be in good hands in their absence. Their old accountant, Lisa Schoonover, had recently returned from Tennessee, and Tomas Marichal (the store manager) was running the store full-time and was planning to buy it, allowing Jake and Janelle to retire.

They spent the next twenty minutes discussing potential strategies for sneaking across the Canadian border, and the risks of minefields—both French and Chinese.

Peter, who had been quiet for most of this conversation, spoke up. "Okay, it's a calculated risk, but here is what I propose. I say that we spend a few months stocking up on supplies that we know the resistance can use. Then we charter a seaplane to take the four of us up there and drop off us *and* the gear at a very remote lake. We make sure that everything that we bring is compatible with packhorse saddles, and we even bring nine saddles with us—six packsaddles and three riding saddles."

"You're kidding, right? I haven't ridden a horse in ten years," Jake said.

"Neither have I, but I can do all things through Christ, who strengthens me."

Rhiannon glanced at her sister, and they both started nodding.

"I actually think it's a great plan," Janelle said. "Even if the Chinese have any sort of air defense up there—which I seriously doubt—if they track us and we drop off the radar, it will probably be at least twelve hours before they'll get anyone up there to check it out. By then, we can have all our gear tucked back in the woods. Then we hike out, borrow a pack string, and pick our way down to Anahim Lake on cattle trails, conspicuously staying off the roads."

Jacob still looked incredulous.

Peter jumped back in. "For years, I've been hearing Rhi rave about Sigutlat Lake, way up in the Dean River country, in Tweedsmuir Provincial Park. It's what, eighty or ninety miles northwest of the ranch? It's a fly-in lake that was used by tourist fishermen. That was where her dad took her by horseback, to catch those famous eighteen-pound trout. The lake freezes up in early No-vember, so I say we get there well before October."

"Is that lake big enough to land on?" Jake asked.

"Certainly. Sigutlat Lake is eight miles long," Rhi said. "And Peter is right. Unless the Chinese discovered uranium up there or something, there will be nobody, and I mean *nobody*, there. There are no more tourist fly-fishermen. A family built a fly-in lodge there, back around 2006, but the last I heard, the lodge had burned down. Hopefully the dock is still there."

"So who would be crazy enough to fly us up there?" Rhi asked.

Jake and Janelle glanced at each other, and then Jake answered for both of them: "Rob, at Smith Brothers."

Smith Brothers Air & Seaplane Adventures had been in business for twenty years. The small company flew charters in Florida year-round as well as in the Lake of the Ozarks region of Missouri each summer.

The company was owned by a former Delta Airlines pilot with thirty thou-sand hours of flying experience. His son and right-hand man was Rob Smith, a former U.S. Air Force pilot with a poorly concealed wild streak. Rob had more than twenty-five hundred hours of stick time, and nearly half of those hours were in seaplanes and pontoon floatplanes. He had made hundreds of takeoffs and landings on lakes.

For many years the company had three small floatplanes and "The Big Plane," a five-seat UC-1 Twin Bee. Then, just a year after the UN capitulation, they gambled and bought the "Really Big Plane," a Cessna Amphibian—a floatplane variant of the recent-generation Cessna Caravan. (Since float-planes were primarily recreational, and the recreational aviation market had not yet recovered, Smith had the chance to pick it up for twenty cents on the dollar.) While it outwardly looked like a typical floatplane, it was scaled up considerably and was powered by a beefy 675-horsepower turboprop engine that burned either JP4 or JP5.

The thirty-nine-foot-long Cessna seated twelve passengers and cruised at 159 knots once up at altitude, and 128 knots on the deck, with a range of 805 nautical miles. The plane's useful load was 3,230 pounds. With a full load, the plane had a takeoff distance of 3,660 feet.

Rob felt guilty about not being more active in the resistance against the Fort Knox government, so he jumped at the opportunity to take the risky charter. His father objected at first, but he eventually relented.

"Looking at the sectionals, I can see that the closest U.S. airport—at least straight-line distance—is the tarmac strip at Port Angeles, Washington. That is a 6,347-foot-long strip that can handle a Boeing 737, so it can certainly handle our puddle jumper, even if we are overloaded and just stagger off the ground. But it's about five hundred miles to your lake. The problem is, it's another five hundred miles back, and our plane only has an eight-hundred-mile range flying a standard profile, and a *lot less* if we try to dodge radar."

"What if we were to refuel up there?" Jake asked.

"You can arrange that?" Rob asked. "We're talking about a crud load of jet fuel. The capacity is 332 gallons, which equates to 2,224 pounds. Depending on how much low-level flying we have to do, we'll probably burn between 260 and 300 gallons of that getting there, leaving only about 65 gallons in the wing tanks when we land."

"Let me make some inquiries," Jake said.

The next day, Jake met with Rob again and presented a solution. "The resistance guy tells me that there is a very active cell in Bella Coola. Apparently it is a cell that is independent of the Anahim Lake group, which I assume is the one that Alan and Claire are in. We can arrange to have a resistance boat refuel you with two hundred seventy gallons of jet fuel—all in five-gallon cans—at the mouth of the Dean River, which is almost impossible to reach overland, but it is only forty air miles from Sigutlat Lake."

"Okay. With two or three minutes per can—since five-gallon cans are slow to pour—we're talking two hours to refuel. Call it three hours, to be on the safe side. I hope you realize that the top of the wing is sixteen feet over the water, so we'll need very calm seas to be able to refuel. It's like standing on a metal roof of a house, but the house is *moving*. If there are swells, it feels like you're surfing when you're up on the wing."

Jake pulled out a map and showed him the water-landing site, and said, "You'll be landing on salt water, but on a very sheltered waterway. The Dean Channel is one of the longest inlets on the coast of BC. So unless there are unusually high winds that day, at most there will be just very small swells."

"What about Chinese troops?"

"Not an issue. We're talking about some remote and unpatrolled coastline, not Vancouver Island. The nearest PLA garrison is in Bella Coola, and there are no roads to the mouth of the Dean. You can only get there by boat or by floatplane. "

Rob Smith rubbed his chin. "So why don't I just drop you and your gear off with the resistance there at the inlet from the get-go?"

"It's on the wrong side of the mountain range, and the Chinese have the only road—Highway 20—very closely watched. They're sure to be checking IDs and they probably search every round-eye vehicle that passes through. Getting thousands of pounds of contraband cargo through would be tricky at best. The intel guys say that they scrutinize the east-west highway routes in particular, since they consider those strategic."

"Well, if you're *sure* you can arrange that, then I'm game. But if your refueling committee falls through, then I'm up a creek without jet fuel," Rob said.

"I'm going to promise them about one hundred pounds of various ammunition and batteries in trade for the fuel, so they'll definitely be there."

"Batteries?" Rob asked.

"Yeah. Most people don't realize it, but modern armies depend on batteries just as much as they depend on ammo, fuel, and MREs. They burn through a ton of batteries for radios, starlight scopes, intrusion detection systems, flashlights, laser aiming lights—all kinds of things. Without batteries, any army is back to nineteenth-century warfare."

"Maybe you should be sabotaging battery factories in China."

All four of them took a four-week immersion course in Chinese. With a better ear for languages, it was Peter who did best in the class. The others were able to absorb only a few words and key phrases. Their instructor—a refugee from Taiwan in her sixties—found it amusing when they asked her how to say phrases like, *"Throw down your weapons,"* and, *"Surrender, or we will shoot."* In the end, only Peter became conversant in Chinese at a rudimentary level. But at least the other three of them remembered their key phrases and one crucial command: Surrender.

For weapons, Rhiannon had a AUS-Steyr bullpup, a capable little rifle, but it used proprietary magazines that didn't interchange with M16 magazines. However, Rhiannon had eleven spares (a mix of thirty- and forty-two-round), so she didn't consider that a big drawback. Meanwhile, Peter had a captured Indonesian Pindad rifle, which was a clone of the FN FNC. It used standard NATO M16 magazines. When Jake asked Peter where he'd gotten the unusual weapon, Peter said, "I got it from an Indonesian soldier who had no further use for it."

Jake would carry an LAR-8 variant of the AR-10 with nine twenty-round steel FN/FAL magazines. The Rock River Arms LAR-8 was designed to accept either FN/FAL magazines or L1A1 magazines. Jake and Janelle both carried SIG P250 pistols chambered in .45 automatic. (Hers had originally been a .40 S&W, but they were able to find a factory conversion caliber exchange kit and some extra .45 ACP magazines.)

For body armor, Peter had a set of the excellent Australian Army–issue Tiered Body Armor System. The TBAS was the equivalent of a Level IV vest in the civilian world. Jake had Level IIIA concealment body armor, and Janelle had Level II. It took some searching, but they also found a Level III vest for Rhiannon. Ironically, that vest was priced *lower* than a less-capable Level II vest being sold by the same store, but because of Florida's hot and humid climate, thicker vests did not sell well after the UNPROFOR withdrawal.

Although U.S. ammunition makers were getting back into production, there were still chronic shortages of many varieties of pistol cartridges, as well as several rifle calibers.

They gathered what they could, following the NLR's published list of ammunition needs.

Janelle also found fourteen boxes of .243 Winchester, intended for her mother's deer rifle.

From three resistance veterans in Florida, they received donations of 144 electric blasting caps, twenty-seven kilos of German C4 in three-kilo blocks, two square yards of DuPont Detasheet in twelve-by-thirty-six-inch rolls, and two hundred meters of detonating cord.

Rob's plane was kept in top condition by the Smith Brothers A&P mechanic. The only changes needed before the trip were temporarily removing some seats and taping over the Unites States N-prefix registration markings, making the plane "quasi-sterile."

55

HINTERBOONIES

I've seen things you people wouldn't believe. Attack ships on
fire off the shoulder of Orion. I watched C-beams glitter in
the dark near the Tannhauser Gate. All those moments will
be lost in time, like tears in rain.

—Rutger Hauer as Roy Batty, in *Blade Runner* (screenplay by
Hampton Fancher and David Peoples, based on
a novel by Phillip K. Dick)

Port Angeles, Washington—August,
the Eleventh Year

Their flight to Washington, completed in stages, was exhausting. After
the initial thrill of lifting off the lake in Tavares, they were faced with
two and a half days of flying across the country in a plane that, despite
its fancy padded leather seats, was still cramped and noisy and lacked a bathroom. After two layovers at motels near small-town FBO airports, they were
happy to arrive on the Olympic Peninsula.

Once they were in Port Angeles, they still had to disable the plane's transponder and remove the plane's emergency locator transmitter (ELT) radio.
They also had to pick up another eighty pounds of batteries and night vision
gear that, by previous arrangement, had been couriered from Spokane, Washington. One unexpected addition to this supplementary gear was a pair of
PF-89s, the Chinese 80mm equivalent of the U.S. LAW rocket. Jake suspected that "the gnomes of Langley" had quietly supplied them. Because they

were Chinese made, they were considered "sterile" and deniable for their upcoming foray into occupied Canada. The addition of these eight-and-a-half-
pound rocket launchers meant that Rob had to rerun his weight and balance
calculations. To compensate for the extra weight, Rob asked everyone to
empty his canteens and hydration packs. This left just a few small bottles of
apple juice for them to sip on the final leg of their flight to Sigutlat Lake.

They rested—or *tried* to rest—for nearly twenty-four hours at the home of
a former resistance leader in Port Angeles. The tension was high. Since they
were just past the summer solstice, there was more than thirteen hours of
daylight at this latitude. Because he would be skimming the water during the
first part of the flight, Rob wanted to take off while it was still daylight so that
he'd have the best depth perception.

As Rob had explained before, they had two potential flight profiles for
their infiltration: The first would be to fly very low in ground effect over the
ocean and then fly nap-of-the-earth over land. The second would be to fly normally and attempt to blend in with Chinese-occupation cargo flights. Rob
ruled out the first option because it would consume too much fuel. They settled on a combination of both plans: They would skim over the water while in
U.S. airspace, but then once they passed over Vancouver Island, they would
pop up and fly at sixteen thousand feet and do their best to look "normal" to
Chinese ground controllers, except for their lack of an active transponder.

They took off at 9:35 P.M., and Rob immediately settled the plane into ground-
effect flying. The water seemed very close. Janelle estimated that the plane's
floats were just fifteen to twenty feet above the choppy water. They were so low
that Rob had to swerve *around* some fishing boats. This seemed harrowing to
his passengers, but Rob laughed about it. The sun was setting over Peter's left
shoulder. The others heard him praying aloud. They reached Vancouver Island
at dusk. Their landfall was just east of Sooke Lake. Rob pulled up to just above
treetop level, and he skirted above the trees for a few minutes. "They tell me that
if you do this right, your tires touch treetops so often that they never stop spinning," Rob joked. In actuality, they were between thirty and fifty feet above the
treetops, but they still seemed unnervingly close. He dipped the plane even
lower, nearly touching the surface of Sooke Lake. It was now nearly dark.

Rob pulled back on the yoke sharply, emulating the profile of a takeoff
from the lake. He then dialed in the autopilot to take them on a heading

directly toward Campbell River, with a steady climb to 15,500 feet. Although the plane's cruising ceiling was actually 20,000 feet, he chose this altitude because it was often used by the three Harbin ShuiHong-5 maritime patrol and utility planes that their intelligence contacts told them were deployed in British Columbia. (These aging planes used this reduced ceiling because their cabin pressurizing systems often failed.)

The rest of their flight would be in darkness, relying on instruments. As they neared Campbell River, Rob descended and turned northwest, following the profile of a routine landing at the Campbell River Airport. Instead of staying on course, he descended farther to just two hundred feet above the Campbell River Marina. Then he turned sharply east and climbed over Cape Mudge to again confuse radar intercept and ground-control operators into thinking that this was now a different plane. He pulled up into a gradual climb and set a heading northeast toward Williams Lake. Then, over Clendinning Provincial Park, he descended below the eight-thousand-foot peaks and turned due north up a broad valley. Once they reached the north end of the valley, Rob said, "From here on we should be outside of Chinese radar coverage, until we get closer to Williams Lake, where I've been told they now have an ATC radar, but no air defense artillery or surface-to-air missiles. Of course, if that intel is *wrong*, then we'll be the first to find out."

He laughed, but the others didn't.

He climbed to 20,600 feet, exceeding the normal operational ceiling of the aircraft. The plane droned on until they reached Big Creek Provincial Park, at the north end of the coastal mountain range. From here, the terrain dropped off into the Chilcotin Plateau. Rob now set a new heading that would take them to Charlotte Lake. At Charlotte Lake, he turned again slightly toward the Blackwater Meadow Indian Reserve. Once over the reserve, he descended to 15,000 feet and made his final turn to Sigutlat Lake. They had now flown seven hundred nautical miles, and Rob was nearing exhaustion.

He turned his head. "I waited until we were this far north to make our final turn because I wanted to be in the shadow of Itcha Mountain. Even if they have an ATC radar at Williams Lake or even at Bella Coola, we'll be outside of their line of sight," Rob explained.

"Which means?" Janelle asked.

"Which means they can't see us on radar. Radars can't see through mountains. So, for all they know, we could be landing anywhere in about a three-hundred-mile radius. And if they have a blinding flash of the obvious and realize that their target is an amphibian floatplane, then they'll realize that there are at least a dozen lakes where we could land, not to mention ump-teen little airfields. To them, we are now a proverbial needle in a haystack."

Jake reached across and gave Rob a high five.

Their descent to Sigutlat Lake was uneventful but stressful, considering that they were making the descent on instruments, and the moon had now set.

"Now, this is where we take a chill pill and just trust the accuracy of the Garmin TAWS," Rob said.

Jake was transfixed, watching the display, which in three dimensions showed Rob's banking turn and descent over the lake. It was like watching a video game or a computer flight simulator. This was a true instruments-only landing, with hardly any outside reference. The only light that he could see was the glow from the engine's exhaust below his window, and just a faint white reflection from the snowy peaks above. As he paralleled the centerline of the lake, Rob had already dropped the flaps and had throttled back.

"Our sink rate is about fifteen feet per second," Rob reported. Closely watching his instruments, he pulled back on the yoke to flare at the last moment and they touched down on the lake in a very smooth landing. After feeling that, he pulled back the throttle. Once they had slowed to twenty miles an hour, Rob pushed the left rudder pedal to turn and taxi to the center of the lake. Then he shut down the engine. "The gauges show one hundred forty-five pounds of fuel. That will be plenty to get me over to the Dean Channel. As for now . . . It's too dark to pull up to the shore safely."

"What about GPS?" Rhiannon asked.

"That won't tell us where a boat or other obstruction might be. Nor do we know the current condition of the dock. It's almost pitch dark out there. "

He popped his head out the door for a moment to sniff the air and look around. He was just barely able to discern the shoreline in the distance. The lake was quiet.

Rob closed his door. "The lake is dead calm, and there is no wind. We might drift a bit, but we should be fine. Wake me up at first light."

With that, he turned off the avionics, took off his headset, reclined his seat, and closed his eyes.

"Cool as a cucumber," Peter whispered.

"That's why we hired a professional pilot with thousands of hours of flying time," Jake replied. "Now, let's take turns getting some rest, too."

That same night, Phil was cuddled in bed alongside Malorie. Tree frogs were peeping in the distance. Phil turned slightly, shifted his arm under his pillow, and let out a soft sigh.

"You awake?" Malorie whispered.

"Yeah." He reached his hand up to gently stroke the side of her head.

After a minute, she turned to face him. "What was that sighing about?"

"I was just praying some more. I'm worried about the lack of progress in booting out the Chinese. I think that we're going to run out of resistance fighters before they run out of PLA soldiers and vehicles. We're down to our last four blasting caps. Without force multipliers, we can't gain the initiative. And if we can't gain the initiative, then we need to seriously consider cutting our losses and—"

Malorie interrupted. "Is this Phil Adams, the eternal optimist, that I'm talking to, or did some strange man sneak into my bed?"

Phil chuckled.

She kissed him and then said, "We just have to keep up the fight and trust in the Lord. Ultimately, he's the one who is in control. Not General Zhou, not you, and not me."

"Amen to that."

As dawn broke over Sigutlat Lake, Rhiannon could see that they were just three hundred feet from shore. Rob started the plane's engine. A flock of bufflehead ducks was startled by the noise and took flight. Rob maneuvered the plane to the tiny, deserted fishing village at the southeast corner of the lake. There were still two cabins standing, but what had been the larger lodge was a blackened ruin. A woodstove and a rusty Servel refrigerator body were still standing near the middle of the ruin.

The wooden dock was a T-shape with its shorter leg paralleling the shore. It was weathered to gray but appeared to be in serviceable condition. Rob

handed Jake a length of rope and had him step out on the pontoon. After Rob
had expertly maneuvered to the side of the dock, Jake was easily able to hop
over and tie up the plane to a cleat. After shutting down the engine Rob jumped
out and added another mooring line. Surprisingly, there were still some floating plastic buffers, and they were able to shift the plane down the dock to
them, to protect the starboard pontoon from any damage. Once the plane was
alongside the buffers, they snugged up both lines.

They were almost immediately attacked by mosquitoes. They wore mos-
quito repellent almost continuously, henceforth. Unloading the plane took a
half hour, and then shifting the cargo to the woods behind the village took
another two hours. All that they left on board was the one hundred pounds of
ammunition and batteries that had been promised to the resistance fighters
who would be refueling the Cessna at the mouth of the Dean River.

Rob shook their hands and said, "I'll be praying for y'all. Before I fly out at
sunset tonight, I plan to take a long nap and then do some catch-and-release
fishing for rainbow trout with a hand line. I hope that I catch at least one big
one. But even if I don't, I'll still have bragging rights."

Rhiannon gave him a questioning look.

Rob clarified. "I mean bragging rights to say that I flew seven hundred
miles into occupied Chinese territory while being painted by PLA air defense
radars and dropped off a team of scrappy resistance fighters along with their
fully automatic weapons, rocket launchers, explosives, and night vision gear.
Then I did some fishing before I flew out. What a great story to tell my grand-
kids, someday."

Rob grinned and gave them a stylized parade float royalty wave. Then he
turned to walk back to the dock whistling "Dixie."

Janelle readied her pack, filling her canteen with filtered water from the
lake, and headed out with a GPS. (Since she was the most confident on a horse
in the bush, it was decided that she would be the best one to hike out and lead
back the horses.) While she was gone, the others planned to gradually shift
the cargo and packsaddles to an agreed location six hundred meters away to a
place even deeper in the timber. There, they would make a cold camp, set up
thermal camouflage, and wait.

It took Janelle three and a half days to hike thirty-three miles east to the
Andy Cahoose Meadow Indian Reserve. The trail was in worse shape than

she had remembered it, with a lot of newly downed timber. By prior arrangement, there was a resistance team summer grazing a herd of cattle and a string of packhorses and mules. When she arrived, Janelle met the First Nations husband and wife team, who were camped in a yurt. They saw her walking in and asked, "Are you Janelle?"

"That's me!"

They wasted no time and soon had two horses saddled, and halters and leads on the rest of the string. While the husband stayed to watch the cattle, his wife, Maggie, would accompany Janelle back to the lake. In addition to their sleeping bags, they each carried an axe and a bow saw to deal with the worst of the downed timber.

With the each horse's lead tied to the tail of the horse ahead, the pack string looked like a herd of elephants. It took them five grueling days to get back to the cold camp. While they could detour around a lot of the fallen trees, some of them were on steep, rocky, or brushy slopes and had to be cleared. By the time that they reached the camp, Janelle and Maggie were exhausted and ravenous, since they had packed only four days' worth of food.

Rhiannon had been quite worried by Janelle's long delay. Janelle assured her she was fine. "But that trail is a mess. We'd better plan on four days just to make it back to the meadows."

Jake and Peter had already organized the loads equally alongside each packsaddle.

There were a couple of ornery mules in the string, but they had them all saddled and loaded within two hours. That afternoon they covered only eight miles before they camped at dark and hobbled the pack string. The next morning they were short one horse, and found that even though it was hobbled, a dappled gray gelding had covered four hundred yards in crow hops. "That's the thing about horses; there's not two of them with the same personality," Rhiannon said.

The next three days were frustrating. Because of the downed timber, they had to break up the string and lead horses individually or in pairs on some stretches. But everyone remained in high spirits, and each night Maggie entertained them with stories of what had happened in the region since the Crunch. Maggie said that she had been a horse packer for the resistance but that she had never personally engaged in any combat. She had lost three toes to frostbite while resisting the French, and had lost her left earlobe to frostbite while resisting the Chinese.

Back at Andy Cahoose Meadow, they shared a barbecue with Maggie and her husband. Like Maggie, her husband knew of the McGregors only by reputation and had not heard any details of what had happened at the ranch since the Crunch. Since they wintered at the Michel Gardens Reserve (fifty miles east of Anahim Lake), they had news only of families in their immediate vicinity.

The next morning as they prepared to head out on the forty-five miles of trail to the McGregor ranch, Jake asked Maggie's husband what he might need from their cargo. "I could use some aught six shells, some .303 shells, and some matches." Jake filled all of his requests, with two hundred rounds of each type of ammunition, and four large boxes of matches. He also added the bonus of a twenty-dollar-face-value roll of Canadian silver quarters.

Maggie accompanied them the next morning on her Morgan mare. The plan was that once they reached the McGregor ranch, she would lead the pack string back to Andy Cahoose Meadow by herself.

The next two days went quickly. They were now on well-maintained trails, so the going was much easier. They spent the first night in the woods near the Blackwater Meadow Reserve. Maggie explained that from here on, it would be safer to camp where there were cattle pastured to confuse "those Chinese thermal things." They spent the next night at the Louis Squinas ranch, which was technically a First Nations reserve, but to all outward appearances was just a typical British Columbia cattle ranch. One family lived there, but the ranch was currently unoccupied because the family was running their cattle for the summer up at a place they just called "Fourteen"—their summer pasture range.

Though they were now quite close to the McGregor ranch, they stayed an extra day; they were getting closer to civilization and needed to transition to night travel to decrease the chance of being spotted by Chinese drones or patrols.

Up until now, they had been riding with handguns on their hips, but with all of their guns stowed, they asked Maggie if it was wise to break them out. She said, "No. If they attack with a gunship, then we're all dead anyway. And if a ground patrol spots us, we're better off trying to outrun them and ride back into the timber. From there, we can set up an ambush."

They left the long guns stowed.

Although it was only a mile to the town of Anahim Lake, and another seven miles to the McGregor ranch, it took them all night to get there. They had to take a circuitous route around the hamlet of Anahim Lake.

They arrived at the ranch at 5:00 A.M. and were greeted by an ambush.

Phil and Malorie were up and cooking breakfast when they heard "Alert zone three."

"Get ready to thermite all of the files and maps!" Phil shouted. Then he and Malorie rushed out of the house and ran down the north draw to reach one of their planned ambush sites. Just as they got into position, the pack string came into the far end of the kill zone. Phil flipped down the bipod legs of his MAG, quickly positioned the Bulldog bag, and clipped on its belt to the gun's twenty-round teaser.

When the strangers were in the middle of the kill zone, Malorie shouted, "Halt! Who goes there?"

Rhiannon, on the lead horse, sharply reined her mount to a stop. She hesitated, and then answered, "Rhiannon McGregor Jeffords, and a group of friendlies."

It took a few minutes in the early light of dawn to straighten out who was who. Phil and Malorie quickly identified themselves as "friends of Ray" and residents of the ranch.

When they reached the house, Janelle and Rhiannon were crying tears of joy as they saw their brother, Ray, for the first time in more than a decade. Their happiness, however, was quickly shattered when they learned that their parents had been killed by the PLA.

56

RECUPERATION

Tears are the silent language of grief.

—Voltaire (François-Marie Arouet)

The McGregor Ranch, near Anahim Lake, British Columbia—August, the Eleventh Year

After all of the panniers were unloaded and the packsaddles were stowed in the barn, they turned out all of the horses in the east corral, which was partly shaded by trees. Here, they reasoned, there was less chance of a Chinese drone operator noticing the sudden influx of livestock.

Maggie stayed for the day. Before she left that evening, she was given a captured FAMAS F1, seven spare FAMAS magazines, five hundred rounds of 5.56mm ball ammo, a custom leather scabbard for the FAMAS that had been handmade at Stan Leaman's ranch, a cleaning kit, and a copy of Malorie's English translation of the French army FAMAS manual. They also gave her five of their packsaddles and their panniers, with the assumption that she would get more use out of them than the McGregors would.

"I'm glad that you got here when you did," Ray began. "The PLA administrators have announced that they're starting a nationwide census in less than two weeks. After that, any adult who is caught without an internal passport will be subject to arrest or perhaps even summary execution."

Rhiannon had three passports: Canadian (lapsed), Australian, and U.S. Janelle had two passports: Canadian (lapsed), and United States Peter had Australian and U.S. passports. Jake had only a lapsed U.S. passport. They decided that Rhiannon and Janelle would queue up for the Chinese passports, while Jake and Peter would try to stay "under the radar."

Fortunately, the Chinese had very few FLIRs. But what the PLA lacked in technological sophistication, it made up for in sheer numbers.

"What we need are force multipliers—technologies or tactics that dramatically increase combat effectiveness. With modern conventional armies, these multipliers are typified by electronic communications, aerial bombardment, intelligence gathering, rapid troop transport, electronic warfare, force concentration, and the use of precision guided 'smart' munitions. In the context of guerrilla warfare, we'll depend on command-detonated explosives and perhaps even toxins," Phil said.

"When we were up against UNPROFOR, they essentially played nice, at first. They also had a relatively small force. But the situation with China is considerably different. The gloves have been off from day one, and this is truly asymmetric warfare. They've got a huge, highly mechanized, and largely armored force with plenty of firepower. Their targeting capability is weak, however. It's almost like Elmer T. Fudd lugging around a big blunderbuss but not knowing where to point it."

"And we're those Wascally Wabbits," Jake offered.

"Right. So we confuse Elmer. We demoralize Elmer. We starve Elmer. We freeze Elmer. We give Elmer stomach trouble. We blind Elmer. We give Elmer sleepless nights. We pour itching powder down Elmer's shirt."

Phil paused to take a breath, and then went on. "Just 'think outside the box,' folks. Arson and sabotage will be key force multipliers. Given the cold climate of the interior, two of our primary goals will be depriving the Chinese of liquid fuels and burning them out of their barracks. I intend to freeze them out of BC over the next winter or two."

57

BIG TREBLE

A clever rabbit's burrow has three holes.

—Chinese proverb

Near Nimpo Lake, British Columbia—September, the Eleventh Year

Their recon mission was a failure. They had been detected, perhaps by a ground sensor, so now Peter and Ray were on the run. After he had shot just four rounds, Ray's FAMAS carbine jammed. He tried the traditional "slap/pull/squeeze" method of clearing the jam, but a glance in the ejection told him that the jam was a dreaded "double feed," which could take a long time to clear. He didn't *have* a lot of time.

"VBT!" he shouted to Peter, quoting one of Malorie's favorite fake acronyms. Recognizing Ray's predicament, Peter laid down covering fire for their withdrawal with pairs of semiautomatic shots from his Pindad SS2.

Ray safed the FAMAS and slung it across his back as he ran.

Nearing a boulder that would provide decent cover, he pulled his Inglis pistol from its stock/holster. He fired two quick shots toward his pursuers. Seeing that Peter was up and running, Ray fired three more times. Then he pulled the wooden shoulder stock from its harness, attached it to the butt of his pistol, and adjusted the gun's tangent rear sight to two hundred meters. Shouldering the gun, he tried to engage the advancing Chinese squad as best he could, firing deliberately. Once he heard Peter firing again (following his own rush), Ray jumped up and started a rush, reloading as he ran.

This series of withdraw-by-fire and rushes went on for several minutes. Peter was briefly stunned when a bullet hit him near the top of his TBAS trauma plate. He realized later that he would probably be dead if it weren't for his armor. Mainly because of their superior accuracy, the PLA squad stopped pursing them after they had taken four casualties. Peter shot and killed three PLA soldiers, and Ray badly wounded another.

After they broke contact, Ray and Peter kept running, heading for dense timber. They were in an area just a few miles from the ambush of the French Gazelle helicopter five years earlier.

They were certain that the Chinese would resume their pursuit once a larger unit arrived to back them up. What they hadn't planned on were scent-tracking dogs.

When the heard the dogs, Ray shouted as he ran, "We've gotta think fast. They may have transponders on their dog collars, so even if the handlers can't keep up with them, they can use those returns to vector attack helicopters in on us."

"There's another VBT for us," Peter said.

If they got pinned down, he expected the Chinese to call for a gunship. It would be either a Z-9 (a clone of the Eurocopter Dauphin) or a Z-10, a more formidable attack helicopter similar in capability to the Augusta 129 or the Eurocopter Tiger.

After running for another minute, Peter said, "Hey! How about treble hook lines?"

"Could work!" Ray answered. "Let's look for a narrow spot."

They found the right spot a few hundred yards ahead where the trail crossed a swale that was hemmed in by trees and some large boulders. The dogs now sounded as if they were getting closer—perhaps only a mile behind them.

They stopped and grounded their weapons. Ray dug into his pack and pulled out his medical kit, which contained several battle dressings and a combat application tourniquet (CAT). Beneath that was a brown plastic clamshell soap box that was about the size of his hand. Inside it was a piece of cardboard with eight separate pieces of 120-pound test monofilament wrapped in notches that had been cut along the sides of the cardboard. Each nine-foot-long fishing line had a three-quarter-inch-wide treble hook tied at both ends.

To save time, Ray pulled out his tanto pocketknife and cut the cardboard in half. He said, "Four for you and four for me. Doggie chest height, naturally."

They quickly unwound the snare lines and started to string them up across the trail.

Phil had taught them the technique. He'd learned it from a Special Forces NCO. The idea was to attach them to a strong synthetic line such as spiderwire fishing line. Typically one end was attached to the hook and the other to the ceiling rafters or doorframes with enough slack to allow the hooks to lie on the floor near the edges of the wall. They could place these in what Phil termed a "fatal funnel"—an interior ambush zone inside a building. According to Phil, using treble snares could delay, distract, and unnerve a SWAT-style raid party, allowing defenders to have a brief period of advantage wherein they could shoot the invaders. The attackers are slowed and stunned by pain, allowing the defenders to spring a trap and fire upon the attackers, all caught nicely inside a restrictive space. The same sorts of treble hook snares were also useful in wilderness areas on trails.

By the time that they were done emplacing all eight snare lines, the barking dogs sounded much closer, perhaps only a half mile away. "Crud, they're gaining fast," Ray muttered nervously.

Ray and Peter grabbed their rifles and resumed running. They had run about fifteen hundred yards when they heard a terrible commotion behind them. They stopped to listen. The many shrieks, howls, and barks from the dogs made it clear that the pack had gotten themselves into a big tangle. The howls went on and on, and both men felt bad to have been forced to harm the dogs the way they did.

Peter uncapped his canteen and took a long pull from it, and offered it to Ray, who also took a sip.

Handing the canteen back, Ray said, "Thanks. I think I have time to clear that jam now."

58

EBB TIDE

All warfare is based on deception. Hence, when able to attack, we must seem unable, when using our forces we must seem inactive, when we are near, we must make the enemy believe that we are away; when far away, we must make him believe we are near. Hold out baits to entice the enemy. Feign disorder, and crush him.

If he is secure at all points, be prepared for him. If he is superior in strength, evade him. If your opponent is of choleric temper, seek to irritate him. Pretend to be weak, that he may grow arrogant.

If he is inactive, give him no rest. If his forces are united, separate them. Attack him where he is unprepared, appear where you are not expected. These military devices, leading to victory, must not be divulged beforehand.

—Sun Tzu, *The Art of War* (Translation by Lionel Giles, 1910)

Prince Albert, British Columbia—November, the Eleventh Year

On November 26, a backpack containing twelve of the Project Jordan Pogo Sticks was captured by a Chinese patrol, following an ambush near Prince Albert. All of the guerrillas were killed, so the PLA had nobody to question about these strange devices. The local PLA commander recognized that they were unusual and suspected that they might be some sort of hand-emplaced sensor, so he ordered that they be sent to the Third Department intelligence section regional headquarters in Regina. "Passing the buck," the Third Department officer rightly claimed that their specialty was signals intelligence rather than technical (materiel) intelligence, so on November 28 they were forwarded to the PLA technical intelligence section in Vancouver. They arrived by train on December 3. One of the sticks was sawed open. The overseeing office recognized the dark gray powder that poured out as either an explosive or an incendiary, so he had his subordinate fetch a representative from the Explosive Ordnance Disposal (EOD) office at the same garrison. On December 4, two of their EOD bomb technicians completely disassembled one of the Pogo Sticks and took detailed photographs, which were relayed via their satellite communications to Beijing.

On December 6, the Technical Intelligence Directorate ordered that the dark gray powder first be tested to determine if it was gunpowder, a high explosive, or thermite. The first test, wherein a fully suited EOD tech exposed a few grams of the powder to the intense heat of a burning piece of magnesium ribbon, confirmed the suspicion that the powder was thermite. A preliminary report was written and forwarded to Beijing.

On December 9, the Technical Intelligence Directorate ordered four of the Pogo Sticks be packaged with extreme caution, heavily padded, and transported to the Technical Intelligence section building north of Shanghai, as soon as possible. The evening of December 10, all ten remaining intact Pogo Sticks were individually and tightly wrapped in bubble pack, and four of them were further packaged in a double box and put on a Y-20 long-range transport plane bound for Shanghai.

On the evening of December 12, the box of Pogo Sticks arrived at the Technical Intelligence section in China. The following morning (December 13 in China and December 12 in Canada), the box of Pogo Sticks sat on a loading dock under armed guard. An argument then ensued between two PLA officers, who both held the rank of major—one of them in Technical Intelligence and the other in Engineering—in charge of an EOD unit. They were bickering about how and where the mysterious cylinders should be un-packaged and who should be in charge. They were still arguing when the box burst into flames, and a searing, white-hot stream of burning thermite poured out of one end of the box.

Then the real shouting began.

59

FLAMBÉE DAY

Victory has a hundred fathers, but no one wants to recognize defeat as his own.

—Galeazzo Ciano

Occupied Western Canada—December 12, the Eleventh Year

At 12:12 P.M. Saskatchewan time (10:12 A.M. in British Columbia) every Pogo Stick with a depressed cap sleeve ignited simultaneously.

Because knowledge of Project Jordan was on a strict "need to know" basis, the mass immolation was as much of a surprise to most of the resistance as it was to the Chinese. Even those who were supplied the incendiaries were not told the exact date that they would be activated—only that they needed to be emplaced "before the first week of December."

There were unfortunate incidents where the Pogo Sticks started fires in unintended places. In one instance a few Chinese gas cans had been pilfered by a resistance unit. These burned down a generator shed and destroyed a pickup truck. In another, a generous Chinese supply sergeant had given some cans of diesel to the headman of an off-hydro tribal village in the Yukon Territory. There, a generator house was completely destroyed.

Even in other places where Chinese vehicles were destroyed, there was collateral damage: a wooden bridge, dozens of civilian buildings and vehicles, and two wooden docks. There were more than 150 Chinese casualties, but no reported civilian deaths.

A few Pogo Sticks had also had their springs removed and surreptitiously hidden under flexible fuel blivets. Huge fires burned out of control at many Chinese fuel depots. Because they had all started simultaneously, the fires overwhelmed the ability of PLA soldiers and the few trained firefighters to respond. Hundreds of buildings burned while motor pools and marshaling yards became infernos. There were also dozens of railroad locomotives and railcars set ablaze, since the Chinese frequently used auxiliary heaters that were kept refueled with twenty-liter cans. This was particularly true with the rolling stock that the Chinese had brought to Canada. (The ubiquitous Manchurian Heaters were used in railcars and in large tents to stave off the cold. They were also used as ration-warming tray heaters for field messes. Now, nearly half of the Manchurian Heaters had fuel cans that had burst into flames.)

There was never an exact count of the number of ground vehicles, aircraft, and generator trailers damaged or destroyed, but it was at least five thousand. Nor were there details on the amount of fuel or the number of buildings destroyed, but it was certainly devastating. And with the winter solstice just ten days away in the Northern Hemisphere, the incendiary attacks came at a very advantageous time. The PLA forces in Canada were largely immobilized. Exploiting the dire position of their opponents, the NLR went on the offensive. They attacked wherever and whenever possible, all through the winter, pressing their advantage. With the loss of the majority of their armored vehicles, the PLA commanders drastically scaled back their operations. At the strategic level, PLA planners started looking for a quick exit strategy for their campaign in Canada.

Occupied Western Canada—Late April, the Twelfth Year

The Xinhua news service announced a "cease-fire and troop withdrawal," on April 25. Its carefully worded statement, which did not include the word *surrender*, announced that all Chinese UN forces would be withdrawn from

Canada on or before August 20. (Sooner, if additional UN transport was provided.) Under the "Completion of UN Humanitarian Mission and Cease-fire Agreement," the Chinese troops would not be allowed to bring any weapons with them, and the only vehicles that they could take with them were ambulances.

60

WEDDING PRAYER

If every Jewish and anti-Nazi family in Germany had owned a Mauser rifle and twenty rounds of ammunition and the will to use it, Adolf Hitler would be a little-known footnote to the history of the Weimar Republic.

—Aaron Zelman, cofounder of Jews for the Preservation of Firearms Ownership

Porthill Border Crossing Station, Idaho— Twenty-two Years After the Crunch

Phil and Malorie Adams pulled up to the border checkpoint with their pickup's radio playing an oldie by the Mumford & Sons. They had enjoyed a pleasant drive down from their ranch near Kamloops.

As he handed his Canadian driver's license to the officer at the booth, Phil wondered how old this young man must have been when the Crunch hit. He surmised perhaps less than four years old. The border patrol officer noted the Resistance Veterans of Canada Association (RVCA) sticker on the Ford's windshield.

Phil caught the border patrol admiring the MP5 submachine gun mounted on the dashboard and the brace of Glock pistols with extended magazines holstered in the center console. "Do you have anything to declare?" the officer asked.

"Just *hello*."

The officer noted that the children in the backseat were both quietly reading well-worn books from the *Little House on the Prairie* series. Phil and Malorie were proud of their kids for being avid readers. Alan Cedric Adams was eleven years old, and his sister, Claire Megan Adams, was eight.

The officer nodded. "Enjoy your visit to the United States, sir, and thank you for your service."

Both the wedding and the reception that followed were being held at the El-kins Resort on Priest Lake. The groom, Leo LaCroix-Kim, had met his bride, Chantal, when they were both attending the University of Idaho. Chantal Tolliver was from the town of Priest Lake, Idaho. Her father owned and oper-ated Priest Lake Country Outfitters, a business that rented snowmobiles in the winter and guided float trips in the summer. They also had a rifle and pis-tol range, where they gave private instruction. In recent years, many of their shooting-school students had been tourists from Japan.

The wedding celebration seemed swarmed with children. There was lots of laughter as children ranging from toddlers to teenagers ran around, pell-mell. The mothers and grandmothers hoped that none of the children would fall or jump into the lake until after the group photos had been taken.

Phil and Malorie greatly enjoyed attending the wedding and catching up with acquaintances. They were amazed at how quickly all of the children had grown up. As soon as they arrived, they immediately found Ray McGregor and his wife, Sylvia.

Ray was wearing a red-and-green Clan McGregor kilt. Sylvia was one of Stan Leaman's second cousins. She was just sixteen years old at the onset of the Crunch and had come to live at the Leaman ranch after her parents had been killed by a Chinese drone strike when she was nineteen. She and Ray had married fourteen years after the Crunch. Ray and Sylvia had a son and a daughter, who were now ages four and six, and Sylvia was pregnant with their third child. Their son was named Alan Leaman McGregor and their daughter was named Claire Malorie McGregor.

Other guests from Canada included Stan Leaman; his wife, Katie; their grade-school-aged children, Philip Alan Leaman and Claire Malorie Leaman; and their infant son, Terrence Billy Leaman. Of their three children, Philip showed the most First Nations traits, with jet-black hair and dark-brown eyes.

Also attending were Ken and Terry Layton, and their sons, Dan, Thomas, and Gray.

Todd and Mary Gray were also there with their four children. There were also three generations of the Altmiller family, who had traveled from Florida.

The guests that were the least well-known by the wedding party were Dustin Hodges and his wife, Sheila. Sheila's son, Tyree, wasn't with them. He was a U.S. Army aviation warrant officer, deployed in the Africa campaign. It was hoped that the Chinese would be pushed out of Africa in the next few years.

Joshua and Megan Kim were there, but could be in Idaho for only three days. They were both working at Field Station (FS) Kunia, Hawaii, operated by the recently reestablished Army Security Agency. Joshua was the site manager and Megan wore two hats as both senior analyst and constitutional protection oversight manager. (The NSA and the military SIGINT agencies now had strict rules that precluded recording the conversations or intercepting the e-mails of American citizens.)

The wedding ceremony had a strong gospel message, and some great old hymns, which pleased Phil and Malorie. The decorations and place cards were all readied in the reception hall. The wedding cake had been made from two full sheet cakes that were cut and pieced together in the shape of North America and then frosted white. "Leo" was written in icing across Canada and "Chantal" was written across the United States. A red line of icing marked the Forty-ninth Parallel, bisected by the shape of a heart.

There was an enormous pile of wrapped wedding gifts on two tables in the back of the reception hall. Phil got a chuckle seeing the large number of distinctively long rectangular boxes. Ever since the ouster of the UN occupiers, guns and ammunition had become standard wedding gifts in both Canada and the United States. Just like giving gold as wedding gifts in India, guns were seen as a lasting store of wealth. They were also considered "invasion insurance." Phil and Malorie added their own large, heavy gift boxes to the pile. They contained a full-auto German MG4; another box with a tripod, links, and small accessories for the same gun; a full-auto QBZ-95 bullpup and six magazines; an ammo can full of 5.8x42mm cartridges; and a pair of Glock 30S pistols.

Everyone was having a wonderful time at the reception. There was a lot of mingling between the tables, embraces, and laughter. As Ray was returning to their table with two cups of punch, he overheard his wife, Sylvia, saying to the bride's father, "Ray has killed dozens of enemy soldiers—mostly with IEDs—but I've only seen him *hit* one man."

"Oh, not that story again!" Ray objected.

"No, let her tell it," Mr. Tolliver said.

Sylvia continued. "It's true. You hush now, Ray, and let me tell this. We were at an RVCA meeting in Kamloops last summer. And there was a roly-poly young man there, bragging his tail off. Based on his age, I thought that he must have been in the resistance to the Chinese occupation. But he was claiming to have resisted the French, too. With Ray and me both standing there, this fellow launched into a cock-and-bull story about how he was with 'a nine-man team that had destroyed eight French helicopters at the Williams Lake helibase.' So Ray played along with him, and said, 'Tell me more. How did you do it?' And this poseur says, 'I'll tell you. We used compound bows to silently take out the three sentries, and then we used TH3 incendiary grenades that had been smuggled to us by a U.S. Special Forces team.'"

Mr. Tolliver cocked his head, and Sylvia went on. "So Ray says to him, 'That was one fine bit of work, sir. I'd like to shake your hand!' So when this fellow reached out his hand, quick as lightning, Ray punched him in the nose."

Mr. Tolliver roared with laughter.

Ray looked sheepish. "Yep, I couldn't control the urge, so I hit him. I'm afraid I made quite a scene that evening. There was blood going down the front of his nice white shirt. I said to him, 'For your information, it was just *me* and my *two* friends who were there that night, not you and that mythical nine-man team. And by the way, we didn't use archery equipment on the sentries, nor did we use thermite on the helicopters. But I'll spare you the *actual* details because I don't want you incorporating them into your own story, if you ever dare repeat it.'"

GLOSSARY

10/22: A semiautomatic .22-rimfire rifle made by Ruger.

1911: *See* M1911.

5Ws: Who, What, When Where, Why. (Intelligence report format.)

9/11: The terrorist attacks of September 11, 2001.

AAA: Depending on context, American Automobile Association or Anti-Aircraft Artillery.

Accredited/Accreditation: The formal approval of a Sensitive Compartmented Information Facility (SCIF) that meets prescribed physical, technical, and personnel security standards.

Acoustic Security: Security measures designed and used to deny aural access to classified information. *See also* SCIF.

ACP: Automatic Colt Pistol.

ACU: Army Combat Uniform. The U.S. Army's predominantly gray "digital" pattern camouflage uniform that replaced the BDU.

AFB: Air Force Base.

AFCENT: Allied Forces Central Europe. (A military command.)

AGL: Above Ground Level.

AI: Artificial Intelligence.

Air Gap: *See* High Side and Low Side.

AK: Avtomat Kalashnikov. The gas-operated weapons family invented by Mikhail Timofeyevitch Kalashnikov, a Red Army sergeant. AKs are known for their robustness and were made in huge numbers, so that they

are ubiquitous in much of Asia and the Third World. The best of the Kalashnikov variants are the Valmets that were made in Finland, the Galils
that were made in Israel, and the R4s that are made in South Africa.

AK-47: The early generation Kalashnikov carbine with a milled receiver that
shoots the intermediate 7.62x39mm cartridge. *See also* AKM.

AK-74: The later generation AK carbine that shoots the 5.45x39mm cartridge.

AKM: *Avtomat Kalashnikova Modernizirovanniy.* The later generation 7.62x39
AK with a stamped receiver.

ALAT: *Aviation Légère de l'Armée de Terre.* (Light Aviation of the Land
Army.)

AM: Amplitude Modulation.

Ammo: Slang for ammunition.

AO: Area of Operations.

AP: Armor Piercing.

APC: Armored Personnel Carrier.

AR: Automatic Rifle. This is the generic term for semiauto variants of the Ar-
malite family of rifles designed by Eugene Stoner (AR-10, AR-15,
AR-180, etc.).

AR-7: The .22 LR semiautomatic survival rifle designed by Eugene Stoner. It
weighs just two pounds when disassembled. Still in production, it has
been manufactured by several American makers since the 1960s.

AR-10: The 7.62mm NATO predecessor of the M16 rifle, designed by Eugene Stoner. Early AR-10s (mainly Portuguese, Sudanese, and Cuban
contract, from the late 1950s and early 1960s) are not to be confused
with the present-day semiauto-only "AR-10" rifles that are more closely
interchangeable with parts from the smaller-caliber AR-15. *See also* AR,
AR-15, and LAR-8.

AR-15: The semiauto civilian variants of the U.S. Army M16 rifle.

ASA: Army Security Agency.

ASAP: As Soon As Possible.

ATC: Air Traffic Control.

ATF: *See* BATFE.

AUG: *See* Steyr AUG.

AUS-Steyr: *See* Steyr AUG.

Authorized Personnel: Those holders of active security clearances who are fully cleared and indoctrinated for SCI, have a valid need to know, and have been granted access to a SCIF. *See also* SAP and SCIF.

AVGAS or avgas: Aviation Gasoline. The most commonly used aviation gasoline is hundred-octane, low-lead (100LL).

AWOL: Absent Without Official Leave.

BAH: Basic Allowance for Housing.

BATFE: Bureau of Alcohol, Tobacco, Firearms, and Explosives (a U.S. federal government taxing agency).

BBC: British Broadcasting Corporation.

BC: British Columbia.

BCD: Bad Conduct Discharge. Also sometimes jokingly called a Big Chicken Dinner.

BDU: Battle Dress Uniform. Also called "camouflage utilities" by the USMC. Most BDUs were made in the woodland camouflage pattern.

Big Chicken Dinner: *See* BCD.

Black: Depending on context: either a classified program or a designation applied to information systems, and to associated areas, circuits, components, and equipment, in which national security information is encrypted or is not processed. *See also* Red and Red/Black.

Black Rifle/Black Gun: Generic terms for a modern battle rifle—typically equipped with a black plastic stock and forend, giving these guns an "all-black" appearance. Functionally, however, they are little different from earlier semiauto designs.

BLM: Bureau of Land Management (a U.S. federal government agency that administers public lands).

BMG: Browning Machine Gun. Usually refers to .50 BMG, the U.S. military's standard heavy machine-gun cartridge since the early twentieth century. The .50 BMG cartridge is now often used for long-range precision countersniper rifles.

Body-Cam: A body-mounted camera, typically worn by law enforcement officers.

BUD/S: Basic Underwater Demolition/SEAL (school). *See also* SEAL.

BX: Base Exchange.

C1: The Canadian Army's version of the L1A1 FAL variant.

C2: The Canadian Army's version of the L2A1 heavy-barrel FAL variant.

C4: Composition 4. A plastic explosive.

C7: The Canadian Army's version of the M16A4 rifle. Produced by Diemaco, and later by Colt Canada. Also issued by Denmark, Holland, and Sweden.

C8: The Canadian Army's version of the M4 Carbine.

CAR-15: *See* M4.

CARB: California Air Resources Board.

Cat: Slang contraction for Caterpillar (tracked tractor).

CAT: Combat Application Tourniquet.

CB: Citizens Band radio. A VHF broadcasting band. No license is required for operation in the United States. Some desirable CB transceivers are capable of SSB operation. Originally twenty-three channels, the Citizens Band was later expanded to forty channels during the golden age of CB, in the 1970s.

CBC: Canadian Broadcasting Corporation.

CBLTV: Canadian Border Logistics and Training Volunteers network. Spoken "Cable TV."

CBP: Customs & Border Protection.

CENTCOM: Central Command. Nicknamed SADCOM by its detractors.

CG: Center of Gravity.

CGF Gallet: The French manufacturer of SPECTRA ballistic helmets. *See also* SPECTRA.

CHU: Containerized Housing Unit.

CI: Counterintelligence. *See also* HUMINT.

CIA: Central Intelligence Agency.

CLEP: College-Level Examination Program.

Closed Storage: The storage of SCI material in properly secured GSA-approved security containers within an accredited SCIF. *See also* Open Storage and SCIF.

CLP: Cleaner, Lubricant, Protectant. A Mil-Spec lubricant, sold under the trade name "Break Free CLP."

CM: Chinese Mandarin.

CMCS: COMSEC Material Control System.

CN: Canadian National (railroad).

CO: Commanding Officer.

CO_2: Carbon dioxide.

Collateral SCI: *See* SCI and SAP.

COMINT: Communications Intelligence.

COMSEC: Communications Security. The measures used to protect both classified and unclassified traffic on military communications and computing networks.

CONEX: CONtinental EXpress. The ubiquitous twenty-, thirty-, and forty-foot-long steel cargo containers used in multiple transportation modes.

CONFIDENTIAL: The security classification applied to information, the unauthorized disclosure of which reasonably could be expected to cause damage to national security.

Continuous Operation: This condition exists when a SCIF is staffed twenty-four hours every day.

Controlled Area/Compound: Any area to which entry is subject to restrictions or control for security reasons.

Controlled Building: A building to which entry is subject to restrictions or control for security reasons.

CONUS: Continental United States.

COPD: Chronic Obstructive Pulmonary Disease.

Co-Utilization: Two or more organizations sharing the same SCIF.

CP: Command Post.

CPR: Depending on context, Canadian Pacific Railway or Cardiopulmonary Resuscitation.

CR1M: Combat Ration, One Man. (Spoken "Crim.") The Australian equivalent of the U.S. MRE field ration. *See also* MRE and IMP.

CR5M: Combat Ration, Five Man.

CRKT: Columbia River Knife & Tool.

CRYPTO: The marking or designator identifying COMSEC keying material used to secure or authenticate telecommunications carrying classified or sensitive U.S. government or U.S. government–derived information.

CSA: Cognizant Security Authority. The single principal designated to serve as the responsible official for all aspects of security program management with respect to the protection of intelligence sources and methods.

CSIS: Canadian Security Intelligence Service.

CSS: Cyber Security Service.

CTS: Computerized Telephone System. Also referred to as a hybrid key system, business communication system, or office communications system.

CTTA: Certified TEMPEST Technical Authority.

CUT: Coordinated Universal Time.

Db.: Decibel. A measurement unit of sound intensity.

DC: Depending on context, Direct Current or District of Columbia (D.C.).

DCI: Director of Central Intelligence.

DCIPS: Defense Civilian Intelligence Personnel System.

DCS: Defense Clandestine Service.

DCS Task Group Tall Oak: Previously called DIA Project Tall Oak.

DD: Department of Defense (typically used as a prefix for form numbers). *See also* DOD.

Det Cord: Short for detonating cord—a plastic tube filled with PETN. It is typically used for connecting multiple explosive charges, so that they detonate almost simultaneously.

DF: Direction Finding.

DHS: Department of Homeland Security.

DIA: Defense Intelligence Agency. *See also* JBAB.

DIAC: Defense Intelligence Analysis Center.

DIAM: Defense Intelligence Agency Manual.

DIOCC: Defense Intelligence Operations Coordination Center. (Part of the DIAC.)

DJ: Disc Jockey.

DLI: Defense Language Institute.

DMV: Department of Motor Vehicles.

DMZ: Demilitarized Zone. In the context of a SCIF, the perimeter network segment that is logically between internal and external networks. Its purpose is to enforce the internal network's IA policy for external information exchange and to provide external, untrusted sources with restricted access to releasable information while shielding the internal networks from outside attacks. A DMZ is also called a "screened subnet." *See also* IA and SCIF.

Document: Any recorded information regardless of its physical form or characteristics, including, without limitation, written or printed matter, data-processing cards and tapes, maps, charts, paintings, drawings, photos, engravings, sketches, working notes and papers, reproductions of such things by any means or process; and sound, voice, magnetic, or electronic recordings in any form.

DOD or DoD: Department of Defense. *See also* DD.

DPM: Disruptive Pattern Material. A British military camouflage pattern, with colors similar to the U.S. Army's defunct woodland BDU pattern.

DRM: *Direction du Reseignement Militaire.* The French Directorate of Military Intelligence.

DRSN: Defense Red Switch Network.

DSArms: An American gunmaking company, founded by Dave Selvaggio.

DShK: *Degtyaryova-Shpagina Krupnokaliberny,* or "Degtyaryov-Shpagin Large-Caliber"—a 12.7mm Russian machine gun, later produced in several other communist nations. Informally called a "Dashika" by some users.

DSS: Diplomatic Security Service.

E Division: The RCMP division that polices all of British Columbia except Vancouver.

E&E: Escape and Evasion.

ELINT: Electronic Intelligence.

ELT: Emergency Locator Transmitter.

EMSEC: Emissions Security. Protection resulting from measures taken to deny unauthorized individuals information derived from intercept and analysis of compromising emanations from crypto-equipment or an information system. *See also* TEMPEST.

EPA: Environmental Protection Agency.

EQ2050: A Chinese Humvee equivalent vehicle.

E-Tool: Entrenching tool. (A small folding shovel.)

ETS: Expiration of Term of Service.

FAA: Federal Aviation Administration.

FAL: *See* FN/FAL.

FAMAS: *Fusil d'Assaut de la Manufacture d'Armes de Saint-Étienne.* The French army's standard-issue bullpup carbine, chambered in 5.56mm NATO. *See also* FÉLIN.

FBI: Federal Bureau of Investigation.

FBO: Fixed Base Operator. Typically used to describe a small private airport's refueling facility.

FÉLIN: *Fantassin à Équipement et Liaisons Intégrés* (Integrated Infantryman Equipment and Communications). The French infantry combat system of the 2000s. *See also* FAMAS.

FEMA: Federal Emergency Management Agency (a U.S. federal government agency). The acronym is also jokingly defined as: "Foolishly Expecting Meaningful Aid."

FFL: Federal Firearms License.

FHJ: 84A twin-barrel 62mm incendiary rocket launcher used by the Chinese PLA.

Field SCIF: *See* Tactical SCIF.

FIST: Fire Support Team.

FLB: Forward Logistics Base.

FLIR: Forward-Looking Infrared. A camera that can detect body heat as well as the heat vehicle engines.

FNC: a 5.56mm NATO battle rifle originally made by the Belgian company Fabrique Nationale (FN). *See also* Pindad SS2.

FN/FAL: A 7.62mm NATO battle rifle originally made by the Belgian Company Fabrique Nationale (FN), issued to more than fifty countries in the 1960s and 1970s. Now made as semiauto-only "clones" by a variety of makers including DSArms. *See also* L1A1.

FN-MAG: A 7.62mm NATO belt-fed light machine gun developed by FN of Belgium. It has been issued by more than eighty countries. The U.S. military uses several variants of the gun, under the designation M240. *See also* M240.

FOB: Forward Operating Base.

FOUO: For Official Use Only.

FRS: Family Radio Service.

FS: Field Station.

FSB: *Federalnaya Sluzhba Bezopasnosti.* The main successor to the KGB.

FSMA: Food Safety and Modernization Act.

Galil: The Israeli battle rifle, based on Kalashnikov action. Most were made in 5.56mm NATO, but a variant was also made in 7.62mm NATO, in smaller numbers.

GAZ: *Gorkovsky Avtomobilny Zavod.* A Russian car and truck maker.

GB: Gigabyte.

GCA: The Gun Control Act of 1968. The law that first created FFLs and banned interstate transfers of post-1898 firearms, except "to or through" FFL holders.

GDP: Gross Domestic Product.

GG: The "Excepted Service" pay-grade category for intelligence and national security positions. (GG pay-grade numbers are roughly equivalent to General Schedule [GS] civil servant pay grades.)

Glock: The popular polymer-framed pistol design by Gaston Glock of Austria.

GMRS: General Mobile Radio Service. A licensed UHF-FM two-way radio service. *See also* FRS and MURS.

GMT: Greenwich Mean Time. Also known as Coordinated Universal Time (CUT).

GPS: Global Positioning System.

Green Door: Slang used in the intelligence community for restricted access to information and/or locations.

GS: General Schedule.

GTK: *Gepanzertes Transport Kraftfahrzeug.* A variant of the German eight-wheeled Boxer APC.

Ham: Slang for amateur radio operator.

HAROPA: The functionally combined ports of Le Havre, Rouen, and Paris.

H-E or HE: High Explosive.

HEI: High Energy Ignition.

Hesco: A military contractor best known for its prefabricated wire and fabric ballistic protection bastions.

HF: High Frequency. A radio band used by amateur radio operators.

High Side: A network for classified traffic. High-side networks are always physically disconnected ("air gapped") from unclassified "low-side" networks. This prevents inadvertent or intentional "copy/paste" of classified information into low-side messages. *See also* Low Side.

HK or H&K: Heckler und Koch, the German gun maker.

HK91: Heckler und Koch Model 91. The civilian (semiautomatic-only) variant of the 7.62mm NATO G3 rifle.

HMMWV: High-Mobility Multipurpose Wheeled Vehicle, also commonly called a Humvee, or in civilian trim, a "Hummer."

HQ: Headquarters.

HUMINT: Human Intelligence. *See also* CI.

Humvee: High-Mobility Multipurpose Wheeled Vehicle spoken "Humvee."

Hydro: Canadian slang for grid power or a power company, or a power bill. In Canada, all grid power is generically called "hydro" power, regardless of its actual origin.

IA: Depending on context, Information Architecture, Information Assurance, or Internal Affairs.

IBA: Interceptor Body Armor.

ICE: Immigration and Customs Enforcement.

ID: Identification.

IDS: Intrusion Detection System. A security alarm system to detect unauthorized entry to a secure facility.

IED: Improvised Explosive Device.

IFV: Infantry Fighting Vehicle.

IH: International Harvester.

IMP: Individual Meal Pack. Canada's standard field ration containing precooked entree packed in heavy-duty plastic-foil retort pouch. The equivalent of a U.S. Military Meal Ready to Eat (MRE).

INFOSEC: Information Security.

Intel: Slang shorthand for intelligence.

IR: Depending on context, Infrared or Intelligence Requirement.

Isolator: A device or assembly of devices that isolates or disconnects a telephone or CTS from all wires that exit the SCIF and that has been accepted as effective for security purposes. *See also* KSU.

IV: Intravenous.

JAG: Judge Advocate General corps. (Military attorneys.)

JBAB: Joint Base Anacostia-Bolling (JBAB), the headquarters of the DIA, in Washington, D.C.

JBLM: Joint Base Lewis-McChord. (Formerly, Fort Lewis and McChord Air Force Base, Washington.)

JP4: Jet Propellant 4, an aviation fuel.

JP5: Jet Propellant 5, an aviation fuel.

JWICS: Joint Worldwide Intelligence Communications System.

Kel-Tec: A Florida gun manufacturer specializing in polymer frame guns.

Kevlar: The material used in most body army and ballistic helmets. "Kevlar" is also the nickname for the standard U.S. Army helmet.

KIA: Killed in Action.

KJV: King James Version of the Bible.

KSU: Key Service Unit. An electromechanical switching device that controls routing and operation of an analog telephone system. *See also* Isolator and Red/Black.

KTM: An Austrian manufacturer of motorcycles. The K and T are for the surnames of the business founders, Kronreif and Trunkenpolz. The M is for Mattighofen, Austria, the name of the town where the motorcycles are built.

L1A1: The British army version of the FN/FAL, made to inch measurements.

LAR-8: A variant of the AR-10 rifle that accepts FN/FAL or L1A1 magazines.

LAW: Light Antitank Weapon.

LC-1: Load Carrying, Type 1. (U.S. Army Load Bearing Equipment, circa 1970s to 1990s.)

LDS: The Latter-day Saints, commonly called the Mormons. (Flawed doctrine, great preparedness.)

LDSH: Lord Strathcona's Horse. A regular armored regiment of the Canadian army, headquartered in Edmonton, Alberta, Canada. Members of the regiment are commonly called Strathconas or Strats, for short.

LGP: *Le Gouvernement du Peuple* (The People's Government).

Line Conditioning: Elimination of unintentional signals or noise induced or conducted on a telecommunications or information system signal, power, control, indicator, or other external interface line.

LLDR: Lightweight Laser Designator Rangefinder.

LNO: Liaison Officer.

Low Side: An unclassified network. High-side (classified) networks are always physically disconnected ("air gapped") from low-side networks. This prevents unintentional or intentional copying and pasting of classified information into low-side messages. *See also* High Side.

LP: Liquid Propane.

LPCs: Leather Personnel Carriers.

LP/OP: Listening Post/Observation Post.

LRRP: Long Range Reconnaissance Patrol.

LZ: Landing Zone.

M1 Abrams: The United States' current main battle tank, with a 120mm cannon ("main gun").

M1 Carbine: The U.S. Army semiauto carbine issued during World War II. Mainly issued to officers and second-echelon troops such as artillery-men, for self-defense. It fires .30 U.S. carbine, an intermediate (pistol-class) .30 caliber cartridge. More than six million were manufactured. The folding-stock version designed for use by paratroopers was designated M1A1. *See also* M2 Carbine.

M1 Garand: The U.S. Army's primary battle rifle of World War II and the Korean conflict. It is semiautomatic, chambered in .30-06, and uses a top-loading, eight-round en bloc clip that ejects after the last round is fired. This rifle is commonly called the Garand (after the surname of its inventor, John Garand). Not to be confused with the U.S. M1 Carbine, another semiauto of the same era, which shoots a far less powerful pistol-class cartridge.

M1A: The civilian (semiauto only) version of the U.S. Army M14 7.62mm NATO rifle.

M1911: The Model 1911 Colt semiauto pistol (and clones thereof), usually chambered in .45 ACP.

M2 Carbine: The selective-fire (fully automatic) version of the U.S. Army semiauto carbine issued during World War II and the Korean conflict.

M4: The U.S. Army–issue 5.56mm NATO selective-fire carbine. (A shorter version of the M16, with a 14.5-inch barrel and collapsing stock.) Earlier issue M16 carbine variants had designations such as XM177E2 and CAR-15. Civilian semiauto-only variants often have these same designations, or are called "M4geries."

M4gery: A civilian semiauto-only version of an M4 Carbine, with a sixteen-inch barrel instead of a 14.5-inch barrel.

M9: The U.S. Army–issue version of the Beretta M92 semiauto 9mm pistol.

M14: The U.S. Army–issue 7.62mm NATO selective-fire battle rifle. These rifles are still issued in small numbers, primarily to designated marksmen. The civilian semiauto-only equivalent of the M14 is called the M1A.

M16: The U.S. Army–issue 5.56mm NATO selective-fire battle rifle. The current standard variant is the M16A2, which has improved sight and three-shot burst control. *See also* M4.

M60: The obsolete U.S. Army–issue 7.62mm NATO belt-fed light machine gun that utilized some design elements of the German MG-42.

M240: The U.S. military variant of the 7.62mm NATO FN-MAG light machine gun. *See also* FN-MAG.

M249: The U.S. military variant of the 5.56mm NATO FN Minimi light machine gun.

MAG: *See* FN-MAG.

MAG-58: *See* FN-MAG.

Maglite: A popular American brand of sturdy flashlights with a machined aluminum casing.

MAPEX: Map Exercise.

MC: Master of Ceremonies.

MCRU: Mobile Control and Reporting Unit.

MG3: A German belt-fed light machine gun, chambered in 7.62mm NATO.

MG4: A German belt-fed light machine gun, chambered in 5.56mm NATO.

MI: Military Intelligence. *See also* CI, HUMINT, and SIGINT.

Mini-14: A 5.56mm NATO semiauto carbine made by Ruger.

Minimi: *See* M249.

MOIS: Ministry of Intelligence and Security, the Iranian spy agency. *See also* VEVAK.

MOLLE: Modular Lightweight Load-carrying Equipment.

Molotov cocktail: A hand-thrown firebomb made from a glass container filled with gasoline or thickened gasoline (napalm).

MOS: Military Occupational Specialty.

MP: Military Police.

MRAP: Mine Resistant Ambush Protected (vehicle).

MRE: Meal Ready to Eat. *See also* IMP and CR1M.

MRI: Magnetic Resonance Imaging.

MSS: Depending on context, Ministry of State Security or Modular Sleep System.

MTBE: Methyl tert-butyl ether. An oxygenating additive for gasoline.

MultiCam: *See* OCP.

MURS: Multi Use Radio Service. A VHF two-way radio service that does not require a license. *See also* FRS and GMRS.

MVPA: Military Vehicle Preservation Association.

MWR: Morale, Welfare, and Recreation.

NAB: Naval Amphibious Base.

Napalm: Thickened gasoline, used in some flame weapons.

NATO: North Atlantic Treaty Organization.

NBC: Nuclear, Biological, and Chemical.

NCO: Noncommissioned Officer.

NFA: The National Firearms Act of 1934. The law that first imposed a two-hundred-dollar transfer tax on machine guns, suppressors (commonly called silencers), and short-barreled rifles and shotguns.

NiCd: Nickel cadmium (rechargeable battery).

NiMH: Nickel Metal Hydride (rechargeable battery) improvement of NiCd.

NIMTC: Navy and Marine Corps Intelligence Training Center.

NIPRnet: Nonclassified Internet Protocol Router Network. This network replaced MILNET. It is now known as the Unclassified but Sensitive Internet Protocol Router Network, but still commonly called "Nipper Net."

NIST: National Institute of Standards and Technology.

NLR: *Nous sommes la résistance*. (Translated: "We are the resistance.")

NOC: Nonofficial cover. (Clandestine agent.)

Nondiscussion Area: A clearly defined area within a SCIF where classified discussions are not authorized due to inadequate sound attenuation. *See also* Secure Working Area.

Norinco: The China North Industries Corporation. A weapons and military vehicle maker.

NRO: National Reconnaissance Office.

NSA: National Security Agency.

NSA-Net: The National Security Agency's secure intranet. Commonly called "the high side."

NSA-W: NSA Washington.

NSTS: National Secure Telephone System.

NSWC: Naval Special Warfare Center.

NWO: New World Order.

OB: Order of Battle.

OCONUS: Outside the Continental United States.

OCP: Operation Enduring Freedom Camouflage Pattern, commonly called by its civilian trade name, MultiCam.

One-Time Pad: A manual one-time cryptosystem produced in pad form.

OP: Observation Post. *See also* LP/OP.

Open Storage: The storage of SCI material within an accredited SCIF in any configuration other than within GSA-approved security containers. Open storage is approved while the facility is unoccupied by authorized personnel. *See also* Closed Storage.

OPORD: Operations Order.

OPSEC: Operational Security. The systematic and proven process by which potential adversaries can be denied information about capabilities and intentions by identifying, controlling, and protecting generally unclassified evidence of the planning and execution of sensitive activities. The process involves five steps: identification of critical information, analysis of threats, analysis of vulnerabilities, assessment of risks, and application of appropriate countermeasures.

OSINT: Open Source Intelligence. Gathering intelligence from public, unclassified sources, such as periodicals. OSINT *sources* are unclassified, but once analyzed, they become classified, usually at low level.

P90: A bullpup 5.7x28 caliber personal defense weapon, manufactured by FN.

PAL: Possession and Acquisition License. (For firearms, in Canada.)

Paracord: A contraction for Parachute cord.

PCS: Permanent Change of Station.

PDD: Presidential Decision Document.

PEDs: Personal Electronic Devices.

PETN: Pentaerythritol tetranitrate.

PF-89: The Chinese 80mm equivalent of a LAW rocket.

P.I.: Philippine Islands.

Pindad SS2: The Pindad Senapan Serbu 2 Indonesian variant of the FN FNC 5.56mm battle rifle.

PLA: People's Liberation Army (China).

PM: Prime Minister.

P-MAG: Polymer magazine.

POL: Petroleum, Oil, and Lubricants.

POV: Privately Owned Vehicle.

PPCLI: Princess Patricia's Canadian Light Infantry. A Canadian army unit, headquartered in Edmonton, Alberta, Canada.

Pre-1965: U.S. silver coins with 1964 or earlier mint dates, usually with little or no numismatic value. They are sold for the bullion content. These coins have 90 percent silver content. Well-worn pre-1965 coins are sometimes derisively called "junk" silver by rare coin dealers.

Project Tall Oak: A fictitious DIA working group, later renamed DCS Task Group Tall Oak.

ProvGov: Provisional Government (in the United States).

PSYOPS: Psychological Operations.

PV: Photovoltaic (solar power conversion cell or array). Used to convert solar power to DC electricity, typically for battery charging.

PVC: Depending on context, Poly-Vinyl Chloride (white plastic water pipe) or Progressive Voice of Canada.

PVCL: People's Voice of Canadian Liberation.

QBZ-95: Bullpup-style assault rifle manufactured by Arsenal 266, part of Norinco and Arsenal 296, under Jianshe Corp., China South for the People's Liberation Army. These bullpups shoot the Chinese 5.8x42mm cartridge, which was rarely exported, and only for military contracts.

QRF: Quick Reaction Force.

QSZ-92: A semiautomatic pistol designed by Norinco that shoots the 5.8x21mm cartridge.

RAC: Radio Amateurs of Canada.

RBC: Royal Bank of Canada.

RCG: Restoration of Constitution Government.

RCIED: Radio-Controlled Improvised Explosive Device.

RCMP: Royal Canadian Mounted Police.

RDX: Research Department Explosive.

READOUT (Multi-Net): A classified acronym.

Red: Designation applied to an Information System(s), and associated areas, circuits, components, and equipment in which unencrypted national security information is being processed. *See also* DRSN.

Red/Black (Switch): Red commonly refers to clear text-sensitive information, while Black refers to either encrypted or unclassified signals. The Red/Black switching security requirements and their criteria were declassified in 1995.

Reg: Slang for regulation.

RFI: Request(s) for Intelligence.

RINT: Radiations Intelligence.

RORO: Roll-On-Roll-Off. A type of cargo ship designed for transporting vehicles.

RPG: Rocket-Propelled Grenade.

RPV: Remotely Piloted Vehicle. *See also* UAV.

RRSP: Registered Retirement Saving Plan.

RSOC: Regional Security Operations Center. (Formerly Regional SIGINT Operations Center.)

RTA: Radio Traffic Analyst. *See also* TA.

RTB: Return to Base.

RTV: Room Temperature Vulcanizing (silicone sealant).

RVCA: Resistance Veterans of Canada Association.

SAD: Special Activities Division.

SADCOM: *See* CENTCOM.

SAEDA: Subversion and Espionage Directed Against the U.S. Army.

SALT: Size, Activity, Location, Time. An intelligence report format. *See also* SALUTE.

SALUTE: Size, Activity, Location, Unit, Time & Duration, Equipment. An intelligence report format. *See also* SALT.

SAM: Depending on context, Surface-to-Air Missile or Sources and Methods.

SAP: Special Access Program. Any approved program that imposes need-to-know or access controls beyond those normally required for access to CONFIDENTIAL, SECRET, or TOP SECRET information. Commonly (and erroneously) called "above top secret," SAP compartmented information is actually considered *collateral* to the TOP SECRET security level.

SBI: Special Background Investigation.

SCI: Sensitive Compartmented Information. This is classified information concerning or derived from intelligence sources, methods, or analytical processes, which is required to be handled exclusively within formal control systems established by the director of Central Intelligence. *See also* SAP and SCIF.

SCIF: Sensitive Compartmented Information Facility. An accredited area, room, group of rooms, building, or installation where SCI may be stored, used, discussed, and/or electronically processed. Also commonly called a vault.

SEAL: Sea-Air-Land (Team). The U.S. Navy Special Operations Force. *See also* BUD/S.

SEARCHLIGHT: An NSA administrative webpage.

SECRET: The security classification applied to information, the unauthorized disclosure of which reasonably could be expected to cause serious damage to national security.

Section: Depending on context, either a 640-acre area of land measuring one mile square, or an intelligence working group (or the telecommunications equipment thereof).

Secure Working Area: An accredited SCIF (or portion of a SCIF) used for handling, discussing, and/or processing of SCI, but where SCI will not be stored. *See also* Nondiscussion Area.

Secwepemc: A First Nations tribal group in British Columbia. Also known as the Shuswap.

SID: System Identification.

SIG: Schweizer Industrie Gesellschaft. A major Swiss gun maker.

SIGINT: Signals Intelligence.

SIN: Social Insurance Number. (The Canadian equivalent of a U.S. Social Security number.)

SIPRNet: Secure Internet Protocol Router Network.

SITTEMPS: Situational templates.

SMLE: Short Magazine Lee-Enfield. A British family of bolt-action rifles that were in service for more than seventy years. Most were chambered for the .303 British cartridge.

SMS: Short Message Service.

SOCC: Security Operations Control Center.

SOCOM: Special Operations Command.

SOP: Standard Operating Procedure.

SPECTRA: The synthetic material similar to Kevlar used in ballistic helmets issued to French, Canadian, and Danish military units. In France, the SPECTRA helmet is also known as the CGF Gallet Combat Helmet. *See also* CGF Gallet.

SQL: Structured Query Language. (Used with database software.)

SS2: *See* Pindad SS2.

SSB: Single Sideband (an operating mode for CB and amateur radio gear).

SSO: Special Security Officer.

STE: Section-Terminating Equipment. *See also* STU.

Steyr AUG: The Austrian Army's 5.56mm bullpup infantry carbine. Also issued by the Australian Army as their replacement for the L1A1. Often called the AUS-Steyr by the Australians.

Strat: Slang for Strategic.

STU: Secure Telephone Unit. (Spoken "Stew.") *See also* STE and NSTS.

STU-III: A third-generation STU phone. (Spoken "Stew Three.") *See also* STE and NSTS.

SUV: Sport Utility Vehicle.

S&W: Smith and Wesson.

SWAT: Special Weapons and Tactics. (SWAT originally stood for Special Weapons Assault Team until that was deemed politically incorrect.)

TA: Traffic Analyst/Analysis. Study of communications patterns to determine unit relationships and dispositions. *See also* RTA.

Tactical SCIF: An accredited secure area used for actual or simulated war operations for a specified period of time.

Tall Oak: *See* Project Tall Oak. (Later renamed Task Group Tall Oak.)

TARP: Depending on context, Threat Awareness and Reporting Program or Troubled Asset Relief Program.

Task Group Tall Oak: *See* Project Tall Oak.

TAWS: Terrain Awareness and Warning System.

TBAS: Tiered Body Armor System (Australian army issue).

TBD: To Be Determined.

TDY: Temporary Duty.

Technical Truck: A pickup truck equipped with a pedestal-mounted machine gun.

TEMPEST: Telecommunications Electronics Material Protected from Emanating Spurious Transmissions. The now unclassified U.S. government code word for emanations security. *See also* EMSEC.

TEP: TEMPEST Endorsement Program.

Thermite: A mixture of aluminum powder and iron rust powder that, when ignited, causes a vigorous exothermic reaction. Used primarily for welding. Also used by military units as an incendiary for destroying equipment.

Third Department: The PLA's signals intelligence-gathering and analysis arm.

TIG: Tungsten Inert Gas. (A welding method.)

TNT: 2,4,6-trinitrotoluene is a colorless or pale yellow and odorless crystalline high explosive.

TO: Tall Oak.

TOC: Tactical Operations Center.

TO&E: Table of Organization and Equipment.

Topo: Short for topographical.

TOP SECRET: The security classification applied to information, the unauthorized disclosure of which reasonably could be expected to cause exceptionally grave damage to the national security. *See also* TS and SCI.

TPZ: Transportpanzer. A variant of the six-wheel Fuchs (Fox) APC.

TRU: Thompson Rivers University.

TS: Top Secret.

TSCM: Technical Surveillance Countermeasures (Surveys and Evaluations). A physical, electronic, and visual examination to detect technical surveillance devices, technical security hazards, and attempts at clandestine penetration. *See also* TEMPEST and EMSEC.

TSEC: The system for identifying the type and purpose of certain items of COMSEC material.

Type 92: *See* QSZ-92.

Type 95: *See* QBZ-95.

UAV: Unmanned aerial vehicle. *See also* RPV.

UDT: Underwater Demolition Team.

UN: United Nations.

UN-MNF: United Nations Multinational Force.

UNPROFOR: United Nations Protection Force (Security Assistance Command).

UPS: Uninterruptible Power Source.

U.S.: United States.

USB: Universal Serial Bus.

U.S.-Controlled Facility: A base or building to which access is physically controlled by U.S. individuals who are authorized U.S. government or U.S. government contractor employees.

USMC: United States Marine Corps.

VAB: *Véhicule de l'Avant Blindé* (Armored Vanguard Vehicle).

VAC: Volts, Alternating Current.

Valmet: The Finnish conglomerate that formerly made several types of firearms.

Vault: *See* SCIF.

VBCI: *Véhicule Blindé de Combat d'Infanterie.*

VBT: Very Bad Thing.

VCI: *Véhicule de Combat d'Infanterie* (infantry combat vehicle). A variant in the VBCI family of wheeled APCs.

VCP: Vehicle Control Point.

VDC: Volts, Direct Current.

VEVAK: *Vezarat-e Ettela'at va Amniyat-e Keshvar.* The Iranian intelligence service *See also* MOIS.

VPC: *Véhicule Poste de Commandement* (command post vehicle). A variant in the VBCI family of wheeled APCs.

VTT: *Véhicule de Transport de Troupes* (troop transport vehicle). A variant in the VBCI family of wheeled APCs.

VW: Volkswagen.

WAN: Wide Area Network.

WD-1: U.S. military-issue two-conductor insulated field telephone wire.

Wi-Fi: Wireless Fidelity.

XL: Extra Large.

Z-9: A Chinese military utility helicopter. It is a license-built version of the French *Eurocopter AS365 Dauphin*, manufactured by Harbin Aircraft Manufacturing Corporation. The attack variants have fixed-mount 23mm cannons.

Z-10: An attack helicopter developed by the People's Republic of China.

Z-19: A Chinese reconnaissance/attack helicopter developed by Harbin Aircraft Manufacturing Corporation for the People's Liberation Army Air Force and the Ground Force Air Force.

ACKNOWLEDGMENTS

Special thanks to Mr. X., who articulated the dilemma of those trapped in and near the D.C. Beltway, bound by golden handcuffs.

Also, thanks to "Joe Snuffy." Despite having his own successful career in military intelligence, and many job offers, he chose to live a simpler life, and avoided the golden handcuffs.

This book's title is a shared homage in honor of:

- The veterans of the U.S. Army Fourteenth Armored Division ("The Liberators");
- Those who designed and built the Consolidated B-24 and PB4Y-1 "Liberator" heavy bombers;
- The aircrewmen who flew B-24 Liberator bombers in World War II. In particular, I thank Lt. Col. Alvin G. "Al" Millspaugh, whom I met when I was a teenager;
- George Hyde, the German-born designer of the American FP-45 Liberator pistol made during World War II;
- And Cody Wilson, the inventor of the twenty-first-century "Liberator" 3D-printed pistol.

This novel is also dedicated to the memory of famed cattleman Richmond P. Hobson Jr., the author of *Grass Beyond the Mountains*, which describes the early cattle ranch settlement of the interior of British Columbia in the 1930s. The largely roadless country north of Anahim Lake is *still* one of the last frontier regions in North America.

I also want to express my thanks to the many other folks who encouraged me, who contributed technical details, who were used for character sketches, and who helped me substantively in the editing process. They include: Fred Burton (a former DSS counterintelligence agent, now Stratfor's vice president for intelligence), Roxanne B., Frank B., Dave B., Cheryl, Mr. C. in Cocolalla, the DCS Guy, E. in Afghanistan, Erin in Bella Coola, Frank and Fern, "Enola Gay," Harry, Josh H., Buddy Hinton, Hugh, Jeff C., Jerry J., the intrepid float-plane pilot Rob J., Reggie Kaigler ("DEMCAD"), Steve K., "Ken and Terry Layton," Norm of Anahim Lake, Mr. O. of the Secwepemc, J.I.R., Patrice, Randy R., S. in Kamloops, Brian S., Tamara, an unnamed fellow ASA veteran, and an unnamed defense attaché.

Last, but far from least, my sincere thanks to my editor at Dutton, Jessica Renheim, for her amazing skill in making my scribbling seem coherent.

James Wesley, Rawles
The Rawles Ranch
September 2014

ABOUT THE AUTHOR

Former U.S. Army Intelligence officer and survivalist **James Wesley, Rawles** is a well-known survival lecturer and author. Rawles is the editor of SurvivalBlog.com—the nation's most popular blog on family preparedness. He lives in an undisclosed location west of the Rockies and is the *New York Times* bestselling author of *Expatriates: A Novel of the Coming Global Collapse; Founders: A Novel of the Coming Collapse; Survivors: A Novel of the Coming Collapse; Patriots: A Novel of Survival in the Coming Collapse*; and a nonfiction survival guide, *How to Survive the End of the World as We Know It.*